MORTAL SINS

Also by Anna Porter

HIDDEN AGENDA

MORTAL SINS

A NOVEL BY

ANNA PORTER

NAL BOOKS

NEW AMERICAN LIBRARY

Copyright © 1987 by Anna Porter

All rights reserved. For information address New American Library.

Published by arrangement with Irwin Publishing Inc.

NAL BOOKS TRADEMARK REG. U.S. PAT. OFF. AND FOREIGN COUNTRIES
REGISTERED TRADEMARK—MARCA REGISTRADA
HECHO EN BRATTLEBORO, VT., U.S.A.

SIGNET, SIGNET CLASSIC, MENTOR, ONYX, PLUME, MERIDIAN
and NAL BOOKS are published by NAL PENGUIN INC.,
1633 Broadway, New York, New York 10019

Designed by David Shaw & Associates Ltd.

Library of Congress Cataloging-in-Publication Data

Porter, Anna.
Mortal sins.
I. Title.
PR9199.3.P624M67   1988   813'.54   88-5173
ISBN 0-453-00616-7

First NAL BOOKS Printing, October, 1988

1 2 3 4 5 6 7 8 9

PRINTED IN THE UNITED STATES OF AMERICA

For Puci and Julian

My thanks to Maria des Tombe for research, Jean Marmoreo and Michael Weinstock for medical facts, Jim Young, who is a real coroner, Bob Wilkie and Malcolm Lester for encouragement and corrections, John Pearce for his forbearance, and Lorant Wanke for remembering how to get to Eger.

MORTAL SINS

ONE

She lifted the heavy tear-shaped brass knocker and let it fall. The sound was like a sharp high-pitched drumbeat that echoed back and forth between the two gray marble pillars of the porch. The pillars served to dwarf the unwary visitor, in case the broad granite steps, the armed guard at the gate, and the towering poplars lining the long, winding driveway had failed to cut her down to size already. The driveway, according to *Business Week*, was paved with a fine gravel of meteorite. The marble was from Carrara, where Michelangelo had chosen his. "Awesome" was the word that came to Judith's mind. One of Jimmy's favorite words had finally found a fitting occasion.

The meticulously carved oak door opened about ten inches, wide enough to afford the thin white-haired man inside a thorough inspection of the visitor. Only his eyes moved. The rest of his body, elegantly draped in three-piece black suit and matching bow tie, was poplar-straight.

"Yes?" he asked, barely moving his lips.

"Hello," Judith said brightly. "I'm Judith Hayes. I'm here to see Mr. Zimmerman."

"Yes," he repeated, "you are expected." He opened the door wider and made room for Judith to enter.

"May I?" He was already behind her, expertly lifting the burgundy coat, her best, by the shoulders and slipping it over one stiffly held arm. *God forbid he should notice the lining's frayed down the back.*

"Please follow me," he suggested with a slight nod toward the marble-tiled reception area. The pink marble ran partway up the wall, formed a small ridge, and stopped where the white and pink flocked wallpaper began. There were several large horse prints in gold-painted frames, a small nude female statue on a pedestal —

1

probably Greek — a Byzantine crystal chandelier, and a marble-top table with a huge silver dish that served as an ashtray. To the right, a white-carpeted staircase with oak banisters.

The butler turned left, swept past a pair of closed doors with shiny brass handles, and pointed the way through a third.

"Mr. Zimmerman will be with you in a moment." He bowed slightly and signaled her to enter, then turned ceremonially and left.

He's been watching too much *Upstairs, Downstairs,* Judith thought.

The waiting room offered few comforts. A library of brown leather and gold ran from floor to ceiling. In the center stood a huge oblong table of dark mahogany with heavy carved legs and a straight-backed chair placed dead in the middle of each side. Gold candelabra. In one corner a Queen Anne writing desk with its round-shouldered chair, gold letter opener, and Victorian inkwell and pen.

She remembered her mother had once bought a yard and a half of leather-bound books to fill an empty space in the living room. "You're not *supposed* to read them," she scoffed at Judith's father. "They're the decoration. Nobody *reads* leather-bound books..."

Curious, she approached the shelves only to confront an army of *Encyclopaedia Britannica* and Winston Churchill.

Near the gray stone fireplace, she found two maroon wing chairs facing each other, turned slightly toward the dead logs and two bronze wolfhounds. She chose the chair farthest from the door. The touch of cold leather made her shiver.

She tried a number of casually relaxed positions, ending up with legs crossed, knees tilted to one side, arms akimbo, and desperately needing a cigarette. Times such as these brought to mind why she had begun to smoke in the first place — exactly 24 years before the day that she'd last quit. It had been her first New Year's Eve party. She'd worn a red taffeta dress with frills at the neck and wrists, a bow in the back. Marjorie, her mother, had puckered her lips in anticipated disapproval as she warned James to make sure he brought her home by 1 A.M. The Big Concession. The dress had been a hideous miscalculation. She stood out in the crowd — a clumsy, oversize red blob. But she had been most aware of her hands, hanging like useless talons at the ends of what she believed were her simian arms. And then James had offered her a cigarette.

"Mrs. Hayes — I apologize." A deep baritone voice whisked her back to the present before she'd taken one whiff of the sinful weed.

He stood in the doorway, his head mere inches from the top of the frame, his shoulders almost blocking the light from the hall. He instantly dwarfed the room. Six-foot-four was what *Business Week* had said: "The man bestrides the earth like a Colossus..."

"Mr. Zimmerman?" Judith asked, quite unnecessarily, as she struggled to her feet.

"I was caught by the phone just as I came to greet you. Blasted things have come to rule our lives." There was a touch of an accent on "things," but she may have been waiting for it.

He was striding toward her with jaunty, energetic steps, his jacket flaps swaying with the motion, his right hand already extended. Once he reached Judith, he cupped her hand in his own broad-palmed hands, dry flat fingers that scraped her wrist. His face, as he looked down at her, seemed impossibly far away. She had to crane her neck to meet his eyes. They were a bright, transparent blue, set wide apart, shaded by almost white eyelashes and thick, jutting gray and white eyebrows. A columnist had once conjectured that it took a full ten minutes each day to untangle and shape them.

His hair was white and starting to recede into a widow's peak. His skin seemed bronzed and leathery, the deep wrinkles around his mouth and eyes like squint lines against the sun. The toll exacted by all that tennis, sailing, golf. Or was it from sitting in the bleachers watching his Chicago baseball team, now training somewhere in Florida?

"Would you like something to drink?" he asked. "Coffee, perhaps? Some wine? Tea?" He pushed a button under the arm of the other maroon wing chair.

"Tea, I think," Judith said, although she had intended to request a gin and tonic. On reflection, the atmosphere was all wrong for gin.

"Tea for the young lady, Arnold, and coffee for me. Double espresso, please," he said, not glancing behind him, where the butler had materialized in the doorway.

Judith gave a small internal whinny at the "young lady" and told Zimmerman how pleased she was that he had agreed to the interview. He hadn't granted one since 1977, and that had been rather a formal exchange conducted at his New York office. No photo opportunity.

"You don't find *this* formal?" Zimmerman asked, indicating the room. His pale eyes had fixed on Judith's face, the white lashes steady, the corners of his mouth pulled into a polite, quizzical smile.

"It's more formidable than formal," she said, "but it is your home, and I appreciate being here." She was pulling her notebook out of her purse — setting up the props.

"Don't you use a tape recorder?" he asked.

"No. I trust my notes." Judith had hated tape recorders ever since hers had broken down ten minutes into a habitual bank robber's confession and she hadn't noticed it wasn't recording.

"Jensen had a handsome Japanese job which he stuck on the desk in front of me," Zimmerman went on. "Apparently he hadn't the foresight to speak into it himself. That made it very difficult later to discern what his questions were. Or what I had said yes to. A clever journalistic trick, I'm told." He gave her a long, calculating look. "What do you think?"

Judith had read the Jensen story and hadn't found it particularly clever, except for the bit about the old lifeboat theory, where Zimmerman had agreed that if the whole world were fed and clothed at the expense of the wealthy nations, there would be no standing room left for anybody, and we'd all drown. "Jensen is out of work and that's not very clever," she said.

Zimmerman laughed. "I know," he said, keeping his voice light. "You're never out of work, are you, Mrs. Hayes?"

"Can't afford to be," Judith said.

Arnold served her tea in translucent bone china on a silver tray.

"Perhaps we could start there," Judith suggested. "Why you've agreed to talk to me, when you've been avoiding the press for some ten years."

"Avoiding?" His head tilted to one side, he contemplated the word for a second. "No. I haven't been avoiding the press. I merely haven't had time for it or reason to befriend it. In America there is a tacit assumption that men in business, like politicians and movie stars, owe the press, on demand, interesting explanations for their actions. They are expected to be available for astute comment, for photographs, for revelations about their personal lives. What's astounding to me is that so many businessmen comply. I've tended to consider the whole thing an intrusion, and not fair to my family and associates — such as they are. Besides, I derive no joy from seeing my words in print." When he laughed his whole face wrinkled up, layer by layer, radiating outward. "But all that has changed now. Right?"

"Has it?"

"Clearly," he said with mock earnestness, "or we wouldn't be here."

"Why has it changed?"

"Perhaps I'm tired of being a recluse. Perhaps I'm learning public relations. Or I want to curry favor with the Chicago sports fans. Or I liked what Marsha Hillier had to say about you. Does it matter? Fact is you're here, so let's get on with it." He sat back, crossed his elegantly tailored pant legs, placed his elbows on the arms of the chair, and intertwined his fingers in relaxed anticipation.

Lovely. Next. "Let's talk about Pacific Airlines," said Judith. "You told the remaining shareholders that its management team would be ill suited to administer an average Albanian household —"

"No disrespect to your Albanian readers," Zimmerman interrupted.

" — and that your first move as chairman would be to cut the fat off the corner office gang. That's pretty tough language coming into the stewardship of a new company. I wondered whether you used it partly in retaliation for the battle they waged to keep you out."

"Only partly. Mostly, I never cease to be amazed at the lengths executives will go to keep their Lear jets. Their primary responsibility should be to the shareholders' investment they have been entrusted with, not to their own job security. Now and then the two coincide. Not so at PA. During the past four months, that group of management gurus devoted all their time to hunting for another buyer. A white knight," he whispered conspiratorially, "and a blind one, too, I bet, who couldn't read financial statements or work out for himself why Pacific was declaring a loss, the second year running, when American Airlines' profits are up again, and National is diversifying its asset base. There is nothing wrong with Pacific that a new team can't correct."

"You have fired the top executives?"

His eyebrows shot up to affect a look of exaggerated innocence.

"I've been hoping they'd all leave in protest. After all, I've been questioning their competence in public. It would save us all a lot of bother if they admitted defeat."

"Will you run the company yourself?"

"Men like me, Mrs. Hayes, run things. We're good at discerning larger patterns, but not at filling in the details. Joe Willis, the new president, will take care of those." He emptied his coffee cup with a loud slurp and put it back on the silver tray. "More tea?" he asked Judith.

She shook her head.

Zimmerman summoned Arnold for more coffee for himself.

"Mr. Dale, a member of the Pacific Airlines board since 1983, has hinted that the union was concerned about your — "

"Did you say concerned?" Zimmerman hooted. "Now there's an understatement. Afraid, panicked, terrified, maybe — but definitely not concerned. It doesn't take a genius to discover I'm not a man to stand around discussing increased benefits, fewer working hours, and ironclad job security while the company goes down the tube. The unions have run Pacific Airlines for 15 years. They even have two representatives on the board. They've bought themselves a namby-pamby management which has let them have it their way all those years. Well, they've had their chance. Now it's my turn." He was leaning forward in the chair, his shoulders squared, every bit the fighter — or at least playing the part with conviction.

"You have some 14,000 people with union contracts at Pacific. You can't run the airline without them — "

"I can't? Hmm..." Once more that quizzical smile. "I doubt if you have examined all my options. Similarly, I doubt if they have. When they do, they'll realize that I aim to put PA back on its feet, with or without their help. It's their choice which." He watched Judith writing for a second, then he asked, "In their place, what would you do?"

"I don't know all the facts," she said. "But I guess I wouldn't give in too easily."

"Would you put your job on the line? On a point of principle?"

Another trick question? "Yes, I think I would."

Zimmerman nodded. "You have the luxury of immutable principles. Most people don't."

Before she had a chance to respond, the door flew open to admit a small, balding man with gold-rimmed glasses, fur-collared coat, and blue silk scarf. He carried two immense attaché cases that looked as if they weighed more than a man his size would want to lift. To Judith's surprise, he tossed the cases onto the mahogany table and continued his progress toward the fireplace.

Zimmerman completely ignored his presence.

"God, Paul," the man shouted, pausing to catch his breath, "I've been trying to get you for two hours. The damn phones are out or something. Both your lines busy, busy, busy. Drove me crazy. In the end, I figured I'd need you to sign things, so I braved the damn *blizzard* and I came myself —" Blizzard? A few desultory flecks of snow wafted against the windows.

He had either just noticed Judith, or only now decided to acknowledge her. His squeaky voice rose another note. "But you're not alone..." He spread his short legs, rocked back on his heels, and stuck both hands into his pockets. "Well..."

Zimmerman inclined his head to one side. "Judith Hayes, meet the illustrious Philip Masters, my current mouthpiece and occasional counsel. Mrs. Hayes and I were in the midst of reviewing my interest in Pacific."

"You were?" Philip Masters squawked, staring at Judith.

Zimmerman chuckled at Masters's consternation. "In a manner of speaking. Mrs. Hayes is working on an abridged version of my life story. It's what they call, in her trade, a personality profile."

"And Pacific Airlines?" Masters spluttered.

"We had to start somewhere," Zimmerman said.

"Hello," Judith said noncommittally. She had read about Masters and hoped to talk to him about Zimmerman. Masters was thought to be the keeper of the secrets — a smooth negotiator and a tough opponent. He had been with Zimmerman since 1949, first acted for him in a dispute over a piece of land in Ste-Agathe, Quebec, was a wizard at real estate law, and had eased Zimmerman's way into the more than 100 million square feet of office and shopping mall space he now owned in the U.S. and Canada. He spent much of his time lobbying for favors in Ottawa and in various state capitals.

"But Paul — " Masters rocked even farther back on his heels, till Judith thought he was in danger of landing on his ass.

Zimmerman cut him off in mid-sentence. "I invited Mrs. Hayes," he said. "She is a friend of Marsha Hillier, Colonel Hillier's daughter."

"Oh," Masters said. "And who do you work for, my dear?"

"I free-lance. But this story is for *Finance International*," Judith said. She hadn't even flinched at "my dear."

"Sort of like you, Philip, a hired gun," Zimmerman said. "She'll work for whoever makes her the best offer." His voice was gentle despite the slam it aimed at both of them. Judith was surprised that

Masters didn't protest. Perhaps he was used to this sort of banter. He merely turned his back and started for the table and his two briefcases. "Right, Philip?" Zimmerman didn't let go.

"I don't take any job that comes along, only the ones I choose," Judith said to fill the void.

"More luxuries," Zimmerman murmured. "How very convenient."

Masters spoke at last. "As I mentioned," he said with a tight grin, "I have a few things for you to sign. Closings today. Shouldn't take more than ten minutes. Maybe Mrs. Jones —"

"Hayes," she muttered.

" — will excuse us?"

Zimmerman stood up slowly. From the careful way he lifted himself, palms steady on the arms of the chair, Judith guessed he had arthritis or rheumatism — the only hint so far of his age.

According to Who's Who, Paul Zimmerman was 58 last July. Born in Hungary. Educated in Montreal. No degrees listed. Sixteen chairmanships, including Loyal Trust, Monarch Enterprises, Domcor, Royal Bus Lines, New York Securities, Southern Airlines (Pacific Airlines hadn't made it into the current edition), Wheatsheaf Resources, and a bunch of oil and gas companies that Research had indicated were each in the $12-million to $25-million net worth range. Monarch itself had seven separate subsidiaries, each wholly owned, each with its own CEO reporting to the holding company.

His listed charitable activities included the United Jewish Welfare Fund, the World Wildlife Fund, the Jerusalem Foundation, the United Jewish Appeal, Canadian Aid to Refugees, and the Weizmann Institute.

Two children: Arthur, born 1961, and Meredith, born 1977.

Wife: Brenda. Research said she was born in Montreal in 1950, had a BA in English literature from McGill, and had married Zimmerman in 1975. Her main interest was shopping. There had been an earlier wife — 1950 to 1973 — name of Eva.

Zimmerman claimed no clubs and no interests. He went to great lengths to protect his privacy. He hated to be photographed and on one occasion had wrenched the camera from a photographer's hands, torn out the film, and knocked the photographer to the ground in the ensuing struggle. The photographer had sued for assault. Zimmerman had settled out of court for a reported $150,000.

With Zimmerman's gaunt frame now towering over him, Masters seemed ridiculously short and rotund. His meticulously cut vented dark blue jacket could not hide his bulging paunch. Judith bit her bottom lip till the pain overcame her desire to giggle. It was the thought of the two of them, side by side, striding into some momentous corporate meeting.

"Mrs. Hayes, if you wouldn't mind," Zimmerman said with a helpless shrug. "Perhaps Arnold could show you around the house while Philip and I go through these papers. I expect you'll want to see the place, anyway."

Arnold was already there, waiting for Judith. His pinched cheeks implied that he had several more important tasks to attend to and that, like Masters, he didn't approve of journalists.

"Goodbye, Mrs. Hayes," Masters called after them. "Please give my regards to Mr. Webster."

A nice touch, that, considering that Webster owned the magazine Judith was writing this story for.

"Perhaps you'd like to see the gallery?" Arnold asked without enthusiasm. "Mr. Zimmerman collects Impressionists."

"A good idea." Judith much preferred Impressionists to pink marble.

It was the right decision. Zimmerman's collection, though it had barely been mentioned in the press, was spectacular and, she suspected, one of the best in private hands. The paintings were displayed in a large oblong room, with a shimmering blue and gold patterned Oriental rug occupying the center. Each painting was lit by its own wall fixture, and each had a small brass plate for identification. Judith noted two Delacroix, one Degas, three Turners, some Corots, a green canvas by Odilon Redon, and several Monets. The Degas was a marvelous glowing blue ballet dancer bending over her shoe. The Gauguins were all early, except for a still life of khaki pears and orange cauliflowers on a pink plate.

Judith recorded them all in her notebook. "Has Mr. Zimmerman been collecting paintings for a long time?"

"Twenty years," Arnold said. "These are not all of them. There used to be more." He took a step back from Judith's elbow and positioned himself near the bay window. She assumed he regretted speaking two sentences in a row.

"Maybe you would like to see the garden?"

She had read about that, too. Terraced, Italian, two artificial waterfalls turned on during the summer, a skating pond for the winter, three hills he had made for tobogganing, a warm pool with sauna and fake palm trees, Japanese lanterns at night. The whole thing was estimated to have cost $2 million. He had built it for his new wife, Brenda, apparently because she felt the woods that had originally occupied the space had blocked out the sun. Zimmerman himself, Judith had read, had taken to jogging three miles slowly around the garden each day, protected from public view by the tall stone fence and the electric wiring along the top of it. In the winter, the snow was removed from the paths in the mornings. The exercise, an unidentified friend had told Jensen, provided his thinking time. He made most of his investment decisions while on the run.

Judith joined Arnold at the window. "Must be beautiful in the summer," she said.

"Mmm," Arnold concurred. "If you would like to walk around..."

"I'd rather not," Judith said firmly. "Much too cold now to appreciate it." She picked up a finely painted statuette from the windowsill. It was handcrafted, the figure of a woman in peasant garb, her full skirt spread out around her ankles as she posed, her knees drawn up, her hands gathered around some flowers. She was a fragile light blue, with apricot cheeks; a tiny smile lit up her face. "She's rather beautiful."

"Zsolnay," Arnold said. "From southern Hungary, near Pécs. Mr. Zimmerman has had a number of them brought over." He took it from her and carefully replaced it. "They are rather valuable."

"Really," Judith growled. *And here I was, about to smash it.*

They were both saved from further conversation by Zimmerman. "My apologies again," he said. "I wish one could predict every crisis." He turned on another light that brightened the room to a gallery effect. "You like the paintings?"

"They're beautiful. But why the Impressionists?"

"You think they're too informal? They were very popular with dealers in the '60s: a little risqué, yet still with recognizable shapes and forms — later they got most of us into abstracts. Except for Ken Thomson. He stuck with the old Krieghoffs, crafty devil." He chuckled.

"No other reason?"

Zimmerman contemplated. "I like their sense of reality. No pretense at an ordered universe. No symmetry of design. They painted their impression of the truth — as they saw it. With some collusion by the viewer, who was left to inject his own interpretations. Look at this woman of Degas; she has a perfectly blank face. You and I are forced to imagine who and what she was."

He seemed amused by the trouble Judith was having, balancing her notebook on the crook of her left arm, while her right hand tried to keep up with his patter.

"Have you studied art?"

"No," she said, not wanting to remember her disastrous year in art history.

He had turned to one of the paintings, a small Renoir, and was closely examining the gold-leafed frame. "This has been chipped," he said to Arnold who was hovering nearby.

"I haven't studied business either," Zimmerman said with a chuckle. "Yet I seem to get by. Have you seen any of my buildings?"

"Of course," Judith said. They dominated Toronto's downtown skyline. "Everybody has."

"They are like giant jigsaw puzzles with an almost infinite variety of pieces. The catch is to assemble them first in your head, or you'll never realize them in concrete and be there to collect the rent. In this business, you can't make small mistakes, only big ones."

He led her back into the hallway. "What's your deadline?" he asked.

"Four weeks," Judith replied, surprised by his change of tone.

"I'm afraid Philip was wrong. Our little signing session is likely to last a couple of hours, maybe longer. Can we resume another day?"

"When?"

"Perhaps you'd care to join us for dinner Sunday? A few friends are coming to celebrate with me."

"What's the occasion?"

He didn't answer immediately. He stopped and turned and seemed to be thinking about the answer. His ice blue eyes were fixed, unblinking, on her face, with a gaze so intense and questioning she felt uncomfortable and looked away, over his shoulder to the incongruous glass case full of dead butterflies behind the Greek statue near the gallery entrance. Each butterfly was pierced through the center by a bright gold pin. The tiny incandescent wings glistened in the amber glow of the chandelier lights.

"A bit of a late birthday party," Zimmerman said finally. "And I want you to be able to observe the man I have been. Otherwise the transformation would mean little to you."

TWO

The first person to arrive at Brandy's on the 27th of February was Sylvia Hogarth, the 22-year-old newly hired waitress. Normally the owner-manager opened the doors himself, set up shop, checked the kitchen for supplies, and made sure of the morning deliveries of fresh meat and vegetables. But on the 26th he had asked Sylvia to work the extra couple of hours — on double pay — because he needed to spend the time in Greey's office upstairs, attempting to negotiate a five-year lease renewal.

That was why it was Sylvia Hogarth who discovered the body.

The man lay on his side, in the alcove entrance to Brandy's bar-restaurant, his head at an angle, against the door, his back curved around the bright orange lettering on the doormat. The letters stood out clearly on the photographs taken by the Identification Bureau: WELCOME.

His right arm was hooked around his chest. His left arm covered his face, the elbow pointing upward, as though he was trying to shut out the light. He wore a heavy navy blue woolen overcoat, a gray mohair scarf, and black rayon socks with old-fashioned garters.

In the beginning, Sylvia Hogarth had thought he was sleeping. Although the area around Brandy's had long ago become a fashionable hangout, there were still a number of old derelicts around. No denying the proximity of Jarvis Street with its flophouses, cruising whores, and charity homes for the needy. In winter some of the derelicts took refuge over hot air vents around the St. Lawrence Market a couple of blocks away; that was against the law, but the police didn't bother them. Constable Peter Giannini from 52 Division had been known to slip them a dollar or two himself, as had Detective Inspector David Parr of Homicide. They both shopped at the market on Saturday mornings.

Sylvia Hogarth had waited for a few moments, she said, not knowing what to do, then asked the man politely to move on. When he didn't respond, she nudged his foot, gently — "I barely touched him. Didn't move his leg. No" — with the toe of her shoe. That's when she noticed that he wasn't wearing shoes. "It's snowing, you know, and about 10 below, so I figured he can't have been wandering around without shoes. Perhaps somebody stole them off him during the night. That's what I thought. So I stepped over him and opened the door. His arm sort of flopped down and then I could see the blood on it." She swallowed hard. "I've never seen a dead man before." She looked over her shoulder toward the fancy doorway where the backup from 52 Division had cordoned off the scene for the photographer.

"You phoned then," Parr prompted, patiently.

She shook her head. "I think I must have screamed, because a man heard me and stopped. He phoned the police. That's him over there." She pointed at a young man in an Irish knit sweater, now sitting under a floppy tropical tree at one of the window tables with Constable Angus Stewart, who was taking his statement.

Neither Sylvia Hogarth nor the owner-manager, who had been called down by now, had ever seen the dead man before. It had been difficult enough to convince Sylvia to look at the man's face, and even when Giannini had succeeded, she would only glance at it for a second before she turned away, bringing her handkerchief to her lips. She thought she was going to be sick if they made her look again.

Parr wished other people in the area of Church and The Esplanade were as squeamish. They were all jostling for a better view, and the five uniformed men were having a tough time keeping them back.

Parr waited for the Identification Bureau to finish its work before he moved in for a closer look. Staff Sergeant Levine of the Criminal Investigation Branch had called him down after he had examined the body. Levine had thought there was something unusual about this homicide. And he had been right. Levine had a knack for spotting the interesting ones.

The most interesting thing about the dead man was that he was distinctly not one of the local derelicts. He was carefully and expensively dressed. The overcoat was brand new, or near as dammit. His gray suit, Parr noted enviously, had the silk finish of one of Bill Brady's best imported materials; his shirt was silk, too, and probably handmade, judging from the extra-wide cuffs held together by a pair of pearl cuff links with gold connecting pins. There was a squashed brown and blue check felt hat half hidden under the body, as if it had been thrown there before the man fell.

Strangely, he wore no shoes.

The third striking thing about him was the manner of his death. Two bullets had entered his body: one through the right temple, the other through the throat. Both shots had been fired at close range — the burn marks around the wounds testified to that. Either shot alone would have been fatal.

The damage to the back of the man's head was terrible. A piece of his skull had been blown away by the blast, as had some of his brain. Parr guessed that the killer had used Remington-Peters bullets, the ones that explode on impact as the copper-sheathed nose peels back. But he would have to wait for the autopsy to verify that. What he didn't have to wait to determine was that the body had been carried here from some other place and bundled into the doorway. There was barely enough blood to account for the bullet that had traveled through the neck, let alone the one that had exploded in the man's head. Big pieces of skull and brains were missing.

"Well?" Levine asked, bending over Parr's shoulder and gazing into the dead man's open mouth. The lips were drawn back in a silent scream as if he had known he was about to be killed.

"A lot of gold fillings," Parr said. He shut the eyelids over the staring black eyes, though he knew the pathologist wouldn't like that. It was instinct mixed with some grudging respect for the dead. He stood and brushed the snow off his knees. He saw Levine was watching him expectantly.

"They're on their way to pick up the body," Levine said. "Anything else you want to check first?"

"I'd like to find the scene of the murder."

Levine nodded vigorously. "I've already called the dispatcher, sir. More men are on the way." It was only at times of great excitement that Levine called him sir, or when the Chief was around. They had known each other too long.

Again, Parr examined the man's face. He was about 60 years old. The gray, sallow skin had taken on the texture of starched plastic as it sagged back from the cheekbones. The wrinkles under the eyes had bunched up in the outer corners as the muscles had relaxed. The hair had receded, though the man had gone to some trouble combing a few long strands over the top of his head.

The hands were wide and suntanned, a deep bronze color, in contrast to the whiteness of his face. A thin pale circle around the ring finger of his left hand showed that he had been wearing a wedding band. Parr lifted it gently to take a closer look at the cracked knuckle.

"Anything in the pockets?" Parr asked.

"No identification whatsoever, sir," Levine replied.

"Nothing *at all*?"

Levine shook his head. "A bit of glass," he said with a grin. He pulled open the dead man's jacket. "There," he said, pointing at the shirt pocket. A couple of tiny blood drops had frozen onto the outside of the pocket. When Parr bent over them he saw they were small pinpricks that had penetrated the shirt.

"Glass," Levine said lightly. "Could make it easier for the boys to find the place where he'd been bumped off, wouldn't you say?"

Parr grunted in agreement. Levine was good at his job. One day he'd make inspector. But what Parr wanted right now was a cup of hot coffee.

He asked the IB men to let him have a report by the end of the day. He figured Levine would hound the pathologist. He'd visit the coroner's office himself tomorrow. He wished everyone a good morning and left for the St. Lawrence Market to see if Madame Roche still brewed the best coffee in the city.

THREE

Since 10 A.M. the letter had sat on the mantelpiece unopened. Judith had put it there right after succumbing to the old garden-variety feeling of greed that often possessed her at month's end and snatching the mail directly from the mailman's hand. There were three checks outstanding, and a tiny bonus from *Reader's Digest* for rerunning an old story about her father, the closet bard. Only two of the checks had come, accompanied by an urgent note from Ma Bell about settling her overdue account. Then there was the letter with the Chicago postmark.

The handwriting was, unmistakably, James's. The initials had elaborate squiggles to disguise their identities, the middle letters were neatly rounded little morsels, upright and in perfect formation. Judith remembered when all of James's writing had been like that, minutely controlled. Then he read, somewhere, that doctors were known for distinctive, though often illegible, handwriting and developed the ornate squiggles.

The last letter from James had been well over a year ago, and she had been sorry she ever opened it. He had attempted to give her advice about Jimmy's adolescence, though he hadn't seen the kid in two years. Judith suspected her mother had put him up to it — "the boy needs a father's hand" and all that. Just because his marks were lousy.

The alimony payments came from a Bay Street legal office — in Canadian dollars and never on time.

Judith made herself coffee and scrambled eggs. Anxiety always made her ravenous. She searched, in vain, for the bacon, some ham, and even, in desperation, the cottage cheese she had purchased in deference to her diet. That the cottage cheese was gone surprised her most. Kids usually hated it.

She ate two slices of toast with real butter — another *no* on her low-calorie strategy, but she had a perfect excuse on the mantelpiece: she needed all the fortification she could find.

The plan for this morning had been to work quietly on her Zimmerman notes. Instead, she tidied the kitchen and stacked last night's dishes, with the dinner plates grouped by color (the pink ones had come from James's parents — they used to have little gold lines around the edges) and the peanut butter glasses on the bottom shelf (out of habit; it had been some years since Jimmy had to reach for a glass). In the Hayes house 1987 was supposed to be the year of the dishwasher, but it hadn't happened yet.

Behind the canned Zoodles, she discovered a package of Betty Crocker's Chocolate Chip Snackin' Cake mix, poured it into an 8-by-8-inch tin, followed the too simple instructions on the side of the box (she tried them in French, for a challenge), and slammed it into the oven. All that absorbed a mere 15 minutes, despite the rusty hand mixer.

At noon she poured herself a glass of port, put on her old Frank Sinatra record about walking with the lions, curled up in her favorite shabby brown armchair, and tore open the envelope with one quick movement before she could change her mind.

In the top right-hand corner, in raised script, the paper displayed James's professional qualifications and the address of his clinic. "Dr. James W. Hayes, Veterinary Surgeon..." The W stood for Wadsworth. It really did. James had been assigned it by his father, the itinerant salesman, who had hoped to be written into the will of some distant cousin called Wadsworth. Later, James had tried to pass the initial on to Jimmy, but Judith had dug in her heels. No baby should have to be called Wadsworth.

The words were admirably spaced, the whole letter wonderfully centered. James took pride in the presentation of his work.

My dear Judith,

Who's he kidding?

Another year has gone by, filled, I'm glad to say, with challenge, learning, and a measure of happiness. I hope the year has been kind to you as well. I fear, though, when talking to Jimmy and Anne, that you are still having difficulties in your life and I know, I am, to some small degree, to be blamed for that.

Ugh...

My analyst is convinced that I have found a way to deal with my day-to-day problems, and he has encouraged me to take more responsibility for past actions and emotions.

A small choking noise erupted from deep in Judith's throat and surfaced as a squeak.

She finished her port in one gulp and poured herself another.

To make a long story short —

Not quite short enough...

— I feel the time is right for me to visit with the children. They must be given the opportunity to relate to me, one on one, at their own level and within their own environment. As you may recall, their visits here have been somewhat strained.

And mercifully brief and far apart. Nothing for several years after the separation, only letters and gifts for birthdays and Christmas. The first visit had been arranged by James's lawyer — the same fellow who sent the monthly installments — with Judith's lawyer, who was not really Judith's lawyer but a friend she occasionally dined with, and who gave her interests about as much attention as he accorded other charitable institutions. As the old saying goes, you get what you pay for.

During that first memorable visit Jimmy had been bitten by a poodle in James's care. The dog, it turned out, was not suffering from feelings of deprivation at having been moved to downtown Chicago from his Iowa farm, as James had assumed. He had rabies. Jimmy had spent the rest of his filial visit in Billings Hospital, screaming for his mother every time the doctor stuck a needle in his stomach. Judith had flown to Chicago to hold his hand and bring him home as soon as they'd let her. In the hospital cafeteria she had emptied a bowl of carrot soup over James's head and had to be restrained by the nursing staff from beating him to death with the blue plastic tray.

The next, and last, visit was two years later, and much less adventuresome. They had had a minutely scheduled timetable with outings to the Art Institute, Frank Lloyd Wright's home and studio, Lincoln Park Conservatory, the Shedd Aquarium, and a daylong excursion to the Museum of Surgical Sciences and Hall of Fame. Then they had gone sailing on James's new 24-foot yacht, with his current belle, and confirmed that Anne had inherited her mother's tendency for seasickness. Anne might have mentioned this before they took off across Lake Michigan, but didn't want to talk to her father about something so personal. After all, she barely knew him.

Afterward, when Judith asked Jimmy how they had gotten along with their father, all he said was "He runs one hell of a tour."

   I realize, in hindsight, that we were not yet ready for one another then. Now we are. When I spoke to Jimmy on the phone last weekend, I knew the time was right. He needs me. I expect the same is true of Anne, too, but perhaps her needs are less pressing than Jimmy's. And this is as it should be. A boy needs a role model —

Oh no. Not a role model!

   — and no matter how hard you've tried, you cannot be that for him. Don't jump on your high horse, Judith, I'm not being critical. You've done a fine job bringing them up. But Jimmy is nearly a man himself now. It is my turn to do my duty —

No amount of port could alleviate that line. And, knowing James, he would truly have conned himself into his new role. He would probably have had a faraway look in his eyes as he penned those words. She'd been half expecting it, since his last garbled call about getting Jimmy interested in animal science. For Christmas he had sent the two kids a huge aquarium — perhaps a reminder of the Shedd — personally delivered by the owner of Exotic Aquarium Services. Luckily, all the fish had died within three weeks so Judith didn't have to remember to feed them any more. Anne had flushed their limp, slippery bodies down the toilet and they had converted the aquarium into a major-league flowerpot that now happily housed the philodendrons.

   — and I hope I can count on your help, or that at least you will not throw obstacles in my way. While I've not been of much assistance to you, myself, these past few years —

Closer to ten, actually...

   — I do intend to do my share now. There is a convention of small-animal vets in Toronto next week. I will be arriving Monday evening, the 2nd, and expect to stay for two weeks. I've already mentioned my plans to Jimmy and Anne. They have agreed to dine —

Dine!

— with me at the hotel Monday night. I beg you, Judith, not to make it difficult for them.

Yours,
James

She followed her nose into the kitchen, took Betty Crocker out of the oven, and loosened it around the edges. While waiting for it to cool, she checked the school calendar. March 2nd really *was* next Monday. Under the date, next to Jimmy's swim tryouts, in Anne's neat blue pencil it said DAD.

She set to frosting half of the chocolate cake, cut it into bite-sized chunks, and ate it.

Then she vacuumed the living room, vigorously cleaned the upstairs toilet bowl with Sani-Flush, and shoved a load of Jimmy's shirts and underwear into the vintage 1960s washing machine in the basement.

When none of this worked, she dialed Marsha's number.

Marsha and Judith had been friends since Grade 7 at Bishop Strachan School for girls. Back then, they had been best friends, so close the head prefect suggested they not be allowed adjoining desks — they would be too distracting for each other. Years later, the friendship deepened as their paths diverged — Marsha scaling the executive ladder on the New York publishing scene, Judith eking out a meager living from words in Toronto.

"Judith, for Chrissakes, what's happened?" Marsha's reassuringly familiar, wonderfully deep, amused voice was full of concern and expectation.

Already Judith felt better. Marsha's voice usually had that calming effect on her.

"Nothing yet, but it's all about to. James is coming, if you can believe it. He is planning on *relating* to Jimmy and Anne, and he wants to be a *role model*. He actually thinks Jimmy needs him, and he wants to do his *duty* ..."

"He told you all that?"

"In a letter. What am I going to do?" She had failed to keep the whine out of her voice.

"Nothing," said Marsha after only a moment's thought. "You're going to sit it out, calmly. James has clearly hooked onto a new analyst. The last one was intent on having him identify his personal goals and needs, putting him in touch with his feelings, forcing his innermost fears and childhood deprivations to the surface, so he could wallow in them. Relating wasn't on the menu... New shrink, new priorities. With luck, this too shall pass."

"But the kids?"

"They'll deal with it in their own way. Jimmy knows all about rabid beasts now, and you can't go sailing in Toronto in March. They know he's coming?"

"Yes. They've known for a while. That's another thing that bothers me. Why in hell didn't they tell me?"

"Because they're smart. What's the point of getting you all riled up a minute sooner than necessary? Who likes to break bad news?"

"They want to see him."

"So? He's their father. It's not an issue of conflicting loyalties. Why shouldn't they see him?"

"Do you suppose Mother's had something to do with this? She's been talking about Jimmy needing 'a father's hand.'"

"No point blaming the visit on Marjorie. Last time you won a battle with her you were 16, and that was a costly victory."

Ignoring her mother's insistence that she spend the summer at her grandparents' cottage in the Muskokas, Judith had gone to stay with Marsha's family on the North Shore. She had loved the semblance of opulence at Marsha's, the freedom afforded the three children. Although they had nannies well past the age when nannies were an acceptable alternative to parenting, none of them had to report in on what they did each day and why.

Marsha and Judith had drunk beer and Colonel Hillier's vintage port and cruised the beaches in Marsha's new red convertible with custom-made license plates that said NO. 1 CAT.

For three weeks afterward, Marjorie had refused to speak with Judith, and when the grandparents died a year later, she had managed to make her feel guilty for their deaths.

"What am I going to do?" Judith repeated.

"Make some tea. Don't drink anything stronger than tea, and don't eat sweets. You can't handle crisis when you're fat and hung over. Have your hair done, buy a new dress, go out with a friend, keep busy. By the way, how did you get along with Zimmerman?"

"Went well, I think."

"You think?"

"Well...I felt as though he was orchestrating the whole thing. He had choreographed the interview, knew what he wanted me to ask, had an agenda for his answers, had me scheduled to see what he wanted me to see. He was overly cooperative. And I don't see why."

"I warned you he was going to be cooperative. He has no reason not to trust you. After all, I arranged the introduction. From his point of view, that means you're the safest ray of limelight he's likely to get."

"Why?"

"He used to know my father. He's been a guest at my mother's summer place on the North Shore. He thinks we move in the right circles to celebrate a man for his ability to make wads of money and keep it. Funny thing is, Mother has always despised him, but never let him know."

"Any particular reason?"

"With Mother, it's anyone's guess. Mine is she thinks he became too rich too fast. As third generation after the potato famine, she's always had delusions of class."

"How well do you know him?"

"Well enough to flirt with, but not enough for a serious conversation. Strong cocktail party stuff."

"I'm going to his home for dinner Sunday night."

"Super. That gives you an excuse to have the hair coiffed, buy the new dress...you know."

"Thank you, I'll try," Judith agreed reluctantly, before hanging up. She had never found hairdressers relaxing. The time they wasted annoyed her, as did the whole pretentious performance, and the results were rarely worth it.

The doorbell had been ringing for a full minute or so, in rhythmically persistent bursts, and it wouldn't stop. With her shoulder to the wall Judith could peer through the side window and just see the back of whoever was standing on the porch.

There was no mistaking the angle of the shoulders nor the worn blue overcoat with the faded blue collar. She opened the door to view the rest of Detective Inspector David Parr leaning against the doorpost, his hand still on the bell, grinning.

"It's kind of hard to tell from here," he said, "but that may have been a not unreasonable rendition of 'Colonel Bogey.' What do you say?"

Judith shook her head. "More like a fire alarm," she said. "Best part is when it stops."

"That's part of 'Colonel Bogey,' too. May I come in?" he asked, standing first on one foot, then the other as he loosened his overshoes. "Not much hospitality in these parts today."

He kissed her, a little too casually, on the top of her head. They had been seeing each other for a good year or so now, yet the relationship had failed to settle into a comfortable groove. She ushered him into the living room. He threw his overcoat onto the back of the couch and himself into the armchair they both liked. He was looking at her expectantly. "Did you wonder how I knew you were here?" he asked.

"Lucky guess?"

"Uh-uh."

"Binoculars?"

"Gave that up when I came off the regular beat. It's the path to the front door. Snowed last night. About an inch of new snow. Pair of big duck boots going, pair of smooth boots also going — two kids. Heavy gumboots in and out: mailman. Nothing else by the front door. I know the back door's stuck because I spent two hours battling with it last weekend. Deduction: you haven't been out yet." He hooked his forefinger into the collar of his shirt and loosened his tie. "Awful day," he said with a sigh.

"You can say that again," Judith concurred, perching on the arm of the couch near his coat. "I was about to make tea. Would you like some?"

"Tea?" he asked, looking at Judith with renewed attention.

"Tea," she said. "And I don't want to talk about it."

David shrugged. "Like me to start the fire? Damn cold in here." While the kettle boiled he scooped out the ashes and set up the logs. Jimmy had stacked them against the back door, which was very likely the reason why the door was stuck in the first place. All damp oak.

Judith brought in the mugs of tea and studied David's back as he worked. He had broad sloping shoulders, slightly hunched forward; the muscles stretched the rough tweed of his jacket. She remembered the first time she saw him; she'd thought he looked more like a college professor than a policeman. He'd been wearing that old heavy tweed jacket with the extra-large brown buttons, and his shirt was creased, open at the neck where his tie was always askew. She had promised herself she wouldn't fall in love with him, but it hadn't quite worked.

"Did you happen to be passing by?" she inquired.

"Not exactly. I needed some respite," he said, settling back on his haunches, watching the fire race through the newspaper before it caught the kindling. "I've been at the top of Spadina Road since noon. An old woman's been found with her head bashed in. Killer used the poker and left it in the fireplace. No fingerprints. He went around wiping the door handles, the cups, even the cards. Very efficient."

"Cards?"

"Tarot. She was a fortune-teller."

Judith shuddered. She still couldn't get accustomed to David's line of work.

"What was her name?"

"Cielo. Italian for heaven or sky," Parr said. "With a soft *c*. Wasn't her real name, though. She used it only for professional purposes. Did you ever consult her?"

Judith shook her head. "Haven't tried a fortune-teller in years."

"My second homicide today," David sighed. "All that wretched paperwork. But at least with Madame Cielo we can hope for an early burial. The other one's likely to drag on for weeks. No clue as to who the guy is. Someone went to the trouble of removing all his identification. Even the ring from his finger." He didn't tell Judith about the deep scrape marks along the knuckle of the man's ring finger, nor that the joint had been pulled from its socket when the ring was wrenched off.

He wandered into the kitchen for a second cup. "Judith," he called over his shoulder, "I'm sorry about the other night."

"You are?"

Judith was about to follow him when the front door crashed in with the combined weight of Jimmy and his closest friend of the moment, Duke (his mother had a lifelong crush on John Wayne). They hurtled into the living room in a blurred movement of flailing arms and legs, yelling and laughing till they hit the couch. Jimmy tossed his knapsack into the corner smack up against the record player.

"Hiya," Jimmy said with a smirk. Recently he'd taken to smirking whenever he saw David and his mother together.

"Boots. Boots!" Judith shouted in retaliation. "How many times do I have to tell you..."

"Keep your shirt on, Mom," Jimmy said, hopping back to the front door on one foot as he struggled to remove the boot from the other foot.

Duke thumped down where he was, lifted both feet in the air, and began to untie his World War II American army specials. "Sorry," he growled, in a voice of poignant hurt. After all, it wasn't his house. Or his mother. Very likely his mother encouraged trampling mud into the carpets because it reminded her of the Old West.

"C'mon," Jimmy said, digging Duke in the side with his foot, and headed into the kitchen.

"How about dinner Sunday?" David asked.

"Where's the peanut butter?" Jimmy yelled.

"Don't know," said Judith. "Can't," to David.

"Can we finish the ice cream?"

"Saturday?"

"I think so," said Judith.

"Thanks," said Jimmy.

"Creeps," Anne asserted from the doorway, addressing no one in particular. She slammed the door behind her. "I'm definitely not going to the dumb dance now. Stupid little show-offs. *No way.*"

"Ain't Zitface going to be surprised?" shouted Jimmy from the kitchen.

"What happened?" Judith asked, solicitously.

David waved limply and made his escape.

The phone rang.

Anne clutched her books to her fast-developing chest. Her hair stood at angry attention, her chin jutted out as it used to when she was defiantly wading through the terrible twos.

"Mrs. Hayes?" asked the polite voice on the telephone.

"Yes?"

"This is Deidre Thomas, Mr. Zimmerman's secretary. Mr. Zimmerman wondered if you would like the car to pick you up on Sunday."

"Sunday?" Judith pondered vaguely.

"For the party," Deidre Thomas explained. "Mr. Zimmerman is expecting you at his residence at seven o'clock for cocktails. Dinner will be served at eight."

"Sounds lovely," Judith said, realizing she hadn't even thought about dinner at the Hayes residence today. If she hurried, there might still be time to cook the pot roast, but only just.

"You *are* planning to be there," Deidre's voice persisted.

"Of course," Judith said. "But I'll drive there myself."

"Mr. Zimmerman thought Geoff would pick you up at 6:30 — "

"Thanks all the same," Judith said. What was the matter with this woman? Had she been programmed to have her driven to the party and nothing less would do?

"If you're quite sure...," Deidre said, hesitant.

From Zimmerman's mention of it, Judith would never have guessed that she was such an important part of Zimmerman's late birthday party. After all, they had just met.

FOUR

"You know you're welcome to look at him any time you want," Dr. Yan said testily. "Ours is but to serve." He sighed theatrically and took another cigarette from his gnawed-looking package of Camels. If he must smoke, Parr thought, why in heaven's name those? "Though what you think you're going to accomplish by staring at the poor bugger again..." Yan shrugged and spread his small manicured hands, palms up. "Perhaps you're looking for a flicker of recognition from him?"

Parr chose to ignore Yan's customary bullying. "I'm hoping for *something*," he said. No point getting into a battle with the coroner. He could be a brilliant strategist when it came to slowing down the works.

Parr glanced around Yan's office. It had been painted sky blue and outfitted with orange straight-backed chairs, black side tables, pea green filing cabinets, and matching green ashtrays: 1950s Holiday Inn.

"Still no idea who he is?" Yan asked.

Parr shook his head. "Nothing. Pockets were empty. Fingerprints not on file. Shirt handmade, no store name. Sent his mug shot out to all divisions, no response. Somehow, I doubt if there will be. By the looks of him he was a clean-living guy who was in the wrong place at the wrong time."

"A mugging?"

"Possibly. I don't think so. Too deliberate for that. Moving the body, for instance, for which there's double evidence. You put the time of death between 10 P.M. and 1 A.M., but Brandy's was open till midnight and the staff left by the front door without tripping over him at 1 A.M."

"Did you read the pathologist's report?" Yan asked. "Not that I want to discredit your professional hunches."

27

"About the blood-alcohol content? Sure. Been checking the bars in the area. No luck yet. Damn hard to pick out a guy — any guy — in a Thursday-night crowd, unless he's a midget, wears a clown outfit, or has a light bulb on his forehead. This one's sort of elderly average. And even if we got lucky and he'd been knocking 'em back in a bar with a waitress who has photographic recall, she'd have trouble with the photograph. People look different when they're dead."

"Some do," Yan agreed, glancing pointedly at Parr. "By the way, would you mind taking your goddam foot off my chair?" he asked with a fixed grin. "It's new."

"Right," Parr said, launching his butt off the coroner's desk as he swung his feet from the orange plastic seat cushion. "Well off. Somewhat overweight."

"Only around the middle," Yan said. "Healthy heart and lungs. You could try checking tennis clubs. Well-developed triceps and deltoids, right arm only. Lumpy flexor pollicis of the right thumb."

"Anything else?" Parr asked.

"Sure." Yan butted his cigarette in the ashtray. "Lots. He had lousy teeth and an expensive dentist. Probably calcium deprivation as a child. The back molars are gold, front bicuspids filled with porcelain. Another goes and he's into a whole new set. Or would have been."

Parr opened the door for the coroner and followed him out.

"In some countries people used their mouths as vaults," Yan continued. "Lots of gold teeth in case you had to get out in a hurry."

The elevators had obviously escaped the decorator's attentions. They were pre-war antiques with folding wrought-iron doors that clanged shut with such force that young cadets usually took the stairs at the morgue.

"He had been married a long time," Yan continued. "At least 20 years, I'd guess. Quite an indentation on the ring finger."

Storage was in the basement. Despite the cold and the overwhelming ministrations of Lysol and lemon air freshener, there was a faint smell of decaying flesh, or so Parr thought each time he came down here. Through all his years on the force, he had never become accustomed to it. In a room to the left of the main area, a couple of white-smocked pathologists were working on the fortune-teller. Parr waved at them as he passed the open door.

The room where the bodies were kept resembled a giant rectangular filing cabinet, painted antiseptic white.

"There are traces of brown stains on the first joints of the third and index fingers, right hand," Yan said, pulling on the handle of the drawer labeled NO NAME. "Nicotine. But you got that before. From the teeth."

Stretched out naked on the sheet-covered aluminum slab inside the drawer, the body seemed much less human than it had when curled up at Brandy's welcoming door. The wounds on the throat and forehead had turned pale blue, the blood was caked dark brown.

Yan picked up the right hand and propelled the fingers toward Parr. "Cigars," he stated with a triumphant grin. "Discoloration of the tip of the thumb and under the thumbnail. See?"

"Yeah."

"Comes from grinding the butt in the ashtray. Don't get so much with a cigarette. You don't smoke, do you?"

"Used to," Parr said. "Pipe."

"Right," Yan murmured, dropping the dead man's hand. "You're the type."

Parr decided it was better he didn't know what Yan thought of as the pipe-smoking type.

Since yesterday, the pathologist must have dug into the man's chest for more of the glass they'd found in his breast pocket. There was a cut above the nipple the length of a finger. Yan's chalk mark surrounded the incision, dark green around the waxy yellow skin. They had found a much larger piece of glass embedded in the brain.

"The glass came from a car window," Yan said. "Some kind of expensive smoked job used to break the sunlight."

"What make?"

"Don't know yet. They're checking with manufacturers."

"Killed in a car then," Parr asserted. "Glass shattered by the bullet that passed through the throat. Clean line of exit. Only shards in the chest."

Yan nodded.

"What do you make of the serial number on the left arm?" he asked, pointing at the upper left arm.

"Concentration camp," Parr said. "Probably Jewish."

"Of course," Yan said, impatiently. "What else?"

Parr held the arm with thumb and forefinger, looking at the six-digit number, indigo blue, stretched sideways and blurred, but still neatly printed.

"Auschwitz," Yan said, finally. "You can tell from the series. Very practical, the Germans. Systematic, like the Japanese. That's why they're so good with computers."

Parr had heard Yan had spent some years in a Japanese prisoner-of-war camp. Lost both his parents during the war. He was still given to red-faced rages over his secretary's Toyota Corona and the Minolta Forensic used to photograph details of the bodies.

"He'd have been about 14, I'd say, when they checked him in. Still growing. Or trying to. That's why the numbers are stretched. They grew with him, poor bugger. That puts him between 55 and 60. Must have been one strapping strong kid to survive that nightmare."

Parr replaced the arm gently beside the body.

FIVE

There are some overwhelming advantages to being an observer at a party, Judith observed to herself. Somewhat like dropping into a play where you're the only one without a script, a role, or the benefit of rehearsal. Zimmerman's party was well into Act I.

"I hadn't planned on getting into the textile business," the man in the olive green bow tie told Judith. "A fluke really. Met this guy at a dinner of Parker's, said he'd inherited the shop from his uncle. Couldn't make a go of it, and cared less. I like a challenge." The man swirled the champagne around in his long-stemmed glass. "We were up 20 million last year."

"Double what it was when he started," the capacious woman in the red décolleté added. "Eddie's got a knack for making things work. Not like *some* people, buying and selling companies like used furniture." She glanced at Eddie, smiling benevolence and pride, almost maternal. "Whatever he touches," she sighed.

"Except, perhaps, for wine," remarked Philip Masters as he pushed past with a full glass in each hand. "Can I get you something, Judith?" he squawked.

"No, thanks," Judith said, determined to follow Marsha's advice and nurse only one drink before dinner.

"We were okay in wine, you sleazy sod," laughed the face above the green bow tie, "till you lot decided to take your pound of flesh — "

"Eddie," hissed the large woman, her head swiveling rapidly.

"Rather an unfortunate choice of words, wouldn't you agree, Judith?" Masters said lightly.

"What I meant was — " Eddie stammered.

"I know what you meant," said Masters. Then he grinned. "You couldn't afford it, Eddie. Can't live in a house if you can't carry the mortgage." Then he half turned his back on Eddie and his wife,

31

either to indicate, rather crudely, that the conversation about wine mortgages was over or to get a better view of Judith's neck, which was at about his eye level. "Paul has asked me to take care of you for a while," he said. "Don't drift away."

"Charming," Judith said, as they all watched him maneuver his way toward a blue lace woman who was waiting for one of the glasses he carried.

"You know Jane?" Eddie inquired.

She didn't.

"A marvelous woman. Masterminded last month's Creeds benefit for the blind. The Botanical Gardens extravaganza for the ballet, last year. Shaw Festival fund-raiser auction, too, I believe."

"Has he finally succeeded in getting her on the National Trust board?" the red décolleté asked sweetly.

"Just," Eddie said.

"Odd that Paul would invite you to such a gathering of old friends, having met you only a couple of days ago," said the red woman, whose name turned out to be Susanne. "Especially as you're a journalist."

"You've known him a long time?" Judith asked after agreeing that it was indeed odd.

"Twenty-five years," Eddie said. "I was his first customer in the Aspen resorts. Those days, it was hard to sell units in Aspen, if you can believe. Now they're lining up at a million a shot. Turned out to be one hell of an investment. We've tried a few other odds and ends since, nothing major. Paul's interests jump from opportunity to opportunity. I'm more of a sticker, if you know what I mean."

"What happened to you in the wine business?" Judith asked.

Philip was back before Eddie could answer. He stopped a few inches from Judith's chin and looked her over, clucking appreciatively and somewhat theatrically. "You're very lovely this evening," he said. "Lovely and not so threatening."

Judith, who couldn't remember when she had last looked threatening, took a small step back and collided with an athletic man in his 50s who had been keenly engaged in debating decorating styles for his home in Florida. A couple of times in the conversation Judith had tried to abandon the textile business and join decorating, for a change, but couldn't make the transition. Eddie needed an audience.

"When was I ever threatening?" she said.

"Our first meeting was...well, frosty? Would you agree to frosty?" Philip didn't wait for her to agree. Insecure? Maybe. "That's it," he said, thoughtfully. "I worry about people with a chip on their shoulder. They're apt to be dangerous."

She felt the blood rush to her cheeks, but she was not going to ruin her chances of getting the story for *Finance International*. The Renault needed muffler repairs and she'd promised herself a new couch. However tempting it might be to toss the drink at his balding head, hell no. She sipped on her gin and tonic.

"Me too," she said. "I worry about people with chips on their shoulders. Lot of it going around these days."

Masters chuckled.

"Don't let him get to you, dear," said Susanne in a stage whisper. "It's just his style. Thrust and parry. Right, Philip?"

Masters continued to ignore her. "Come," he said to Judith. "You must meet the others." He held her by the elbow. "Have you met Brenda Zimmerman yet?"

She hadn't. Arnold, who was rather dashing in tails and white gloves, had ushered her directly into the tuxedoed, bejeweled room and left her there. She had stood for a while surveying the bright lights, the bowls of exquisitely arranged lilies of the valley, the shining faces, the women's colorful dresses. In the background, someone was playing the piano. Two waiters in crimson jackets wove around the small clusters of noisy people. There was not one familiar face among them.

It was precisely for such an occasion that she had bought the Boots Anti-Perspirant-Deodorant with aluminum chlorhydroxide.

Masters directed her to the far end of the room where the grand piano snuggled against the gold-brocade ceiling-to-floor drapes. Under a dignified portrait of herself — in black velvet, with fan and tiara — a tall blond woman, around 35, maybe 40, in a strapless burgundy gown, was gesticulating at two grave men. They were both very still and attentive. She had the self-conscious beauty of someone who knows how to inflict it on others. Her long slender arms flew in the air as she emphasized a point; the array of woven silver bracelets on her wrists made a soft tinkling noise. She wore elaborately designed silver rings, one on each finger.

When she laughed, she threw her head back, presenting her soft, blue-white throat and coming precariously close to dislodging her ample breasts from the uncertain confines of the burgundy dress.

"You must be Judith Hayes," she said with high-pitched enthusiasm, before Masters had been able to make the introductions. "How very nice that you could come. Paul's told me all about you. Well..." She elongated the "well" as she appraised Judith with a narrowing of the eyes, as though she were scrutinizing a new pet. "No wonder he's so enchanted with the story. Right, Philip?" She nudged Masters with her elbow. "I'd no idea writers came in such splendid packaging." She clapped her hands in child-like delight, her rings and bangles clanging musical accompaniment.

"We do our best to provide amusement and variety," Judith said, with a mock curtsy.

"This," Masters said, "as you may have guessed, is our hostess. And on my left, the resolutely pious Rabbi Reuben Jonas, our spiritual caretaker." The man with the steel-rimmed granny glasses winced and adjusted his hand-tied bow tie by turning it, once, clockwise. Miraculously, it stayed put.

"This week," Masters continued, "he's in persistent pursuit of $5 million for the United Jewish Appeal, having already fleeced us for the new university in Tel Aviv. Sometimes I wonder how many universities we need in Israel."

"One can never have too much education," the rabbi said, with practiced intonation. "Only too little."

Brenda held up her rings in supplication. "That was last week, Reuben."

"And Chuck Griffiths," Masters said, indicating the other man. He had a shiny, tropical tan, thick gray hair, and a spectacular gold watch. "He has just accepted the unique honor of being caller at the good rabbi's fund-raiser."

Griffiths shuffled his feet in obvious discomfort.

"Or hasn't Reuben told you?" Masters squealed.

Brenda reached out her champagne glass for the passing waiter to fill. "Always the last to know, eh, Chuck?" Her voice was loud and sharp. Around them, heads turned to watch as Griffiths gulped his drink, the ice hitting his upper lip. A drop of yellow liquid trickled down his chin and landed on his tidy white collar.

"I'd mentioned to Philip I was going to approach you," the rabbi said quickly. "I thought perhaps...inasmuch as you haven't yet... Obviously, you're the ideal choice. We'd be most grateful."

"Thanks, Reuben," Griffiths said quietly. "I'd like to think about it for a day or two."

"What's to think?" tinkled Brenda. "It's an honor, and you know it. But if the shoes don't fit...well..." She trailed off into another elongated "well," threw her head back, and once more challenged the burgundy dress to hold on.

Griffiths and the rabbi asked the waiter for fresh Scotches on the rocks. The rabbi then took Griffiths by the arm, murmured something to Brenda, and led him off toward the dining room.

"A little hard on him, weren't you?" Masters asked.

"Was I?" Brenda said with feigned surprise. "A man should be able to occupy his wife." Then she returned her attention to Judith.

His wife?

"Paul says you take notes of everything. Is that right?" Her lightly penciled eyebrows curved up above violet eyes shaded in a range of violets.

"Only when I'm working," Judith replied.

"And tonight? Are you working tonight?" Brenda asked eagerly.

Judith patted her enormous black handbag affectionately. "I brought my notebook," she said. "I guess Mr. Zimmerman thought this would be an easy way to meet his close associates all at once." *A hideous idea.*

"I suppose you'll have to write about the little woman, won't you?" Brenda tilted her head in an attitude of abject meekness. "Every great man has one, lurking just offside in the shadows. Behind him. Encouraging. Supportive..." She trailed off.

"Brenda," Philip Masters said in a voice a teacher might use with a troublesome child.

"Oh yes," purred Brenda, smiling flirtatiously over the top of her glass. Her tongue darted out and licked the rim. "I love the way champagne tickles. Don't you?"

"Mmm," rejoined Judith, helpfully.

"Faithful retainers, that's another must for all great men. In my opinion, and Hilaire Belloc's, they ought 'not to play the old retainer night and day.' Nothing personal, dear Philip." She turned to Judith. "We're friendly rivals for our lord's attentions."

"Ready for another?" Masters asked, grabbing Judith's half-empty glass.

"Philip's had a bit of a head start," Brenda confided. "Some 20 years, I think. We've been married 12. Met in the Bahamas. At the Colony in Nassau. One balmy night under the stars, surrounded by those fabulous white Roman columns in the garden. He was wearing a white suit. A storybook romance. Love at first sight, wasn't it, Philip?"

Masters smiled distractedly. "I don't think I was with you," he said.

"You weren't?" Brenda squealed. "How silly of me. Of course you weren't. No matter how faithful, a guy can't be expected to retain all the time. He's allowed to miss one or two inconsequential events. Nothing major, though. Right?" she asked Judith.

Again at a loss for a script, Judith said, "Mmm," which appeared to have worked last time.

"Have you met Meredith?" asked Masters.

Relieved at the distraction, Judith admitted she hadn't.

Brenda clapped her hands and jingled her bracelets. "Wonderful, wonderful," she shouted. "You can see how his mind works, all logic, and deduction. The two of us would almost add up to a whole brain — he's all left brain, I'm all right. Intuitive, telepathic, romantic. I used to write poetry when I was young. Wasn't very good, though. Do you read poetry?" she demanded.

Judith remembered English 101 and the last time she had to memorize a poem. "Some," she said cautiously. Later, there had been e.e. cummings and a brief crush on T.S. Eliot. *We are the hollow men.*

Brenda took her by the hand and propelled her toward the grand piano. Judith was surprised at the physical strength of her grasp. Brenda's silver ring left a slight indentation on Judith's palm.

"That's Meredith," she explained.

Meredith Zimmerman was perched on the piano stool, playing Liszt energetically. Her soft ash blond hair, tied with red ribbon, cascaded down over her back and swung rhythmically as she hammered the keys. Her high forehead and emphatic cheekbones echoed her mother's face; the wide jawline and white-blond eyelashes mirrored her father's. The starched white collar and the blue taffeta dress spread around her reminded Judith of picture-perfect little girls on Victorian postcards with titles like "Dusk at Chichester."

"Isn't she simply wonderful?" Brenda asked, gazing adoringly at her daughter.

Meredith looked up, beamed at her mother, and carried on with the Liszt.

"A professional," Masters said. "Trained with Malenkov from the Warsaw Conservatoire. She has all the discipline."

"Amazing for a ten-year-old," Judith said, thinking of Anne's painful piano lessons, the hours of monotonous practice, the battles trudging along to Mrs. Moore's on Howland Avenue. After two years of merciless persistence, Mrs. Moore had admitted defeat. "I can use the money, my dear, but I cannot sit here and rob you blind. I do have a conscience." Jimmy had inherited the secondhand piano and the apprehensive Mrs. Moore.

"The best," Brenda sighed. "'She walks in beauty like the night...all that's best of dark and bright.' You know it?"

"Keats," Judith guessed.

"Byron. You have children?"

Judith nodded. "Two." She'd always had trouble keeping those damned Romantic poets apart.

"How very fortunate," Brenda said, and squeezed Judith's arm. "They're such a joy."

"Not invariably," said a new voice at Judith's elbow. "From time to time even the noblest intentions misfire —"

Judith turned to look into the narrow face of a gawky young man wearing a dark mauve tuxedo, red bow tie, and matching cummerbund.

"— and what you get is someone like me. Isn't that right, Brenda?" He grinned, revealing an uneven set of shiny teeth and shiny pink gums. His skin was pale and dry, and though he could hardly have reached 30, the lines had begun to set into grooves around his mouth and eyes. His face was dominated by a thin protruding nose with pointed tip and flared nostrils. The strenuously moussed white-blond hair stood damp and rigid, in a peak over his forehead. The overall effect was that of a yellow-tufted blackbird with bright red neck feathers.

"Well," said Brenda, stretching the e. "Arthur."

"Arthur Zimmerman, Judith Hayes," chimed Masters.

That accounted for the watery blue eyes, the blond hair, eyelashes, and eyebrows. A watered-down version of the old man.

"Hayes, Hayes," mused Arthur, as though searching his memory for clues. Then he clicked his fingers. "Gotcha," he said. "You're the reporter person. Right?" He squinted at her.

Judith allowed that this was so.

"Papa suggested I should be pleasant to you. And I do so try to fit in with Papa's plans, don't I, Philip, old chum?" He deposited a languid hand on Masters's shoulder. "Would you be a good sport and get me another small libation?"

"Arthur spent some years in England," Brenda whispered. "Harrow, I think. Hence the phony English accent."

Masters shrugged off the hand unobtrusively as he turned to greet a gray-haired woman in an orange gown of homespun wool. "I guess the good doctor couldn't make it?"

"Being pleasant is such thirsty business, don't you think?" continued Arthur. "But then you wouldn't know, would you, Philip? Not quite your stock-in-trade. He doesn't exactly have to be nice to anyone," he explained to Judith. "So he isn't."

The waiter returned Arthur's glass filled to the brim, wiped his hand on his vest, and left.

"Bravo, darling," Brenda shouted, clapping again. Others joined in the applause as Meredith stood, all dimply smiles, and acknowledged the adulation. She bobbed her blond head, flicked the pony-tail back into place, and straightened her dress. Arnold, a vision of courtliness, appeared, proffering Meredith a silver tray and a champagne glass.

"We allow her just a touch at a party. She's always loved champagne," Brenda said.

"I used to take violin once," Arthur said, brushing his forehead with his wrist, as if to erase an unwelcome thought. "In Vienna, mostly. Papa was determined I was the new Yehudi Menuhin. A fine try, but no Stradivarius, as you might have surmised. Must be on your side of the family," he said *sotto voce* to Brenda, "all this divine perfection. Either that, or second time lucky."

Paul Zimmerman had suddenly appeared by Meredith's side, gathered her in his arms, and lifted her high in the air, her head thrown back, her feet flying. Her small patent-leather shoes grazed the grand piano as he twirled her around and around, her arms firmly clasping his neck. "Oh, Daddy," she shrieked in a voice of scolding and delight, "Daddy, put me down!"

For a second, pictures of James and her son — his son — flittered through her mind, pictures she had long ago relegated to her mental archives: James throwing Jimmy in the air, his arms and legs spread wide, floating, then whirling him around so fast she'd been frightened he might drop the boy or hit the walls with his feet, but he never did. Jimmy had whooped and hollered with glee, curiously unafraid. Often she'd found him lingering near the door around six o'clock, making funny little gurgling noises and jiggling up and down with suppressed excitement, waiting for his father to come home. How at age two he could sense the time, she never knew.

Tomorrow Jimmy would be "dining" with his father at the Four Seasons Hotel. A quite unreasonable jealousy stabbed at Judith as Arnold began to usher the guests in for dinner.

SIX

Two tables had been prepared for dinner. Both were decorated with hyacinths and more lilies of the valley, gold-bordered table-mats, festive maroon napkins in soft cones, and an array of silver cutlery and silver plates under blue-patterned porcelain dishes. When Judith picked up her napkin, she realized it sparkled because the maroon cloth had been woven through with gold thread. An army of crystal glasses, four for every guest, glowed soft amber in the light of two giant candelabras.

The tables were side by side, each set for eight people, six on the sides, one at each end. Paul Zimmerman occupied the head of one table and Brenda the foot of the other, a traditional Ma and Pa arrangement, once removed.

Judith had been popped onto her chair by the reluctantly dutiful Masters, who had escorted her into the dining room. In addition to the tiny wreath of red rosebuds and violets, the pink card above her plate displayed a handsome script-rendering of her name.

"No half-measures for Paul," Masters commented as he left her. "Either he likes you or he doesn't. In your case, I had hoped he would make an exception."

"Meaning what?" Judith asked warily.

"Wait for the jury to come in," he cackled humorlessly. "But already he's got you sitting on his right."

On his left was Jane Masters, pale and statuesque in blue lace. Judith guessed her to be at least a foot taller than Philip, but she admitted to some malice in her estimate. Above the lace Jane wore a solid gold choker with a single pearl in the center, and diamond earrings. Her constant smile was as fixed as were the diamonds in their setting. Her conversation ranged through an update on the findings of the Unfair Advertising Committee in Washington, with particular reference to cosmetics, to a plot summary of *I'll Take Manhattan*, soon to be made into a five-part miniseries with joint Canadian-American financing. She modestly admitted to casting her vote for the project. As a new member of the Telefilm Canada board, she felt constrained to push for commercialism in the face of declining funds.

"The time has come," Zimmerman agreed with exaggerated vehemence, "for a touch of reality in the arts. So many people lining up for handouts. Haven't we indulged them too long?"

Judith noted that he had leaned heavily on the curved wooden arms of his chair when he sat down. His knuckles had turned white with the effort of lowering his massive body with dignity. There were tiny beads of perspiration on his forehead and upper lip.

"On the other hand," he continued, "when the Lorenzo de' Medicis are all seeking other pleasures, what are the arts to do but turn to the state for nourishment?"

He turned to Arnold and ordered the first wine to be served. "A modest little Mâcon-Lugny," he said. "An '83. Not a great year, but pleasant enough." To Judith, he confided that he had once assumed mild pretensions as a wine connoisseur, even hired a man in Paris to buy him a cellarful of white Burgundy, northern Rhône, and Alsace, and to teach him the necessary vocabulary. "In the end, I couldn't keep it up," he said. "Felt like a fool with all that sniffing and gargling. Never cared much for the stuff anyway. May have seen too much of it when I was a child. Little town I come from in Hungary is famous for its wine. Maybe the only place in Hungary anyone has ever heard of — Eger. Makes a red wine called Egri Bikavér. Bull's Blood, to you. Ever had it?"

It was a cheap red and Judith had bought it fairly often, though hardly for its distinctive aroma. On a good day it was only tart, on bad days it left a sour taste in the mouth. "I've tried it," she admitted. "Never knew it was famous."

"They ruin the flavor when they bottle it for export. The Algonquin in New York used to bring in its own. Only place in North America I've tasted the real thing."

"Last summer," Jane said, "we donated a case of Hermitage La Chapelle to the Festival Auction. Imagine, it fetched over three thousand. It was the year, I think...'80? '81? Philip took a wine cruise once around the Mediterranean."

Zimmerman glanced at Jane for a moment, preoccupied with

his own thoughts. She smiled firmly. Judith worked on her cream of asparagus soup with croutons. Then Zimmerman, who hadn't touched his soup, proposed a toast to Jack Goodman, "now freed of the restricting confines of ITT, and at the helm of Domcor — an organization with drive, promise, and a well-greased piggy bank to tap for smart investments."

Domcor, Judith had read, was one of Zimmerman's older companies. Valued at $20 billion or so by *Fortune,* it had held onto a consistent high rating in the Top 500. Its only problem, they said, was too much cash in the treasury. It had made a grab last fall for Quaker Oats of Chicago but had backed off after a month of ugly public haggling.

Goodman, it turned out, was sitting on Judith's right. She recognized him as the back-to-back neighbor with the boundless interest in Florida decorating styles. He was brightly energetic, cheerful, an enthusiast. Whatever it was he had to do with the greased piggy bank, Judith had no doubt he would do it well.

"It's been a terrific ride, Paul," he said. "So far. Give it a year or two and I'm going to need a new challenge, though. Trouble with Domcor is, it's hard to improve on perfection."

"Right," a gravelly voice from the end of the table said. "Just keep it from the marauders, Jack. No more, no less. We don't need another round of legal hassles."

"If I lay off all bets, Adrian," Goodman asked, "are you and Paul going to give me a shot at Pacific Airlines?"

"Anything you want, Jack, you name it," Adrian rejoined. "Long as it isn't Monarch. Paul isn't ready to retire."

Judith returned her attention to Paul Zimmerman. He seemed deep in thought, not listening to the bantering between his associates.

"It was my father who introduced me to wine," he said at last. "On Sundays we would all gather for dinner at noon around a wooden table with my mother's heirloom napkins you weren't allowed to touch once your hands got messy. She washed them every week and hung them on the line to dry. My father had the only knife in the family, his *bicska.* A pocketknife. I saved up for mine till I was nine. He cut the bacon, and he poured the wine. Each of us had an earthenware mug, for milk, water, tea, on Sundays for wine. Not the brassy red you know, a leafy green white wine called Leányka. That means something like 'little girl,' but friendlier." He wiped his damp forehead with the back of his hand, his pale blue eyes fixed somewhere over Judith's shoulder. His voice had become soft with the memories. "My mother had been a very beautiful woman. You wouldn't have known it by the time I arrived. I was told by my father's friends. She had been one of those dark-eyed beauties that come along once in a while, they make a man shiver. Like Meredith."

"Your daughter?" Judith asked, surprised.

"She'll grow into one of those. I used to know another girl called Meredith when I was a boy. She was perfect..." he trailed off. Gazed around the table, as if trying to recall where he was. "Have you ever been in love, Mrs. Hayes?" he asked at last. "She made my chest ache. You know that feeling?"

"Oh yes," Judith said with instant recognition. "What happened to her?"

Zimmerman sighed. "A long story, that," he said. "Maybe I'll tell you about it later."

She waited a bit, then asked about his mother. How did he remember her?

"Dressed in black, like the peasant woman she was, thin-faced, narrow shoulders, broad hips; she wore a shawl over her head. She said very little. Those days women weren't to speak unless they were spoken to."

"Barbaric," Jane said.

"No one could keep my mother quiet at dinner," Judith said. "But she never allowed wine or liquor in the house. Only sherry." Toward the end, her father had taken to carrying around a mickey of Scotch in his breast pocket next to his crumpled pieces of paper. Like Brenda, he used to write poetry.

The Beef Wellington was rare, the carrots and noodles over-cooked, but there were some delicious mushrooms the waiter served sparingly. "Morels," Goodman explained. "They're difficult to find here. Paul took a fancy to them some years ago in France, when we were looking for a place he and Brenda could use in the south. The problem with those old houses is they need so much repair before you can move in, don't you think, Jane?"

"Worst part is coming up with the right people to do it," Jane agreed. "Far as I can tell, the lot of them rip you off at every turn. Their little eyes light up with dollar signs as soon as they spy an American."

"And did you find the place?" Judith asked.

"Eventually. Near Nice. It needed a lot of work, though, Brenda will tell you. She's spent months getting it right."

The second wine was a rich smoky red. Zimmerman picked up his glass and squinted through the wine, stirring and swirling it around. "Hard to imagine that life now," he said, "with all my guests here and all my money." He smiled at Judith. "Money does impress. Strange, don't you think? My father was one of the poorest men in town. Dirt poor. So poor some days we had nothing to eat but grapes. We stole fruit in the summer. In the winter we starved. You know the old joke about how to make Hungarian omelet? First you steal the eggs..."

Zimmerman put down his glass and returned to drinking from a water tumbler of amber liquid Judith thought might be ginger ale. He hadn't had more than a sip of wine all evening. Nor had he eaten his food. He had pushed the meat about on his plate, shoved the vegetables to the sides, played with them, as a child might.

"He worked in the vineyards," Zimmerman continued. "Picking grapes. That's what my father did. In the late fall, after the harvest, there were these great wooden vats full of grapes and all the men and boys in our part of town would take turns climbing into the vats to squish around the grapes and trample out the juice with our bare feet. For days afterward our legs were purple up to our knees. Little kids waded in up to their waists."

He hooked a finger inside his starched shirt collar and loosened it. The diamond stud snapped and jumped out of sight. Zimmerman either hadn't noticed or didn't care. He drank more of his amber drink. "It's the air I remember most. Clear, fresh air full of the rich scent of grapes and raw wine. He had so much life then. He died young." He banged his chest with his fist. "His heart."

He mumbled something else, but Judith couldn't quite make out the words.

He sat still, his shoulders slumped forward, his arms resting on the table. He was gazing into his plate where the blood had congealed around the *boeuf en croûte* and soaked into the noodles, turning them pink. He shook his head from side to side, once, with a quick, jerky movement. He took a deep breath. "I'm sorry," he mumbled. "Sorry. Sorry. Sorry." Then he fell, face first, into the noodles.

For a moment nobody moved. Jane, still frozen in an attitude of exaggerated interest, dropped her knife with a clatter. Conversation stopped. Judith jumped up, bent over him, listening for his breath. Her hand reached out to touch his massive shoulder. But Brenda was already there, her arms around him. As she pulled him back, his head lolled to one side and crashed into the back of the chair. His mouth had fallen open, his eyes stared up at the ceiling, his face, all pink from the beef blood on one side, was yellow-white on the other.

Brenda screamed.

SEVEN

Brother Twelve and the Indian hadn't stopped at the Harbour Light since 1975. Brother Twelve claimed he had once preached to a Methodist congregation in Bismarck, Manitoba, and simply couldn't countenance the ministrations of the competition. The Indian said he hated all white men's religions even when accompanied by soup and a bed for the night. Parr suspected that, in both cases, it was a point of pride.

Daytime the two men spent in parks up and down Jarvis, at the lower end of Church, and across Sherbourne south of Queen. Summer nights they slept on the benches. The winters were toughest. They got by with underground parking lots, subway entrances, underpasses, and those downtown buildings that still allowed vagrants to sleep over the hot air vents at night.

At 8:30 A.M., the Indian dropped by Madame Roche's for coffee. He had been hopping around the four corners of St. Lawrence Hall since 7:30 A.M. and had collected some $20 and change. His collection technique varied from day to day, but the most fruitful routine involved a combination of dreadlocks, tambourine, and a fierce, sullen, threatening face he could never maintain for more than an hour at a time.

He liked his coffee thick and black and he never asked for credit or any favors. Here he was a paying customer, like any other. He had pulled a black knitted tuque over the dreadlocks and was warming his hands around the cardboard cup when Madame Roche noticed his shoes. They were brand new, shiny, dark brown leather lace-up brogues.

That's why Madame Roche called Detective Inspector David Parr.

Parr found the Indian and Brother Twelve on a bench in Regent Park. It was where they spent most mornings, waiting for the Dove to open for business at noon. It was a sunny, cold, crisp day. Brother Twelve was counting his change, laying out the coins slowly, quarter by quarter, dime by dime. It was a laborious process. He wore dark blue knitted gloves with the fingertips cut or worn away. The Indian had stretched out crosswise on the bench, the back of his head supported by his clasped hands, his elbows high, his face turned to the sun, his legs blocking the path.

He wore four or five multicolored pullovers, a checked hunting jacket, an army coat circa World War II, an old pair of baggy woolen trousers. His shoes, as Madame Roche had observed, were brand new. Years ago, as Parr remembered, the Indian had worn a good pair of rubberized working boots, but he had never had anything as swish as these brogues.

"Good morning," Parr said, positioning himself on the path next to the legs, but careful not to block the sun.

The Indian pushed his tuque farther down on his forehead in slow motion. Then he squinted up at Parr. "Hello, Officer," he said in his early-in-the-day croaky voice. "How's everything with you today?"

"Good, good," Parr said, wondering how come the Indian had such a memory for faces. "Yourself?"

"Can't complain," he said and shut his eyes again. "Can't complain at all."

"I can," Brother Twelve said, "but I can't say as anyone wants to hear it." He had shifted all the change into the inside pocket of his long overcoat, wrapped his wilted scarf around his neck, and hunkered down to roll a cigarette from a handful of butts.

"Some fancy shoes you got there," Parr said, coming to the point. He nudged one shoe with his foot so there would be no mistake about which shoes he meant.

"Oh yeah?" the Indian said, inspecting his toes with interest.

Parr tried a more direct approach. "Where did you get them?"

The Indian shrugged. "Don't know."

"Where were you last Thursday night, the 26th?"

Brother Twelve looked up from his task to ascertain that he'd heard right, then he began to laugh — a deep, shaky, mirthless laugh.

"How the hell would I know where I was last Thursday night, man?" the Indian asked stiffly. "I don't even know where the hell I was last night. Or last year. And I don't give a shit. I don't know what goddam day it is now, nor never mind some bleedin' Thursday away back. Why don't you just come right out with it? What are you looking for?"

There was no sense running them in. But if that was the only way he was going to get at those shoes, he had no choice. That's what he told the Indian. "A man has been murdered and dumped into the doorway of a fancy eatery, foot of Church and Esplanade. He'd been robbed of everything including his shoes. You're wearing brand-new shoes that look like they'd fit him."

"Never killed anybody," the Indian said, starting to take notice.

"Not since the bleedin' war, anyhow," Brother Twelve added.

"Best way to prove that is to let me take the shoes. We have a bunch of people up on Jarvis Street who can figure out if they belonged to the dead man. You can wait there while they do." Parr was trying to sound reassuring. He didn't succeed.

"You mean you want to run me in?" the Indian yelled.

"For an hour or so, that's all."

"On what charge?"

"No charge. You'd be helping the police."

"That's grand, man, truly grand. Me helping the police. You hear that?" he said to Brother Twelve, who was laughing again.

"Either that, or I'll charge you with obstructing justice. Or assaulting a police officer."

"That's five days," the Indian said, outraged. "I ain't goin' in there for five days, man. You know I didn't do nothin'. You know I wouldn't kill anybody. I've been hangin' around here some ten years, man, never got in any trouble. Mind my own business..." The fight had gone out of him at the prospect of not being there when the Dove opened. Nor the next day. That's what Parr had been counting on.

"Get you back by noon, sharp," he promised. *If the shoes aren't the dead man's.*

The Indian sure hated the inside of a police car. Parr suspected he hated all closed spaces and locked doors, and lost confidence away from his buddy. He'd pulled his coat tight round his shoulders, turned up his collar, and stuck his hands in his armpits. He was shivering. "The shoes were a gift, man," he said, as though he'd just remembered. "I was under the archway at the market. Late night. Dark, anyhow. A heel of red to pass the time. Big black car came by. Driver threw them at me. There was even a five-dollar bill inside. Some pages from the Book. That's God's own truth. People do that, man. They come and throw us stuff. Makes them feel better."

But that wasn't true either. Later, when the shoes came off and were hustled away to Forensics ("Let those bastards get a whiff of this..."), the Indian said he had fished them out of the cream-colored garbage bin on the corner of Church and Front, back of the Flatiron Building. It was on his daily route. His property. No one else dared put one finger to that bin. The shoes had been inside a plastic bag. White, he thought. Though he had worn them for two or three days they were still like new. Size 14 silk-lined brogues. In the center of the lining the manufacturer's trademark had been stamped in gold: Dack's Fifth Avenue, New York.

By now, Yan was beginning to bitch about the body cluttering up his morgue. "Man with 14 points of definite identification features murdered near a crowded Yuppie hangout and you turkeys can't find one goddam relative to collect the remains."

There had been no reaction to the mass postings of the mug shot and personal details, though they had been run in some of the major papers now, and no recognition from the dentists. There was still hope the ad in the *Dental Journal* would bring in something.

The *Canadian Jewish News* had agreed to run a picture but they didn't have an issue going to press for another week.

The silk-lined shoes turned out to be the 1986 best-selling Dack's Classics for the fall season, and the Fifth Avenue store in New York thought they might have sold a thousand of them since they first came out. They were willing to look at the photograph, but couldn't see how anyone would remember a face. That meant asking for help from the NYPD. The chief problem with them, however, was they generally had more bodies of their own lying around than they knew what to do with, and this one was off their lot.

At least someone had come to collect Madame Cielo. She had a daughter in New Orleans married to an enterprising Cajun cook. The two of them ran a small restaurant on Canal Street that hadn't yet made a cent. Mother, whose real name had been Barbara Fleming, had supplied the seed money and frequent extras, most recently a check for $3,000 to pay back taxes. Desjardins, the son-in-law, claimed all this was a repayable loan, though neither he nor the daughter could recall exactly how much they had borrowed over the past three years.

Mrs. Fleming's well-kept bank account recorded a total of $24,500 going to Mrs. Desjardins, but it had suffered little deprivation. The old lady had had bonds, stocks, retirement accounts, and term deposits totaling over a quarter of a million dollars — not bad for a small-time fortune-teller.

The daughter claimed she was as surprised as anybody. Her father hadn't left money, and she had no idea her mother had become so prosperous.

The Madame Cielo business generated cash only, in uneven bursts ranging from $100 one week to $5,000 the next. She deposited regularly from a brown envelope, Fridays at the Dufferin branch of the Canadian Imperial Bank of Commerce. The tellers remembered her bringing the cash in a variety of denominations. Her totals, entered in a large blue binder, were always accurate.

There had been no cash on the premises on Spadina Road and no blue binder.

There were eight witnesses to swear, if necessary, that the Desjardins were both in the restaurant the night of the murder.

Stewart and Giannini would spend the next week interviewing the neighbors. After the lousy day they'd had tracking the rest of the garbage from the Flatiron Building's garbage bin, it would be a welcome change.

EIGHT

Following Zimmerman's death, the press was unrestrained in its appreciation of all his good works. The *New York Times* gave him a corner of the front page, recycled the old picture from *Business Week*, and called him a "titan." The *Globe*, tastefully, put him on page 2 (same photograph) and labeled him a "Canadian philanthropist." He deserved a full column in the *Wall Street Journal*, with a list of his holdings and predictions of trouble at Pacific. None of the family had spoken to the press, and "the family's spokesman" said the funeral was going to be private. Donations were to be sent to the United Jewish Appeal.

Only the *Star* mentioned that the funeral would be at Forest Hill Catholic.

Though he complained about the last-minute changes he still had to make in the funeral arrangements, Philip Masters readily agreed to Judith's request for an interview. He seemed almost eager to fix the time, get it over with.

Paul Zimmerman had been dead only one day. Judith was halfway into the *Finance International* story. "Some small changes in direction, I think, Judith," Giles had suggested helpfully. "It's one of the largest corporate empires in America. We'll still want to know where it came from, but do try to find out where it's going as well. Perhaps a new header piece. Maybe a sidebar or two. Backgrounders. Profiles of family members. Close associates. That sort of thing. None too often one of our writers is right there when..." He paused to find the correct phrase, and gave up: "...the subject croaks."

"Right." For $5,000, American, he could have all the sidebars he wanted.

Time to recheck her *Who's Who*. Philip Masters, she discovered, was a CM, a QC, a B.Comm., and an MBA. Born in 1925 in

51

Montreal to Stephanie Goldberg and Colin Masters. Attended Queens, McGill Law School, Osgoode Hall, and Harvard Graduate School of Business Administration. Senior partner in Masters, Goldberg, Griffiths, with 22 directorships, most in conjunction with Paul Zimmerman's holdings. Director of all seven subsidiaries under the Monarch umbrella, as well as of the Monarch Enterprises holding company. There were a number of development companies, the Bank of Massachusetts, Linden Industries (real estate and gold, with a recent interest in construction), two hospitals, the ballet, the New York Philharmonic, the NYC College of Art, the Boston Museum, and an assortment of Jewish charities.

He belonged to eight clubs, including Edinburgh Golf, The Leash, Lyford Cay, Checkers, Long Island Lawn Tennis, Vail Golf Club, and the Royal Hunt. His interests, in contrast to his appearance, were all sports. No children.

Masters, Goldberg, Griffiths was on the 24th floor of the Monarch Building at Bay and Richmond. It was a black, antiseptic tower with two-level underground shopping, bank, waterfall, escalators, and four sets of elevators. No parking lot.

The 24th floor was gray plush carpeting, white walls with Christopher Pratt prints, a semicircular receptionist's desk with matching receptionist. Masters's secretary was exchanging light-bulb jokes with her. They were both writhing with laughter when Judith announced herself.

"Mr. Masters is waiting," the secretary said, recovering her composure. She looked like a life member of a strenuous fitness club, broad-shouldered, muscular, tanned, and tall. Masters must have a penchant for surrounding himself with tall people. "You're late," she observed, with a tight smile, motioning Judith to follow her.

Judith checked her watch. Only ten minutes late, which, considering she had had to abandon the Renault six blocks away behind a semi in a no-parking zone, was not too bad. "Being late for an appointment," Marsha had told her, "is not so much rotten manners as an insult. It's telling the other person your time is more important than theirs. It's like having a secretary place your calls." Perfection came easier for Marsha.

The quality of art took a sharp downturn along the corridor: sunset photographs and pencil sketches of 19th-century Indians in full feathers. Masters's office was in the far corner. It was two sides glass, two sides framed photographs of Masters with assorted friends, pets, and clients. In one he was dressed in Western garb, riding a white quarterhorse, his short legs stretching around the horse's ample sides. In another, he and a young Zimmerman were leading a pair of ridgeback hounds with numbers on their sides.

The younger Paul looked remarkably like Arthur. There were pictures of Masters pitching the ball for the Blue Jays (he had been one of the original sponsors), in morning coat and top hat with Zimmerman, with E.P. Taylor and the Queen at Woodbine for the Queen's Plate.

"Coffee?" the statuesque secretary asked.

"No, thanks."

For a moment Judith thought she had been left alone in the room, then Masters popped up from behind the three-foot-high red plaster and plexiglass tower that occupied the pine side table near the center.

"It'll be the tallest tube building in the world," he said, patting the top of the tower. "And that colour is real. Red Napoleon granite blocks from northern Sweden, polished by hand in Italy, cut into 42,000 perfect pieces, each marked for its exact position on the face. It'll be the most distinguished landmark in the city."

"The new Harbourfront Tower?" Judith asked, getting down on her haunches and looking up at it from the tiny people's perspective. There were not only tiny people, but tiny trees, benches, and azure blue lakefront with tiny sails. Right out of Lilliput.

"We started construction a month ago," Masters said. "Our first joint project with the Restman group. Come to think of it, our first joint project with anyone. Zeidler's design. We had hoped Paul would be around to see the opening. He was so proud of it. And he did like putting one over on the Reichmanns." He winked at Judith, as if to suggest she knew what he meant, which she didn't.

"First Canadian Place," Masters explained. "It's been the tallest tube to date. Won't be this time next year. Paul's always liked competition. A striver. A winner. What you'd call a Type A personality."

"I wouldn't," Judith murmured, "but I know what you mean."

Masters asked: "Why don't you sit by the window? Super view. You can write while I walk about. Never too comfortable sitting." Another Type A.

"That stuff," Masters continued, "it's jargon. A kind of shorthand. Don't misunderstand me, he wasn't typical in any way. One of a kind. Created the whole damn thing with his own hands. From nothing." He was pacing behind her. When she turned, he said, "He told you how we met?"

Judith shook her head.

"Montreal, 1948." He pronounced every word: "Nineteen hundred and forty-eight," as though pausing over the numbers would bring the memory closer. "I was 23, a graduating student at McGill, celebrating old McCarthy for allowing me to article with him. There were six of us at Le Vieux Coq. Champagne toasts, Scotch chasers. That sort of thing. We were showing off for the girls at the next table. Started tossing some glasses into the fireplace, Russian-style." He giggled. "The waiter asked us to leave. We were so outraged by his impertinence — and we were drunk, must have been drunk — we refused to pay. Next morning the maître d', still dressed in black tie and red cummerbund, arrived at McCarthy's and told me if I didn't ante up, he'd have to see if the senior partner had the money. From petty cash, he told me. That was Paul Zimmerman. Six-foot-three, ham-handed handsome, dreadfully uncomfortable in his tight-fitting clothes. A few years younger than me, but had *he* lived!"

Masters poured himself a glass of water from a big plastic jug on his desk and stood before a brownish photograph of Zimmerman and himself, arm in arm, in front of a two-story building and a Ford Model A. Zimmerman's long arm reached down, Masters's elbow bent up — they were both laughing.

"That was his first piece of land," Masters said. "I negotiated the loan for a pittance. I used McCarthy paper to get the Bank of Nova Scotia in. Amazing what a letterhead will do. Even now. God knows how he talked Eaton's and Simpsons into it, but they came, too. He was still working at Le Coq nights. Weekends he scrubbed down washrooms at the Montreal General. And he read Latin and economics at Loyola; he said he didn't study, he 'read.' Funny, that. He spoke English with an accent so thick you could cut it with a knife, but for some reason he wanted to be fluent in Latin. I suppose, in retrospect, that was a European thing. Owning land makes you prosperous, knowing Latin gives you class."

"In Hungary?"

"Especially in Hungary. They are as class-conscious as anyone in Europe, maybe more. Some hangover from the old Hapsburg

Empire. Everything is a question of breeding. Same with horses — can't buy yourself a winner no matter how much you're prepared to pay, it's all in the breeding." He smiled up at the photo of himself riding the fat quarterhorse. "Paul didn't much care for money, not for its own sake. He thought it dehumanizes." He stopped pacing near Judith's shoulder, rocked back on his heels, hands in his pockets. "Naturally, I didn't agree with him."

"For a man who didn't think much of money, he did expend huge bursts of energy stashing it away," Judith said.

"Sure. He was exceptionally good at it. Driven. Tireless. But it wasn't for the money. At least, not for its own sake. Or for the power it generates. The challenge, I think. Proving he could do what he set out to do, every time. Not to anyone else, only to himself. He didn't much care how the rest of the business community viewed him. He almost enjoyed being seen as an interloper, a robber baron. He had no interest in joining clubs, in seeking acceptance. He was, except for the few friends you saw Sunday night, a loner."

"He'd known all the people he invited that evening, except myself, a long time?"

"All of the men, more than 20 years. Let's see, now..." He looked around his wall of photographs till he found a group shot of some white-clad people waving from the guardrail of a white yacht: "Monte Carlo, 1965. We were all there. The Bonniers — he's had his ups and downs, but never a doubt they stayed close to Paul. Eddie's a hard worker, he hangs on one deal at a time, not a risk-taker, like Paul. Couple of times he stayed in too long. You heard the other night about his wine business."

"Did Paul lend him the money?"

"Not exactly. We bought some shares in his new venture and bailed out when we had to. That's all." He pointed at another couple in the photograph. "Reuben and Vera Jonas. You met the rabbi already. Vera was away with her family in England. Her mother's been ailing. Jonas is one of the best fund-raisers in the city — no, the world, I venture. Over the years he's snatched millions from Paul, and all for good causes. In January alone Paul donated over $700,000 for the new university in Tel Aviv. Adrian Parker, down the end of your table, he's with Ross, Wilkinson. He's been advising us on investments since '63, when he was still a junior accountant and he was all we could afford. Now he's one of the best in the business. Couldn't have done the PA deal without him. Jack and Alice Goodman. He *is* Domcor now. Super manager. Paul and I tried to tempt him away from ITT for years. I met him at law school. Same as Chuck Griffiths, my old law partner, now heads Loyal. You might have noticed Martha. She wore a low-cut dress made of some diaphanous material. Made her look like the tooth fairy. She's a pretty little thing, only been married ten years. Chuck's second wife."

"Who's the dark-haired woman next to Paul Zimmerman?" A full head of curly black hair and blue eyes. White pants skin-tight across her round hips.

"That's Eva, Arthur's mother," Masters said curtly.

"Is she coming to the funeral?"

"No. She lives in Europe now," Masters said, as if that explained why she wouldn't come.

"Is she included in the will?"

"She is well taken care of already, as is Arthur. But we haven't read the will yet."

"You know who the chief beneficiaries are, though, don't you?"

"Obviously Brenda and Meredith, in trust."

"And what will happen to the companies?"

Apparently relieved that she had veered off personal matters, Masters grew effusive again. Sure, they would all miss Paul's particular brand of genius, but they were superb organizations with strong executives at the helm. Monarch's board would elect a new CEO. Pacific was on the way to a turnaround, the management team was in place. In six months, at most, they would be into calmer waters. Paul knew how to select his teams.

"I saw the funeral notice in the *Star*," Judith said. "Why did he pick Forest Hill Catholic for the service? Wasn't he Jewish?"

"He used to be. I don't know why he changed his mind. Frankly, I doubt if he believed in God in the end."

"Oh," Judith said. She was remembering Zimmerman tipping head first into the plate of *boeuf en croûte* with noodles. Such would be a time when a passing thought of God could be most useful.

Masters pulled a blue folder from a drawer and tossed it to Judith's end of the pine carpenter's bench that served as his desk. "I assembled this for you: a list of his major holdings and a chronology of his acquisitions, from the first building. Back when we started in New York no one else would think of risking money there. The city was virtually bankrupt. His timing was impeccable, as was his judgment. The Reichmanns came after him. Everybody did. He knew when to take chances."

Judith didn't reach for the folder. That would have been a sign she was ready to leave. "When you said we had hoped he'd be around for the opening of the Harbourfront Tower, what did you mean?"

"We? Paul and I, of course."

"Why *wouldn't* he have been there?"

Masters stared at her for a second. "I guess Paul didn't tell you," he said, his voice rising to a squeak again. "Never did say why he agreed to the interview, did he?"

"I thought..."

Masters sighed theatrically. Then he leaned over his desk toward her, supporting himself on the palms of his hands, arms straight, like a small bulldog about to pounce.

"Paul was dying. Heart. He'd known for almost a month. But we thought he had at least another year."

NINE

The Forensics report on the glass shards Yan had dug out of the man's chest arrived on Tuesday. Yan's initial information that they had come from some expensive vehicle was correct: light-refractors from a Jaguar XJ-S. "Good news is," the Chief told David Parr, "that there are no more than 250 XJ-Ss in Toronto, perhaps another 2,000 throughout Canada. If we can track his car, we'll know who he was."

"I'll treat him with more respect now," Yan clucked over the phone. "Not everybody I see has the wits and good taste to die in an XJ-S. Any chance you get him out of here by noon?"

Parr was quite certain he wouldn't. If a man had the money for an XJ-S, he had the relatives who'd want to speak up when he was dead. Unless he was from another country. American missing persons reports, for example, rarely meet up with "Whose body is this?" queries in Canada. Another small breakdown in communications that would hearten any nationalist. Canada is nobody's backyard, after all. Canada has a whole separate set of administrators.

Parr decided to follow the shoes to New York.

He didn't bother with Dack's Fifth Avenue. Giannini had sent the long form of the press release and photo kit to the manager, who said they didn't remember this or any other customer, except for a few regulars. Not remembering was his prerogative. Helping the police of another country was a nice thing to do, but not a civic duty.

Parr took a cab across the Queensboro Bridge to the 107th Precinct. The cabbie grew solicitous when he heard the address. He'd been driving cab for some 15 years and he'd been there before. The general assumption in the city was that Queens shouldn't need more than a token family peacekeeping force — they liked to think of it as the garden borough, the family borough, full of hard-working, middle-class citizens who kept their noses clean. There were 16 understaffed precincts for a total population of almost 2 million. Every time there was a murder in Queens, the district attorney took it as a personal insult, a mean-spirited attack on his re-election platform. He was particularly outraged when something hit the papers, as the Sorel murders had four years ago. A small-time cocaine dealer named Sorel had been offered a once-in-a-lifetime opportunity at big game. To prove his credentials, he'd had to kill a couple of dealers who had become unstable. In his enthusiasm for the task, he took out their families as well. They had all lived in the Fresh Meadows housing complex in Queens, well within the 107th Precinct's territory and Captain Joe Martelli's range of responsibility.

When Sorel hightailed it to Canada, Martelli followed. He hadn't enlisted official help because he didn't want Sorel arrested in Canada and tied up in endless extradition proceedings; he wanted him back across the border so he could close the case and get the DA off his back. Martelli met David Parr after he was arrested for impersonating a police officer at the Harbour Light on Jarvis, where Sorel had sought refuge for the night. The Salvation Army colonel in charge knew what a police badge looked like, and he was pretty sure it didn't have a silver star, except in the movies. Parr had Martelli released and tore up the constable's report; they exchanged stories over a bottle of Red Label, and in the morning Parr helped run Sorel to ground, then handed him over to Martelli on the far side of the Peace Bridge. Sorel knew enough to squawk loudly to his lawyers, but not enough to finger Parr, so the DA got his man and Martelli owed Parr one — or, as Parr figured it, several.

The 107th's premises made 52 Division seem like a suite at the Waldorf-Astoria. The squad room was painted a grimy gray, the venetian blinds were broken and hung on a frayed string, the floor was spattered brown-green and sticky underfoot, the cluttered desks left barely enough room for one man to pass in between, the whole place smelled of stale sweat and cigar smoke. Parr smiled at the sergeant behind the desk. "Martelli in?" he asked.

"Uh-huh," replied the sergeant without looking up from his paperwork.

Parr went around him and through the squad room to the back

where Joe Martelli's small glass cage attempted to give him the status that went with the job. No one paid any attention to Parr. Helluva place to break into, he thought, but then, who'd want to?

Martelli sat hunched over his desk, the phone held between his chin and shoulder, his shirtsleeves rolled up to his elbows, his holster draped over the back of the chair. He was a big-boned, chunky man in his mid-40s, his hair an unruly mess of damp black curls, his complexion the pale sort that hints at a five-o'clock shadow early in the day. He was doodling on a piece of yellow paper and occasionally grunting into the receiver. When he saw Parr, he grinned, cupped the phone with his hand. "Undercover filing his weekly... Why don't you sit...," he whispered.

Parr got himself a drink from the watercooler. When he came back, Martelli had hung up and was leaning back, appraising him. "Still the crazy professor," he said. "I don't know where you get your threads, David, but they remind me of my wasted youth at Columbia. Beautiful. What brings you to the big city?"

"I've been wanting to give some guy a decent burial," Parr said. "Body's been waiting in cold storage a week now, and no one's come forward to claim it. He was dumped in a doorway late at night, and by the look of him, there's a story. Muggers in Toronto don't often do random killing."

"And you think he's from here?"

Parr spread out the photo, the coroner's report, and the detectives' words on the shoes.

When Martelli finished reading, he asked, "So what do you want me to do?"

"Check through your missing persons records for the past week, maybe as far back as ten days. All points. He could've been from any city, visiting New York, buying shoes. And, yes, please have a man go double-check on Dack's. Some guy in uniform with time to spare. If nothing else makes them remember, that will. Uniformed cops are bad for business."

"What do you think happened to him?"

"He was killed at close range, I'd say, unexpectedly, by someone he knew well enough to sit in a car with. The killer then had the good sense to strip him of anything that might have identified him. At first I figured he might have been a mule, but there was no trace of drugs in the clothing, and wear marks showed his feet filled the shoes pretty tight. He wasn't a user. But he could have been a carrier of some kind. The killer might have been looking for something in the shoes."

"Have you talked to the horsemen?" Martelli asked, as he rolled down his sleeves and strapped on his gun. With one hand, he tested his chin for stubble.

"Got some cute girls in missing persons?" Parr asked.

"One."

"I only call the RCMP when I'm told to. Haven't been told to so far. They're too damn high-handed."

"Comes from running around in those stiff tunics," Martelli suggested. "Four o'clock, I'll meet you at Ashley's, seven or eight blocks down, near the old Sunnyside Garden site. Ask anyone in the neighborhood, just don't sound like a cop when you're asking. They might send you to Westchester."

Parr spent the time till four o'clock prowling around Queens, Forest Hill, Shea Stadium, Corona Park. He had no trouble finding Ashley's on his own.

It was a fake Irish pub, with stained wooden beams, leaded glass windows, orange lanterns, and a long, beer-stained bar. The barman wore a green shirt with a shamrock outlined in white on the breast pocket. He told Irish jokes in a Southern drawl.

When Martelli arrived, he touched his forefinger to his temple, feigning a salute. "Took early retirement from the force in Birmingham," Martelli explained. "Couldn't adjust to the changing times." He pulled some folded sheets of paper from his coat pocket. "I think we've got your man," he said. "Name of Harvey Singer, 57 years old, lived at 120 West 59th Street — not a bad neighborhood. Central Park South. Wife Gloria, of the same address, filed a missing persons report on Saturday."

"That's two days after he died..."

"We double-checked the shoe joint. He bought the shoes in December by American Express. They kept the stub. They keep tabs on all their customers so they can let them know when the sales are. Any idea what those shoes cost?"

Parr shook his head.

"Guess."

"A hundred? One fifty?"

"C'mon, you can do better than that."

"Two hundred," Parr ventured.

"Three hundred shmeckers, buddy. Those babies cost more

than a holiday in Florida. And it turns out Singer bought three other pairs since last summer. At full price."

"Did his wife report a car missing?"

"No. She said he left home on foot, Thursday around noon, and never showed up again."

"Did she say where he was heading?"

Martelli smoothed out the sheets of paper and laid them on the bar. "Says here she thought he was visiting his accountant."

"So why didn't she report him missing on Thursday night, or Friday?"

"She didn't say. Here, you can have these." Martelli gave Parr the reports. "Are you going to give her the news?"

"Yes," Parr said. "But first I'll have to confirm with her that the Auschwitz serial number checks out. Wish me luck."

"You won't want me to file anything till tomorrow?"

"Right. I'd like to talk to her alone. Thanks, Joe."

TEN

Judith examined her face in the hall mirror. It was a small whitish oval, surrounded by a bush of auburn hair. She had planned to cut if all off on her 40th birthday but, in the end, had lacked the courage. The area around her eyes was greener than she had intended, leaving a darker green reflection in the semicircles under the eyes — a sure sign she needed more sleep than she'd been getting the past few days. There were freckles on her nose. She had always had freckles on her nose, but they turned invisible in the hall mirror, because she had positioned it some three feet from the nearest source of light. The idea was not to see freckles — or any other glaring imperfection — immediately prior to leaving the house, and to acquire the steely mien of firm-jawed determination Judith was convinced she needed to do daily battle with the world.

The evening required more than adequate steel. She had been conned into having dinner with James and the kids. When her mother had first extended the invitation to a "family" meal, she had omitted to mention that she viewed James as a life member. At the best of times, Judith loathed meals at her mother's, but tonight's was sure to set a record. The last half-hour had been spent talking Jimmy out of the pair of torn jeans he saved for special occasions and into the new pair he hadn't yet massacred with the bleach. As a concession to his growing feelings of insecurity, she had ironed out the seams. "I'm going to look like an idiot," he claimed, insisting that no one ever wore new jeans.

"If no one wears them, how do they get old?"

Anne had put on the skirt she kept for church and family events. It was a red and black print, with which she paired her bright blue, crumpled, long-tailed shirt. No one, it turned out, would be seen dead with her shirt tucked in either. She completed the outfit with tennis socks and duck boots. Withal she affected a look of grim forbearance that was her habitual expression for visits to her grandmother. "I wonder what your mother has in store for us today," she said wearily, as they piled into the Renault. Whenever Anne referred to her grandmother, she left no doubt as to where that relationship properly belonged.

"I don't," Judith muttered to herself. It was to be an evening of painful pretense in which all participants assumed polite stances, dabbled in small talk, praised the food, ate hearty, and never once alluded to the fact that two of the people present had endured considerable anguish so they wouldn't have to be together.

She was not disappointed.

Marjorie greeted everyone at the door with busy smiles, her apron at the ready, a wooden spoon poised for action in her left hand. "James," she called over her shoulder to the living room, "will you do the honors?" offering her soft powdered cheek for a kiss to Anne, then Jimmy, in turn. "Still working on the soup, dear," to Judith. "Decided to make tomato. On special at Loblaws. Hothouse. All this week — you know..." They both knew Judith wouldn't know. "Such a cold night out..."

"Maybe I could help?" Judith asked, choosing tomatoes over James, but her mother was ready for that.

"A sherry will do you good," she said, scurrying toward the kitchen. "I have milk for the children." The children glanced at Judith balefully.

James stood, arms crossed, leaning against the doorpost where the living room met the hallway. At first glance, the most extraordinary thing about him was his unusual height. On second glance, Judith realized with a start that James had very likely not grown an inch — it was just that she had grown used to the same features in smaller packaging. Jimmy, without benefit of role model, had developed the same lurching posture, the same awkward fake casualness that went with feeling ill at ease.

"Hiya, Dad," Jimmy yelled with irritating familiarity as he bounded by Judith, jabbed James's shoulder playfully with the side of his fist, and barreled into the living room, out of the line of fire.

Anne stayed somewhere behind her mother, watching.

"Well," Judith said with supreme effort. "Well." The second "well" was not nearly as clearly enunciated because, quite unexpectedly, her throat had dried up.

"I would have come to get you," James said, "but Mother needed some help with the shopping." He had peeled away from the door frame and approached Judith cautiously. "How are you?" he asked, pacing the words to show each one mattered, his voice dropping to a whisper meant just for her. Ah yes, she remembered that tone: James placating a tearful cat-owner. "Don't you worry, Mrs. Smithers, we'll take good care of Mufty..."

He hadn't changed much in four years: hair thinner, but still a springy blond (like Jimmy's), skin looser under the eyes and an extra fold below the rounded chin, charcoal gray eyes (Anne's), forehead wider than she remembered, perhaps because of two deep lengthwise lines that lent him a permanently concerned air. That, too, could be very useful in small-animals practice.

"Fine," Judith said forcefully. "Thank you."

"Kind of Mother to have us *all* to dinner, don't you think?" He was clearly working on the principle of once a mother-in-law, always a mother-in-law. "Sherry, or would you prefer something stronger?"

"Very." Anne answered the first question, seeing that Judith wasn't about to do so. "How's the shoulder, Dad?"

"Moving," he said bravely. Judith remembered that look. Once she had fallen in love with it. She wondered if the pale shadow of that feeling still lingered. Somewhere. Memories, they say, never die.

"Stronger," she asked. "Please."

"Good," James said, leading the way into the living room. "I had kind of anticipated you might and invested in a bottle of Gordon's. Like a martini, or has that sort of stuff been swept out by the health wave?"

"Straight up," Judith suggested. "Thank you."

"Mother doesn't approve, of course — never has — but she didn't protest. She thinks of me as a visitor, I guess." He chuckled at that absurd idea, poured gin into the good crystal glasses, and topped them with a dash of sherry. He extracted four green olives from a plastic bag in his pocket and dropped them into Judith's glass. He swirled them around with his index finger and handed her the drink. "Young lady here," he winked at Anne, conspiratorially, "tells me you're still the olive addict you once were. Could've sworn you took to drinking martinis because you didn't think it was chic to eat olive on the rocks."

Anne tried to wink back but it wasn't too successful. If James was going to stay around she might have to take winking lessons.

"Aren't you?" Judith asked ingenuously.

"Aren't I what?"

"A visitor."

There was a crash to the left where Jimmy collided with Granny's Japanese armoire.

"A nice drink, don't you think?" James was going to ignore her rudeness. "You do remember the sherry?"

She did. When they were studying for exams James used to carry a mickey of gin in his pocket and sneak sherry from the DeLisles' house in the evenings. He'd had to sneak the mix because they were almost never alone for more than a few minutes. Judith's mother would sit in the far corner of the room knitting or listening to the radio. There was no question that Judith was to be a virgin on her wedding night.

"Are you still taking us skiing?" Jimmy asked, disengaging himself from the armoire.

"That all depends on your mother," James said decorously. "I told you that. Not my decision. Naturally, I would enjoy having the opportunity of skiing with you at Collingwood..." All this to Judith.

"They can't ski," she said lamely.

"I know," James replied. "All my fault. Should have taught them years ago. A couple of real athletic types and they still can't ski...but not too late. Never too late for anything in life if you make up your mind. Doing something new together is much more conducive to nurturing lasting relationships than simply being together. And I have a lot of catching up to do." He sighed and eased himself into Judith's father's wide leather-backed easy chair. "Perhaps you'd like to come, too?" he asked.

Judith gritted her teeth and arranged her lips in a smile. "I don't think so."

"Yeah," chorused the kids. "Dad's an expert at slalom," said Jimmy. "Last year he and Inge went to Innsbruck. That's in Austria. Four weeks straight skiing."

Marsha, Judith reminded herself, had said that the kids liking their father did not mean they liked Judith less. Easy for Marsha to say.

"Where is Inge this year?" Judith inquired pleasantly.

James spread his hands in a "search me" gesture. "It's all over," he said sadly. "Inge was not prepared to make a commitment yet, and I couldn't handle another superficial relationship. Too many mismatched emotions." Then he brightened. "A fortunate bit of timing, nevertheless. Otherwise she might have insisted on coming with me to Toronto and that would have impinged on our time. Couldn't have been as open between Jimmy and me then." He glanced at Jimmy, then he noticed Anne by the bookcase. "And Anne," he added quickly with a touch of husky emotion.

Judith was relieved to note that Anne joined her in looking sheepish at this bit of Jamesian analysis. Those years of training in common sense hadn't, after all, abandoned her when confronted with her father's dubious charm.

"Would you *like* to go skiing?" Judith asked her.

"Guess so," Anne shrugged.

"Of course she would," James said. "Friend of mine from vet school has a spot up the mountain. Belongs to a private club, yet — Craigleith, you know. We'll leave sharp at 6 A.M. and I'll have you running downhill by noon. And it's a good place for you to start making connections. The right kind of people, and all that. What do you say, Jude — all up to you now. Wouldn't dream of cutting across your bow..." He had leaned closer as he talked. His nose pointed at Judith's. (Had he always had a dimple in his chin?) He affected a painfully earnest look. "I need this time... You do understand..."

"I suppose," she said, as she contemplated the manifold injuries persons could sustain while James was teaching them to slalom.

"It's a school holiday," Jimmy said.

The phone suddenly bellowed from the hall. Everybody froze.

Clearly, Marjorie had at last acknowledged her fast-deteriorating hearing and installed a sadistic loudspeaker system. Luckily, it was cut short on the second deafening roar.

"Judith," Marjorie said on her way in carrying a silver tray with stuffed eggs, celery hearts, and small round toasts with pâté, "the telephone is for you." Her mouth pursed with patent disapproval as she deposited her tray on the coffee table. "Dinner's almost ready."

The caller was Stevie, Judith's next-door neighbor. "This is probably crazy," she said breathlessly, "but I think there's someone in your house."

Stevie was the only person on Brunswick Avenue who had taken Neighborhood Watch to heart. She had conned the Canada Council into giving her a grant to write about family patterns in the Lower Annex area. That meant Stevie spent a good part of each day sitting on her balcony with a pair of binoculars and a bottle of Portuguese wine.

"There is?" Judith asked, not too concerned. Stevie was given to inventing the occasional crisis if nothing happened on the street for a week or so. Last week there had been a haunting across the street, last month an attempted kidnapping. In July she had called the fire department to put out Judith's barbecue.

"Yup," Stevie said. "I saw them moving around upstairs. Light went on and off — flashlight, I bet. I thought of calling the police, but..." She no doubt remembered Judith's lack of tact when the fire brigade knocked down her door. "It's better to check first. You do have a lot of friends, God knows."

"Did you see anyone come in?"

"No. And it's not the detective, his car isn't down the street by the hydrant where he puts it. I checked." Of all Judith's friends, Stevie particularly liked David. Occasionally she'd sit on her back porch flagrantly smoking hash, hoping he'd come and arrest her.

"You're quite sure?" Judith asked, still doubtful.

"Sure I'm sure." Stevie was indignant. "I'm sitting not ten feet from your bedroom window and I see this light come up the back wall where your pictures are...now it's moving over where you keep your typewriter — "

"I'm on my way," Judith said and hung up.

"Back in ten minutes," Judith said to her mother, as she raced out the door. "An emergency. At the magazine...," she lied. Explanations took too long.

Snow had started to fall heavily. The streets had turned soft and mushy under the tires. The Renault's rump fishtailed as she tried to ease it into the careful traffic down Park Road. Already there was an accident at the foot of the hill. She didn't allow herself to think that someone had really broken into the house. She preferred to believe that Stevie was up to her old tricks.

As she rounded the rim of Sibelius Square, she could already see the police car in front of her house, its lights flashing.

A small crowd had formed on her steps. They were huddled in coats, their shoulders pulled up, arms crossed, faces expectant. Everyone watched as she parked the car across the street. She met Stevie and a young policeman coming out of her door.

"Waited and waited, Judith," Stevie said apologetically. She wore her black hooded cloak, red high-heeled boots, and full evening makeup. "When you didn't show, I assumed you must have got stuck in traffic, so I phoned for Parr. They sent these guys," she shrugged helplessly. "Did the best I could under the circumstances, don't you think?"

"You Mrs. Hayes?" the policeman inquired.

"Yes," Judith said and pushed past them into the house. The living room looked the same. Her woolen mitts were still lying on the floor near the fireplace where she'd dropped them on the way out. The kitchen was, as always, untidy, lunch dishes in the sink, Coke cans and glasses all over the counter, Anne's homework spread out on the table surrounded by muffin crumbs.

She raced up the stairs, two at a time, and met a second policeman backing out of Jimmy's bedroom. He was walking very slowly, examining the carpet around his feet. Between two fingers of his right hand he carried a small plastic bag. He looked up at Judith, curious, but noncommittal: "Yes?" he asked. He was terribly young and sure of himself. There's no doubt about it, policemen are getting younger, Judith thought.

"I live here," she explained.

"Hmm," said the very young policeman, still noncommittal.

"Well?" Judith prodded. "Has somebody broken in?"

"Can't tell yet, ma'am. Haven't been here long enough. We were responding to a call. I can see how someone could've got in, though, and out again." He smiled knowingly. "Anything missing?"

Judith rounded the corner into her room, where Stevie claimed to have seen the intruder. The bed was exactly as she had left it, unmade. Her flannel nightgown was curled in a blue ball on the floor with a pillow, near the shoes she had decided not to wear at the last moment. The clothes-closet door was open, her beige nylon slip still hanging on the doorknob. On the dresser, her assorted bottles and jars of lotions and creams stood in their customary disarray.

Only her desk looked different. She had left her clean white copy of the typed Zimmerman story neatly stacked to the left of the typewriter. Each page had been numbered in sequence and laid face down on top of the last one. She had reached midway down page 16. Her green stenographer's notebook had been to the right of the typewriter, closed.

Now some of the typed pages were in a jumble all over the

desk, a couple of them had fallen on the floor, and her notebook lay open on the chair.

"How does it look?" Stevie asked from the doorway.

"Not terribly good," Judith said. "Someone's been rummaging around in my story."

"Didn't I tell you?" Stevie shouted triumphantly. She was waving her arms around in excitement and peering over Judith's shoulder to see what was on the pages she'd typed.

"How did you know I was at my mother's?" Judith asked, as she stacked the pages back in their original order. They were all, much to her relief, still there.

"Saw you and the kids pile into the car. Anne was wearing her skirt — and it's not Easter Sunday."

"How did you get in?"

"Kids' key under the mat."

"You both writers?" the policeman asked.

"She's a journalist," Stevie said, pointing her thumb at Judith. Stevie must have been passing herself off as an author again.

"Is anything missing?" the other policeman asked impatiently. He was still holding the plastic bag.

"Not so far as I can tell, but..."

"Did you keep money or valuables in here?" The first policeman looked around.

"Don't have any," Judith said. "The typewriter, TV set, Jimmy's stereo, two radios, records, tapes, hair dryer..."

"Perhaps he didn't have time to rob you, because I called the police." Stevie said with pride. "They came with the siren and lights flashing, the whole megillah. So he escaped before we came in..."

"Through that room," the second policeman said, indicating Jimmy's room with his plastic baggie. "Window was open, damp mud on the carpet."

They all followed him out and into Jimmy's room where the mess was messier than usual and the mud worse than usual, damp, and in direct line with the window.

"Mind if I close it?" Judith asked.

They didn't. "Not much more for us to do then," the older policeman said. "If you find something missing, you call. Okay?"

"Thanks."

"Do you know what this is?" The younger policeman showed her the plastic bag.

Close up, the contents looked like tobacco with bits of large seeds mixed in. Judith shook her head.

"Cannabis?" Stevie asked, sniffing at the bag. "Grass, you know," for Judith's benefit.

The policeman nodded, his lips pressed together.

Stevie giggled nervously. She had loosened her cloak from her shoulders to reveal her form-fitting angora sweater and the long string of pearls she wore on special occasions.

"Whose room is this?" the policeman asked.

Judith searched the room with her eyes, as if she were trying to remember whose room it could be. There was a football helmet in the corner, a sweatshirt with number 6 emblazoned on its front, a grimy Adidas bag, a fishing rod on the wall, football posters, a signed photograph of Wayne Gretzky, near the dresser a pair of black hockey skates, by the window a brown bear with button eyes and yellow raincoat wearing a Blue Jays cap on his head.

A giant burst of panic welled up from her stomach and caught in her throat as she reached for the bag. "My son," she whispered, swallowing hard. "He's just a child," she added in a rush. "He doesn't..."

They were all silent for a moment. Then the very young policeman let out a long sigh, shook his head from side to side, and dropped the bag into Judith's hand. "You should talk to him about this," he said gruffly. "Fast."

"I will..." Judith mumbled gratefully.

Stevie saw them out the door. She was duly rewarded by being the first person to greet David Parr.

ELEVEN

"I'm afraid I'm hopelessly middle-class, after all," Judith said almost apologetically. "There was a time I thought I was a free spirit. *Some* free spirit. It turns out that, just as you say, I'm encumbered by a variety of outdated behavioral codes and patterns. So why fight it?"

"If you change your mind, send him over so I can teach him market smarts," Stevie suggested. "Stuff he had is stale, third-rate Mexican. He's been taken, if you know what I mean. G'night." Stevie swung her long flaxen hair over her shoulder — had nobody told her the '60s were over? — and flounced out.

"Why don't you let James do his parental bit and lecture Jimmy on the evils of drugs? He's been begging for an opportunity," David said. "Problem with being an absentee father is you never get a chance to tackle anything important. You're stuck in the role of court jester, devising the next round of entertainment when this one palls. I think Myrna took some perverse joy in not allowing me to discuss anything she felt was important for Susie's future. Whatever problems there were, she kept them from me. I know she did."

He was beginning to sound petulant, Judith thought. Would James sound exactly like this talking to Inge about Jimmy and Anne? Never mind "of course not," would he?

David went on, "Never once mentioned Susie had anorexia till they took her into Sick Kids."

"Didn't you notice?" That slipped out before she'd had a chance to check it.

"No," he said, inexplicably. He had crept up behind her and started to kiss the back of her neck.

"And which of your selves are you wearing when you talk about Jimmy?" Judith asked, ignoring his touch. Must be James's proximity making her so bad-tempered. Or the break-in. Or dinner with Mother. Or the grass in Jimmy's room. "The wronged husband? Or the observant friend of the household who's had occasion to behold the young criminal in action?"

"Neither," David said. His arms circled her waist, his palms pressed her hips against his. "As your lover," he whispered. "I want to have more of your *good* times. Let *him* take some of the heat," he said into her left ear a second before he started to nibble it.

She turned her face into the rough tweed jacket front; the warmth, the faint smell of old pipe tobacco, a whiff of after-shave enveloped her in recent memories of love, and then forgetfulness. It had been like this with David for some months now — the warmth and the forgetfulness, each taking its turn. She had already decided there wasn't going to be any permanence, only shared moments when David was less pressured by the Chief, or the Commissioners, when his job wasn't at the center. Most likely, even without the Commissioners, the job would remain the obsession he had allowed it to become, a daily test of his ability to solve problems. A common enough affliction, but not easily curable.

"Dammit, David, you have the worst sense of timing," she said in the end. She pulled his hands back from the hollows of her hipbones where they had naturally settled. She was going to leave all the unsaid anger unsaid. "I'm supposed to be at my mother's for dinner, someone's broken into my home, I can't think of a single reason why I'd feel inclined to make love."

"You can't?" he asked querulously. "That's because you lack spontaneity. Outweighed, most likely, by a delicious inherited sense of orderliness."

"Orderliness?" she asked, leaning against the drawers, smiling to lighten the tension. "Orderly is hardly the word that would come to mind looking around this place."

"I think you throw stuff around to protest your innocence," David said, picking up on her tone. One of the reasons she loved him was his willingness to switch moods. "It's your idea of putting distance between you and your perfect mother." David had relaxed and stretched out on the bed, his ankles crossed, his arms intertwined behind his head.

"Long as it keeps me sane," Judith said, coming closer to him, testing the ground. "Any ideas why someone might be interested in my Zimmerman story?"

"Yes," David said lightly, "I, for one, might be very interested. So might a lady named Gloria Singer, whose husband was murdered in Toronto last week."

He obviously enjoyed her look of total bewilderment. He didn't continue until she had hopped onto the bed next to him, all expectation, arms akimbo, forehead knitted, waiting. "You were about to elaborate on that, weren't you?" she asked in exasperation.

"I might," David said. He was still playing for time, gazing at the ceiling, his eyes half closed as if he was suddenly tired. "Only I thought you were in a hurry."

"For God's sake," Judith yelped impatiently.

"All right, then," David gave in. He told her about following Singer's shoes to New York and his brief meeting with Gloria Singer, who took the news of her newfound widowhood with extreme ill grace. "There is such a range of reactions to a violent death in the family: tears, depression, hysteria. Hers was anger. At Toronto, mainly. And Canada and all things Canadian. She said they'd never been up in this 'damn godforsaken country.' I guess she was outraged that he should have died in a place he had no business being in. When he'd been gone a couple of days she began to sift through his bureau for clues to his whereabouts, and there, among the debris of a lifetime, she found these." David had reached into his jacket pocket and pulled out a handful of newspaper clippings. "She practically threw them at me."

They were some of the same Zimmerman stories that Research had clipped for Judith when she was getting ready for the first interview. There was the Pacific Airlines takeover from the *Wall Street Journal*, with several follow-ups from the Toronto *Globe and Mail*, business section, *Forbes*, Zimmerman outbidding the Belzbergs for a sizable chunk of downtown Philadelphia; the *Time* feature on the tactics he used with the Montreal city fathers to let him build the largest indoor shopping mall in the world, *Newsweek* on his acquisition of the Black Hawks, *Time* and the *Wall Street Journal* on Loyal, a mention of his sponsorship of the Jerusalem Foundation in Canada, and the little squib from *Business Week* about his paving his driveway with meteorite. The *Business Week* story also dealt with his New York real estate deal.

"And they were tied together with this," David said, pulling from his other pocket a long black ribbon.

"Rather melodramatic, don't you think?" Judith asked.

"Yes, under the circumstances, but I can't imagine why she'd have made that up."

"Did he know Zimmerman?"

"She never heard him mention the name."

"Perhaps he knew him through his business."

"Possibly. He was a retired clothing manufacturer. Nose to the grindstone. No boards, no takeovers, nothing. His son is running the business now. They make ladies' dresses in wool. Far as I can tell, all they had in common was they were both Jewish and now they're both dead."

TWELVE

Jimmy denied all knowledge of the "stash." If it was found in his room, someone else must have put it there for the express purpose of causing him trouble. His own suspicions fell on the police, mainly because he'd been reading the new Dorothy Uhnak police procedural and become convinced that the police stopped at no breach of ethics to get their man. This time, their man was a 16-year-old at North Toronto who had been unsuccessfully promoting low-grade grass around the ninth-graders. Jimmy thought the police had planted the "evidence" to coerce him into being a stoolie. Naturally, he was sure David was involved in the deception.

As a low-ranking second choice, he allowed for the slim chance that, instead of the police, the bag had been dropped by one of his friends whom he had sorely misjudged, but he didn't know which one. There had been more than 20 visitors to his room in the past couple of weeks, not including the football team last Saturday morning on their way to practice at Winston Churchill Park.

How they had all fitted into Jimmy's room was a mystery to Judith. They must have stood shoulder to shoulder in three tidy rows, the shortest in front, so they could all see the two *Penthouse* centerfolds Jimmy had kept under his mattress. She didn't want to throw them away till she'd been able to discuss them with him, and the right opening lines to that discussion hadn't yet presented themselves.

Question is, how can you tell if your kid's lying? Answer: you can't, but if *you* can't, no one else can. You're *supposed* to be the expert on your own kid. And Judith's expert opinion was that Jimmy was telling the truth. In turn, that left the problem of who put the marijuana in Jimmy's room and why.

All in all the skiing trip had begun to look good: it would take Jimmy out of circulation for a few days and give Judith the time to finish the Zimmerman story before she dealt with the baggie problem.

James, expensively attired in red-striped black stretch pants, hand-knitted mohair sweater, Sporting Life red on black down-filled ski jacket, and knee-high fur-lined sheepskin boots, collected them at 10 A.M. Judith had left the two packed army-surplus canvas sacks on the porch. She didn't go to the door. Two hours with James last night had been more than enough companionship for old times' sake, especially with her mother playing plaintive accompaniment to Judith's dutiful spooning of tapioca pudding. Marjorie's reaction to the break-in story had been an elegant snort of derision. She had been used to better excuses for Judith's shortcomings.

It was too late to attend the funeral. By the time she arrived the procession had left, the news crews were packing in their gear, an elderly man in a fur coat was collecting blue sheets of paper people had carelessly discarded on the sidewalk in front of the church. When Judith picked one up, he eyed her suspiciously, then returned to his task. They were hymn sheets for the service: Psalm 51. The words were all supplied on one side, the music on the other with only the first verse.

> Have mercy upon me, O God, according to thy
>   loving kindness:
> According to the multitude of thy
> Tender mercies blot out my transgressions...

There was still a small cluster of people on the corner of St. Clair Avenue but no one she recognized. She was on the point of approaching them anyway and introducing herself when she saw a familiar figure, in black overcoat and yarmulke, emerge from the church and slowly descend the steps. He turned up his collar and pulled on a pair of knitted gloves. Tucked under his arm he carried a black leather-bound book with gold-edged pages.

She pretended to read the hymn sheet while she waited for him to draw parallel. "Rabbi Jonas," she said, when he was near. "I'm Judith Hayes. I do hope you remember..."

He didn't. He glanced at her with complete lack of curiosity from behind his fogged-up granny glasses, then tried a small apologetic smile. "I'm afraid I don't quite recall, Miss..."

"We met at the Zimmermans' last Sunday when... Actually we

were introduced by Mr. Masters," Judith rushed on. "I'm writing a story about Paul Zimmerman for *Finance International* magazine." She sighed. "A terrible tragedy."

The rabbi nodded stiffly, agreed, and began to move away.

"I wonder if I might have a word with you about him," Judith asked in her most ingratiating voice. "There was still so much he wanted to tell me, when he died. Philip Masters thought you could help me."

"I'm walking back to Beth Elohim, if you want to walk with me," he said. "Though I doubt there is much I can add," he said curtly. "I didn't know Paul very well."

"You didn't? I thought you'd known him since '55?"

"Hmm...'55? That would be about right," he said, nodding. "In '55 I had just graduated from rabbinical school. My first year helping with the United Jewish Appeal."

"He was already on the board?" Judith prodded.

"No," Jonas said. "He wasn't then. In '55 he wasn't involved in anything much beyond making his business grow. He had built a couple of shopping plazas, was putting up apartment buildings somewhere in Pittsburgh — Chicago, too, I think. They had Monarch already. Named after the butterfly. Paul was fascinated by butterflies."

"Did you persuade him to become involved?"

"In the United Jewish Appeal? I don't think so. He had already persuaded himself. Paul wasn't one to be swayed by anyone else's views. He listened to everyone, then he made up his own mind. Philip's father had been a great supporter since the war and I'd known Philip off and on since McGill. Met Paul for the first time at one of Philip's parents' functions. Black tie — that kind of thing. Paul, with his height, shoulders like a wrestler's, that blond hair, stood out like a giant oak in the shrubbery. I was surprised he was Jewish. He looked more like a Viking, or a Hun. We got talking about the Arabs and the Israelis, and Israel's chances of survival. The need for a home for the Jews. The war. The horrors... It was Paul who asked me about the United Jewish Appeal. He said he wanted to help."

"And he did," Judith prompted.

"Yes," Jonas said thoughtfully. "You could say that."

"He contributed somewhere over a million dollars last year alone."

The rabbi was walking briskly, looking mainly at his feet. He didn't bother to reply.

"And he was involved with the Jewish Welfare Fund," Judith continued, "the Jerusalem Foundation, and the Weizmann Institute. In the past ten years he chaired 12 fund-raisers for causes you've been involved in."

"That many?" the rabbi asked, surprised. "Hmm."

"That many, plus the extraordinary donations for the universities in Israel and the Israeli bond drives. I would have thought you came to know him reasonably well in that time."

"A natural enough conclusion, but alas, the wrong one," he said. "Paul Zimmerman was a hard man to get to know."

"Wasn't he a member of your congregation?"

The rabbi thought about that for a while as they marched across Spadina dodging traffic. "I suppose he wasn't," the rabbi said. "He certainly didn't come to shul. But you don't judge a man by his attendance record. You know him by his actions. Paul Zimmerman was a good man."

Judith was sorry she had abandoned her daily walks program some weeks back. In fact, she was sorry she had altogether abandoned physical fitness years ago when she had discovered it was boring and time-consuming. Rabbi Jonas had built up to a steady speed, swinging his arms from the shoulders, head down, chest forward. She was half running to keep up with him.

"Did you know he was dying?" she panted, close by his heel.

"No. I did not. I've heard it since from Brenda. Quite frankly, that took me by surprise, too. But then, we had very few personal conversations. I am deeply sorry about that. I wish I had known and been able to help him."

It seemed to Judith he had speeded up once they reached the uphill portion of Bathurst. Her impression that he was trying to get rid of her was strengthened when he said evenly, "Anything else I can help you with, Mrs. Hayes?"

"Well, yes...there is..." Judith lurched ahead so she could get the question out without losing him. "I was wondering why he decided to be buried by the Catholic church."

"Why," the rabbi repeated. "Why indeed? We have an old custom of answering a question with a question, Mrs. Hayes. Sometimes in the course of a response, the question answers itself. In this case, though, I very much doubt this will happen. I am told that his will endowed the church with a fund for renovating its 19th-century organ. As far as my friend Father O'Shea knows, Paul never attended a service." He stopped suddenly and looked at Judith. "Perhaps," he smiled at her, "he wanted to cover all the bases. Jews, like everybody else, can panic under threat of death. It's only human." He set off again in the direction of the synagogue. "We'll say Kaddish for him," he said over his shoulder. "Goodbye, Mrs. Hayes," he added when he noticed she wasn't following. "And if you get a better answer, let me know."

"Goodbye, Rabbi Jonas," Judith said, one hand pressed to her side where the stitch was. She took a cab back to her car and drove home to recover.

A message from Philip Masters said that Brenda would see her after all, but not in Toronto. She and Meredith were flying to their Bermuda home as soon as the formalities were over, and certainly before the end of the day. If Judith wanted to join them there tomorrow, she was to let him know.

Though Mr. Masters hadn't yet returned, Goodith, his statuesque secretary, did have all the details for Judith's trip. The car would pick her up at 7 A.M., drive her to Buttonville Airport, whence the PA Lear, number 421, would take her to Bermuda. Mrs. Zimmerman's driver, Geoff, would meet her there. She could expect to be back in the evening.

There had also been a telegram from Paris. "A Mrs. Zimmerman," the operator said. "Shall I spell it for you?"

"From Paris?"

"Paris, France. Spell...?"

"No."

"The message reads: 'Paul was murdered stop signed Mrs. Zimmerman, Meurice, Paris.' Shall I repeat that?"

"Please."

It didn't improve on second reading. Judith wrote it down carefully, asked the operator to mail it, phoned David Parr, and repeated it to him, twice.

"Must be the first Mrs. Zimmerman," David observed sharply. "Do you suppose she's a nut?"

"There is a lot of that around. On the other hand, she may be right."

"You were sitting next to him, for Chrissakes. Did he look like he was murdered?"

"How in hell would I know? Anyone could have slipped poison in his food or drink. There were 16 people at the party. Why don't you get an autopsy?"

"Sure. He was buried this morning with all the pomp and circumstance allotted a man of his exalted position and wealth, and you want me and a couple of the boys to run round to the cemetery this afternoon with shovels and dig him up. Because his ex-wife sends you a telegram. Terrific. What do you say we sleep on it?"

"I'll phone her at her hotel."

"Good idea. Better than your first one, I'd say."

She told David she was planning to be in Bermuda the next day interviewing the second wife.

"One little thing you could look into for me," David asked. "We've been interested in Jaguars since Singer's body was found, and it seems Zimmerman had one. An XJ-S, 1987, he'd imported direct from London. A couple of days ago, the same day he died, it was shipped to Bermuda. I'd like to know if all of its windows are intact."

"Why?"

"There were glass shards in Singer's chest."

THIRTEEN

Mrs. Singer's sense of outrage at her husband's sudden death had not abated by the time she arrived in Toronto to identify the body. David, who had the unhappy task of accompanying her from the airport to the morgue, was even grateful for her sustained fury. From past experience, he knew that anger he could deal with, grief he could not. In Homicide you get your share of both.

Mrs. Singer was shorter than he remembered, shorter even than the diminutive Yan. A slight, compact woman with wavy white hair piled high on her head, a silver fox coat that boosted her narrow shoulders, a heavily lined face that had been exposed to tropical sun. She wore too much makeup for anyone to tell if she had been crying. When Yan pulled back the sheet, she drew her mouth and eyebrows into a grimace of acute pain, touched her fist to her stomach or heart with a sharp intake of breath, nodded, turned on her heel, and walked, very erect, out of the examining room. David followed her outside.

At the door, she swiveled around and looked up at him, dry-eyed. With one hand she clasped the collar tight around her neck, against the wind and, he thought, for comfort. The other hand disappeared between the folds of her coat. "I suppose there will be some formalities," she said. "I should like to attend to them right away. Then I want to take Harvey home."

"Papers to sign. A few more questions. Shouldn't take long," David said. "Perhaps you'd like to take a rest now..."

"I would not," Mrs. Singer said firmly.

"We have booked a room for you at the Four Seasons."

"I have no intention of staying in this godforsaken city one more second than absolutely necessary," she said, her voice rising. "The arrangements are made, the plane is booked, the undertaker is waiting. Now why don't we just get on with it?"

She was silent all the way up Yonge Street to the thoroughly unremarkable building Homicide occupies near Woodlawn Avenue, across from the fashionable gourmet food store Parr patronized for special occasions. Giannini had come up from 52 Division with all the forms.

She did not remove her coat while filling them out and answering the routine questions. David wondered why neither her son nor her daughter-in-law accompanied her on the journey. A nasty duty for anyone alone, but particularly for a woman of her age. When he asked about it, she said she was perfectly capable of handling her own affairs. Family and friends would attend the funeral the next day. She could think of no reason to subject them all to this. Could he?

She had brought a dark suit for the body to travel in, a clean shirt with his initials embroidered on the cuff. She had not brought shoes because David had omitted to tell her that Harvey's were booked into evidence and that, in any event, he had promised to return them to the Indian when the investigation was over.

He and Brother Twelve had managed to establish an alibi for the night of February 26th, after all. Between 10 P.M. and 1 A.M. on the 27th, they had been seen by seven different constables from 52 Division, sleeping on the grille next to what used to be Julie's Mansion midway up Jarvis Street. At least three of the constables had requested the two men to move on, found them unable to do so, and left them there. The owner of the new restaurant at Julie's was known to be kind to vagrants and hadn't filed a complaint.

There had been no stolen Jaguar reports that night, or since.

"Was it unusual for Mr. Singer to go for trips without telling you in advance?" Constable Giannini asked ingenuously. He had been working on a theory of Singer-as-philanderer. A crime of passion, maybe.

"He had never done it before, if that's what you mean," Mrs. Singer replied indignantly.

"Was there anything unusual about his departure on the 26th of February?" David asked.

"Not that I noticed."

"Can you describe your morning for us?"

"Do you imagine this is going to help find who killed him?" She was looking at David with undisguised animosity.

"Possibly," he replied patiently. "I know these questions must seem trivial and some are painful to answer, but you must recognize that our purpose is to serve justice, and I assume you want the same." He sounded pompous even to himself and Giannini could not suppress a wince, but David was a believer in verbal cushions for the bereaved. Inexplicably, they worked.

Gloria Singer was no exception. She now described Harvey's morning without protest. They had woken up at their usual time, 7 A.M. It was still dark, and she had let the dog out onto the balcony. Harvey had put on the water for coffee. She had bought an automatic espresso-maker at Christmas, but never learned how to use it. She was scared of the hot steam. That's why Harvey made coffee. She had brought in the *New York Times* from the doormat. Harvey had dressed.

"Was there anything unusual in the way he dressed that day?"

"No."

"He wore rather expensive shoes, near new."

"He liked to dress well."

"Always?"

"Since we retired in 1982. Left the business to Melwyn and Elaine. Harvey wanted our son to have the challenge of making his own way. We were going to enjoy the money we'd saved." She stopped for a sharp intake of breath, but did not break down.

Giannini offered to get her coffee, which she accepted.

"He had his suits made of English wool, his shirts came from Japan and Italy. Bought his shoes at Dack's. And he bought an apartment on Central Park. Why shouldn't he? Till '82, we had lived in the Bronx."

"He must have made a considerable amount of money, then?" Parr asked cautiously.

"You could say that," Mrs. Singer announced. "And we didn't think we'd live forever to spend it." She slammed her coffee cup onto the desk, spilling some of the black liquid over Giannini's papers. She whispered something under her breath that sounded like "Damn him."

David waited for her to recover her composure, then asked if she'd go on with the events of February 26th.

After he dressed, Harvey had joined his wife in the kitchen. They read the paper, talked.

"What did you talk about?" David asked.

"Nothing special. A dinner party. The kids. Koch's speech. I

asked if he'd read the brochures on Venice I'd left for him next to
the bed. We were going to Venice on the way to Israel next month.
We went in '85 and '83 as well. Every second year. We had planned
once to retire to Israel, but Harvey couldn't stand the climate. He
didn't like the heat. And he loved New York."

She had started to relax, and that was dangerous. Her eyes
became damp as she stared out the window.

"Then he put on his coat and left," David said quickly.

Gloria Singer stiffened again, swallowed. "No," she said. "He
went to the study. I washed the dishes. Let the dog in. Made the
bed. He came into the bedroom to tell me he was going out. Must
have been near eight by then, because I'd turned the light off.
There was some sun, I think. He said he'd be back in the evening."

"Did you ask him where he was going?"

"Yes. But I was annoyed he was leaving for the day without
warning, I'm not sure how it came out. I'd planned to go over to
the Nobels' that afternoon for bridge. I was sure I had told him
earlier. He'd been rather... preoccupied the past few weeks."

"Preoccupied? How?" Giannini asked eagerly.

"Just preoccupied," Mrs. Singer said irritably.

"Was he ignoring plans you had made?" David asked.

"Yes, he was. I don't know what, he was worrying about
something. Week before, he forgot we had theater tickets. Started
to forget his bridge evenings. He even forgot my birthday in
January. Hadn't done that once in 30 years. He bought me this coat
to make up for it." She stroked the furry sleeve affectionately. "Stupid.
Stupid. Stupid."

"Where did he say he was going?"

"I thought he said something about his accountant. Fred Kaplan
did all Harvey's numbers. Last time he'd been down to see Kaplan,
they had lunch and went to a ball game in the afternoon. He didn't
get back till past midnight." In such circumstances Gloria Singer
would be the kind of woman who did not bother to camouflage
her opinion.

"Did he go to Mr. Kaplan's?" Giannini asked.

"No. And Kaplan wasn't expecting him. He was the first person
I called when Harvey didn't return that night. When did he get
to Toronto?"

"He came in on American at 2 P.M.," Giannini said. "He was
booked to return at 10 P.M. the same night."

Gloria Singer shook her head. "Doesn't make any sense. No goddam sense at all."

Giannini nodded sympathetically. It didn't make sense to him either.

"You're certain you never heard him mention Paul Zimmerman?" asked David.

"If he did, I don't remember. I found those bits from the papers in his desk drawer. Only reason I even bothered to look twice was the black ribbon. Nothing else had a black ribbon around it. Have you asked the Zimmermans if Harvey was up here seeing them?"

"Not yet," David said. "As I said, they have had a death in the family, too. Any other unusual things in the drawers?"

She shook her head. "Odds and ends, photographs, old tobacco. Before he started on cigars, he used to roll his own. Matchboxes. Some little things he'd collected in the old country when we were there last year. Memorabilia, I'd call it."

She was unaware of any new friends her husband might have acquired, new habits — except for his forgetfulness; there had been no mysterious parcels or letters through the mail, no unusual phone calls. Nothing.

For identification, she had brought along Harvey's driver's license, his Blue Cross card, and his naturalization certificate. He had become a U.S. citizen on June 1, 1950. He had no birth certificate. That had been lost in the war, as had his parents and most of his relatives. He was in Auschwitz from 1944 to 1945.

David detailed Giannini to accompany her and her husband's body to Air Canada. He drove to the Bridle Path.

There was no guard at the entrance to the Zimmerman estate, and the gates were open. The long, winding driveway was lined with tall poplars, their nude black branches trimmed into mushroom shapes. The ground-floor windows of the mammoth house were man-height and -width, ballooning out of the main structure and protected by wrought-iron spikes of a mid-18th-century British variety, an exaggerated version of the Queen's own at Buckingham Palace. The overall effect was somewhat bizarre.

He parked at the side where the road widened to the size of a tennis court. There were two other cars snug against the flowerbeds, one a Cherokee Chief Jeep, the other a white Ferrari. He walked around the Ferrari, admiring its glistening lines. He could almost smell the fresh leather of the soft bucket seats. Now there, David thought, is a true work of art.

The garage itself jutted out some twenty feet from the main building. Two of its triple doors were shut. Through the third, David could make out the outlines of an old Rolls Silver Cloud and a saucy little Morgan convertible, all battened down for the winter. As he came closer, he saw a young, broad-shouldered man in dungarees bending over the hood of the Rolls, polishing.

"Hello," David called out cheerfully.

The man straightened, put the cloth down on the hood, and glowered at him. His blond hair was cropped short and square. His pinched, red-nosed face was much too small for his bulging neck muscles and sloping shoulders. A bodybuilder, David thought. It takes all kinds. "Deliveries at the back," the youth told him. "Service entrance."

"I am not delivering," David said. "I'm a policeman. Can I talk to you for a second?"

"What about?" He had not become any friendlier.

"Your name, for starters."

"Why?"

David showed him his identification. "Detective Inspector David Parr," he said. "And yours?"

"Michael Ward," the young man admitted reluctantly. "I have no trouble with the police. I work here, see? Part-time, keeping the cars spick-and-span. That's me job, see?"

Why was he so defensive? "When is the last time you took care of the XJ-S, Michael?" David asked, calculatedly adding a hint of menace.

"I didn't bloody steal it," Michael snapped. "They shipped it off to Bermuda last weekend, dammit. Never stole nothing in two years and you know it." He'd backed up against the Rolls, feet braced, head down, like a bull trying to decide whether to charge.

Been to jail, then. Theft?

"Of course you didn't," David said softly, knowingly. A trick he had perfected years ago. "All I asked is when you cleaned the Jaguar last."

"I dunno. Last week," Michael shouted. "What's it to you?"

"Think now, Michael, can you place the time more accurately?" David persisted.

Michael was looking down at his toes, shoulders hunched forward, shaking his head from side to side.

"Perhaps I can help you in some way, Officer," asked a well-modulated voice from the shadows.

The side door connecting the garage to the house had opened and a tall thin man emerged, dressed almost entirely in black. Black trousers, black patent-leather shoes, and buttoned-up black tunic that accentuated his thinness. With his sparse hair, pale and narrow face, long lantern jaw, and flat forehead, he reminded David of an old, black-and-white movie figure of Count Dracula, Max Schreck's version. Approaching slowly and steadily, his arms and torso stiff and immobile, he appeared to be wheeling along.

David was so fascinated that he didn't respond at once to the polite query. The man had come up to the Rolls and interposed himself between David and Michael Ward. He repeated his question, this time putting more emphasis on the "I."

"I was asking about the Jaguar," David said finally.

"You were?" The man raised one thin eyebrow. "Why?"

"We've found pieces of an XJ-S on the scene of an accident last Thursday night, the 26th," David said. Potential witnesses often forget everything when you mention the word "murder." "I was inquiring about the whereabouts of the Zimmermans' Jaguar that night. And on the following day."

"As far as I know, it was in the garage. However, you could ask Mrs. Zimmerman directly. She is in Bermuda, but I would be pleased to furnish you with the telephone number. We had the car shipped to Bermuda last Sunday. That would have been the 1st. The day Mr. Zimmerman died."

"And who might you be?" David asked, pulling out his notebook.

"Arnold Nagy. I'm the general manager of the household, and Mr. Zimmerman's butler," and with a tasteful sigh, "may he rest in peace."

"Was the car used only by the Zimmermans?"

"Yes. Including Mr. Zimmerman's son, when he is in town."

"I was about to ask Michael here if he noticed some damage to the car on Friday."

"He didn't work Friday."

"Saturday, then, or Sunday, before it was shipped off?"

Michael had returned to vigorously polishing the Rolls. He made no effort to answer. Arnold filled in for him, as before: "He didn't work those two days either. He had vacation time coming and took extra days around the weekend. He came back Tuesday morning."

"Could someone other than the family have gained entrance to the garage during those four days and taken the Jaguar out?" David didn't bother with Michael any more.

Arnold thought about that for a while. "Yes," he said, "I expect that would be possible, but chancy. We usually have a guard at the gate. He would certainly have noticed such an irregularity."

"Where do you have the Jag repaired? Normally."

"At Downtown Fine Cars."

"And who would take the car there?"

"Geoff Aronson, Mr. Zimmerman's chauffeur."

"I'd like to speak to him."

"I'm afraid that will not be possible. He is in Bermuda, with the cook and Mrs. Zimmerman's maid. Perhaps it would be best if you asked Mrs. Zimmerman all these questions, Officer. Though, frankly, unless it is frightfully urgent, it would show some respect for her bereavement if you could defer the call for a few days." Arnold spoke English as though he had learned it from old books.

He did not invite David into the house while he fetched the phone number, and he made sure, subtly, that David was not left alone with Michael Ward. He sent the young bodybuilder down to the greenhouse with an errand.

"How long have you been with the Zimmermans?" David asked when Arnold returned.

"Twenty-two years this winter."

"Did you ever meet Mr. Singer? Harvey Singer from New York, an associate of Mr. Zimmerman, perhaps?"

"Singer...," Arnold repeated thoughtfully. "Hmm. Can't quite place the name, though maybe..." For a second, David was sure Arnold was going to say yes. But what he quite distinctly said was, "No. I don't believe so, Officer."

Nevertheless, David was sufficiently encouraged by the hesitation that he decided to call on Deidre Thomas. She was located on the all-marble top floor of the Monarch Building. She had been Paul Zimmerman's secretary for the past eight years. She was an unusually curvaceous 50, with a wide red leather belt connecting the ample halves, both of which she had chosen to accentuate by wearing a tight-fitting blue knitted dress. She smelled of expensive cologne. It was her face that betrayed the 50 years, though she had applied considerable skill to disguising the fact.

She seemed pleased to see David. Since Zimmerman's death she had been working hard, organizing masses of files for Philip Masters. "Death," she remarked matter-of-factly as she led David down to her office, "requires an enormous amount of paperwork."

David said he thought that would very much depend on the amount of money you left behind, which, in his own case, would not pose a serious problem.

Miss Thomas giggled conspiratorially. "Mr. Z. certainly took good care of me in his will," she said. "Two years' guaranteed pay and no obligation to stay beyond the month it'll likely take to get all this sorted out."

Her office was more than four times the size of David's, and a lot better lit. She had a Persian carpet, four mahogany filing cabinets — legal size, a thin designer lamp with movable parts, a bushy plant near the ceiling-to-floor window that offered a superb view toward the lake, and a giant IBM memory typewriter with black box attachment.

"Kind of Mr. Zimmerman," David said.

"Very," Miss Thomas agreed. "And now, though I don't want to rush you, can you explain why you wanted to see me?" She had positioned herself next to the window, hands on hips, a little expectant smile on her face.

Despite the fancy-dress, David thought, a woman to take seriously. "I'm attempting to track down the movements of a man who appears to have known Mr. Zimmerman and may have been in touch with him last week. He was in Toronto Thursday last. Name is Harvey Singer. He's from New York." He had avoided the past tense; no sense in alarming Miss Thomas.

"Singer...Singer...," she mused, slowly walking over to her desk. "Yes, the name does ring a bell. I think..." She opened her desk diary and leafed back to Thursday, the 26th. "Yes, I do have his name down here. He called Mr. Zimmerman in the morning, around 10:30 I think, because Mr. Z. wasn't in the office yet. He came in shortly after 11, after his meeting with the bank."

"Did Singer leave a number?"

"No. He said he'd be calling back, but I did take his name, see?"
She showed David where she had written the name on the separate
daily message sheet her diary provided.

"And did he?"

"Call again? Sure he did. Mr. Z. took the call."

"Mr. Zimmerman knew him, then."

"Must have. He never took calls unless he knew who was at the
other end of the line. Otherwise he could have spent the whole day
on the phone. Everybody wanted something from him. Lawyers,
government officials, charities, foundations, reporters, politicians,
you name it."

"Did Mr. Singer come to see him?" David asked.

"He didn't have an appointment. They could have met later in
the evening, of course. I didn't keep track of all Mr. Z.'s movements, only his business agenda." She said Z the British way:
zed. She sat down behind her desk and swiveled the chair around
to face David. In the process her skirt rode higher up her thigh,
affording a panorama of long, athletic legs in blue lace stockings.
He wondered idly if she was married, and if not, if she might be
free for dinner some evening.

David cleared his throat. "Right. Well then, do you recall his
ever being here before?"

"No, I don't. But his name did sound familiar. That's why I
asked Mr. Z. if he wanted to talk to him. Tell you what, though."
She crossed her legs, one ankle hooked around the other, and
grinned up at David. "I'm checking through all my records and all
his files anyway. If I find something, I'll call."

Constable Giannini spent most of the afternoon annoying everyone at the Downtown Fine Cars body shop, from the manager to
the apprentice repairman. None of them had seen the XJ-S since
December, when Geoff Aronson had had the tires changed.

FOURTEEN

Once she had flown first-class to Rome, courtesy of Alitalia. She had been working on a story about winter tourists in Italy for the now defunct *Star Weekly*, and Alitalia had decided to treat her to the best it had to offer: a fabulous combination of spacious seats, endless wine, champagne, five-course meal, thick socks, traveling bag, and an attentive stewardess. She had felt like Cinderella, savoring every moment, knowing it wouldn't last.

But none of that experience of how the 2 per cent lives had prepared Judith for the Lear number 421 at Buttonville Airport or the crew of two whose sole function was to get her safely to Bermuda. They had donned their uniforms this morning just for her, the TIGHTEN SEATBELTS NO SMOKING request had only her for an audience, and they had prepared the breakfast of coffee, croissants, and eggs Benedict with one customer in mind. There was no check-in counter, no waiting in line, no more fuss about boarding the plane than if she'd taken a cab.

Clearly, the rich have less time to waste than the rest of us.

In Bermuda, Customs and Immigration came to the Lear to glance at her passport and welcome her to the island. The pilot himself helped her out of the plane.

She wore her black high heels and stockings with the black and gray woolen suit Dorrit had saved from her last fall sale, and her all-purpose black bag carried a notebook, makeup, face cream, and, by a stroke of genius, a change of underwear. She had selected the clothes to look appropriately somber but had quite forgotten that Bermuda in February is rather like Toronto in the spring. The sun was already reflecting warmly off the tarmac. If the interview didn't make her sweat, the sun would.

She was greeted by a young man with freckles and a red peeling nose shaded by a blue cap with gold braid around the rim.

It made him look very much like an officer in the British navy, and the rest of the uniform, including the brass buttons, added to the impression.

"I'm Geoff Aronthon, Mrs. Hayes," he said with a slight lisp. "I'll be driving you to Xanadu."

"To where?"

He was flustered. "Mithis Simmerman thent me to drive you to Thanadu," he said, his lisp becoming more pronounced. "Mithis Hayeth, aren't you?"

"Yes," Judith admitted. "But didn't you say Xanadu?"

"The Simmerman home in Bermuda."

Of course. Brenda hadn't stopped at Byron, she'd gone on to Coleridge. It would make a hell of a sidebar: "In Xanadu did Kubla Khan / A stately pleasure-dome decree..." Would there really be fountains, towers, and hanging gardens?

Geoff handed her into the glowing green Cadillac and exchanged some pieces of paper with the flight crew. "You've been here before?" he inquired as they swished out the main gate.

"Never," Judith said.

"...On the left is the Governor's mansion, coming up on the right, St. Peter's Church and the old cemetery." Geoff occasionally broke into his running commentary on the pink and white sights to honk his horn and wave at someone. At the corner of the Sacred Heart School, a group of brown-uniformed schoolgirls set up a cheer, whistled, and hooted as he slowed the car for the lights.

"Your fan club," Judith observed.

"Jutht kids," Geoff said, retreating into his lisp. He had a low embarrassment threshold.

"Seems like you're one of the locals."

"Been coming here for 10 or 11 years. Get to know a lot of people. You know."

"You've worked for the Zimmermans all that time?"

"Yes, ma'am. Started in '76 as a garage boy. I was in the army before then," Geoff said, looking in the rearview mirror to seek eye contact. When he found it, he added: "A good thing Mr. Simmerman didn't ask for references. I'd been discharged for inthubordination. Not cut out for all that dithipline, I gueth." When he smiled, he showed tiny, uneven teeth.

"This the only car you drive?" Judith asked casually.

"Good Lord, no. There's the Rolls, the Chevy station wagon, the

Cherokee Chief, the Olds, the stretch, the Morgan, the XJ-S, and sometimes Mr. Simmerman lets me drive the Ferrari." His nose glowed as he recited the cars.

"Is one of those a Jaguar?" Judith asked.

"A Jaguar?"

"Yes."

"Why?"

"They're my favorite," Judith improvised. "Always thought if I hit the jackpot, what I'd like most is a Jaguar. They sort of hum when you drive them." Not like old Renaults, for example. They cough.

"Know what you mean," Geoff said, smiling again. "The XJ-S is a Jag. It's got the 5.3-litre V-12 May head engine, four-wheel independent suspension, man, you should hear that baby purr... Mmm-hmm."

"Do you keep it here or in Toronto?"

"Usually in Toronto, or in France. It was the boss's favorite car, too, so we shipped it ahead when they went to the chatto."

"In France?"

"Yeah."

"What's a chatto?"

He glanced into the rearview mirror again. "You know, one of those old places they have in France, it's got a vineyard and a lake. Built three hundred years ago. Mrs. Simmerman had it done over real pretty, though. They spent a week there in May, and another in June last year."

"That's where the Jag is right now?"

"No. It's on its way here from Toronto."

"A shame. Would have been nice to see it," Judith said sadly, feeling she'd done her best for David.

"Coming in this afternoon," Geoff volunteered. "Could take you back in it, if you're still here then."

"Thanks. Great." Her enthusiasm was as real as his apparent pleasure at a chance to show off the baby to a covetous buff.

They had turned into a road clearly marked PRIVATE. To the right, the sloping hills of a well-manicured golf course; on the left, the ocean rolled up onto a gold sand beach. A man in golf shoes and checked Bermuda shorts strolled along the shore. The air was soft, carrying the sweet smell of hibiscus. As they approached the end of the fairway, the scent grew stronger, and stronger still along the shiny hedge that bordered the golf course. As they squeezed through a white gateway, she caught her first glimpse of an extravagant white-gabled house surrounded by pink, blue, and white blossoms. The house had a central cupola and four smaller turrets, one on each corner, and a long, screened-in veranda with pink roses climbing up each of its many square pillars. In front, a long smooth lawn set for croquet. Whatever Coleridge had meant by "stately pleasure-dome," this qualified.

The door was opened by a small brown woman in black tunic, white frilly apron, and starched cap pinned to her short-cropped curly hair. "Welcome to Bermuda, Mrs. Hayes," she said with a slight lilt to her voice. "Would you like to freshen up after your journey, or go straight to the conservatory?"

Judith declined the freshening and followed the maid along a brightly lit passageway with coral pink and stucco walls and light blue mosaic tiles. On the window side there were tiers of pink geraniums in hanging pots and baskets of long-stemmed Swedish ivy. The passageway opened onto an expanse of greenery, dappled with sunlight. "The conservatory." Full of tall palms, hibiscus trees, and oleanders, with a perfectly oval pool with bronze fountain and water lilies in the center. Turquoise and pink canaries were chirping in white cane cages.

Brenda Zimmerman reclined on a green and pink chaise longue near the pool. Her hair was piled on top of her head, but for a few feathery blond strands that had been allowed to escape and fall alongside her slender neck. A soft gold silk dress fell in folds from a raised knee. Except for the array of rings on her fingers, her arms and shoulders were bare.

So much for widow's weeds.

She was gazing out the windows when Judith entered and continued to do so until Judith stood at the end of her chaise. Then she looked up. Her face was pale and faded, her deep violet eyes ringed in red. Two new lines had etched themselves into the corners of her mouth. "Well...," she said softly. "There you are again."

"I do appreciate the opportunity to talk to you, Mrs. Zimmerman. I'm terribly sorry..." Judith felt monumentally awkward and cumbersome in her black winter outfit, with the heavy bag, in her inability to find the right words.

Brenda waved the attempt aside with one languid movement of her right hand, which then reached for the tall glass of wine on the turquoise table beside her. "Do call me Brenda," she said wearily, "and for heaven's sake sit down, take some clothes off, and have a drink."

"Thank you." Judith chose a gin and tonic with lots of ice and lemon. She threw her jacket over the back of the chair.

"A bit overdressed for Bermuda, aren't you, dear?" Brenda asked.

"Happens so rarely, I might as well make the most of it," Judith said, pulling out her notebook and kicking off her shoes. "That's better."

Brenda smiled. "Philip says I can talk to you. That, coming from Philip, is tantamount to a recommendation. He's not very partial to the press."

"I know."

"I think Paul would have liked to see the story done," she added, turning her head away. "Did you come to the funeral?"

"I was late," Judith said. "Saw Rabbi Jonas on the way out." When Brenda didn't comment on that, she went on. "Did you know Mr. Zimmerman was going to have a Christian burial?"

"Not until we read the will."

"The 51st Psalm was his own choice?"

"It certainly wasn't mine," Brenda said, emptying her glass. "Not well up on my psalms, really."

"Any idea why that particular psalm?"

"None." She shook the little silver bell perched on the table next to her. "You ready for a refill?"

Judith wasn't. "Philip Masters said you'll be carrying on with the management of the Zimmerman string of companies."

Brenda looked bored. "Probably."

"Have you decided on the succession at Monarch?"

"You mean between Griffiths and Goodman? No, but that part I might even enjoy."

After the maid had come and gone, Judith decided on a less direct approach. "What can you tell me about Mr. Zimmerman?"

"Paul?" Brenda brushed her face with her hand, as though to smooth the skin. Her long, perfect nails were still painted silver. "He was extraordinary. As I said. He never failed at anything — or he never tried anything he might have failed at. A most unusual talent, don't you think?"

Rather alarming, Judith thought, but she didn't say so.

"He breathed, ate, dreamed his business. His mind never slacked. He had to program himself to relax. When he and Philip were working on the Pacific Airlines takeover, he had to force pauses into his 24-hour days so that Philip could catch up to him. They would spend the night going over papers. In the morning while Philip slept, Paul would go for his run, all the while thinking about what the next move should be. When Philip emerged from his slumbers, drowsy, Paul would be completely refreshed and eager to get going. Some people don't need sleep. Paul was one of those. Napoleon, I read somewhere, was another — " She broke off suddenly, focused her eyes on Judith, tense. "Not that I'm saying he was like Napoleon, you understand?"

Judith nodded sympathetically. Zimmerman was obviously a workaholic with latent megalomania, but Brenda wasn't going to be the one to say so.

"He was as earnest about his pleasures as about his work," Brenda said. "You saw the paintings? Paul had an eye for things. He chose carefully. That includes the people around him. I doubt he was disappointed more than once. And he was a wonderful father ..." Her eyes filled with tears she didn't try to hide. She drank with a loud gulp, swallowing her tears with the wine, "...to Meredith."

"And to Arthur?" Judith asked quickly.

Brenda shrugged. "Arthur can take care of himself. He is an adult."

"You met Paul in Nassau," Judith prompted.

"I told you that already," Brenda said impatiently. "Love at first sight with all the trimmings. Afterward, he sent me six red roses every single day, including Sundays, for six months, till we got married." She sighed. "He knew I was an incurable romantic, and he'd determined I would be his wife. Paul had good taste in everything he chose — including women." She didn't elaborate.

Judith put a little star into her book to try and wend her way back to that remark. "Was he still married to Eva when you met?"

"Why?"

"I thought because you waited six months — "

"Good Lord, no." Brenda waved dismissively. "We waited because I wanted to make sure. He was so damn perfect, so... 'Everything my heart desir'd.' Don't you see, I had to make sure it would last. Kept thinking I'd..." Her voice had sunk to a whisper. She cupped her hands around the glass, staring at it. "Poor old pathetic Eva. She had let him go. Worse. She actually left him and moved to Mexico City with Arthur." She almost spat out the "Arthur."

"Any idea why?" Judith asked gently.

"She was crazy. Still is. This for your magazine or are you just curious?"

Was it her imagination, or was Brenda slurring her words?

"Both," Judith said.

"Good. I hope you'll quote me. Maybe she'll sue for libel." Brenda laughed harshly and suddenly, and just as abruptly stopped. "Did you ask Paul about her?"

"No."

"Then what on earth did you talk about?"

"Mostly his recent takeovers. And he told me a little about his childhood over dinner."

"He did?" Brenda's blond eyebrows shot up. "What part?"

"Some place in Hungary where they make Bull's Blood. His father working in the vineyards and the family not having enough to eat..."

Brenda laughed again. "Oh dear, oh dear, he didn't try that old chestnut on you. Must have been the wine we served."

"You mean he made it up?"

"Let's just say he imagined it. Loved the idea of those rags-to-riches stories. His father was a merchant. One of the wealthiest men in Eger. His mother had all her clothes made in Paris and Vienna. Not even Budapest. He was taught violin on a Stradivarius, had a private tutor and his own library. They went to concerts in Vienna and spent summers in Italy. Only problem was, Hitler invaded and they were Jews." Brenda started to examine her silver nails as though she were searching for chips in the polish.

"What happened to them?" Judith asked hesitantly.

"Same as happened to most of the Jews in Hungary. They died."

"In a concentration camp?"

Brenda shrugged. "I don't know. Paul didn't exactly relish talking about that part of his life. That's likely why he invented little stories about parents he never had, and, having never had, never lost."

"How did Paul escape?"

"It was 1944. He was 16. There were rumors about Jews being rounded up in Germany. His father worried he might be forced into one of the work gangs for the Eastern Front nobody ever returned from, so he sent him off into the Bükk Mountains with some of the other young men to hide. Later he joined the partisans. When the war was over he made his way to Vienna and reported in with the other lost and homeless." Brenda finished what was left in her glass and tinkled the bell for another refill. "Where the real rags-to-riches saga begins is with Paul arriving in Canada by cattle boat in the winter of 1946. He was 17, alone in the world, with nothing but the clothes on his back and a burning desire to succeed."

"He never went back to Hungary?"

"What for?" Brenda threw her head back so forcefully it hit the back of the chaise longue and rebounded. The canaries set up a wild din in response to the thump.

Finally Brenda resumed. "First job he got was on the docks. He was big and tough and could carry the weight of two men with one arm. His favorite trick was crouching on the floor, grabbing a chair by one leg, his arm outstretched, and hoisting it over his head. He could still do that last year. It earned him respect on the waterfront. Also made him a large moving target with a funny accent and a long Jewish name. So one day a bunch of them pinned him down, broke his ribs, and stuck a knife in his stomach. They glued him together at the Montreal General. He stayed there for a year washing floors and cleaning toilets to work off the bill." Brenda smiled. "Last year, he gave them a hundred thou toward the new wing. They never knew why."

"He met Eva there?"

"She was a nurse. Couldn't resist his looks. Few women did." She laughed again. "Know what you're thinking," she said, her voice a childlike singsong, "but you're wrong. Not altogether wrong, but mostly wrong, and anyway what does it matter now he's dead." She shouted the last word, leaning forward, almost spat it at Judith, then buried her face in her elegant hands.

"Mommy?" Judith heard over her shoulder. It was a small, uncertain voice, a little shaky. Meredith emerged from behind one of the citrus trees. She must have come in some time ago. Her bare feet made no sound on the tiles as she tiptoed toward her mother. "Mommy?" She wore a tiny pink bikini with blue ribbons, another blue ribbon held up her hair. Instinctively, Judith reached out to comfort her, but Meredith ignored the outstretched hand and went to stand over her mother.

Brenda looked up and smiled, although she had tears running down her face. "It's okay, baby," she whispered. "It's okay."

Meredith put her arms around Brenda's neck and hugged her

head against her childish rotund stomach. Then she turned her attention to Judith: "We were wondering if you would like to have some lunch," she said, suddenly every inch in command, with a smile like her mother's, but without the touch of irony.

Brenda wiped her face with a white silk handkerchief and took another long gulp of her wine. "Well...," she said — her elongated "well" — "perhaps we should join Philip on the terrace?"

When Brenda stood, the gold dress unfurled with a soft hiss. "What have you ordered for lunch?" she asked Meredith.

"Philip wanted lobsters and some garlicky salad with eggs and little green things, so I had Stephie make me a hot dog. Can't stand all that guck." Meredith led the way out of the conservatory, around past a baroque German cuckoo clock that was just starting to strike twelve and through a pair of French doors to what Judith assumed must be the terrace, though it looked rather more like an open-air Greek museum, complete with classical statues in various states of undress. The whole thing was covered — and would be until April, said Meredith — by an enormous blue-tinted plastic balloon.

In the center was a huge bean-shaped pool. Philip Masters, wearing tennis whites, green visor, and gold-rimmed sunglasses, sat at a stone table near the pool. He was working on a pile of papers, making notes here and there, his elbow close to a glass containing frothy pink liquid, Chinese paper umbrella, and long straw. He jumped to his feet to greet them. "Beautiful day," he shouted.

Only Meredith found it in her heart to agree with him. The white outfit made him appear both wider and shorter than he was, like some overgrown schoolboy with unnaturally aged features. His knees were very rosy in their nudity.

While lunch was served Brenda sunk into gloomy silence, and Philip extolled the virtues of the island and why Paul had decided to build here. "The terrace is Brenda's addition," he said. "It's rather" — he grinned at his lobster — "original, don't you think?"

"Mmm," Judith agreed.

"What Philip means," Brenda said, or rather slurred, leaning forward and fixing Philip with a baleful gaze, "is that it's gauche, self-indulgent, worthless kitsch, and he doubts Paul would ever have had the lousy taste to install it himself. But Philip is much too polite to say so."

Meredith pushed her plate with the half-eaten hot dog to one side, ran to the pool, and dove in with one easy, practiced movement.

Philip didn't say anything. Clearly it was his turn to sulk.

Perhaps because of Philip's discomfort, Brenda brightened. "You'd like to go for a swim?" she asked.

"Didn't bring a bathing suit," Judith confessed. She was sweating inside the clinging woolen skirt and sticky black pantyhose.

"No problem," Brenda chirped. "There's a bunch of bikinis I keep on hand for forgetful visitors. Let's see you for size..." She assessed Judith with one eye closed. "Ten, with an outsized top, I'd say," she pronounced. "Got lots of *those*." She lurched out of her chair and floated off in the direction of the French doors.

For a moment neither of them said anything, then Philip broke the silence: "She's taking it very hard," he said. "She's not used to taking losses. She had a protected childhood, a little princess whose greatest problem was not knowing what to wear to the next birthday party, or whose boyfriend danced with whom. Her acutest problem was whether to mix or match her accessories. She was the only child of middle-aged Jewish parents. A late baby who never lacked for anything. They would have regarded it as a personal failure if she were denied anything *they* could provide for her. She never even encountered anti-Semitism — and that was when quotas and restrictions were still a way of life for the rest of us, when banks and department stores didn't hire Jews, when apartments, resorts, hotels, and even beaches were 'gentiles only.' Nobody ever beat *her* up for being a 'kike.'"

Philip stood up and paced a little, hands clasped behind his back. "I thought, when I was growing up, that experience toughens the man, but it doesn't, you know." He stopped and looked at Judith. "All it does is make you aware of other people's misery. Gives you a firsthand knowledge of what it's like to be the underdog, a feeling of sympathy for victims. That sort of thing. In my case, there was an additional advantage: I took up boxing. You're looking at a onetime welterweight champion for Montreal East, my dear." He poured himself a glass of Perrier. "For Brenda," he said, "coming here may have been a mistake. I told her so, but she did want to get away from where Paul died. Trouble with Bermuda is they'd had some of their happiest times here."

"There's something I've been wondering about since we first

met," Judith said, deciding to put Brenda's absence to good use. "Mr. Zimmerman remarked on your being a hired gun, working for whoever paid the highest price for your services. What did he mean?"

Philip played with his napkin. He smoothed it over his knee, folded it into a neat square, monogram side up, then dabbed his chin with it. "That would have been on Thursday, you say...," he mused.

"The 26th," Judith said.

"Nothing to do with the story, but I guess you'll see the announcement next week anyway." Philip placed the napkin carefully beside his plate. "I had accepted the chairmanship of Amco. He took it a little hard. After almost 40 years I suppose he'd grown accustomed to our working together."

"Your moving to Amco, would that have meant you'd no longer be his lawyer?"

"We hadn't yet resolved how we were going to deal with the long-term association with Masters, Goldberg, Griffiths...He was too angry then to discuss that. So was I, I guess. We were both shouting —" Philip broke off. Meredith had emerged from the water and slipped back onto her chair, a big terry-cloth towel wrapped around her shoulders, her blond hair dripping on the marble tiles.

"You told her," she said. "You said there wasn't any need to tell anybody and then you went and told her." Her big violet eyes were fixed accusingly on Philip Masters. Her voice shook.

Masters bent toward her, placing a limp, placating hand on her bare arm. "Honey, it isn't what you think, I just told her about —"

"I heard you," Meredith screamed. "You think I don't hear things. Just like the last time." She swung from her chair and set off toward the house, running. Over her shoulder, she gave Masters a parting shot: "You *suck*." Then she slammed the door behind her.

"She is highly strung. Like her mother," Philip explained quickly. "She'd overheard my discussion with her father last Thursday. We decided to keep it to ourselves till it was absolutely necessary for Brenda to know. Now is not the time to tell Brenda I won't remain the faithful retainer she's always said I was."

"I don't think Brenda likes you a helluva lot," Judith opined.

Philip smiled. "It's her way," he said. "Bantering. Wouldn't take it seriously. We've known each other a long time. Sometimes, I think..." He picked a lump of sugar from a silver bowl and put it on his tongue. He made a loud slurping noise as he sucked on it. "She resented my being so close to Paul. Female jealousy. You know..."

Judith didn't, but there was no need to say so because Brenda had returned with an assortment of bikinis, all white, with blue ties, "so you can mix and match," she said. "There are changing rooms behind the bar." Brenda herself had changed into an almost strapless pink bikini. The pants were held together by a pair of thin gold chains on each side, exposing her long, brown flanks. Rubens would have gone crazy over her figure: perfect in every detail, only a little too much of it.

It was clear Brenda hadn't lied to Who's Who about her age. Nobody 40 had a figure as seamless as hers. No sags, no droops, no concessions to gravity. Thank God the changing rooms had no mirrors, only oriental birds-on-branch prints, cane chairs, and deliberately rustic woven mats.

Knowing she'd feel rotten standing next to Brenda, Judith hid in a fluffy blue towel supplied by the maid and let it go, reluctantly, with the same movement she used to leap into the shallow end of the pool. The bikini clung to her like wet tissue paper.

Brenda, with the practiced motions of someone accustomed to dealing with unsteadiness, cautiously lowered herself down the ladder at the other end, slid into the water with a girlish squeal, and immediately began to swim vigorous strokes — breaststroke. She kept her head well above water. With her blond hair now piled higher on her head to keep it dry, she rather resembled a swan, or some white-tufted wading bird.

Philip Masters sat on the edge, his pedicured feet lightly dangling in the water. Judith made her way toward him. She slid her soles over the white marble tiles, their touch soft and sensuous to her hot, tired toes. Philip, his visor pushed back on his head, watched her with interest. He was waiting for the next round.

"Did Paul Zimmerman ever talk to you about his childhood?" she asked, not wanting to disappoint him.

"Not a whole lot," Philip said brightly. "Past couple of years he'd begun to get maudlin now and then. Happens to everybody with age. Talked about getting his first bicycle. Happiest day of his life. Biggest deal apparently in that chicken-shit town was getting a new bike. His was orange, except for silver tire guards and the handlebars. Do you remember your first bike?"

"Yes. Not much nostalgia in it, though. Kept falling off all the time." Her father had taught her to ride on an old secondhand ladies' bike with over-elaborate handlebars that resembled oxen's horns. He had run along behind holding onto the seat as she pedaled. Both of them panted and tried to concentrate. Neither was particularly athletic. Come to think of it, that may have been the only time Judith ever saw her father run. "Fool," her mother had murmured when she saw the two of them land sideways into the neighbor's fence. "Serves him right."

She must have loved him once, although Judith never saw that. Before she gave up on him. Before he finally convinced her that he had no ambitions to become the bank president, no desire to have, no interest in the things money could buy. He hid behind his newspaper most evenings, seemingly deaf to her sharp tongue. In the ledger he brought home from the bank each night, she later discovered he was writing poetry.

"Mine was a secondhand Raleigh. I took it to my room the first night," Philip said. "Paul got to enjoy his fully for a day. Then the Russian invasion came and it made bicycles frivolous."

"Did he have any friends?"

"Only one he ever mentioned. Some kid called Feri. They became best friends when they were six or seven. Inseparable. Paul was shy and reticent, tongue-tied, he said. Feri was confident. A talker. They made a good pair." Philip laughed. "Paul sure changed a lot."

"What happened to the other kid?"

"Who knows? It was a lousy war."

"When I came to your office, you told me Paul wasn't interested in making money and didn't want power. Challenge, you said, but you never really explained."

"Didn't I?" Philip mused. "I must have assumed you'd prefer to work it out for yourself. What he wanted, naturally, was to prove himself. Over and over again. He had to make sure he could still do it. It's kind of a DP mentality, you know."

"DP?"

"Displaced person. It's what they called wartime refugees. But the syndrome was nothing new. My grandfather came out of

Ukraine after one of the pogroms. He was 14 when he arrived in Montreal. Not a penny in his pocket. He never stopped trying to prove he could make it, either. Worked 24 hours a day. Got his first grocery store when he was 20 and kept adding new stores till the day he died at age 82. He had 14 stores by then. Sent all his kids to university, though he never had one day of school himself. Hell, he couldn't even read."

Judith floated on her back, gently fluttering her hands to keep her balance. The water felt warm and bubbly, like champagne, the tiny bubbles crisscrossing her stomach, which had begun to feel smooth and silky like the tiles. Her hair fanned out around her head, luxuriant, little waves caressed her scalp. The sun made flashy rainbows along the sides of the big blue bubble.

"Nice. Very, very nice," Philip clucked appreciatively and moistened his lips with his small pink tongue.

Judith, her ears bobbing in and out of the water, pretended not to have heard. Fact was, while she thought she should protest from a professional viewpoint, she felt quite receptive to the compliment. The light cocoonlike warmth had made her feel sensual. Sexy. And that was not a good way to be feeling around a short, balding married man whom she was supposed to be interviewing for her most lucrative assignment of recent years. She checked to make certain Brenda was out of earshot, then decided it was time for one of her lead gambits.

"Eva Zimmerman says Paul was murdered," she announced while watching Philip closely. She hadn't changed position, she just opened her eyes wide.

He stiffened as though he'd been hit by a blast of cold air and clutched his hands together in his lap. Then he pushed his dark glasses higher on his nose as he composed his features into an amused expression. Resuming control came easily to him, but the effort had been visible. "When did you talk to Eva?" he asked carefully.

"She sent me a telegram," Judith said. "Who do you think would have wanted to kill Paul Zimmerman?"

"In a telegram?" Philip's voice rose to its upper ranges. "That's crazy. And typically Eva. She would have had my letter for a few hours, consulted her lawyers, ignored their advice, and gone ahead with whatever destructive nonsense first entered her mind. She is bad-tempered and impulsive." He had relaxed enough to resume dangling his toes in the pool. "As to who would kill Paul, nobody. With the possible exception of Eva herself once she saw the will. Paul left a few odds and ends to old friends, a couple of reasonable bequests to charities; everything else went to Brenda and Meredith — in trust."

"And Arthur?"

"Just his allowance."

"And that would have caused Eva to send that telegram?"

"Hell, no. She doesn't much care for Arthur." Philip chuckled. "Not an easy target for love, that guy. Never was, far as I recall. It's for herself she'd want more money. Eva knows how to spend, and I suspect her investments could use a blood transfusion. Paris is an expensive city, and they don't have free rooms at the Meurice."

"She stays at the Meurice?"

"No, my dear, she *lives* at the Meurice."

Brenda swam closer, pulled herself out of the pool, sauntered over to Masters and flopped on her stomach on the ledge. Her thighs made a funny little clucking sound as she slapped them onto the stone.

Among other things, the wet bathing suit revealed that she was a natural blond.

"Well," she announced with a sigh, "I do like to think your trip wasn't a total waste of time. At least you've had a swim."

"Thanks," said Judith.

"To give thanks is good, and to forgive...," Brenda declared, for no apparent reason.

"I beg your pardon?" Judith asked.

"Swinburne, you know," Brenda said, leaning on her elbows. "A much underrated poet: 'If life was bitter to thee, pardon/If sweet, give thanks; thou hast no more to live;/And to give thanks is good, and to forgive.'"

"Hmm," Judith said noncommittally and prepared to dive for her towel.

"Did you wonder what Paul was talking about when he died?" Brenda asked suddenly.

"When he said 'Sorry'?" Judith inquired tentatively. She hadn't been sure Brenda had heard.

"Yes."

"I guess I didn't," she said. "Do you know what he meant?"

"I believe," Brenda said, "he was forgiving himself for all the things he had left undone." She put her head down, closed her eyes, and went very still.

Judith figured the interview was over. "I was wondering," she said, talking to Masters, but watching Brenda for a reaction, "if you came across a Mr. Singer among Mr. Zimmerman's acquaintances?"

"Singer?" Philip pondered. "Singer...was that the man in the music business, went public last year? Gerald, I think...bought that radio station..."

"No," Judith said. "A man in the rag trade in New York."

"No idea, I'm afraid. Did you say an associate of Paul's?"

"Perhaps."

Philip shook his head thoughtfully. "Sorry."

Brenda hadn't moved at all when she mentioned Singer. Judith pounced on the blue towel, wrapped it around herself, and went to change. All the way, she was aware of Philip Masters's eyes gazing at her rump.

When she was ready to leave, he escorted her to the door. Brenda was still lying immobile by the pool. "I'll see you in Toronto," Philip said huskily.

"More than likely," Judith concurred.

Geoff was waiting in the driveway beside the green Cadillac. He was as disappointed as Judith over not having the XJ-S.

"Had to take it in for repairs, ma'am," he told Judith mournfully. "Windows got all smashed on the way over. Damn tranthport never learned how to take care of fine cars."

FIFTEEN

Doctor Meisner's waiting room was purely functional. It paid no heed to newfangled theories about creature comforts or stress alleviation for patients. The color was basic green, the furniture, army-issue straight-backed chairs, with no distracting pictures on the wall.

There were four other patients in the waiting room. Two wore business suits cut from the same widely spaced pinstriped material, one had overalls. The fourth was a pregnant woman, circa eight months and closing quickly; in deference to the invigorating cool air in the waiting room, she kept on her black mink overcoat, which had clearly been bought just months ago. She had left her black lace-up boots on the plastic mat next to the entrance and was rubbing her toes gently against one another to restore circulation. Those toes brought back memories Judith had thought buried under mountains of emotional rubble: images of James cradling her frozen feet against his warm stomach as they lay in their cramped double bed above the noisy surgery, their hands on her belly, waiting for Anne's next aggressive kick at her confinement. They had felt truly important then. Becoming parents was such a momentous event. They had married because that was what everyone expected them to do. There might have been some fumbling moments of love years before, some excitement in the car on the way home from college dances, groping on his parents' faded chintz couch the odd times they could be alone, but all that had palled with their hopelessly inept attempts at sex once they survived their formal wedding night. Her pregnancy lent some meaning to the marriage and, for a while, spared them further efforts in bed. James's relief at not having to keep up the pretense made him cheerful, concerned, and openly affectionate.

Once Anne was born, they both retreated into their separate, cautious selves.

"Mrs. Hayes." The nurse's sharp voice entered Anne's freshly painted nursery. "If you wouldn't mind..." She was pointing at the door to her left. Judging by her tone, she'd been trying to attract Judith's attention for some time. "Doctor's waiting," she added grimly.

Once Judith had done a story about the hours two doctors kept their patients waiting in the course of a week and what those hours were worth for the patients involved. There had been stormy protest from the medical profession, insulted by her temerity in putting them on the same scales as other people.

Doctor Meisner sat at his desk, facing the window. He had a long, thin neck and was completely bald. Judith made it to the middle of the room before he acknowledged her presence. Then he stretched out one arm and made quick waving motions toward her. This she interpreted as an invitation to sit, and she did so, moving the low-slung green plastic-covered chair so she wouldn't see the bed with the nasty steel stirrups at the end.

When Doctor Meisner finally swiveled toward her, he was still looking in the file he had been reading. He wore horn-rimmed half-moon glasses. "Not much I can add to your story, Mrs. Hayes," he said in his best palliative voice. "Mr. Zimmerman was suffering from a condition known as IHSS. It's a familial, or inherited, heart disease. It was diagnosed in early February. The prognosis for this type of ailment is, generally, fair in the short term. But it is unpredictable. If he followed the regimen I laid out for him, he had every expectation of living a full and happy life."

"For how long?" Judith asked.

"That, Mrs. Hayes, is not within the province of medical science to predict. Anywhere from one month to five years."

"Is that what you told him?"

"At first." Doctor Meisner now glanced up at Judith and smiled. "But that's not the sort of response Paul would find satisfactory. He was a man of action. He had been a patient of mine for 20 years and I knew him well. So I told him that, if I were a betting man, I would guess he had a couple of good years left, and then, who knows?"

"Were you surprised when he died so suddenly?" Judith asked.

Doctor Meisner shrugged. "Not especially. Though...I did wonder why the disease had speeded up at such a rate. IHSS is a deformation. It's known to be slow. He was starting to keep it under control with the drugs and physically, he had always been strong. Yes, I suppose you could say I was somewhat surprised."

"Were you the first physician to examine him after the attack?"

"You mean after he died? No. I was called, but by the time I arrived he had been taken to the Wellesley by ambulance. Doctor Jenning was in attendance. One of the best young men in the field. Paul was dead on arrival." He shook his head. "Nothing could be done. And they did try everything. He must have been terribly disappointed to go so soon. He still had plans, things to complete, you know."

Judith confessed she didn't know. She was thinking what she'd want to complete in such circumstances. Her life insurance policy payments, for one. Perhaps she'd do that will. "His will, you mean?" she asked.

It was an inspired guess. "Yes. He did want to change his will. Must have told you about that, did he? Odd. He was such a secretive fellow. But you're right. He'd been feeling rather badly about Arthur of late. Only son he had, after all, though Arthur wasn't much of a prize, what with his —" Meisner cleared his throat "— his sexual preferences. But he's such a talented boy, and there were so many bridges to mend. Paul knew," he sighed. "Paul knew."

"And Eva, was he going to include Eva?" Judith prompted.

Doctor Meisner raised his eyebrows to further the cause of a knowledgeable nod. "Ah yes, poor Eva. I had so hoped for a reconciliation once. But she wouldn't have it. She wouldn't come back to him. She said it was because of the boy. I never figured out what happened between those two. They had been happy once. Edna and I knew them then, and Edna...well, she and Eva had become friends. Coffee, lunch, I think they had a bridge club. You know, women's stuff."

Oh yeah, hold on to your knitting, lady, this is no place to fight the good fight. "Sure," Judith said between gritted teeth.

"Then one day, poof —" Meisner's hands shot up to show he held nothing but air "— she was gone. Never a word to Edna. Nothing. Paul didn't even know where she'd gone until he had a letter from her lawyer. Crazy female."

Well, at least that checked with Brenda's and Philip's versions. "He wasn't going to include her, then?"

"If he was, he never told me," Doctor Meisner said. "He only talked about Arthur...and — I guess it won't do any harm to tell — about spending some time with himself. Recovering his past, he called it. But that's understandable. Sort of stuff most people want to do when they know they're dying."

"Did he talk to you much about his past?"

"No. About his father, when I asked if there had been a history of heart disease in the family. He died when Paul was very young. So had his grandfather."

"How old was Paul when his father died?"

"Seven. No, eight."

"Before the war, then?"

"Sure, '36 or so." He returned the file folder to his desk. "If you'll excuse me, Mrs. Hayes, I have another patient waiting..."

Judith lingered in the doorway for one more question. "I was sitting next to him when he had the attack. He'd been drinking out of a water glass. Some kind of amber liquid. Could that have been his medication?"

"Possibly. Why?"

"I wondered," Judith said with a reassuring gaze, "if he might have been poisoned."

For a moment Meisner stared back at her, stiff, curious, then he shook his head. "Come on, now, that's ridiculous. Why would anyone want to kill Paul?" He waved Judith out dismissively. "Please tell Mrs. Gordon to send in the next."

When she arrived home, Stevie was sitting in the kitchen drinking sherry, feeling dejected because David had suggested she might have imagined the intruder into Judith's home. She wore her revolutionary headband and black leather boots to show her outrage. There was no point asking how she had got in. She had brought a gift of a melancholy Japanese tea plant that should never have been left out in the cold.

There was a message on the tape from Jimmy that everything was cool on the mountain, which was just as well, considering the 18-below temperatures. No need for the snow-making machines. Anne had progressed to five, whatever that meant, and there was some guy from University of Toronto Schools trying to make an impression on her. They'd be on the hill till the evening, then call again.

The tape registered several clicks and buzzes, then *Finance International* came on, in the person of perfectionist Giles, and announced they didn't think much of Judith's lead. "Death of a Titan" wouldn't have worked even for Theodore Dreiser, and *Finance International* wasn't known for melodramatic leads. Giles was sure Judith would come up with something better, and if she didn't, that was all right too, there were people on staff who could. She should get down to the human interest material, now that she'd finished the investments profile.

"Human interest, indeed," Stevie said, going for more sherry. "What do they know about that? I could give them a human interest story that'd set their ears on fire, and never leave this street," she threatened.

"Charles Griffiths will be in his office between 2 and 3 this afternoon, would talk to Mrs. Hayes" was the last of the messages. It was delivered by a jolly female voice.

Quarter past 2. Still time to reach Dundas Street before 3 if she hurried. She pulled on her aged winter coat, wrapped her head in a woolen scarf, and offered to let Stevie out.

"I don't believe you made it up," she told Stevie, reassuringly. "And I don't believe Jimmy's on drugs. But right now I haven't the time to get to the bottom of it. When I'm finished with Zimmerman, we'll drink the rest of the sherry and figure it out. Okay?"

It wasn't, but Stevie let it go with a sigh. She didn't want to be a burden.

Loyal Trust was one of the brightest stars in Zimmerman's corporate firmament. It had been much in the news after the government's deregulation of the financial industries, as had its brilliant CEO, Chuck Griffiths, former corporate lawyer, partner with Philip Masters in Masters, Goldberg, Griffiths. Judith had already collected Loyal's corporate profile, annual reports, and brief history of recent acquisitions from the PR department. Unlike many companies, Loyal Trust had an open-door policy. It was proud of its results. In the lobby there were photographs of the top sales group's recent trip to the Bahamas, the elevator displayed multicolored graphs of the year's gains, the second floor sported a portrait gallery of smiling directors. There was a Girl Guide eagerness about the receptionist and about Griffiths's chubby secretary. The only long face in the building belonged to Chuck Griffiths himself.

"I have a 3 o'clock meeting, Mrs. Hayes," he told her. "I do like to cooperate with the press, and particularly *Finance International*, but you have to appreciate..." He shrugged.

Judith checked her watch and promised to keep it short.

"I hope you've had all the cooperation you need from the staff," Griffiths continued. "It's been a spectacular year for us. Best in our history. New branches in the Bahamas, Secure Trust in Great Britain, the growth of our American companies... A great pity that Paul won't be here to share the best with us. Tea, coffee?" He had ushered her away from the formality of the desk, into a deep brown armchair in the corner of his office, where he had arranged a small sitting room complete with couch and liquor cabinet.

"They've been wonderful," Judith said about the staff. "I have enough material for a second story, when this one's finished," she gazed earnestly. "In fact, that's a very good idea. The Loyal Trust story." Not much chance he'd fall for that old trick, but always worth a try.

He didn't. He continued to look glum, while he poured coffee from a silver pot and arranged himself facing Judith.

"It's Paul Zimmerman I've come to talk to you about," Judith continued, "and what happened between him and Philip Masters."

Griffiths crossed his knees, stirred his coffee, and registered no reaction.

Judith pressed on. "I assume you know about the parting of ways between them. You were, after all, close to them both. It was Masters's relationship with Zimmerman that propelled you into Loyal, I understand."

Well, that got a rise out of him at last. "Did Philip tell you that?" he asked, his voice rasping.

Judith stirred her coffee, though she hadn't put anything into it. She was hoping her preoccupation could be interpreted as agreement and that Griffiths would go on. Which is exactly what he did.

"Must be his notorious sense of humor again" Griffiths said, but he wasn't smiling. "Fact is, I've known Paul Zimmerman for almost as long as Philip has. We were both interested in land deals, Paul and I. When we met, and I was still a student at McCarthy's then, I had already put a bit of money into a piece of Trois-

Rivières. Paul was working on some deal in Ste-Agathe, so I gave him a bunch of free advice. Not to diminish the help he paid for from Philip, but that was all legal help. Paul and I were friends long before I joined Masters and Goldberg." He brushed a bit of lint off his dark suit. "Hell, we used to take holidays, Paul and Eva, Zelda and I — Zelda was my first wife. We were each other's best men at our second weddings. Nothing to do with Philip that I ended up at Loyal. Paul acquired it through Monarch in '74. It was a deadbeat, tired old firm, a bit of a gentlemen's club. Paul needed someone to shake it up, turn it around. Seemed like a challenge, so I took it. I can tell you, it sure beats hell out of corporate law."

"Who will run Monarch now that Zimmerman is gone?"

Griffiths shrugged. "Still to be determined," he said. There was a hint of a smile on his face.

"Do you know why Masters and Zimmerman quarreled?" Judith asked.

"You should ask Philip that question, Mrs. Hayes. It's nothing to do with me and I make a point of not interfering in other people's battles unless they directly affect my business. All I can say is it was a long time coming. Philip's been empire-building for too damn long and he couldn't expect Paul to turn a blind eye forever. Lawyers get paid for a service, even ones as elevated as Masters."

"What did Philip want?"

"A coronation, I think. He still does. For his old age, he decided he wants to be in the Senate. And nothing — and I mean nothing at all — is going to come between that gilt-edged seat and his aging arse."

"And that's why he left Paul Zimmerman?" Judith inquired with wide-eyed innocence.

Griffiths stood up to confirm her time was over. He began to look over some papers on his desk. "Well, that's all I'm going to tell you about it."

She changed the subject. "Did you agree you'd be Rabbi Jonas's caller at the United Jewish Appeal fund-raiser?"

"I'm still thinking about it," he said distractedly.

"There was that little exchange between Brenda Zimmerman and you at the party — can you tell me what that was about?" Judith pressed on.

"I don't recall any exchange," Griffiths rose, checked his oversize gold watch. "And I'm afraid I have a meeting now."

"About your not fitting Paul Zimmerman's shoes," Judith persisted, "and something about your wife."

Griffiths strode to the door and opened it wide. "I do hope you can find your way out," he said, his lips tight. "Goodbye, Mrs. Hayes."

He closed the door behind her.

As soon as she got home, Judith asked the operator to place a person-to-person to Mrs. Eva Zimmerman at the Hôtel Meurice, Paris, France. Eva had already sent her calling card, and for human interest it would be hard to beat a crazy ex-wife, holed up in the most palatial hotel in Paris, dispatching dire warnings that her former husband was murdered. After a series of hollow clicks and bangs, and a plethora of "Allo"s, a male voice inquired, "À part de qui?" The operator said, "Judith Hayes," which reverberated across the Atlantic and corrected itself into a long whine, and finally a gravelly female voice said, "Yes, Mrs. Hayes. What took you so long?"

"I'm sorry...?"

"I was expecting your call on Wednesday. Did you not receive my telegram?" She pronounced each syllable and placed equal emphasis on all of them. A perfect Zsa Zsa Gabor Hungarian accent.

"Yes, I did," said Judith, "but I'm afraid I was in Bermuda yesterday." Why the hell was she apologizing for not responding immediately to an utterly preposterous telegram?

"How is the lovely Brenda? Taking it like a soldier, is she? And the child...what's her name? Beverly? Alexandra? You know... the little princess?"

"Meredith?"

"Ach yes, Meredit." She pronounced it that way, with a hard t. By making it sound like an uneasy combination of "mare" and "edit," she took a lot out of the name.

"They were fine," Judith said.

"Did you happen to mention my communication to Brenda?"

"No. I did tell Philip Masters, though. He seemed surprised. I wonder what — "

"Philip was not surprised," Eva Zimmerman stated unequivocally. "Philip is the last person who would have been surprised. Anyway, almost the last. When you're so close to the devil you're bound to feel the heat. So what did he say?"

"Mrs. Zimmerman." Judith thought she should bring the conversation around so she was asking the questions, not the other way around. "About the telegram. Why did you send it to me?"

"Who else was I going to send it to? You're working on the story, aren't you?"

"Yes, I am, but that doesn't explain... What I mean is..." She was beginning to feel like Alice conversing with the Red Queen. "Why did you send a telegram saying that Mr. Zimmerman was murdered?"

"Why? Because he was. That's why. And I thought someone should do something about it. Don't you think that's reasonable?"

"Actually...well, yes. But I don't understand *why* you think he was murdered." It was at times like these she wished she'd kept a tape recorder. Giles would never believe this conversation, even if *Finance International* were the kind of magazine to delve into such personal matters as murder.

"Because he told me so. Himself. Paul was expecting to be killed. Perhaps not so soon, but he knew it was coming. He had been anticipating it for years. A matter of destiny — as he saw it, of course. With Paul everything was a question of destiny. We have a way of bringing these things down on ourselves if we expect them, and the waiting becomes a kind of race. For time, you know. Very likely a key to his success — he never knew when he'd be cut off. Personally, I would recommend suicide in such cases — a greatly preferable method. So admirably controllable. But that wasn't his way." When she paused, Judith could hear her breathing — a hard, rasping sound, as though she was having trouble drawing air into her lungs. "Perhaps you'd like to come and visit?" she asked.

"In Paris?"

"Well, that's where I am."

SIXTEEN

Constables Stewart and Giannini had interviewed altogether 48 people on Spadina Road between St. Clair and Eglinton and had gathered a list of suspicious-looking characters a mile long who had been seen in the vicinity of Madame Cielo's over the past two or three weeks. The list abounded in such surprises as a black woman with four white poodles who was driven to and from her house in a stretch limo, two people with eye patches and bowler hats, a green man with a guitar case, a six-foot peroxide blond woman, a dwarf, and a punk rocker with orange hair, spiked black wristbands, and her own blue hearse. David Parr concluded that Spadina Road must have more than its fair share of creative people. The problem was how to weed out the imaginary characters from the real ones. In a redbrick rooming house, there was a young schoolteacher who admitted to having consulted Madame from time to time. Madame's fee varied with the nature of the business. For a simple forecast, she charged her standard $50. For consultation regarding loved ones, her fee escalated to $100. Once, the schoolteacher had asked her if she could cast a spell that would re-establish her relationship with a boyfriend. This particular procedure was tagged at $300 for step one, and heaven knows what happened at step two. As the first stage had involved spraying her friend's brand new Volvo with her own urine while mumbling some extremely embarrassing words, the schoolteacher couldn't bring herself to the second stage.

"So did it work?" Parr asked Giannini after he had listened to the report.

"What do you mean, did it work?"

"The urine. Did it work?"

"I didn't ask," Giannini confessed.

"Kid was afraid she was going to say yes," Stewart said. He was two years older and ten pounds heavier than Giannini and never let him forget it.

"You figure she actually tried it?" Giannini asked.

Stewart shook his head. "Takes all kinds," he said. "But I reckon we've got the motive, all we need is the suspect."

"You do?" Giannini asked.

"Yeah. Streetwise old woman went around collecting large dollops of cash from a bunch of simple marks. She pushed them to do stupid things in exchange for celestial favors and milked them for all they were worth. There's plenty of lonely, gullible people around. Well, one of them, after trying the urine trick, or God knows what else, having run out of savings along the way, got royally fed up and bumped her off. Can't say I blame the poor sot." Stewart sat well back in his chair and looked expectantly at Parr. "What do you think, sir?"

"Well, then," David said. "All you chaps have to do is bring in that poor sot and we can close the file. Case has had a bit of attention in the press, the Chief wants us to clear it up fast. We're due for a couple of breaks."

Parr certainly thought *he* was due for a break. Two unsolved murders and Judith insisting he look into a third was not conducive to feeling happy with himself.

In the morning he had talked the Bermuda police department into checking out Zimmerman's XJ-S, but it had already been cleaned and the glass replaced, and on walking around it they saw nothing suspicious. He could hardly expect the Bermuda police to take much more interest on the basis of unsubstantiated suspicions from Toronto. The Zimmermans were not the sort of people whose cars one tore apart without strong evidence. Perhaps Levine could persuade them to cooperate if he tried in person.

David had Michael Ward checked through the files and, sure enough, he had a mature police record that started when he was twelve. Petty stuff, mostly, till he'd shot and wounded a gas station attendant in 1975 and gone away for a ten-year jaunt. He'd been paroled into the custody of the John Howard Society and they'd found him the job at Zimmerman's. There had been no complaints about him since. Checked in with his parole officer regular as clockwork.

David's luck changed with Deidre Thomas's call at 3. She had found a letter addressed to Paul Zimmerman from Harvey Singer.

"What does it say?" David asked.

"I'll meet you at the Royal York, Black Knight Bar, at 5," Deidre suggested, "and you can see for yourself. Or don't officers of the law ever have drinks with regular members of society?" She sounded coy, which didn't suit her age range.

"Drinks are fine," David said, "but can't wait till 5. How about I pick you up in ten minutes in front of the building and we go for coffee break at Telfer's?"

She didn't hesitate for a moment.

She waited for him at the curb, in ankle-length silver raccoon. She wore high-heeled gray suede boots and a soft peach scarf that wound around her head. When she got into the car she let the folds of the coat fall back to reveal the long shapely legs David had admired the day before.

"You're not married, are you, Officer Parr?" she asked him over the rim of her whiskey sour. "I was reading somewhere that policemen have one of the highest divorce rates in America. Guess that would be true here as well, wouldn't it? Tough being married to a policeman, worrying every night if he's safe. Waiting. Not knowing." She shivered deliciously.

"Statistics don't lie," David said, opening the long white envelope she had given him.

The paper was rather unusual in that it was bordered in black. The sort of paper they use for funeral notices. It was addressed in fine, slanting longhand, well-spaced words, to Paul Zimmerman, Esq., Chairman, Monarch Enterprises. It was dated December 21, 1986, and that matched the New York postmark on the envelope to which it had been stapled.

There was no "Dear Mr. Zimmerman" or "Dear Paul," or any other form of salutation. The letter simply said: "This picture will bring back some memories for you, as it did for me. I hope your nights are long."

It was signed "Singer."

There was a photograph in the envelope, an old black-and-white with serrated edges, showing two boys around ten years old, standing close together, each with an arm around the other's shoulder. One was a good hand's-width taller than the other, so the short one had to reach a bit to stretch his arm up. You could just see the ends of his fingers over the taller one's bony shoulderblade. They were wearing baggy swimming trunks. Both had thin, boyish legs they had spread apart in bravado, showing off for the camera. Above the waist, the smaller boy was a little chubby, which he had gone to some pains to hide by wearing an oversize singlet. The other pushed out his narrow chest, the ribs forming an arch over the hollow of his stomach. They both had short haircuts, one blond, the other dark. The smaller boy wore glasses, and his outer arm was propped against his hip. The taller boy had made a fist with his outside arm and was flexing the nonexistent muscles. Both were grimacing into the sun.

The picture was taken on the grass in front of a small white house with double glass doors and climbing roses. There were some gardenias to the left and the rear end of what looked like a baby carriage.

"I was married once," Deidre confided. "Didn't work out particularly well. It was okay in the beginning, of course, but didn't last the stretch. Not many do these days, I suppose." She mused. "I've been living alone for a few years now. Paul made it easy for me. No regrets. Successfully single, as they say. Only problem is Saturday nights. Damned if I know why, but they're the hardest. I think we were all conditioned to believe that if we were good little girls and kept our legs crossed, didn't argue with the boys, and prettied up our faces, we'd be whooping it up Saturday nights. Doesn't work, though, does it?" She was fingering her whiskey sour, not drinking much of it. "Wish I'd never heard of calories, don't you?"

"How did you mean Paul made it easy for you?" David asked.

Deidre shrugged. "Doesn't much matter now," she said. "He just did." She looked very sad, suddenly.

"Where did you find this?" David asked, putting the photograph back into the envelope.

"In one of our 'bring forward' files," she said. "We were very organized. Reason I remembered the name was that Paul asked me to look up Singer in the New York telephone book. You see, there's no address on the envelope." She rolled her eyes at the memory. "There were dozens of them. I copied the pages for him."

"That would have been late last December?" David asked. "After he got this letter?"

"Probably," Deidre said, thoughtfully. "Hard to isolate the time. All I remember is going round to the central library. We don't have a New York telephone book at the office."

"The 21st is near Christmas," David prompted.

"So?" Deidre said. "Wouldn't stand out much for me. Haven't paid attention to Christmas for years. Best way I know to get through the whole damn holiday period is to try and ignore it. It's such a rotten letdown once you grow up, don't you think?"

David nodded pensively.

"One time I went to an ashram in New Jersey. I read about it in *Time* magazine. Now don't laugh. I thought it might really help me with life, you know."

David didn't laugh.

"What do *you* do Saturday nights?" Deidre asked.

"Not a helluva lot," David confessed. "But my mother never made a big issue of it, so I don't worry about it. What else is there in that file?" he asked.

"Not much. Birthdates. Lists of birthday presents he bought Meredith and Brenda, so he wouldn't buy the same things again. And there were copies of letters to Arthur — that's his son in New York. Letters from organizations he regularly gave money to. That sort of stuff."

"Nothing else from Singer?"

"No. Why? Was this guy somebody famous?" she asked.

"No," said David. "He wasn't anybody special. He just died a few days before your boss did, and I've been thinking there might be a connection."

"But Paul died of a heart attack."

"Singer was murdered. In Toronto last Thursday night." David pocketed the envelope and its contents. "I'll drive you back now," he said.

He had been wrong when he thought that talk of murder might alarm Deidre Thomas. She became positively ebullient. "My," she said, "my, my, my," swiveling her head, bouncing her brown curls. "I've never been involved in a murder investigation before. Do you have any suspects?"

"Not yet," David admitted, "but I'm working on it. I'd like to borrow that file for a day, if I may."

"You don't think Paul had something to do with it himself?" She narrowed her eyes and hunkered down around her glass. David wondered if she was trying to look like Humphrey Bogart. She had looked a whole lot better before.

"I doubt it. I have to get back to work now," he said, "but, if you like, we could go to a movie one Saturday night."

"Tomorrow?" she asked eagerly.

"Why not?"

She pulled the raccoon over her shoulder and headed out the door. "I'll bring the file," she said.

David figured he would have to see Mrs. Singer one more time. He was not looking forward to it.

SEVENTEEN

When David arrived at Judith's, she was packing. It was a process that worked by elimination, rather than thoughtful choice. She had laid most of her clothes out on the bed, lined up blouses on one side, skirts and pants on the other, pantyhose and underwear in one corner, jackets and dresses in the other. In the middle she had built a nice little arrangement of toothpaste, toothbrush, and creams and lotions, and a black felt hat. Boots and shoes were stacked on the night table with the phone.

"You're planning to spend the year?" David inquired from the doorway.

Judith held up a lilac blouse, gray skirt, and brown pants. "What do you think?" she asked, holding them against herself.

"At the Meurice, I'd go for the skirt," David said. "But then, I've never been invited to the Meurice, never mind stayed there. It's a place for black mink, long lamé dresses, and strings of real beads. Royalty stays there, not policemen from Toronto."

"You sound a bit jealous," Judith said, placing the skirt and blouse in the battered blue suitcase at the foot of the bed. She threw the pants on the floor.

"I am," David admitted. "I'm going to have a rotten time in New York with Mrs. Singer while you're at the Meurice with a weird old dame who sounds half interesting."

While Judith continued to stuff clothes into the suitcase, David sat at her typewriter and told her about Mrs. Singer, sending Levine off to Bermuda to check out the Jag the local cops wouldn't touch, the police report on the Zimmermans' garage boy, and his meeting with Deidre Thomas.

"That's the Chloe?" she asked, sniffing the air.

"The what?"

"The perfume you've brought with you. Twenty-eight dollars

for a small bottle, plus tax. Done some close questioning, have you?"

David ignored the innuendo. Chances were Judith knew him better than he knew himself. "She's a fairly sophisticated lady, with some income on the side. Zimmerman bequeathed her a tidy sum, enough that she doesn't need to worry about the next job now he's dead. She's attractive and tough, and I think she was rather more to him than a private secretary. She might know quite a lot about him."

"She's not the only one," Judith said, wrapping her boots in a dry-cleaner bag. "I had the impression that old Mr. Zimmerman may have been a ladies' man of some repute. No one's exactly talking about it, but there are hints. His wife suggested he had been a connoisseur of women, and I have an idea he was in mid-affair with one of his directors' wives when he died."

"A man of formidable libido," said David, with the kind of good-natured smirk men put on their faces when they hear of the sexual exploits of other men — grudging admiration and fellow pride.

"And of few close friends, I suspect, though so far only Philip Masters has been willing to come right out and say so. Except for Eva, that is, and the consensus is she's mad."

David showed her the note and the photograph. "This is what Deidre found in his files," he said. "Is one of these Zimmerman?"

"Very likely the tall one," Judith exclaimed. "An amazing similarity to Arthur Zimmerman. But people change a lot into their teens. God knows, my kids have. Wouldn't recognize the two charming little angels from the galloping behemoths I live with." She had started to pull some of the clothes out again for a second look. "You think the other's Singer?"

David did. He also thought there was something enormously endearing about Judith bending over the well-trodden suitcase, her bright auburn hair on either side of her face, like puppy's ears, her shrunken hand-knitted sweater riding high up her back to reveal the foamy flesh where her hip began. There was the edge of a strange sensation in the back of his throat that he almost recognized as tears, and it struck him again that, no matter how he struggled to disguise the fact, he loved her.

Judith threw two jackets and a dress onto the middle of the bed over the hat, creams, and lotions, and stood back for a critical appraisal. The sweater resumed its uncertain perch, the hair swung back, and David took her in his arms and kissed her. She laughed softly because she'd been expecting him to come to her: she'd been aware of his eyes turning soft as he watched her.

They made love over the dress and jackets and simplified Judith's packing by eliminating a certain element of choice, particularly in the way of hats. It was a warm, tender, reassuring kind of love that was difficult to surface from — the kind Judith found most insidious because it left her doughy, unprepared for the world. David's strong, feisty body surrounded her, made her feel much too safe, protected from the harshness of everyday life. It would be difficult to snap back into the plans for the Paris trip.

She lay with her face toward the window, her eyes shut against the last remnants of daylight. David had pulled the covers over them, and held her, spoon-fashion, close to his chest, as though he had guessed her thoughts. "Would you like to get married?" he asked suddenly, his lips brushing her ear.

It was not the first time he had asked her. It was his substitute for saying "I love you," an expression he assiduously avoided. "It's debased coinage," he'd told her once. "Doesn't mean anything. Suffers from overuse." He never even condescended to an innocuous "me too" over the telephone.

It had been Myrna's way of holding on, her constant cry of need, knowing he had no option but to go on with the ritual of "I love you"s. It would have taken a peculiar kind of bastard to attack such an exposed throat. Myrna was certain that David didn't have it in him, and she was right. The constant mix of pity and guilt — because he had stopped loving her years ago — kept him parroting the words through clenched teeth long after she had already transferred her own cravings to the all-forgiving arms of the Roman Catholic Church.

Being Catholic had imbued her with a new sense of purpose, a secondhand aura of self-worth, an implied superiority she wore like a mantle. Not only did she no longer need his forced expressions of love, they had become an obscenity, as had any attempts at even formal sex. She took to arranging flowers at the drop-in center run by Our Lady of Perpetual Succor, knitted long scarves for the poor, and did penance by handing out warm bowls of Lipton's Noodle Soup at the Jarvis soup kitchen. David used to hope she would find a part-time job, police salaries being what they were, but she treated the suggestion with the scorn it deserved. Doing the Lord's work left no time for such frivolities.

"Maybe," Judith replied. That, too, was as before. She was not yet ready for another kick at the can. Marriage still meant the steady subjugation practiced by James. "Why? Has Myrna agreed to the divorce?"

The telephone spared him a complicated reply. It was Sergeant Levine. He told David that the lab report on Singer's shoes was in. They had found traces of paper fiber in the toe section of one shoe. Singer must have been carrying some document that the killer or killers wanted. The Indian swore on his mother's grave there had been no paper in the shoe when he found it, though he could barely recall finding them in the first place.

"Will you be coming in tonight, sir?" Levine inquired respectfully.

"Why?"

"The Chief was looking for you."

"Why?"

"Search me, sir."

"Smart-ass," David mumbled under his breath when he hung up the phone. "Thinks he knows everything."

"And does he?" Judith asked injudiciously.

David was struggling into his trousers, which had been bunched up around his ankles when he fell onto the bed. One shoe was wedged into the end so tight he had to push and shove to remove it. He made small, unhappy grunting noises.

"For example," Judith continued needling him, "how did he know where to find you?"

"They always know where to find me..." Another grunt... "That's the damn rules... shit." The trouser cuff ripped with a loud fart of a sound, and David sat on the bed again. The rip had finally released the shoe. "Going to look really spiffy for the Chief," he said, dejected.

Judith offered to fix the trousers for him, but he was in a hurry. He said he'd call later and left.

But the only call that evening was James announcing he had reached a new plateau in his relationship with his children, that they had begun to communicate without the mechanisms of false projection they had all leaned on before. Deep down, all three of them understood — which put them all ahead of Judith, who didn't.

"When must they be returned?" he asked petulantly.

"School on Tuesday," Judith said, feeling like the wicked step-mother who had never taken an interest in analysis. "That gives you three more days, probably enough to assuage any remnants of guilt you may still harbor about ignoring them all these years." Could she have tried to be a better sport?

James sighed. "Jude, oh Jude," he lamented, "there was no need for that. None, and you well know it. A little understanding can go a long way to healing wounds, if only you'd try to sublimate your feelings of inadequacy and forgive yourself. Dr. Murdoch says the heaviest burden we each carry around is our own sense of deficiency. You could do a lot worse, Jude, than spend a day or two in Chicago and go see him. Be happy to set it up for you."

"Jolly good of you," Judith said breathlessly, but the irony was lost on him — psychiatry does not encourage humor. "And now, if you don't mind, I'd like to speak to my daughter."

"As you wish... Till Monday night, then." And he dropped the receiver against some hard object so it thundered in Judith's ear.

After a minute Anne came on. "You okay, Mom?" James must have warned her that she wasn't in a relating mood.

"Just fine," Judith said with forced brightness. "I'm going to Paris tomorrow. Only for a couple of days, but it ought to be exciting."

"Oh wow, can I come?"

"Wish you could, darling, but not this time. It's all work and when I finish the story I'll get you the Roots boots. Next week. The suede lace-ups. That's how much money this one's going to bring in." What she meant to say was that she missed them and hoped Anne missed her, but the boots were as close as she could get to saying that sort of thing at a distance.

Anne shrieked with delight. "Great, Mom. Holy! Love ya!" she yelled easily, then went into a long and enthusiastic account of how she'd "bombed" some hill called the Bluff, and it was a cinch, so she was going to try the Rattler tomorrow. She was bringing her feet together now and sashaying down, instead of the abominable snowplow the new guys were still doing, not that there's anything wrong with the snowplow, it's just that only nerds did it; after three days *anyone* can learn to parallel. She'd made a bunch of new friends and met this gorgeous guy in the clubhouse who goes to Upper Canada College and doesn't have a single zit and dresses in jean jacket and blue jeans and skis better than anyone else at all, even Daddy. He's 18 and they were going to go up the first lift together tomorrow.

Jimmy had gone swimming in somebody's indoor pool but he was in great shape for a slob. He'd told Dad he wanted to be a pilot, which was an outright lie because we all know he's afraid of heights, but he was forever trying to impress the hell out of Dad with all kinds of manly talk, like flying and football, and the two of them went down to the hockey rink last night so Jimmy could show off his great skating. "Neither of them can skate worth a damn, but they were both trying so hard they didn't notice."

"Did Jimmy tell him about the marijuana?"

"Not yet. But he said he would. I don't think he had anything to do with it, Mom. If he was on something, I'd know about it. I know everything else he does."

She bubbled on for another minute or two, warming Judith with her enthusiasm, then said goodbye in a flurry of haste to join some new friends at the door.

In preparation for the Paris trip, Judith read through her now voluminous notes on Zimmerman and the people around him, then set out a series of questions for further interviews. Philip Masters wasn't due back from Bermuda till tomorrow. There was no use trying to see Brenda again for a while. But on an impulse, she called American Airlines to see what it would cost to fly to Paris via New York and found it was about the same. Then she called Arthur Zimmerman and made an appointment to see him the next day at 11 o'clock, at his place on Riverside Drive.

If the airspace over LaGuardia wasn't crammed and if there wasn't a traffic jam over the Triborough Bridge, that left room for breakfast with Marsha, and she might even catch up with David in the afternoon.

She put her notes away, finished packing, and collapsed into bed.

EIGHTEEN

At first she didn't know why she woke up. One minute she had been wandering in a dream with an interminable maze of soft sycamore trees placed too close together, the next she was lying in bed, stiff, her eyes open, listening. It was very quiet. She could hear herself breathe. Short, shallow breaths, as though she had been running, which, indeed, she had been in the dream. She had panicked when she couldn't find her way through the peeling bark, and there had been a sound following her, someone close behind, but not yet in sight.

Then she heard it again: the sound of scraping steps, the sound from the dream, except she wasn't dreaming now. She sat up and listened harder, her whole body intent on the noise, trying to hear it more clearly, wanting it to become something familiar, like the kitchen tap, the neighbor's cat pursuing his fickle love, the Persian from across the street, a late-night stroller — anything she'd recognize, so she could blame her imagination and go back to sleep. But the sound remained mysterious. She could now identify it as coming from outside, near the back of the house where the small yard housed the wet wood for the fireplace. The sound of scraping was a rolling log. Then more steps on the back porch, near the door that thank God was stuck and she knew no amount of shoving could open because she and David had both tried.

She reached for the bedside lamp but stopped in mid-motion as she realized she'd be visible once the light was on, and if whatever it was did get into the house, it would know she was aware of it, and that seemed more dangerous than pretending she was asleep or out. She could hide. Her mind raced around the closet spaces, but she made no movement to climb out of bed. She listened as the steps — yes, they were definitely steps — came around toward the side, where a thin alleyway separated her space from Stevie's. How

129

she wished Stevie were out there, that the night prowler was her, hoping that Judith was awake but not wanting to intrude until she was sure.

Her eyes found the electric clock on the table next to the typewriter. It was 3 A.M.

The body outside heaved against the giant garbage pail she shared with Stevie and knocked it over; must be a heavy body because she knew the pail had been full. Its metal top clattered to the sidewalk. A bag of bottles smashed onto the concrete. Then it was coming around to the front. Up the creaky steps, not softly, not hesitating, pounding, purposeful boots making directly for the door. They stopped.

She leaped from the bed and ran toward the curtains. She'd hide behind the curtains and keep listening. She couldn't go into the closet. If someone was coming into the house she wouldn't be cornered in the dark with no means of escape. For some obscure reason, she suddenly remembered a prairie dog she'd seen when she was a child of eight visiting relatives in Saskatchewan. It had drowned in its burrow when the local boys had poured water into its hole. "Usually they come out," her cousin explained, "and we can bag 'em."

Its nose was black and its tiny red tongue hung out from between its furry lips.

The curtain was long enough to hide her feet but not thick enough to hide her shape if someone turned the light on in the bedroom. The phone. She'd have to get to the phone.

The steps started up again. She peered out from behind the curtain, still hoping it was Stevie. It wasn't. The shoulders were too broad. The distant yellow streetlight didn't illuminate much of his frame, but it was a man, and he was wearing some sort of peaked cap. He was on the porch now and she lost sight of him. There was a rustling noise. Was he trying the lock?

She dropped to her hands and knees and crawled toward the phone. She sensed rather than saw where it was, next to the bed. She felt along the small table till she touched its familiar plastic shape, lifted the receiver, and almost dropped it, the dial tone seemed so loud. Could he hear it? She dialed by feel, trying for 911, Emergency, and got it wrong. Then tried again and this time succeeded. The ringing shrilled into her ear. Once. Twice. The operator came on, a bored and sleepy voice.

"This is an emergency. Give me the police." Judith's voice came in a shallow whisper.

Downstairs there was an explosion of shattering glass. Something thudded into the living room, rolled, rattled along and came to a stop — *thump* — at the foot of the stairs. It had sounded like metal when it hit the floor, something hollow. It bounced once.

The voice at the other end of the phone was asking if he could help her. Yes. She gave her name and address and something about there being a man trying to break into her house, then dropped the receiver and stood, listening and waiting.

With the window broken the outside sounds were clearer now. Long strides on the porch, receding. Down the steps thumping along the path, toward the street. The soft banging of boots on concrete. Still going farther away. A car door opened. Slammed shut. The engine started and the car rolled quietly toward Bloor Street. No light through the windows as it passed. He must have left his headlights off.

It was intensely quiet, so still she heard the blood thumping in her ears. Gingerly, she crept toward the banister at the top of the stairs and peered down. A faint yellow light fell onto the sheer curtains in the corner of the living room. A shrill buzzing from the phone. She had suddenly become aware of it — or had it just begun?

In the distance, a dog barked. Under her hand, the wood felt hot and clammy. She slid her hand along and down slowly toward where the hollow object had stopped. Her other hand touched the wall, its shiny smoothness comforting as she homed in on the light switch. She turned it on, took a long deep breath to calm herself, then descended.

The thing lay on the worn brown carpet, smack up against the bottom step. It was wrapped in white paper, and something bright red was oozing from it, spreading over the carpet. The same red ooze streaked across the room from the front window, in splotches and random stripes, and series of drops, like thick blood. As she approached the object, she saw it was cylindrical. She sat on the bottom step and examined it closer. One end was shiny, flat, a silvery surface; the other was open, black and red. That's where the oozing red spread from. All around the can — no doubt it was a can — a folded piece of thick white paper splattered in red, like the carpet. It was held on by a rubber band.

She touched the can, tentatively at first. When nothing happened, she picked it up and, looking inside it, decided it was a can of red paint. She traced its passage from the foot of the stairs back to the window it had been thrown through. The splotches of red along the way were bits of soft paint where the tin had bounced and rolled, before coming to rest. Shards from the broken window lay scattered about on the carpet — large jagged pieces, edged in red. Only one of the panes was broken.

She turned the can in her hands to see if there were any marks on the paper that gave a hint as to why it was there. She loosened the rubber band, her hands now covered in the red paint and sticky. When the piece of folded paper came away, it revealed a perfectly ordinary label on a perfectly ordinary can of Corona red paint. She smoothed out the paper. Inside, where it had been folded over, there was something painted with a brush in crude red letters, all capitals. As she held it under the light the letters formed into a message: STAY AWAY FROM JEWS.

Underneath, there was a second piece of paper glued to the first. It looked as if it had been clipped from a medicine bottle. It was printed in bold type and it read: WARNING. Just below was a skull, the universal sign for poison.

Judith sat in her favorite chair and continued to study the paper. The letters were formed with a thin brush, thin on the down-strokes, flabby on the cross-strokes. Where the brush had been lifted off, little pools of hardened paint had formed. She felt it with her fingers. The writing was dry. Whoever threw the can into the house must have prepared the message hours previously. Corona takes almost a day to dry.

For the first time since she awoke she noticed the cold. She was wearing only a flannel shirt and no slippers and the paint had dribbled onto her toes. They looked unnaturally white against the splotches of crimson. An icy wind blew in the flimsy curtains where the shattered glass was. A car came down the street, much too fast, and stopped in front of her house. Doors opening.

She raced upstairs for her pink and beige bathrobe, before opening the door for the two amazingly young policemen who had already been there once, investigating a break-in, barely three days ago. Her first impulse was to apologize for getting them out again, in the middle of the night, this time with no more excuse than some maniac dropping cans of paint into her living room, and after they had been so kind and let Jimmy off a marijuana charge.

"What happened here?" the older one asked, before she had a chance. Neither of them was looking at her. When she followed their eyes, she noticed there was some dark paint on the outside of her door — that's what they were studying. They both reached for their flashlights at the same time.

What they saw in the glare of the two flashlights was something out of a World War II movie, something so out of place here, so out of sync with the times, that for a minute or two no one said anything. They just stared at it in disbelief: a big painted swastika. It was bright red, like the rest of the paint, glistening wet and streaking downward. It looked as though it had been dipped in blood.

NINETEEN

"There are kooks and crazies everywhere," David said, still try
to reassure her. "These guys aren't dangerous."

"What do you mean they're not dangerous? They blow up sy
gogues in Turkey, slaughter people in coffeehouses in Paris, they
even built some kind of armed camp in Iowa, for Chrissakes
and you're telling me they're not dangerous?" Her voice came
harsh whisper that only David was supposed to hear, but the m
above her bent his knees a little and slouched toward them. S
had taken an aisle seat in the back of the DC-9, which meant th
the lineup for the toilets started at her shoulder.

"They're not dangerous in Canada," David asserted irritably. H
hadn't had much sleep. At 2 A.M. he'd had to interrogate a bike
because the Chief insisted there was some connection between h
fire-bombing the Golden Palace on Queen Street West and a
obscure territorial battle being waged by the parvenu Hong Kong
Chinese gangs against entrenched Sicilian interests in the area
After two hours of listening to obscenities and inhaling undilute
body odor, David remained unconvinced.

At about 4 he had gone over to Brunswick Avenue to board
up Judith's window while she cleaned her carpet with some
evil-smelling acid solution that made his eyes water but expunged
the remnants of the biker's sweat that still clung to his clothes.

"They're a no-account, irrelevant fringe group, but the RCMP
keeps tabs on them anyway. We always know if they're up to
something serious."

"Sure. That's how come the Mounties let Keegstra teach anti
Semitism as part of his grades 7 through 12 history classes i
Eckville, Alberta, for 15 years, before anybody so much as slappe
his wrists."

"It's a free country. Can't interfere with someone else's belie o matter how crazy, long as they don't impinge..." He sighed. "He as charged and convicted. What more do you want?"

"I want them to stay away from other people. That's all. Little ough to want in return for my taxes. You're sitting there telling ie that they can organize themselves into groups, they can march ɔ and down pretending the Holocaust never happened, they can rry flags and swastikas and practice bizarre white supremacist es and there is not a thing you can do about it till they actually tack someone?" She was spluttering with helpless anger, all the ore difficult to contain because she was still trying to whisper.

"That's right," David said. He was half pleased that when she'd pped being frightened, her next emotion was rage. She'd make a ost unsuitable victim. "None of those things you just mentioned onstitutes breaking the law. We can get them for disseminating te literature or for causing bodily harm, or breaking and niering..."

"And how would they have known about my Zimmerman ory?" In her mind, she had started to list all her friends and cquaintances who would have heard about it from her or from one another.

"In your case," David went on, "we can charge them under Section 387 of the Criminal Code. I imagine Giannini and Black are working on that right now. They've been in contact with the Mounties' nuts expert in Ottawa, and they'll know where to look for the guy. They'll likely have someone in custody by the time you return from Paris."

"No one I know would be connected with those people," Judith mused over her third cup of gray American Airlines coffee.

"You'd be surprised," David said. Now that he was no longer defending the laws he had no hand in creating, only in enforcing, he relaxed enough to feel genuinely sleepy. "They don't wear horns, don't carry special ID, they look like the rest of us, relatively normal, together people. Sometimes you pick them out in conversations, the mild, garden-variety bigots. At parties, for example, some charmer will suddenly start in about Jews being too smart for their own good. Or too damn grasping. Or too steadfastly different, or too politically left-wing. Or there'll be some virulent attack on Israel...so much hatred in a rich and lazy country..." He was drifting off softly to sleep; his head dropped onto Judith's shoulder.

She let him sleep. There were a few minutes left before landing at LaGuardia and she had some thinking to do. She searched her memory for stray comments she hadn't noticed at the time, remarks she'd walked away from rather than face some unpleasant-ness and destroy the spirit of a party. Had anyone joked about Zimmerman's fast-made fortunes? Was there something more than bug-eyed envy in the disapproving glances that passed among friends at the Press Club?

The pilot tried a couple of wisecracks about light snow and damp runways, took two labored tries at landing, then managed to slam his tires onto the ground and came to a shuddering screeching halt some distance from the terminal. The passengers loosed their knuckles from the metal armrests and clapped enthusiastically.

David jerked upright in his seat and looked at Judith accusingly. "What happened?"

"Fast landing. Why don't you go and get your cab," Judith said wearily. "Mrs. Singer will be expecting you, and I have to wait for my luggage. Anyway, Marsha's meeting me at Benny's Deli for breakfast. I called her this morning to tell her what happened."

Benny's was Marsha's favorite deli for spicy pastrami and dill pickles on bagel, and for the reasonable certainty that Benny wasn't going to rush you out before the second cup of coffee to make room for another batch of customers.

Judith deposited her suitcase by the counter. Benny looked at it approvingly. "Reminds me of my zeyde," he said with a conspirato-rial grin. "That's the kind of suitcase he arrived with from the old country. Kept it next to his bed for the rest of his life, in case he had to go again."

Marsha sat in a booth by the window on Seventh Avenue. With one hand she was stirring her coffee absentmindedly, with the other she turned the pages of a pile of manuscript she had on her lap. Her head was bent over and soft blond curls had escaped from her tidily sculpted chignon, feathery like baby hair. Her long neck tilted slightly to one side, and there was just the suggestion of a smile on her lips. Some of Judith's most cherished early memories of Marsha featured her in exactly that pose, with the same expression of delight or amusement on her face. They dated back to Bishop Strachan School, when the two of them studied together in the library. Studying with Marsha made it impossible to remain uninvolved with books. She read passages of Plato to Judith as though she had personally discovered him. It was contagious. For a whole year, both of them had been passionately in love with Petrarch, then Hamlet, finally Heathcliff, the old standby for late-blooming teens.

"New manuscript?" Judith asked, sliding into the seat across from her.

"The best," Marsha said. She kissed Judith once on each cheek — "Paris style," she explained. Judith tousled the soft hair back of Marsha's neck and pulled her head into the hollow of her shoulder — like old times.

"Damn good to see you," Judith said, feeling a little bit better even about the broken window, and about David's having taken her at her word and left for Mrs. Singer's without waiting for her luggage.

"Wow," Marsha said, settling back to examine her better. "Now that's full battle gear. New herringbone winter coat with extra shoulder pads, your special-occasion jacket, button-down shirt with long cuffs... You must be expecting a rough day."

Judith laughed. Marsha had always been able to read her. This morning when she dressed, she hadn't even been aware of piling on her most protective clothes.

"Scrambled eggs and lox," Marsha called out to Benny. "You might as well be totally fortified," she said. "You're not actually nervous about seeing Arthur, are you?"

"The story's got me spooked," Judith admitted. "It's not Arthur, it's not even flying to Paris to see Eva, or that some nut tried to warn me off the story last night, it's everything. When this story began, it was fairly straightforward. Now nothing's as it seems."

"In that case," Marsha said, keeping up the light banter deliberately, "Arthur will be a disappointment. He's exactly as he seems. Somewhat spoiled early in life, overpraised for his indifferent appearance, too much easy money..."

"You sound like your mother," Judith remarked.

Marsha shrugged. "I suppose so. But Mother was talking about Paul, who did, after all, make it himself. I'm talking about Arthur, who didn't. First time he met Arthur he was about ten. It was at one of my parents' come-with-the-whole-family Thanksgiving lunches that put the fear of death into all the turkeys along the North Shore throughout the month of October. The barbecue was the size of a Ping-Pong table and they stuck five turkeys on the spit at one time. All the kids were wearing jeans and T-shirts, they chased one another in packs, climbed trees, waded out onto the dunes, and dug for clams; they all got wet and grimy, except for Arthur. He wore a suit. He wore a wide tie with blackbirds on it. And black, shiny slip-on shoes with velvet bows on the toes. He stood near his mother, while the grown-ups had refreshments on the lawn — it was the last of the Indian summer. Little Lord Fauntleroy, with a difference. He stood stock still, listening to whatever the grown-ups were talking about. He kept his hands out of sight — I remember that particularly, because having them behind his back like that gave him a military bearing my cousin George tried to imitate later, waiting for birds to snare in the marsh."

"He sounds formal, not spoiled," Judith said.

"Till the grown-ups went inside. Then he joined the kids down by the boat houses. I had been nominated to kid-duty, sat in the boat house pretending to read. But I was fascinated by Arthur. Everybody acted like he wasn't there for a while, but he waited them out. By the end of the afternoon, Arthur had taken command of the group. He was wilder, more willing to take chances than anybody. He never let a kid off the hook in dare-double-dares. Ginny Simpson almost drowned trying to prove she wasn't afraid of the water. He made George climb to the top of the red oak back of the summerhouse and hang from a limb thinner than my finger..."

"How come?" Judith asked. "Why did they do what he wanted?"

"That's the weird thing," Marsha said with a mouthful of pastrami sandwich. "He somehow intimidated all of them. He was tough. No question he was going to be obeyed. He assumed he was the leader — just out-talked, outwitted, out-argued everyone. Ego that large must have had some home fertilization."

Judith had finished half her lox and eggs. She made patterns on her plate with the rest. "He's gay," she said. "Did you know that?"

"Everyone knows that," Marsha said. "He's been living with an aging art dealer who's into S and M with young men and was even charged once for something-or-other when a boy was severely beaten."

"What happened?"

"Nobody knows. The boy dropped the charges."

"Do you remember Eva, too?"

"Barely. That day she wore a broad-brimmed beige hat with feathers. That's about all I recall. My mother remarked that she was beautiful." Marsha chuckled. "Back then that was a sign of disapproval. My mother thought Eva was too foreign."

"Wasn't Paul?"

"I think Eva had more trouble with English."

"When they divorced, it was Paul your parents chose to stay friends with."

"Friends?" Marsha snorted derisively. "They didn't stay friends with either of them. Paul remained socially acceptable because he had the money, that's all. Large dollops of money could, even then, buy you acceptability. Being Jewish, of course, it took more money than for a Christian. Not that anyone ever asked Paul Zimmerman for his articles of faith, that would have been in bad taste. But he was rather proud of being Jewish. He often said so. That sort of relieved everyone else of pointing out the fact." Marsha stared at the pickles on her plate. "It took years before I realized a lot of them thought he shouldn't have made it across the Atlantic. Some were as bad as the Nazis, just never had the chance."

"What do you mean?"

"Racists, like your night visitor. It's just a matter of degree, and opportunity for doing harm." Marsha pulled on her soft leather gloves and coat. "Come on, I'll drive you there."

On the way they talked about James and the kids and how Judith wasn't to worry about his finding a way to their innocent hearts. "What irks me most," Judith said, "is the stupid phoniness of it. His ululations about his own banal feelings. He's using them as tools."

"True, but that's not it," Marsha pronounced as she pulled up in front of Arthur's house on Riverside Drive. "What gets to you is you're jealous of him. You're the one that puts in all the hard time to raise them and he's a distant romantic figure they might fall for because he never had to tell them to brush their teeth."

"And will they?"

"Fall for him? No. They're too smart."

They both looked up at the high, narrow, redbrick house across the street. It had thin, arched windows with leaded panes, a stone porch with iron railings and a lantern, and a white door with a circular window at about eye level.

"Call me when you're through," said Marsha. "If you come down to my office, we'll go around the corner to New York, New York, and try a bottle of Pomerol '78. It'll set you up for Paris."

Judith watched her drive down the street a little too quickly. The white Chevy fishtailed at the corner, then regained its poise. As it turned the corner, Marsha gave her a thumbs-up sign. Judith thought fondly of her old Renault, which rarely got up enough steam for a fishtail.

She pressed the button to the left of the iron lantern. The door opened almost immediately. "At last," Arthur said with exaggerated forbearance. "I thought you were going to spend the rest of the day in that car, waiting for me to come out and visit with *you*." He ushered her into the glaring white entrance. "Who's your friend? She seemed familiar."

"Marsha Hillier."

For a moment he searched his memory, his eyes turned toward the bas-relief angels that decorated the ceiling, his yellow eyebrows knitted, a puzzled frown across the fragile, white forehead. To add to the theatrical effect, he touched the back of his forefinger to his brow, his elbow lifted high. "Oh yes," he said. "The colonel's lovely daughter, with the deep-set blue eyes, who fancied herself so utterly composed till..." A little smile flashed across the thin face. "But never mind, Mrs. Hayes, I won't waste your time with idle chatter. Come in, come in."

His hair had only a touch of mousse today. It was cut even shorter than on the night of the party, and was a lot limper. What his clothes lacked in exuberance, they made up for in a show of affluence. The beige jacket was low-key Pierre Cardin, the darker pants narrow, tailored silk and wool, with a glow all their own. His shirt, a modest blue, was pure silk, as was his neatly tied cravat. Blue with white spots.

"Now, I've never quite figured out why he was a colonel, when the old buzzard never made it to any war I know of. Would you like to come into the living room, or the study?" A courtly gesture of the hand, first left, then right. "Perhaps a tour of the house would provide appropriate color for your piece? A throwaway for those *House and Garden* aficionados?" When she told him she'd rather he made the choice, he led her into the living room, which had the color scheme of a Ron Bloore painting — all white. It was glaring even in the gray light of the dismal snowy day. A long, soft couch covered in velvet, leather chairs, wall-to-wall carpet, shaggy goatskin rugs, a thick white and cream wall hanging above the couch, white lacquer fireplace with black interior, rough-textured walls, and black-and-white prints in stark thin black frames. In the center a long white marble table; to one side of the fireplace a white china cat, its back curved, ears back, tail high, as if about to pounce. On the other side, a small replica of Michelangelo's David, on a tall white pedestal.

"Welcome to the palace of the Ice Queen," Arthur said in a high falsetto voice. In the bright light, his face was even more pallid than she'd noticed earlier. There were soft pouches under his eyes. It was hard to believe he was only 26. "In some countries, as you no doubt know, white is considered the color of mourning. China, for example." He motioned her to one of the white leather chairs. "We may as well start here, don't you think?"

"I do appreciate your seeing me," Judith said. As she sat down, the chair made a restrained whooshing sound of escaping air. "So soon after your father's death." Safe to start with the formalities.

"Oh. Oh. Oh." Arthur laughed, a forced, high-pitched laugh with little choking sounds. For added effect, he threw himself onto the couch, his arms and legs spread out as if convulsed by laughter. "You thought I was mourning for my father, didn't you. Now, don't deny it, you did, right? You thought that's why all this white?"

She didn't deny it.

"Wrong!" he said, composing himself at last. "I wouldn't mourn him if he was the last man on earth and I was facing total loneliness for the rest of my life. The only kind thing that old bastard has done for me in recent years, my dear Miss Hayes, is to die." He said "dear" as "deah," his personal version, she remembered, of a British accent.

"I'm sorry," Judith mumbled. "I had assumed, because I last met you at his party, that you were...friendly," for lack of a more appropriate word.

"You assumed wrong," Arthur said flatly. He extracted a long, brown cigarette from a china box on the table, tapped it, filter end down, on the top of the box, and lit it with a gold Ronson lighter he'd pulled from his pants pocket. "Fortunately, not inexcusably wrong, as I was at that party and you might easily have confused me with the adoring throng surrounding the now late financial wizard."

"If you hated him so much, why did you go to his party?"

"I went because I was summoned. This humble abode, you see, as well as some other less visible joys of my life here, are rather dependent on a meager allowance he'd been generous enough to dole out for me. Since I've come of age, of course, he was no longer obligated to continue supporting me, but, alas, I'd become rather accustomed to not having to make a living. Work, I rather think, is greatly overrated in American society. Don't you agree?" He gazed around the bright room with apparent enjoyment. His whole demeanor was theatrical, every gesture pushed beyond its natural content to become a satire of itself.

"I've never had time to consider work as anything but a necessity," Judith admitted, rather prudishly. "Why were you summoned?"

"That little secret, I'm afraid, went with him to his just rewards." He gestured downward with the index finger of the hand holding the cigarette. He had long thin fingers, pale and dry as his complexion. They were wrinkled at the tips as though he had spent too much time underwater. There was a long, purple mark on his wrist that stretched back under the elegant cuffs. It stood out luridly against the whiteness of his skin. "When he called, he warbled on about some special occasion he had planned that he wanted to include me in. Whatever it was, I'm sure we were spared a nasty surprise. I can't imagine his planning anything pleasant that would include me." He blew smoke at the ceiling, exposing his thin blue-veined throat with prominent Adam's apple.

"Doctor Meisner told me he was planning to change his will in your favor. Perhaps that's why he called?"

Arthur shook his head forcefully. "No. He did the new will in January. He was going to bequeath me a couple of million dollars, not a whole lot, but it might have gone some way to soothe my grief." He chuckled. "Trouble is a man changes his mind once, he can change it again, and that, I'm told, is what he did. He changed the will again."

"And you believe that?"

"If you're asking whether I'm planning to contest the will, the answer is, I'm not. That'll save you the embarrassing question." He stifled an imaginary yawn. "I'm not interested in spending the next two years mucking about in some Toronto courtroom. I don't like Toronto, and I don't like courtrooms. I particularly dislike lawyers. First one I met was Philip Masters, and as far as I'm concerned, the legal profession never recovered from that initial shock. This on the record?" he inquired with affected coyness.

"Yes, for the record," Judith said, continuing to make notes in her book. "Why do you hate Philip Masters?"

"Because he is a despicable, puny-minded, self-serving, immoral, dishonest son-of-a-bitch, a fact that has been a constant with him for more than 25 years, but only became apparent to my father, the sharp-eyed business wizard, in the past couple of months." He was speaking with such animation and so fast that spittle formed on the corners of his mouth. He wiped it with the back of his hand, elegantly. "That, presumably, is why he fired his ol' buddy, finally, a couple of weeks ago," he continued. "The trouble with a bloody pirate like Zimmerman *père* is he cannot conceive that he is not the only son-of-a-bitch on the block. He had so little integrity himself that he had to believe that Masters had enough for both of them. You know, the old friend, come-what-may, stick-with-you-right-or-wrong syndrome. All that shit." He seemed fatigued after his outburst and relaxed back into the softness of the white couch.

"I suppose you know why he was fired?"

"You suppose right. And I've been expecting it for years." He gestured, palm upward, eyebrows shooting upward. "Have you seen where he lives? You haven't? The mansion on Bridle Path, the condominium in London? Do you know how much he's stashed away for those rainy days — may they come on him soon? You don't? Well, this should give your avaricious readers something to chew on: about six million, all to himself and the dreadful dragon Jane. And you're going to want to tell them how he did it, but the pity of it is you can't prove it, because what he did was push-pull financing. You can get Zimmerman to underwrite your costs, but before you count on that going down, you'd better grease my palm, because I'm the fixer. And once you start playing my game, all the wild cards are mine. Only I can make sure the funding doesn't dry up. If you bleat, you lose everything — that's how he operated all these years, or since his wily mind cottoned onto the opportunity. It's not very original. Regular heavy-duty flimflam game." He giggled. "Get it?"

"I think so. I went to see Chuck Griffiths yesterday. He told me — "

Arthur interrupted. "He didn't!" he shouted, and clapped his hands together, like a child. "He didn't. He didn't," Arthur repeated, giggling with enjoyment. "He told you about Martha and the old goat, did he? Well..."

"Not in any detail," Judith said and waited for more. She had been about to tell him what Griffiths said Masters's designs were on the Senate, but Martha sounded more interesting.

"Randy old bastard he was, but she's quite a piece herself. My, did the lovely Brenda hit the matrimonial roof. Whoof! A rocket. Took two double martinis to calm her. But then it takes that much just to oil her wheels. Poor baby can't get the juices going without a big one. Now that reminds me, Miss Hayes — Mrs. Hayes, right? I'm sorry. Perhaps you'd like a small libation? Scotch, gin, vodka? What's your pleasure?" He was already out of his couch and bending from the waist, overly solicitous, to take her order.

"Coffee, I think," Judith said. She followed him into the kitchen. It, too, was painted white with black outlines, and it gave the impression of having been cleaned by Spic and Span for a commercial about to be shot. Not a spot of dirt, not one dish out of place. The tiles were genuine inlaid stone, not the plastic imitation James and she had laid down on their first kitchen floor in darkest Leaside. There was a plethora of handy gadgets, the kind all housewives are advised to have. Microwave, meat grinder, Mixmaster, Cuisinart, toaster, griller, ice-maker, quick-and-easy broiler, miniature gas barbecue, and a wall of esoteric kitchen instruments that included a fancy Russian egg scooper, like the one Jimmy had bought Judith for Christmas. In the corner a bean-grinder and percolator.

"Brazilian? Vanilla-flavored? Armagnac? Chocolate and coconut for the sweet tooth? Yankee blend? What's your poison, my dear?" He moved with a light, easy dancer's walk, a bit too close to a mince, and pirouetted to face her when he reached the percolator.

"No-frills black," she said, "and you can call me Judith. It's simpler."

"And you're divorced, besides. Probably don't much like him, so why would you like his name? Been living alone for ten years now, with two kids, on Brunswick Avenue. No known vices except for the occasional romance — "

"How the hell do you — Damned im— " she spluttered uncontrollably.

"Not me. Not me," Arthur said, his hands up in a palms-forward gesture to ward off her anger. "It's Paul you should damn. But you're too late for that. He's already damned. Paul had you investigated." When he saw she had stopped spluttering, he turned to the coffee, measured three spoonfuls into the grinder, then faced her again. "It was his normal behavior. Can't blame a chicken for laying eggs, or a rat for eating its young. I've just finished telling you, the only person he ever trusted was Masters. Everyone else was taken apart, examined, scrutinized, categorized, labeled, and shelved." He poured the ground coffee and some water into the percolator, switched it on, and perched on a chair by the white lacquer table. On the wall above his head there were framed *New Yorker* cartoons and an embroidered kitchen towel hanging from a thin piece of wood. It was cross-stitched rather crudely, she thought, for effect: "A home is a place where two people fool each other for a while. Good luck, babies..." There was a happy-face in one corner of the cloth, and a face with a downturned mouth in the other end. The downturned mouth was kitty-corner from "babies."

"I didn't know," Judith said.

"He wasn't exactly excited about seeing reporters," Arthur said. "After he checked you out, he thought you'd be safe. You know. The kind who records what she's told. Not a specially inquiring mind." Arthur sighed contentedly. "But he was wrong, wasn't he?"

Judith took two white porcelain coffee mugs from the shelf to the right of the percolator and set them beside the machine.

"I'm having vodka," Arthur said. "Sure you won't change your mind?"

"If you don't contest the will, how do you plan to avoid working for a living?"

"Simple. I've reached what we might call an amicable settlement with Brenda. She will continue my modest level of support, unchanged, during my lifetime, which, to give the lady her credit for smarts and forbearance, she estimates at less than the aggregate of whatever her legal costs would have been together with the whole or a sizable chunk of the original two million. Do not underestimate the lovely Brenda. She thinks she has a bargain, first-born son and all." He poured the coffee, then asked her to follow him into the study. Once there, he went behind the black leather bar in the center of the room and mixed himself a generous Bloody Mary. "Besides," he said, swirling the ice around with a finger, "she assumes I'm not long for the world. She's been reading about AIDS of late." He stubbed his cigarette into a black and red ashtray shaped like a hollow bull.

The whole room had suffered from someone's overwrought interpretation of Spanish style. There were black iron latticework dividers on either side of the bar, which looked like something out of a Sears assemble-it-yourself Barcelona special, the wallpaper was red and black flocked, the carpets Moroccan, black leather chairs, heavy mahogany tables, incredibly clichéd toreadors and bulls in frames on the wall, and a tourist poster of the Costa del Sol. The contrast between the conscious kitsch of this room and the stark design of the other was jarring, contradictory. Arthur was obviously enjoying her consternation. He leaned over the bar, his long fingers clasped around the glass, head slightly tilted, the exaggerated smile etching itself more deeply into his features.

"What do you think?" he asked.

"About what?" Judith asked noncommittally, taking in the sights.

"*Not* about the room. About the AIDS idea. You think she has a fighting chance?" Arthur affected a flirtatious look.

"I don't know," Judith said, a touch embarrassed. "I've only researched your father."

Arthur shrugged. "As you like," he said. "It used to drive the old man crazy, my flagrant gaiety. His being dead will take some of the enjoyment out of it. Maybe all the enjoyment out of it. A pity, when you've evolved a whole life around a single theme, don't you think? The old man told me the Nazis tried to exterminate all homosexuals, lest we infect the master race. He thought them wise, except for botching the job. They left too many alive. He told me in loving detail of the experiments they conducted using homosexuals. He loved stories of torture and debasement." He hissed the words, slowly, savoring each sibilant and observing Judith for reaction. He seemed pleased when he saw her wince. "He used to tell me about them when I was a kid. His idea of bedtime stories. Thought it would frighten me off."

"I thought his own parents were killed by the Nazis," Judith said.

"I doubt if he had parents." Arthur finished his drink with a loud gulp and fixed himself another. "He bought me a butterfly net when I was five and taught me how to catch and kill the poor sods. Gave me a daily quota. He made me watch them flex and stretch their bodies, thrash their wings trying to escape the pins he'd thrust through their thoraxes." He demonstrated by flapping his elbows up and down, erratically, and jerking his neck back and forth. "Amazing how long it took some of them to die." He relaxed again, smiled, put his elbows on the bar, and intertwined his hands under his chin. "Did he show you the butterfly collection?"

"There was a big glass case full of butterflies near the entrance."

"We used to have four of those," Arthur said. "I remember the day I decided to become a homosexual. What I actually wanted to be was a raving, strutting cross-dresser, a drag queen. I tried on my mother's evening clothes and waited for him to come home. I sat on a bar stool, like this, dangling my stockinged feet. Mother's black sling-back shoes had slipped off, I had her feather boa wrapped around my neck, the dress off the shoulder, coquettish." He arranged himself on the bar stool, knees crossed, one shoulder turned toward Judith. He smoothed down the shoulder of the jacket, before he put his chin over it, looking back at her from under half-closed eyelashes (white-blond as his father's had been), his cheeks sucked in, his lips pursed. He tossed one end of the imaginary boa over the other shoulder. "Oh my," he said, his voice high, "did we ever have ourselves a scene. And I was only eight years old. Oh what a wonderful day. More coffee?" he asked, descending from the stool.

"Please," Judith said. She followed him out into the kitchen. It was good to get away from the bulls for a while. "Your mother says he was murdered," she told him matter-of-factly.

"Very likely," he said, after only a moment's thought. "Though it couldn't have been easy to accomplish with a houseful of jolly party-makers. I suppose you can ask her about it in Paris. Did she say who did it?"

"No."

"Hmm. I do so hope she doesn't have me in mind. It would be ever so troublesome to have to fight with her again. I'm rather fond of the old dear."

For her second coffee, he offered her a choice of venue: either of the two rooms already explored or a third, upstairs, with a view of the river, the games room. She chose the first room: more games sounded distracting, and she found plain white more accommodating than Spanish modern. When she asked him about the contrast between the rooms he said that somehow contrasts suited his mood swings. "Decorating is a form of artistic expression," he explained. "It's what I do. Father had hoped I would take an interest in the arts. He didn't have time himself, one of his few frustrated ambitions. Too busy making the next million. And the next one. I think I've already told you what a flop I was at violin lessons. Only pleasant part of that ordeal was getting away from him. For some reason he took it into his head that Mother and I would stay behind in Vienna so I could learn violin. Vienna is the only place for violin lessons. They also make marvelous, simply marvelous, tortes."

"Yet he had an extraordinary collection of Impressionists," Judith said, taking him back to Zimmerman. "His own selection?"

"That's your first silly question, Mrs. Hayes. Why would he run around the world searching when he could have the best hired brains money could buy? Jeremy bought all his art. That's how I met Jeremy: he introduced us. Lovely bit of irony that, don't you think?"

"Who is Jeremy?" she asked, though she had already guessed.

"My lover, of course. I assumed you knew. He's up in the bedroom. Resting." Arthur stretched out on the white couch. His languid arm reached for another cigarette. "I think you'll find him...interesting. He is a self-contained man. Doesn't need anyone or anything — he allows us lesser mortals to inhabit his life from time to time; we're decorative, rather than functional. It's an attitude that renders him unbuyable, virtually incorruptible. I like that. Back where I come from, it's a rare commodity."

"If the relationship between you and your father was as unpleasant as you say, why did he decide to write a new will that featured you at all?"

"Why? He was buying me off, naturally. Unlike my lover, the illustrious Jeremy, I am totally corruptible."

"What was he buying?"

"My silence. I had discovered a nasty little secret, and he was willing to pay me handsomely to keep it that way."

"Then why did he change his mind?"

Arthur shrugged. "I guess he must have decided the secret wasn't worth as much as he had originally estimated."

"Will you tell me what it was?" Judith tried. "Obviously it's not worth anything now."

"No," Arthur said firmly. "I've no intention of telling you, or anyone else, Mrs. Hayes. I never intended to in the first place. I merely threatened him with it. Perhaps that's what he realized when he changed his mind. If he changed his mind."

"Did anyone else know about...this?"

"I'm sure they did, but I doubt if you'll get them to tell you either, my dear." He stood to stretch his legs. "How about that tour now?"

The games room was full of arcade games of all kinds, even

pinball machines. The walls were covered with masks made of wood and metal with leather straps dangling from their ears. They were decorated in garish colors. The floor was shiny black arborite. In the center there was a huge mechanical bull festooned with streamers.

"You want to try it?" Arthur asked.

"Perhaps some other time," Judith demurred. "What about Brenda? He did love Brenda, didn't he?"

"I suppose," Arthur said, putting a quarter into the Pacman machine. "In his fashion. I would have tired of her ages ago, but then I do not share any of my father's tastes or predilections. Nor he, mine." The game had already kicked into action, but he continued talking while he worked the levers with both hands. He was clearly an expert.

"But he had an affair with Mrs. Griffiths," Judith persisted.

"He had affairs all the time, didn't mean anything. Liked pretty women, that's all. He was quite discreet as a rule, but Martha decided to publicize this one herself. For some reason, she figured she'd harangue him into divorcing Brenda and marrying her. The fool." Arthur had piled up 20,000 points and was getting an extra little yellow man.

"How did Chuck Griffiths take it?"

"Lousy. If Mother is right, I'd put him down for a suspect. He kept up the facade, but underneath he was seething. And my charming father, true to himself, kept his foot tight on Griffiths's throat. One of his basic business tenets: once you've stepped on a snake, keep your foot firmly on his neck or he'll turn on you." At 50,000 points Arthur's little yellow guy was gobbled up by the more colorful square fellows, and the machine declared him dead.

"How did he do that?" Judith asked.

"He owned the majority of Loyal Trust, paid Griffiths's salary, guaranteed his bank loan, held the mortgages on Griffiths's own properties — he had him totally in his pocket. If the poor bugger came up for air, he'd slap him back so fast he'd have skid marks on his ass." Arthur led the way to the gallery. "Jeremy's private collection," he explained. "Hopper, de Kooning, Andrew Wyeth, Jackson Pollock, couple of Harold Towns, three good Matisses, a fair Renoir, a Vuillard landscape, a series of Van Dyck drawings, studies by Tiepolo. Except for a couple of odds and ends, he stayed away from Impressionists."

It was a magnificent room, each piece of art individually lit, each wonderful in itself. The effect was overwhelming.

"Alas," Arthur said, "some of them are only visitors. Jeremy still dabbles in the business, for the love of it." As they walked past the open bedroom door, he called out to him: "Jeremy, my love, won't you say hello to the nice lady?"

From the black-draped four-poster bed in the middle there came the low groaning sound of a wounded bear.

"Next time," Judith suggested.

"Sure. You can try Jeremy and the mechanical bull at the same time. It should be quite a day." He was so pleased with that thought he practically bounced downstairs. "I'll make you some light lunch," he offered.

It was a shrimp salad with mayonnaise dressing and toast. He told Judith about his "lovely mother," Eva, who had idolized her billionaire husband. Seemingly she had no will of her own and no life except the one she lived through Paul. She showed scant interest in Arthur. He didn't recall her ever trying to shield him from his father's anger; she may have felt he deserved punishment. He thought, though, that their breakup may have had something to do with him. Being only ten at the time, he couldn't be sure. Later, Eva blamed him for her own loneliness.

When they had eaten, he called a cab for her. She had only one remaining question: "What was it you were about to tell me about Marsha Hillier, when I arrived?"

"About how she lost her cool?" He laughed. "I suggest, my dear, you ask *her* about that. You are, I was told, supposed to be friends?"

TWENTY

Mrs. Singer was not pleased to see him. The apartment was a mess, her things half packed, she had been living out of suitcases for a week. She was going to Israel. With Harvey gone, there wasn't much to keep her in New York. The New York Police Department still had Harvey's death under investigation, but she knew the statistics: she wasn't holding out much hope.

She offered David a seat among the debris of what had once been their living room. The furniture was covered in yellow plastic, the floorboards were bare. Next to the door there was a thick roll of carpet tied up with string. On the way in, he noticed the mezuzah had been removed from the doorframe. Its absence left a light mark on the wood.

She cleared a spot for him to sit, between two boxes, on a straight-backed chair with thin bandy legs. Through the stiff plastic, he could barely discern the blue and gold embroidery on the seat cushion.

In the cardboard boxes on either side there were picture frames, china figurines, birds and shells, cigar boxes, even a pair of gold-embossed baby shoes. The junk of a lifetime. On the mantelpiece, the only remaining decoration, an oval white frame with a photograph of two people in winter coats, their arms around each other, squinting and grinning into the camera. Her hair was looser and more silvery, the face younger, but there was no doubt the woman was Gloria Singer. He would not have recognized the man. The picture he had fixed in his mind was of a face frozen in a silent scream, the lips drawn back to reveal those pathetic gold fillings, black eyes staring at the sky. The expression was shock and horror, perhaps disbelief. Parr had long ago learned to discount the expressions of dismay on the faces of the dead — most people were surprised by their own dying — but he still found it hard to make the connection with the photograph.

He felt too large and heavy for the daintiness of the chair and was relieved to be able to lumber over to the photograph for a closer look. It made him feel professional, rather than fat.

"That's Harvey and me in Hungary last year," Gloria explained. "Our first trip back since the war. And the last. We'd been planning to go for a number of years, but Harvey always postponed it. He wanted to go...and he didn't. It's my last picture of him."

"I expect you both had some memories you'd rather not revive," David surmised, thinking of Singer's arm with the neatly tattooed six-digit number. "Was the trip worthwhile?"

"Oh yes," she said, smiling at last. Her skin brightened when she smiled and the resemblance to the photograph grew stronger. All that gruffness was covering up the pain. She put down the long-stemmed vase she had been wrapping in tissue paper — the whole apartment must have been a study in daintiness — and came over to him. "We went to London first, we'd never been there either. Harvey booked us into Grosvenor House, right on Hyde Park. Beautiful high-ceilinged rooms. A real surprise. We took a boat up the Thames, all the way to Hampton Court. Boy, and was it cold! Flew to Budapest from Heathrow. They served champagne all the way and we discovered we both spoke better Hungarian than we thought. He was tipsy when we landed. It's because he was nervous. Harvey didn't usually drink." She beamed, half ashamed, half proud, like a mother talking about her child's exploits. "He joked with the passport control people. Can you imagine? After all that waiting and planning, I thought maybe they weren't going to let us in."

David was glad Gloria had started to loosen up. "Specially in Hungary," she said. "As though we were trying to slip in unnoticed. And stay." She took the picture from him, wiped the glass with her sleeve, and put it back on the mantelpiece, angled so as to face the window. "We stayed at the Gellért Hotel for two days. It was sunny for December. We sat on the balcony mostly, watching the boats go by. He had been there once when he was only six, with his parents. Before the war. But he remembered the room. It was all yellow and green flowers, on the furniture, the wallpaper, even the drapes. He said his father wore a cream-colored suit, his mother a flowing creamy dress with big sleeves. They ate on the balcony overlooking the river. So did we. We had all our meals there. Apparently his father knew all about boats, and every time one went by, he would tell Harvey and his mother what it was. Became a bit of a game, then, his pointing at a boat, Harvey and his mother racing to be the first to call it. If the first guess was wrong, the other person automatically won." She took a deep breath and gazed out the window. "In those days, of course, there were more sailboats and pleasure cruisers. Most of the ships up and down the Danube now are cargo ships and tourist boats. There isn't the variety."

When he was certain she wasn't going to continue on her own, David cleared his throat and muttered something inane about his grandfather having been a sailor. That turned the switch back on.

"They had changed the decor," Gloria said resentfully. "The whole damn place is different now. But he did find the same room. And for our last night, he found his father's favorite restaurant, on the Pest side. It's called Százéves, which means something like 'one hundred years old,' but Harvey said it was a lot older than that. It had been 'one hundred years old' when he was a child. There used to be wooden platters and gypsy music. Harvey still remembered the words to some of the songs..." She swallowed hard, her face turning soft and tearful. "The gypsies played music in the camps. The Nazis got them, too." She had tried to sound matter-of-fact, but her voice cracked midway. She glanced at David to see if he had noticed. When he gave no sign of acknowledgment, she went on: "For the last week, we went to Eger."

David let that sit for a while. Eger. He asked her to spell it.

"E-G-E-R, a small town in the Bükk Mountains, about a hundred kilometers from Budapest. It's a historic site, but the reason we went is that Harvey was born there." She turned from the window now, looked at him with curiosity, the light gone from her eyes. "Anyhow, memories won't bring him back. And they're not what you came for."

Maybe they were, maybe they weren't. David wasn't sure what the key was he had to turn. He fished the old photograph with the serrated edges out of his wallet, flattened it by holding it between two palms, rubbing one palm over the other, as though trying to warm it. Levine had once told him he had a lousy habit of rubbing his palms together. Some primeval practice denoting that his ancestors were usually cold.

"I'm curious about this photograph," he said, holding it balanced on his fingertips. "Your husband sent this to Paul Zimmerman last December 21st. Was that right after you came back from Hungary?"

"Yes," she said. "It must have been...," she hesitated, "a few days later. We were back more than two weeks before Christmas."

"Do you recognize the people?" he asked.

She pushed her glasses higher up on her nose and studied the photograph as he held it toward her. Then she took it out of his hand, angled it up to the light, and shook her head slowly. "No," she said thoughtfully, and returned the picture to David. "I don't think so. It's pretty old, though, isn't it?" She didn't wait for him to agree. She pulled another pair of glasses from a dark brown purse, put them on her nose and looked again. "People change," she said, her lips pursed carefully. She looked more purposeful with the half-moon glasses. They were tortoiseshell, long, narrow, slanting slightly upward for a catlike effect. "Why did he send it?" she asked. "I mean, was there some sort of explanation with it?"

There was also a change in her voice. Caution, and maybe something else. Was it fear? He had been trained to recognize such things, but it didn't last. Only a flicker. "It came with this letter," he said, showing her the enigmatic note. He watched her closely as she took it from him, held it up to her face to read it. Her expression held nothing but surprise.

"I can't imagine what he could have meant," she said. "I didn't know he had ever met Zimmerman. I told you that. I never even heard of the man till I read those clippings I gave you. Do you believe Paul Zimmerman had something to do with Harvey's death?" she asked, her mouth forming the words too carefully.

Yes, David was sure now, she was being overly cautious. "Possibly," he said, though he had no reason to surmise anything other than that the photo was supposed to cause Paul Zimmerman some embarrassment. A few sleepless nights.

In 30 years on the force, he had learned to read the signs. She was holding out on him.

"Funny," he tried, "first time I saw it, I thought it was a blackmail note. You know, Mr. Singer with those expensive shoes from Dack's? Perhaps he'd gotten tired of watching the other side have all the fun. It happens." He added a sympathy-laden tone to that remark but it didn't work.

"Harvey was straight as they come," she stated indignantly. "He was a mensch. A real mensch, if you know what I mean." (David didn't, but he nodded anyway. He could guess.)

"We were married 30 years," she said. "I ought to know. And it's not that opportunities weren't there, because they were. In this city — " she waved angrily with her hand " — you can have anything you want if you don't care how you get it. Every time, Harvey would rather have less. Besides, he'd made quite enough for us to be comfortable. Not rich, but comfortable." She ran her fingers through her hair, which showed signs of having been to the hairdresser. David could never understand why women liked their hair stiff.

"There's nothing wrong with liking fancy shoes," Gloria added, a bit defensively. "A respectable weakness, that. Harvey also loved good cigars."

Okay, David thought, that's not the right direction. She isn't concerned about my discovering a blackmail scheme.

"You said he'd seemed preoccupied. He forgot your birthday in January, didn't pay attention to plans you'd made, arrangements to see friends. That sort of thing."

She nodded, yes, but said nothing.

"After your return from Hungary," David went on. "There was this letter, the photograph, and his going to Toronto without telling you, February 26th, to see Paul Zimmerman. He phoned Paul Zimmerman that day, at least twice. They may have met shortly before... your husband's death."

She drew a small white handkerchief from the sleeve of her fresh paisley dress and carefully dabbed her nose. "Paul Zimmerman died, didn't he?" she said.

"Not until Sunday," David said. "Anyway, Zimmerman died of a heart attack." He was suddenly a lot less sure of that than he had been when joking with Judith about opening graves. Gloria's fear was almost palpable.

"So they say," she said quietly. "Perhaps I'm getting paranoid, but I think there are still too many Nazis in Canada. Your government let them in, knowing what they'd done and would do again, given a chance. You gave them asylum."

David shuffled his feet uncomfortably. "We didn't exactly give them asylum, we just didn't turf them out. There's a difference. Anyway, they're mostly dead now. Near as dammit, dead."

"Not dead enough," she murmured. "And not soon enough, either."

"If you're trying to tell me you think some leftover SS trooper killed them both — " he stopped short of telling her he thought she was crazy " — how do you explain the note he sent to Zimmerman?

Why on earth would he want Zimmerman to have sleepless nights? It sounds sort of like a threat to me."

"Or a warning," Gloria said.

"And you've never seen this photograph before?" David asked quickly.

"Not that one," she said. She went over to a stack of shoe boxes on top of the TV set and returned with a red and white Bata box. "I did find these," she said, handing him the box. "They look like they were taken around the same time. They were in one of his drawers in the study."

David put the box on his knees. It contained a mélange of postcards, a silver-colored yarmulke, a locket with a little girl's picture inside, and photographs. Each group was held together by a rubber band, and each package labeled. The label on the package of small black-and-white photographs with serrated edges was: EGER.

"That's all that's left of Harvey's childhood years," Gloria said. There was pride and resentment in her voice as well as the fear he had heard before. "Everything else was burned or looted by the Germans and the locals," Gloria continued. "The house was completely destroyed. There's a sweetshop on the site now. We bought some bonbons there." She showed him a photograph with a two-story house. It had dark shutters and creeping vine on one side. A man and a woman stood in the doorway. He held her by the arm, protectively. She was leaning against him. She wore a short skirt, fashionable in the '30s. Her blouse had an embroidered design across the front. Her white high-heeled shoes had bows across the front. Her hair was bobbed and there was a white spot to one side of her head — either another bow or a flower. He wore a floppy hat, short jacket, and plus fours. They were both very young.

"His parents," Gloria said, almost unnecessarily. "They both died in Auschwitz. They lasted over a year, which is not bad for survival in that camp. My parents didn't last two months. This is Harvey, about six years old." She pointed to another picture in the deck. A serious-looking boy in short pants, jacket, and tie. "He was on his way to a birthday party. His brother," another serious-looking boy, but taller, dressed more formally, in long pants, "and sisters," two squirmy little girls with ponytails and ballooning white dresses. David didn't ask what happened to them all.

Then there was a group shot of ten boys in black bathing togs. They were various ages and sizes, all sitting on the edge of a swimming pool, their feet dangling into the water. David instantly recognized the chunky, angular boy in the middle, sitting next to his shorter, dark-haired friend. Again, they had their arms around each other's shoulders. They were grinning in much the same way.

On the far side, near a water sprinkler, were Harvey Singer and his older brother.

"Do you know any of these other people?" David asked her gently.

"I'm from Budapest," Gloria told him. "Didn't meet Harvey till after the war. I didn't know any of his friends. All I can say is which is him and which is his brother. And there is Ferenc Lantos from the sweetshop I was telling you about." She pointed at the kid next to Harvey's brother. He had a mop of blond hair and long, thin arms with big ungainly hands he crossed over his belly. "We met him in Eger," she said. "Harvey had known him before, of course, but I hadn't. He was so glad to see Harvey had...survived. Hadn't seen each other since before the war."

"How did you get the photographs?"

"Ferenc. He'd found them in the debris of the Singers' house and kept them all these years. Some people never forget," she added, and he saw there were tears in her eyes.

From the Plaza lobby David called Singer and Singer Clothiers in the Bronx and asked to speak to Mr. Singer. Mel, his name was, short for Melwyn. They weren't expecting him in the factory for a few days. Had he tried the showroom on Seventh? The receptionist in the showroom was no more helpful. Melwyn, she thought, was taking a brief vacation in Florida.

Maybe Joe Martelli would talk to him when he returned.

TWENTY-ONE

Judith had never liked Marsha's office. There was normally a fortresslike quality to it, secretarial guards questioning intruders every few steps. Even on a Saturday you had to sign in with the uniformed man on the ground floor, who summoned the ever-present and indomitable Miss Stanley, who finally led the way to Marsha's office. Judith's relationship with Miss Stanley had, for the past ten years, straddled a fine line between mutual suspicion and open enmity. Miss Stanley thought Judith wasted Marsha's precious time — there were already too many demands on her from divers unworthy quarters; Judith found Margaret Stanley presumptuous and inflexible — an image that Margaret would have enjoyed hearing attributed to herself.

The offices along the corridor were of uniform size and shape, like monks' cells. More important people were on the window side, with views over the blue and white glass towers of Fifth Avenue; others had overhead fluorescents. None had curtains, carpets, or more than two extra chairs. There were a few tentative reaches for individuality: small potted plants, posters, family portraits, book jackets, a crocheted seat cushion. Marsha's space was distinctly superior: it made a conscious statement that set her apart and above the others. She had a rug, curtains to block Fifth Avenue, drapes for show on the inside wall, plants, prints, coffee table with couch and chairs, a safe, a liquor cabinet with discreet sliding doors, an armchair on rollers, and an imposing oak desk. The windowsill, like her coffee table, was piled high with manuscripts, her desk covered with letters, folders, envelopes, and handwritten notes. Knowing Marsha as well as she did, Judith guessed the notes would be reminders to herself. Marsha was proud of her unerring memory for facts, comments, events — all with the aid of these little mechanical assists.

She was reading, leaning back in her chair, her boots on the desk, when Judith arrived behind Margaret Stanley's solid form. "The Pomerol will have to wait till next time," Marsha greeted her cheerfully. "You and Arthur must have established a lasting friendship... I expected you over two hours ago."

Did she imagine the note of wariness in Marsha's tone? There hadn't been any tension between them since they were young, and then that was the price you paid for getting to know each other. Each had carried her own baggage of mistrust and childhood wounds into the friendship; each had had to test the other's dependability and loyalty till they were sure.

"I think it was a useful interview," Judith said. "I've got at least three more suspects, should it turn out Eva Zimmerman is right, and I've learned a mass of improbable bits and pieces about Zimmerman himself." She watched Marsha reshuffle her papers, place them gingerly on the desk, brush the flyaway hair from her face. There was a seriousness about her, an air of concentration, as though she was listening, but not to what Judith said — more to the resonance in her voice. When she came around from behind her desk, she wasn't looking directly at Judith.

"I could mix you a nice martini," Marsha said. "Stirred, not shaken, as the great secret agent used to say. I still have a supply of olives from your last visit." She shut the door, drew the curtain on the corridor side, and set about making the martinis. "How did you like him?" she asked.

"Not much," Judith said. "He's spiteful and lazy — envious, I think. Not a bad actor, though; on first acquaintance it's difficult to tell when he is acting. He's learned to cover his tracks admirably." Ordinarily she would have waited to see what Marsha might say. But today she had a plane to catch. "Unlike you, for example," she added.

"Oh," Marsha said nervously, her back still turned as she busied herself with the gin and ice.

"What is it?" Judith asked patiently. "What haven't you told me about you and Arthur?"

"What did the little snake say?" Marsha demanded angrily.

"Not a helluva lot. He implied you'd want to tell me yourself. After all, he said, we're supposed to be friends. Aren't we?" Hard as she tried, she couldn't keep the hurt from her voice.

"Shit," Marsha stated emphatically. "Shit. Judith, I had really hoped I wouldn't have to... Damn it all, there are some things I do I'm not proud of and I don't see why..." She abandoned the gin and ice and sat next to Judith on the couch where she could see her favorite skyscrapers. "It doesn't have anything to do with your story. Otherwise I would have told you in the beginning. Even now I don't want to talk about it... but I guess you're entitled to know."

She took a deep breath. "The truth is, I fucked Paul Zimmerman," she announced. "Not one of the highlights of either of our lives, I might add." She glanced over at Judith to see what her reaction was. When she saw nothing but surprise, she continued. "It was last summer. Mother organized one of her Sunday brunches for the rich and famous and, having successfully begged off all of her social occasions for over a year, I went. For my sins. Which, as I just said, multiplied that day. To make the event endurable I had some Bloody Marys on arrival and a lot of Mother's cider and junk punch. Then wine, I think. The afternoon became somewhat hazy, though I do recall I was trying to keep silent through the meal in case I stumbled over my words.

"Then, while they served coffee and brandy, I wandered down to the summerhouse on my own. I had taken my shoes off so as to navigate with some certainty of staying on the path. I was worried about falling into Mother's famous rosebushes, in full bloom still, and, as you might expect, excessively thorny. Paul was already in the summerhouse, I think. We didn't talk much. It was a hot, drowsy day, with lots of buzzing and chirping outside, you know, real birds and bees..." She chuckled.

"I didn't even take my dress off. He had his pants around his ankles. We were lying on the stone floor, and that was the best part of it, or at least the only memorable part. The cold stone floor felt very pleasant against my back. At some point while we were thus entangled, Arthur paid us a visit. I didn't hear him come in; there's one of those swing mesh doors on the summerhouse, it's very quiet. What I remember is what he said. 'Never tire of it, do you, Dad,' he said. In that falsetto voice of his. Then he wished me good day and left. I saw his face over Paul's shoulder. It registered total disgust."

Judith had gone to get the martinis. She handed one to Marsha. "What happened next?"

"Not a whole lot," Marsha said, taking a drink. "We didn't go on with it, if that's what you mean. I think Arthur's appearance sort of put us off our stride. Paul told me he hated the son-of-a-bitch.

Not the mild dislike some of our parents feel for us, but real hate. And it wasn't said in anger — he didn't mind being found by Arthur; not half as much as I did. It was undiluted loathing."

"Did he tell you why?"

"Yes. He told me Arthur was too much like himself as a child."

"That's all?"

"All I remember," Marsha said. "Next day Paul sent me flowers."

"No wonder he was prepared to let me interview him on your recommendation," Judith said, half joking, half angry that Marsha hadn't told her sooner what her credentials were.

TWENTY-TWO

There was no excuse for what he was doing. Deidre Thomas was much too eager, much too expectant for David to pass off this invitation as a casual come-on in the line of duty. Saturday night was her special time, and he had no business building up her hopes. He wasn't going to deliver. He had more than his hands full trying to cope with Judith.

Deidre had designed herself for the evening. She wore a black mink coat, a form-fitting baby blue velvet dress and jacket, long natural beads, and chunky gold earrings with large diamond studs. His first thought on seeing her in the lobby of her $2,000-a-month, minimum, apartment building was that Paul Zimmerman had been even more generous than she had admitted. His second thought was: he had no excuse for letting her believe he was interested in her. She was overdressed for the movies, hence his third thought: she'd be expecting him to take her to dinner, as well.

He had had an exhausting day, flying to New York and back, followed by a nasty confrontation with the Chief over having no one to charge in either the Singer murder or the fortune-teller's. Then there had been a messy exchange with Giannini over the young policeman's suggestion that they should forget about the paint-can-thrower at Judith's house — there had been no serious harm done, and they were busy on the Cielo case. He had planned to rest at the movies, but Deidre had picked *Crocodile Dundee*. It's hard to sleep with a theaterful of people guffawing in your ears. He bought her a family-size bucket of popcorn and a large Coke, hoping she'd have enough to eat to forget about dinner, but when the movie was over, she announced she'd been lucky to get reservations for two at Dunkelman's. Amazing, on a Saturday night. It had been Paul's favorite restaurant, and she had used his name to get in.

Gnawed by guilt for building up her expectations in the first

162

place, David didn't argue. In the restaurant she removed her astonishingly high-heeled black boots and put on some equally high-heeled silver shoes she'd brought with her in an elegant black bag. "A woman has to be prepared for all eventualities," she explained with a wink. The bag also harbored a chiffon nightgown, toothbrush, face cream, and a brush.

"Why the nightgown?" he asked, for something to say.

"Because it's the most beautiful thing I have," she told him, leaning closer over the table. Fortunately, the tables were lit by candles. David was sure most women's faces benefited from candlelight, but over 50 it was a godsend. The warm glow toned down the rouge on her cheeks and cast the loose pouches under her eyes into shadow.

He ordered some Italian wine she agreed would be adequate (but no more...) and grilled fish. She had a dozen oysters; she said they were good for the libido. She talked about her ex-husband and dancing lessons she'd taken last fall to get her ready for the samba and the Brazilian Carnival she had planned to attend with Paul. He had business interests in Brazil. She was conversationally curious about who had killed whom in Toronto this past year, and what were the most unpredictable murdering types.

She had with her Zimmerman's "bring forward" file and the "confidential" file he had kept under Z for Zimmerman, but she didn't think this was the right time and place to look them over. Perhaps they could go back to his place after dinner so he could read them at his leisure.

He lied that his apartment was being repainted.

She held his arm in the car and invited him to her place for coffee, brandy, and a read through the files. "Not much there, but I can't leave them with you," she told him. "Philip Masters has asked me to deliver all the documents to him by the end of the day tomorrow, and there'd be hell to pay if he found out I've given you some."

Back at the apartment she seated him in a reclining armchair by the gas fireplace and poured him some sweet liqueur that made his teeth sweat. It was the kind of armchair one sees advertised on television, complete with movable parts, footstool, headrest, even a games-table attachment, where she put Zimmerman's files. She turned on the blue gaslight under the artificial log in the fireplace and sat in front of it on a goatskin rug.

"Where did he keep these?" David asked.

"In his office. Philip Masters has already collected all the Ps for 'personal.' But we didn't have any secrets there. Or here."

She was right, there wasn't much in the files anyone would have considered confidential. In the Z file were his own newspaper clippings, marked in thick yellow felt pen where he thought the comments were especially flattering. It seemed he had liked the bit about bestriding the universe like a Colossus. The earliest clipping was from the Montreal *Gazette*, dated May 1950, a small photograph of a storefront. Underneath, he had written in block letters: THE FIRST.

In "bring forward" there really were lists of presents for Brenda and Meredith. Each gift was marked with the appropriate date, and birthday, Hanukkah, or anniversary. Brenda's gifts were mostly jewelry but included such trifles as a Morgan, a Palomino, and a Lazer. There were many letters thanking him for donations and contributions.

There were two letters from Arthur Zimmerman. The first was dated January 2. It thanked Paul for his gracious recent offer to amend the disposition of the "spoils," but suggested something more "immediately equitable" might be worked out in light of the financial needs of Arthur's distinctive "lifestyle."

David hated the word "lifestyle" for a number of reasons, not the least of which was that he didn't think policemen could afford one.

The second letter, dated January 29, was as brief as the first: "I acknowledge receipt of your little package," it read. "It went a long way to relieve our hardship through the month of January. But February is nigh upon us, and Jeremy and I think this may be the ideal month for a vacation in Jamaica. Costs, alas, are running amok on that island, as everywhere else. I am concerned I might even have to approach Brenda for assistance to see us through."

It was signed "Respectfully submitted, Arthur."

"Do you know what was in the files Philip Masters took?" David asked.

"Financial records, mostly. Banking. Checks. Statements. Do you want to see some of them?"

"Yes," David said. "The canceled checks. Personal bank records. Can you borrow them?"

"I'll see what I can do," Deidre said, running her fingers up David's legs inside his gray pants, all the way up to his thighs.

"Oh no," David sighed with silent resignation.

TWENTY-THREE

She had never been inside the Meurice. She had walked by it a number of touristy times, on the way to the Tuileries from the Place Vendôme, past the most famous jewelry shops in the world, along the Rue de Rivoli where only rich dogs dare piss on the sidewalk. She had even stopped once to sneak a look at the yellow marble floors, the soft gold lights behind the glass doors. She had wondered if she could afford one drink in one of the oldest and most opulent hotels in Europe, but had never dared venture into the Copper Bar. Today she was ready for the grand entrance.

It had been an exhausting flight, surrounded by late-night revelers on the way to an IBM sales executives' meeting in Paris and a family with three small children returning home to Turkey after a vacation with distant cousins in Newark. Judging by the uninterrupted wailing of the children, Judith thought the cousins might be offering eloquent prayers to their God, thankful to be rid of them.

It was still dark when they landed, but by the time the semi-striking airport staff had slowly removed the luggage, it was daylight. Paris was shrouded in cold mist. There was a blue-white crispness to the slate-colored roofs, an echoing winter coldness to the wide avenues. The cab driver was stiffly polite and made no protestations about hefting Judith's overnight bag from the seat. It was distinctly not the tourist season. He was not in the mood for insulting foreigners.

The man at the reception desk, all black uniform and white gloves, had her reservation card ready. "Madame Zimmerman," he said, "has been expecting you, Mademoiselle. So difficult at Orly this morning with the strikes." His eyes turned heavenward. The French don't like disorder, even when it's their own.

166

"I'll inform Monsieur Ligeti you're here. Pierre will take your bag to your room. Third floor. I think you'll like the view, it's toward the Louvre. We do hope you will have a pleasant visit." He was filling out her arrival form, smiling uninterrupted. "Only one night? That is right?" Incredulous.

"I'm afraid so." She too found the idea of being here for one night utterly preposterous. It had been two years since she'd been in Paris last. A stiflingly hot mid-July, with Anne and Jimmy in the Hôtel Lindbergh in the heart of the Halles district, a short walk from Île de la Cité, Notre-Dame, and, on the other bank of the river, St-Germain-des-Prés. They had shared a small airless room too close to the noise on Rue Bonaparte, but it was the best holiday she had ever had. She had loved showing them Paris.

Pierre — was his name really Pierre? — wore a brilliant red tunic with three rows of brass buttons and a round fezlike cap that sat jauntily tilted forward on his head. He had the same smile as the man behind the front desk.

"Monsieur Ligeti will meet you in the Quatre Saisons Salon when you are ready. He will show you to Madame Zimmerman's suite."

Judith's room was long and narrow, with a queen-size bed and tempting thick towels. She showered and changed into her low-key blue woolen skirt, the least crumpled of all her best clothes in the suitcase, layered her face with makeup base, brushed her hair over her shoulder, and left in search of the Quatre Saisons.

It was a chilling blue and orange surprise on the ground floor, off the sumptuous passage toward the lobby. The Four Seasons themselves appeared as baroque stone figures with heavy half-draped bodies, Romanesque furled hair, and symbolic carry-on knickknacks, like a sheaf of wheat and a basket of flowers. They stood in ten-foot-tall wall niches backlit in orange, with massive stone pillars on either side of them. In the middle of the salon there was a four-sided couch formation, blue with orange outlines, its center occupied by a wild outcrop of green ferns that reached for the gold ceiling, the blue columns at its corners sporting a purple-based table lamp each. Seemingly random sets of delicate round tables and backless orange chairs stood around the circumference. The overall effect was so uninviting that she didn't consider sitting down anywhere.

The room was empty. She wandered about energetically to

restore circulation to her still-sleeping body. Still no one came. She took to hopping from one orange square of the carpet to the next, avoiding the black lines.

"I do so hope you are Judith," said a robust little man who had materialized in the doorway. He wore a chocolate brown zip-up jogging suit, white Adidas shoes, and a towel around his neck. His face was tanned and shiny, thin gray eyebrows, jutting jawline, deep laugh-wrinkles radiating outward from his lips. His hair was receding, combed over in wet strands to cover the bald patch. She guessed he was around 50, possibly more. "It's been much too quiet around here these past few days. Not enough gaiety, I told Eva, not enough variety. What is the use of living in Paris if we can't catch the lightness of spirit? You are Judith Hayes, aren't you?" He ran across the expanse of orange and blue to grab her by the hand when she agreed she was herself. "You were doing very well there with your jumping, though you did touch the black line with the heel a teeny bit when you last landed, and I'm sure that's against the rules." He squeezed her hand in a warm, damp handshake. "'Step on a crack, break your mother's back.' Do please excuse my watching, I do love games." He had a deep resonant voice, a faint foreign accent with British overtones. There was an infectious enthusiasm about him she found immediately attractive.

"You must be Mr. Ligeti."

"Yes. Yes, of course," impatiently. "You've heard about me, have you? Do come, no sense wasting time down here when Herself is waiting. Ah, but it is good of you to come," he prattled on, leading her toward the elevators. "I had my doubts, I must confess, always have had about journalists. They don't go out of their way nowadays like they used to for a good story. It's all that electronic stuff, makes them lazy. All they want to do is entertain, no effort to dig below the surface, short attention spans. Like their audience." He chortled happily as he ushered her off the elevator at the top floor. "We were just thrilled when your telegram arrived. Thrilled." He knocked on the double doors in the alcove they had reached, waited a moment, then opened the door with his key.

Immediately they were assaulted by the aggressively loud sounds of Beethoven's Ninth Symphony as it wound toward the entry of the chorus.

The room was bathed in soft gold light. "Eva!" he shouted. "Eva. She's here." He turned apologetically to Judith. "She does

like her Beethoven loud," he said. "Maybe in deference to a man
who kept composing after he'd gone deaf, she's trying to make us
both deaf. As well as blind."

There were peach-colored carpets, soft beige drapes, pink hyacinths in earthenware pots against the mirrored wall.

Eva was curled up at one end of the C-shaped white sofa, her
legs pulled in under her, her black skirt fanned out in soft folds.
Her head was bent forward and to one side, listening to the music,
absolutely still. A mauve macramé shawl covered her shoulders
like a tent. Her hands, wearing beige lace gloves, lay in her lap.

There was a faint smell of lilacs.

Ligeti ducked behind the sofa where the stereo set and massive,
full-size speakers occupied the back wall. He turned the volume
down to bearable and faced the room again with a grin of joyful
expectation. The woman lifted her face. Her hair formed a gray
halo of curls around her head. "Now why did you have to go and
do that?" she asked querulously, her voice a deep, gravelly tenor.
"You know I like it to drown out all the noise. I am tired of hearing
myself breathe." The same accent Judith remembered from the
phone conversation — light on the consonants, each syllable
receiving the same treatment, no inflection.

"Judith Hayes is here," Ligeti pronounced from behind her. "She
is late, but she has come. Isn't that great? Isn't that what you
wanted?" As though he was talking to a child — humoring her.
"Come in, come in," he called to Judith who had stopped a foot or
two from the doorway watching Eva Zimmerman as she turned
her face this way and that, her light blue eyes scanning the room
but not focusing on her.

"Hello," Judith said as she approached.

At once Eva's eyes seemed to settle on her, the pale narrow face
fixed in concentration. "Ah yes, please, do come in. Do sit beside
me. We don't much stand on ceremony around here. No time for
that, is there, Miki?" She had high, almost Asian cheekbones, a
round childlike forehead, gently arched eyebrows, dark hollows
around her eyes. A light jagged line ran from the right corner of her
mouth toward the outer edge of her right eye. The scar gave her a
permanent quizzical half-smile that somehow suited the rest of her
expression. She wore no makeup. It was easy to see that she must
once have been a stunning beauty, and even now, her features had
a fineness unmarred by age.

She patted the couch next to her, saying "Sit, sit" to Judith.

Ligeti joined them, bringing a silver tray with coffee, white china cups, cream, sugar, and a half-bottle of Grand Marnier.

"One or two?" he asked Eva.

"Three, this morning, I think," she replied.

He poured three teaspoonfuls of liqueur into Eva's cup with the coffee and winked at Judith. "And for you?" he asked.

"Too early for me, thanks," Judith said.

"Nonsense," declared Ligeti. "We'd like to welcome you to Paris. It'll make you relax. We'll chat for a while. We'll rest a little. No rush." He put a generous helping of liqueur into her cup.

"It'll keep you warm. Take it," Eva commanded. "You'll need all the warmth you can get if we're going to talk about Paul Zimmerman. He's not a warm subject, mmh? Miki, how does she look?"

Ligeti gazed appraisingly at Judith. "Hmm," he said, touching his forefinger to his chin. "She is tall, five-seven or so, long auburn hair, thick and shiny, amazing sea green eyes, small pert nose, thick eyebrows, generous mouth. I'd say she's slender and maintaining it... Forty, maybe thirty-seven, a bit insecure, but then who wouldn't be, arriving here without sleep, some crazy pair of Hungarians talking about murder..."

"Would you mind telling me what's going on here?" Judith tried to maintain a polite tone.

"She's blind, don't you know," Miki said. "Cataracts. Won't hear of an operation, though I've been trying to persuade her, God knows... She's afraid of the knife."

"I've always had a visual imagination," Eva said. "So difficult to talk to someone I can't see. Miki's my eyes. Hope you don't mind."

Judith said she didn't.

"Some blind people paw all over your face to get an image. That's so personal. Doubt if you'd like it. Invading your space, I think they say." She drank up her coffee and asked for more. She prattled on some more about how much she could judge people by the quality of their voices, the feel of their skins when they shook hands. Then she stopped abruptly and turned her watery eyes to Judith. "But we were going to talk about Paul. That's why you came. So. Where do we begin?" She sat forward, attentively, her small, childlike hands still resting in her lap.

"You said on the telephone that Paul Zimmerman was expecting to be murdered," Judith said.

"That he did. Exactly," Eva said solemnly. "And so often, it had become a joke. I'd ask him if I should get my widow's weeds ready and he'd tell me I'd look superb in black. He'd tell me I'd look beautiful in anything. From the day he first set eyes on me, he thought I was the most beautiful woman he had ever seen — bar one. But that's another story. Miki, did you know he had been in love once before? You did? Miki knows everything about me." She listened for a sound, and when Miki cleared his throat, she grinned in his direction.

"He told you he was going to be killed?" Judith asked.

Eva knitted her brows in concentration, as if she had just recalled where she was and why. "Oh yes," she said distractedly. "He was anticipating his own death. Every day. We were both war children, you know. We remembered the war, death seemed as natural then as eating. Or sleeping. One never knew when. And Paul, he was certain death would come and get him. At first I didn't take it too seriously. Why should I? But he had this recurrent vision. More than that. A certainty. We kept in touch after I left him. We would talk on the phone. Once a month he came to see me — here, or in Barbados. London. Wherever I was. I decamped in 1971. Perhaps you knew that? You didn't? Philip gets paid to be discreet. I should have done it sooner to save Arthur, but I was such an optimist. Kept believing it would all work out in the end. But some things don't." She launched into some long story about how to tell the difference between a pessimist and an optimist.

Both Eva and Miki broke into peals of laughter till Eva started to choke. Miki pulled a little blue object from his pocket and placed it in her hand. She thrust one end into her mouth and drew long rasping breaths from it.

"It's a respirator," Miki explained. "She has asthma. Or emphysema. She doesn't care to know which."

Eva wiped the perspiration from her face, adjusted the cream-colored silk scarf under her throat, pulled the shawl tighter around her shoulders, and started to talk again. "I never told Paul about this," she said, waving the respirator around. "I stopped seeing him altogether when it was clear he'd start to notice. I didn't want him to see me this way. Miki?" she called, and he came up behind her, put his hand over her shoulder, and held it, reassuringly. Her hand covered his. "Even the phone has become difficult the past few months. The last time Paul came, Miki pulled down the blinds so we could be in semi-darkness. He told Paul I had a migraine headache." She sighed. "It's such a great pity. A terrible pity."

Miki nodded happily and poured more coffee.

"Did he tell you who was going to kill him?" Judith asked.

"No. He never did. He said it was better for me I shouldn't know. He had ghastly nightmares sometimes, and I would shake him awake. We would stay up, talking, till the fear passed. But he never said what it was. Some shadow from the past. And I would ask him why he didn't go to the police. He was so efficient in everything else. He said that would be useless."

"Why?"

"I don't know why."

"Could have been his imagination. He must have had some dreadful memories from his childhood, maybe that's all. We all have nightmares."

Eva shook her head. "No. This time it was for real. He called on the first day of the New Year. He said the game was up. Those were his words: 'The game is up, Eva,' he told me. He sounded so sad, really, not scared as he used to. I think even disappointed. As if he had waited all this time, and when death came to stalk him, as he had expected he would, it was not all he had imagined."

"He said 'he'?"

"That's what he said. Doesn't necessarily mean his killer was a man, though. It's sort of traditional to refer to death as a man, don't you think, Miki?"

"Perhaps she would like to hear what Paul said?" Miki asked. He was taking Beethoven off the stereo and searching through a stack of white-spined tapes on the shelf above. "First of January, 1987," he said. "We didn't get the whole thing, because we never knew when it was going to be Paul or someone else important, so the tape had to be clicked on by hand. But we did get most of it."

"Not as rotten as you may think, Mrs. Hayes. I don't record conversations to use against people. I record them so I can hear them again. Don't you reread your letters sometimes?"

"Now and then," Judith said.

"The good ones only. Second time you can read between the lines. That's how I listen to the tapes — I can hear nuances I missed before. Especially Paul's — he always had more to say than he knew. He was a man of so many dimensions." Her voice had dropped to a whisper. "Such a waste," she said. "Please, Miki."

The tape was already rolling. Judith recognized Paul Zimmerman's voice saying: ". . .I don't yet know what choice this leaves me. But I have to think about you and Brenda and Meredith. Especially Meredith. I've always felt she was more than just my daughter. So much like someone else I once knew."

"And Arthur?" Eva's voice asked.

"I suppose also Arthur, but he already knows. He is collecting his fee for keeping quiet. I've had to amend the will in his favor. Did he call you?"

"No. You know I wouldn't help him, Paul. Not against you."

"I know," he said. "I may never be able to speak to you again, Eva. I don't know how it will come or when. The only thing I know is they're going to kill me —" a pause "— and that I wish I could see you again."

"When?" Eva asked.

"I'm not sure, but it's a matter of weeks, at most. And you know, I hardly care when. I'm dying anyway."

The tape ended as abruptly as it had begun. "Problems with the machine," Miki explained.

"Could have been another of his nightmares," Judith said.

"Not this time," said Eva. "I know the difference. I knew him better than anyone. Better than Brenda. He'd put on too much veneer by the time he met her, too much civilization. When I met Paul he was a raw youth, and tough as they come. And I, for one, would like to know who in hell killed him and why. And how he knew all those years they were going to come for him. Makes a great story, don't you think? I just love intrigue. I used to read mysteries when I could still see. Such fun unraveling the string till you caught the killer." She stretched, straightened her legs, and stood, steadying herself against the sofa's arm. "Who knows, perhaps I'd like to shake his hand. It's rumored that pain fades faster from one's memory than happiness. Don't you believe it."

She walked directly toward the window, stopped an inch from the glass, reached for the brass handle, and pulled the window open. "I think I need fresh air," she said, breathing deeply. "Is it sunny, Judith? It feels warmer than it has any right to in March, and I can tell it's sunny." She held her face up toward the light.

When Judith went to stand beside her, she was surprised at how small she was, a pale China doll.

The view over the Tuileries' bare trees was clear all the way to the Louvre in one direction, and over the double towers of an old church to the top of the Eiffel Tower in the other. "Oh yes, it's a beautiful spring day," Judith agreed. She longed to be outside, away from the stifling peach-colored room.

Eva must have read her thoughts, because she suggested they take a short walk in the gardens. "Marvelous for your health. A little respite for both of us. Miki, do please get my coat."

"What a superb idea," Miki enthused, clapping his hands. "We shall walk in the gardens." He dashed off through a doorway and returned with a black sable coat and button-up leather boots for Eva. He knelt to help her on with the boots. "We'll meet you in the foyer," he told Judith. "Marie," he called over his shoulder, "Marie, envoyez le chien. Nous allons dehors." Whereupon a small round ball bounced out of another doorway, rolled across the frothy carpet, and leapt into Eva's outheld arms. It licked her face while she squealed with girlish delight.

"Mumu speaks such perfect French," Miki said. "He doesn't understand another language, but he is fluent, better than I am, in French, n'est-ce pas, chéri?"

A maid in black dress and white pinafore brought a thin gold chain and a sparkling red ribbon for Mumu's leash. Judith went to get her own new coat, which seemed surprisingly shabby.

TWENTY-FOUR

"There's not another hotel like it. It has hordes of ambience," Miki stated, as much for the benefit of the smartly obsequious doorman as for Judith. "Eva did try the Crillon, but it's overstated. Too modern. Catering to the Americans — or what the French think the Americans want. The Meurice has a sense of the past. It used to be known as the 'hotel of kings.' Did you know, our suite has been occupied by Queen Victoria and some kings of Spain, Denmark, and Italy. For months it was Salvador Dalí's home. It's the view from our window that persuaded von Choltitz not to blow up Paris."

He had donned a sealskin jacket over his jogging pants. He held the end of Mumu's gold chain in one hand; with the other he guided Eva across the Rue de Rivoli and down the steps into the gardens.

Mumu was about the size of a chipmunk with somewhat longer legs. In addition to the red ribbon around his neck, he wore a tiny white barrette to keep a tuft of longish hair out of his eyes and a stylish jacket of red wool that made him look like an idiot. As soon as they descended the steps he made a rush for the stone lion and lifted his leg against its massive base. Obviously he needed to restore his self-esteem.

Eva was taking long deep breaths, her mouth open, gulping air. "Feels so much cleaner in the winter," she said, gasping. "We're not overwhelmed by the attentions of the whole world. You can walk in the gardens without clusters of tourists clogging up the paths. Miki, are there buds yet? Has the grass begun to sprout?"

"Soon," he told her reassuringly. "It'll be full spring in another couple of weeks."

Mumu had found something brown and sticky and began to roll in it, making a mess of his jacket.

"I saw Arthur yesterday in New York," Judith began.

"Must have been an interesting day for you," Eva said, smiling. "He is a rather unusual boy." She emphasized "unusual."

"You said if you had left Paul Zimmerman sooner, it might have saved him. What did you mean by that?" They were walking down the central pathway toward the main alley that stretches all the way to the Louvre in one direction, toward the Champs-Élysées in the other. The trees were stark, bare, and forbidding. In the absence of lush summer foliage, the naked statues dotted among them were grotesque imitations of human bodies, caked with grime.

"He was a very sensitive boy," Eva said, "and I allowed his father to break him — to toughen him up, as Paul put it. It's difficult in hindsight to understand how I could have permitted the boy to be tormented that way. Paul had some notion that a son had to be strong, that to survive he had to know how to withstand pain, and how to inflict pain without flinching. I suppose he told you about the butterflies?" She had put her arm through Miki's and walked next to Judith but leaning away from her. That, and the thick sable collar rolled high around her chin, made it hard to hear what she was saying. "First time he made Arthur kill the butterflies, the boy vomited. Then Paul beat him."

"And you? Did you let him?" Judith asked.

"She had no choice — " Miki said quickly, but Eva interrupted him.

"Of course I had a choice, silly. We always have choices. I just made the wrong one. In those days I believed he could do no wrong. That if the boy had to get tough, he had to get tough. What did I know about boys anyhow? I'm not proud of it now. I hated Paul as much, in the end, for what he was as for what he made me become. But I have no excuses, only explanations. I think my father sensed something in him that didn't ring right, but my mother was as much in love with him as I was. He had a way with women. The two of them would often stay up nights playing cards and tippling — if that's all they did. At the time, I was jealous. Astonishing, isn't it, Miki?"

"She is never jealous of me," Miki agreed wistfully. "I have more freedom than any man I know. It worries me sometimes, chérie. Do you think it should, Judith?"

"It depends," said Judith, wondering whether he was Eva's lover or her gigolo, now that she had eliminated the possibility of his being just a faithful servant.

They had reached the middle of the gardens and began to wander slowly toward the octagonal pool near the Obélisque. The last time Judith was here, the terraces and stairways around the pool had been crowded with tourists and young mothers with children. There were hundreds of colorful toy sailboats on the water. Today it was deserted. She could hear the gravel crunch under their feet. Eva sat on a bench near the pool and put on a pair of dark glasses with emeralds embedded in the frames. "Is there anyone else here?" she asked. Her voice echoed around the stone layers.

"No," Miki assured her.

"I was 18, a student nurse at Montreal General. My father had a store on St. Urbain Street. An old-fashioned drugstore, where you could buy everything you wanted. I loved the smell in that store. I still remember all those wonderful aromas of soap, spices, fresh dill pickles. Paul barely spoke English and had never learned Yiddish, so we always spoke Hungarian. He learned English fast. He was arrogant, confident, and more aggressive than anyone I had ever met. He was going places, and I think Mama wanted me along for the ride. She wanted all the things for me she'd never had, and by God, did I get them. And I loved it, Judith; don't ever let anyone convince you that money isn't fun. It's...well...look around you. Another poor old blind woman: who'd give a damn if she starved, or froze to death in the gutter tonight. Me, I'm living at the Meurice and I'll have *entrecôte bouchère aux herbes* for my dinner, and maybe you'll join me in a bottle of Château Lafitte Rothschild 1957 — an excellent year. I've enjoyed it all, oh dear, yes. But there was a price to pay. And some of the price was paid by Arthur. That's what I regret the most." She gestured as if to swat at a nasty thought. "Too late now. It was too late when we left. Did he tell you how his father would lock him into the cellar so he would conquer his fear of the dark? That he bought him an Arabian stallion, and when Arthur didn't want to ride it, tied him to the horse with a rope and whipped them around the paddocks? When Arthur fell off, he continued to whip him. Not hard, but enough to make the boy roll into a ball in the mud, trying to protect his head with his arms..." She trailed off, her breathing loud and rasping again. Miki put his hand over hers and pressed his fingers between her gloved ones. Judith noticed she wore a huge red ruby over her leather-covered ring finger.

"Did Paul talk much about his own father?"

"Not much. But he said he was beaten a lot as a child. And it was what he'd needed. He deserved it. They say it passes from parent to child and on through the generations." She sighed. "I'm glad Arthur won't have children. I think he learned how to inflict pain too well. In Mexico when we first moved there he continued the games he'd played with cats."

"What games?" Judith asked, but she could already imagine and wasn't sure she wanted to have the answer.

"Killing games, with sticks and fire and knives. Mutilating games. The object was to allow the cat to live as long as possible in agony."

"Perhaps we should start back now," Miki said. "You're cold."

Judith hadn't noticed she'd been shivering, but she was glad of the pause. As they walked around the Octagon, she asked Eva about Paul's family and rehearsed the two versions of the story she had already heard. "In one version, his father was a poor vineyard worker who could barely afford a meal for his family. He died young of a heart condition — the same one Paul himself had when he died. His mother served meals — when they could afford to eat — on hand-carved wooden plates. In the other version, his father was a genteel bourgeois who lived in a mansion and hired tutors to teach his son to play his Stradivarius. In this version, Paul went to a private school in Vienna once he turned 12, and the family spent summers in Italy. Brenda says his parents died in a concentration camp during the war."

"I heard both versions," Eva said. "In the beginning, only the one with the private school, but when he had a bit to drink he'd talk about the other version. I thought he had such a lively fantasy life, and why not? Too much reality is bad for a man's soul. All day he lived by reason and logic, that's how he built his fortune. At night, let him have his anguish and his desires, let him make up any past he wanted. Tell you one thing, though, I never heard him play the violin."

"Maybe you should go to Hungary, Mrs. Hayes," Miki suggested.

"Oh yes," Eva agreed. "That would certainly tell you about his parents. You'd find out what his demons were..."

Mumu squatted down for a dump at the corner of Le Nôtre's bust, then began to pull Miki toward the hotel.

"Just before he died, I heard him say 'Sorry' three times."

"Oh?" asked Eva with curiosity. "Really? And did he elaborate?"

"No. He didn't have time."

"Let's hope he meant Arthur," Eva said. "There is a lot of room there for 'sorry's."

"What was it that finally made up your mind to leave him?" Judith asked. "I mean, why then? Why not sooner?"

Eva sighed. "I'd hoped Arthur might have told you about that night. Did he show you his arm?"

"I saw a scar, if that's what you mean."

"Runs from his wrist to his shoulderblade. Arthur would dress up in my clothes to irritate his father. First few times he was punished as usual, with a belt. That last time Paul went crazy. He burned him with a flaming piece of wood from the fireplace. He sat on the boy's head and held him down while he poked at his bare arm..." She choked. She bent over, holding tight onto Miki's arm. Judith thought she was weeping. Miki gave Judith an angry glance and motioned with his chin for her to leave them alone.

"I'm all right," Eva said. Her breath came in painful gasps. "Did you see this?" she asked, raising her head, taking off the glasses and holding her face up to Judith. There were tears running down her cheeks. Eva put a tentative finger to her right cheek where the scar ran from the corner of her mouth up to an opaque blue eye.

"Yes," Judith said quietly.

"Of all that I may ever have done in my life, I'm proudest of this scar," Eva said. "It was the first time, the only time, I stood up for my son. That night. I tried to pull Paul away from Arthur. Paul struck me with the hot poker across the face. You wonder why he's let me go? Though he loved me still. And I, God help me, have always loved him — always will. But if that boy blackmailed him now and then, more power to him. He deserved every dollar he got."

TWENTY-FIVE

Judith never discovered what *entrecôte bouchère aux herbes* was. Eva didn't want to have dinner. Nor did she think she had anything to add to the earlier interview. She was exhausted and she wished to rest her lungs and the rest of her body. Miki, now attired in a splendid maroon velvet jacket, gray pants, and glossy evening shoes with black satin bows, came to Judith's room to inform her that they had decided not to continue for today. If Judith would stay in Paris for another day or two, they could cover the cost incurred, but tonight Eva was going to "repose."

Judith argued that she had to be home because of her children, an idea quite foreign to Miki — "surely the nanny would accommodate" — who confessed he'd never indulged in children and considered them extraneous to the discussion. "She was, you could see for yourself, exhausted," he told her. "These are subjects she would rather not discuss. Don't you see? She is unwell. Because she does not like to consult with doctors, we cannot tell how serious her illnesses are. But we know she must rest."

"She did invite me here to talk," Judith protested. "I can hardly be blamed for what she chose to tell me. And it is rather a long way from Toronto if all I am allowed is four, five hours."

"Quite. Quite," Miki agreed. "But you must not judge by the quantity of time. It's quality that counts, don't you see?"

He offered to take her to the airport in the morning, and to compensate with opera tickets for tonight. He could arrange for the escort.

Fortunately, Judith fell asleep and didn't wake up till seven the next morning when breakfast arrived courtesy of Mrs. Zimmerman.

When she called to say goodbye, Eva seemed quite revived. "You must find his killer," she told Judith. "Someone at dinner that night. One of those people knows something. Also try his rabbi.

Let me know how you fare. Perhaps we'll see you again? That would be all right, if you wished. After you've been to Hungary. When you have more of the answers."

Miki came to the room to help direct the bellman with her suitcase. He was as bright as the first time she saw him. "A pleasure taking care of such a lovely woman," he said. The car, a white Silver Cloud, came with its own driver in blue tunic and cap. "I never did learn how to drive," Miki apologized. "No opportunities, really." Halfway to Orly he handed her a thick envelope, with "Hôtel Meurice" engraved in blue script on the top left-hand corner.

"I can't accept this," Judith protested firmly, thinking it was reimbursement for her Paris flight.

When she tried to give it back, he asked: "Don't you think you should open it first?" He watched with exaggerated interest while she slit it open with her index finger.

Airplane tickets from Montreal to Budapest. She pulled them out, stared at them, then at Miki.

"Come on," he said impatiently. "You haven't finished looking. It's not an Easter-egg hunt."

Next to the tickets there was a voucher for a rental car and prepaid confirmed reservations for March 10 to 15 for a hotel called the Park, in Eger. Judith looked even more puzzled.

"I thought a clever woman of your profession," said Miki, "would have worked it out by now. Surely you'd want to go to Eger if you could. Chances are your magazine won't send you. For us, the expense is so negligible, it's worth it. Only obligation on your part is to tell us what you discover about Zimmerman."

When she checked in at the Air France counter she discovered that an unknown benefactor had upgraded her ticket to first class.

TWENTY-SIX

Staff Sergeant Levine returned from Bermuda with several little plastic bags whose contents he delivered to the chief pathologist on Yan's staff. It had been a long time, Levine told David, since he'd had as much fun as he'd had with the police department in St. George. While they had seemed rather formal and uncooperative when Parr first tried to enlist their help, they turned out in numbers to accompany Levine for his complete run-through of the XJ-S.

Rather than get openly involved in Toronto's murder investigation, they had waited till Brenda Zimmerman drove the car to Fulton's Spa, as she did most days for her morning dancercise class, then they towed it away. This gave Levine and the lab man he had brought along a full two hours to crawl and scrape around inside the car.

They knew her routine, the hours she kept, her friends, and, very usefully, her habit of parking illegally rather than expending the extra effort to reach the lot at the back of the building. "Mrs. Zimmerman considers herself royalty," Staff Sergeant Graham of the Bermuda constabulary explained with a wink. "She isn't governed by the same rules and regulations as us lesser mortals. And while I don't wish to speak ill of the bereaved, if she kept her liquor consumption under control she'd not have to bother with quite so much dancercise." Graham was the first black man Levine had ever met with a Highland Scots accent.

For several years they had resisted the temptation to tow her car off, simply accepting the promptly paid fines delivered by young Geoff, the chauffeur. But Graham admitted he had always wanted to tow the Jaguar, and when the others went back to the station, he stayed behind to see Brenda's face. Her expression of disbelief and consternation, he later reported, had been worth the wait.

She had flung herself back into the building, hair flying, eyes wild. The green Cadillac appeared about ten minutes later, young Geoff running around to open the door, standing by as she bounced into the car, running again to the driver's seat and tearing off at 20 miles over the speed limit toward the police station. Mrs. Zimmerman was furious and didn't care who knew it. She stormed in, demanding to see the captain. She didn't believe they didn't have captains in Bermuda. ("That's what comes from watching too much Yankee TV," Graham remarked to Levine. "At least she's not asking for a white man." He guffawed.) Finally she had no choice but to settle for Graham, who insisted she fill out all the required forms and pay the towing charge before he released the car.

That gave Levine and his teammate the extra half-hour to put the XJ-S back exactly the way they had found it. A vision in perfection. There was no question both the right side and front windowpanes had been replaced. They had snipped off some varnish from the elegant wood around the passenger side of the car for analysis. They found faint stains on the leather interior and a splatter of dark spots on the ceiling, which Levine was convinced were blood. Most important, they discovered a hole about the size of a bullet in the leather padding of the right-hand door.

"Careless, that," Levine remarked with the enjoyment of an explorer who has just come upon some Inca gold.

"When does Mrs. Zimmerman come back to Toronto?" David asked.

"She may never," Levine said. "I saw the house and, if I were her, I'd never leave it. Specially as she can imagine what nasty questions are being asked in Toronto."

The lab report confirmed Levine's guess. The splatters were human blood, mixed with Lysol, Ajax, Fine Furniture Polish, Leatherette, and an unidentified acid-base lightener that had made them almost invisible. The hole in the door had been thoroughly cleansed, difficult to establish what kind of bullet had entered it. The angle suggested the shot had come from above. The lab didn't rule out that it had been a hollow-point copper-jacketed Remington-Peters, but it would take time to be so precise.

The carpeting had been completely replaced in the past few days, as had the window on the passenger side. In fact, no one had used the car on that side since the new carpet had been installed.

Again, Levine commented, whoever cleaned the car hadn't had much experience covering up a murder. They had done a lousy job.

David concurred. If only he could establish that Singer was blackmailing Zimmerman and if he could figure out why, that would make Zimmerman Singer's killer: he would have had motive and opportunity.

In the afternoon, Joe Martelli called. He had finally cornered Melwyn Singer, in his apartment on East 49th Street. He hadn't been to Florida for months. He had taken a few days off with his family to ease the pain of his father's death. He had not been able to face the factory or the showroom, both built by Harvey. Zeydie, as he called his father, had been much loved by his family.

When Martelli asked why he hadn't accompanied his mother to collect the body from Toronto, Melwyn said his mother wouldn't tell him when she was going. She had insisted she would go alone. She hadn't wanted him or her daughter-in-law along. Nor had she consulted him about her move to Israel.

Melwyn was a small, rotund, peaceable kind of guy, not the sort to stand in anyone's way. Joe figured he might have felt a little hurt she hadn't even asked for his advice. He also figured Melwyn wasn't much used to this type of behavior from his mother. Overall, they had been a tight-knit family. The two small boys who wove in and out of the conversation would pipe up now and then to ask about Bubbie. She'd left for Tel Aviv last night. Said she'd call when she'd established herself in an apartment.

Melwyn said his parents had been very close, in a conventional sort of way. Affectionate, but formal. Martelli knew what he meant right away: it was the same with his parents, though they were Italian.

The only false note had been in Melwyn's repeated assurance that there had been no noticeable changes in his father's demeanor since last Christmas. Martelli was used to shifts in witnesses' moods. There was no doubt Singer was hiding something, but Martelli had no authority yet to push.

"All that," David said, "is about to change. We know how and where his father was killed. It's now a question of establishing by whom and why. Shall I go through the proper channels to ask for assistance?"

"Only if you have a lot of time," Martelli said. He was as disparaging about bureaucratic hassles as David. "I can go back and pretend I already have the authority. If that's okay with you."

It was. David told him about Levine's day in Bermuda and, with some withholding in personal matters, of what he had learned from Deidre Thomas. He had already reported on his meeting with Mrs. Singer.

The more he thought about Gloria Singer, the more annoyed he became. He leaned back in his worn standard-issue black chair, stared out the grimy window at the indifferent view across the street. Not even a tree. A couple of cold pigeons pecking away at leftover crumbs outside the French delicatessen. "Joe," he said at last, "does it ever occur to you that if your mind worked just a little quicker, or if you were prepared to bully people a little more, you'd be farther ahead in your career?"

"Often. Why?"

"I blew my chance with Gloria Singer, and it was the last one I'll ever get. The department isn't about to send me to Israel. She knew something and she didn't want to tell me about it. She was frightened. That's why she was so anxious to keep her family away from Toronto. And that's why she was in such a hurry to get her ass over to Israel. She thought her own life was in danger." He put his feet up on his desk. At times like this he wished he was still smoking a pipe. It used to help him think.

"It all ties into whatever they discovered in that place they went to before Christmas," Martelli prompted.

"Eger," David spelled it out. "Some obscure little town in the northeast of Hungary. Both Paul Zimmerman and Harvey Singer came from there. There is something they both knew that killed Singer, and may have killed them both."

"And you think Mrs. Singer knew why Harvey was killed?" Martelli asked.

"And more than likely by whom as well." David glared balefully at the cracked ceiling.

"Well, we got one more kick at the can. Can't do it today, we've got our tenth murder of the year in Queens. Domestic, I hope. But I'll get over to Melwyn's tonight for sure. You guys in Toronto don't know how good you have it, being able to puzzle over who did each one of them and why. Down here we're just glad if we can pin it on somebody, then get on with the next bloody little number." Martelli sounded wistful.

After David hung up, he continued his study of the pigeons. There were only four people, Arthur had told him, who ever drove

that car: Paul and Brenda Zimmerman, Arthur now and then, and
Geoff Aronson, the chauffeur. Ward had access, but not the keys.

Singer could have been blackmailing Zimmerman, and
Zimmerman could have decided to kill him. Stupid to mess up his
best car, but there's no accounting for bad judgment. On the other
hand, Michael Ward might have done it — on someone else's
command. Or Arthur — for his own reasons. The chauffeur?
Unlikely. In theory, the car could have been stolen in order to
murder Singer and implicate Zimmerman, but why then was the
car shipped immediately to Bermuda? Brenda and Arthur were
plausible suspects, but neither of them came from Eger, which had
to be the link between Singer and Zimmerman.

He was about to leave for the Zimmerman mansion when
Betty, his secretary, called to say there was a woman to see him.
Downstairs, with the constable at reception. A Ms. Thomas.

His first impulse was to take the back stairs to the emergency
exit at the rear. "Does she know I'm here?" he asked.

"Yes," Betty said with a question mark in her inflection.

"Thank you." It would have been stupid anyway to involve
Betty in the subterfuge. She had ways of leaning on his weaknesses
to get long holidays and leaves of absence whenever the spirit
moved her.

Why did his minor indiscretions have such a compulsive way
of turning into major embarrassments? He pulled on his jacket, his
salt-stained rubber overshoes, and his overcoat. At least he would
seem to be on his way out.

Deidre was sitting on a black plastic chair near the door,
reading a magazine. She wore her familiar high-heeled boots and
the long raccoon. Her hair was in stiff bubbly curls that only a
hairdresser would inflict on a woman. He hoped her hair appointment had been made long before she decided to come to see him.

"Hello," he said awkwardly.

"I was on my way to lunch with an old friend," Deidre said,
with a warm smile. "Coming by here I thought, wouldn't it be nice
to surprise you. So this is where you work," she said, looking
around the waiting room as though she hadn't been sitting there
already for five minutes. "Very..." She paused for inspiration.

"Drab?"

"It's not what I expected." She flashed her eyelashes at him.

"Homicide Bureau sounds so frightening. This is just an office, really."

"And not much of one at that," David said briskly. "I'm on my way out just now, Deidre. Can't stop to talk. I'll call. I said I would — "

"I've got something for you," Deidre interrupted. She reached inside her coat and pulled out a brown paper package about half an inch thick. "It wouldn't fit in my purse," she said. "I've got to put it back this afternoon while Philip is out with a client. Between 2 and 3. So if you wouldn't mind copying what you want while I wait..."

The package contained Paul Zimmerman's canceled checks issued since the end of April 1986. He flicked through them once, quickly, then again without losing the order they were in. There were regular checks for Arthur and Eva Zimmerman, $20,000 for him each month, $100,000 for her. She would probably get by on that even at the Meurice.

There were no unusually large cash withdrawals until the 7th of January: that day he had removed $50,000 in cash. And a further $50,000 on the 3rd of February.

David copied the checks himself. He could have asked Betty, but that would force him to sit around with Deidre making conversation.

"Are you busy this week?" she asked when he handed back the package.

"Yes. I'm sorry," David mumbled, ushering her out.

"All week?" she asked, her voice quivering.

"I'll call you," he said as warmly as he could muster. He'd bloody well make himself, he thought on the way to his car, and he'd tell her then that there weren't going to be any more Saturday nights.

TWENTY-SEVEN

Arnold Nagy was no friendlier today than he had been the first time David met him. Only difference was he allowed David to enter the house. But that was all. He didn't even invite him to sit. They stood circumspectly observing each other in the extraordinarily pink reception area that reminded David of a posh 1950s Montreal bordello, even before he noticed the tasteful female statue in the corner. It was difficult for David to imagine what kind of mind Paul Zimmerman must have had to choose the decor.

Arnold was dressed in a stiff pinstriped three-piece suit with thin black tie, white shirt, and very shiny shoes — possibly because Betty had phoned ahead to say David was coming, but more likely Arnold always comported himself in the manner of a British gentleman's valet. With pomp and discretion.

"A police matter, you said, I believe, Officer." He repeated David's opening line, his face expressionless.

"Homicide, actually," said David.

He was disappointed with Arnold's lack of response. "Yes?" said Arnold, raising one thin eyebrow. He clasped his hands behind him, assuming the position of polite expectation.

No sense beating about the bush. "A gentleman by the name of Harvey Singer was murdered in Toronto the night of February 26th. Perhaps you remember my asking you about him when I was last here?"

Arnold remained motionless.

"We believe," David continued, "Mr. Singer was shot in Mr. Zimmerman's red XJ-S Jaguar."

Still no reaction. Was he accustomed to people being knocked off in the family's automobile?

"Could you tell me where you were between 9 P.M. on the 26th of February and 1 A.M. on the 27th?"

"Certainly," Arnold said thoughtfully. "Glad to." As if he had been asked to move an ashtray. "That was a Thursday night, I think. Correct?"

"Right."

"I watched *Lifestyles of the Rich and Famous* from 9 until 10. Then *Night Heat*. Went to sleep at 11 o'clock. Thursdays are my nights off, weekdays. I normally take Sundays as well, but I don't suppose you'll be interested in that."

"No," David stated categorically. "Was there someone else with you the night of the 26th?"

"No. I went to my quarters after Cook served my dinner at eight. I live alone."

"Anyone see you?"

"Not unless someone was spying on me and I cannot think why someone would."

"In that case you would not have known where Mr. Zimmerman was that night, would you?" David tried to check his hostility. Arnold Nagy, unless he traveled under an alias, had no criminal record and had every right to spend Thursday nights watching television and doing whatever else he wished.

"On the contrary," Arnold said patiently. "I dressed Mr. Zimmerman at 6:30. He was dining at Mr. Griffiths's home. He had been expected to be there by 6:30 for drinks, the actual dinner beginning at 7:30, but he had been late working with Mr. Masters. I set his clothes out at 5 and waited to be called on before I returned to my quarters. I checked the library clock when Mr. Masters left. That's how I know it was 6:30. I asked Mr. Zimmerman if he wished me to call the Griffithses to say he would be late. I did telephone when he left."

His memory for detail was astounding. "You wouldn't happen to know when he came home?" David inquired.

"Not exactly. I do know that when I woke at around midnight and went to the kitchen for a glass of milk, the car was in front of the garage doors."

"Which car?"

"The Rolls."

"He drove it himself?"

"*No*," Arnold protested, as though the very suggestion that Paul Zimmerman would drive his own Rolls was an insult. "Geoff Aronson drove him."

"Who was driving the Jaguar that night?"

"No one," Arnold declared. Another question he had been expecting?

"How can you be so sure?" David's annoyance was growing minute by minute as they stood firmly planted in the general pinkness. "How can you remember so clearly what you and everybody else was doing almost two weeks ago?"

Arnold drew up his lips in what must have been his rendition of a smile. "You were here last Wednesday asking questions about the same evening. Then, too, you were inexplicably curious about the XJ-S, and who drove it. I made it my business to remember everything about that night and where we all were, in case you came back."

"You thought I would come back?" David asked quickly.

"I thought you might."

"Why?"

"Because you hadn't finished with all your questions."

"Not because you assumed I would check on Michael Ward?"

Arnold shrugged almost imperceptibly. "That had occurred to me," he said. "It wouldn't have taken much to discover that he had been incarcerated."

Now there's a fine word, David thought. "I want to speak to him now, if I may," he asked politely.

"I'm afraid that will be impossible," Arnold announced. "He left the day after you came here to question him. We have no forwarding address. As his parole is over, I assume he didn't have to give one. Is that right, Officer?"

David didn't reply. He focused on the huge glass case over Arnold's shoulder, with its vast collection of dead butterflies. "We are going to search the garage, and maybe look around the house, then," he said. "This is a murder investigation, Mr. Nagy, and we assume we will have your full cooperation."

Arnold hesitated. "Have you informed Mrs. Zimmerman?" he asked.

"Yes. She has been told."

Arnold insisted he would call her himself to confirm her permission. He left David cooling his heels in the doorway while he used the phone in the library. David examined the butterflies more closely: 15 rows of 15, each expertly stretched to display its full wingspan. The colors were iridescent blues and reds, oranges and yellows. Their bodies lay flat, each set of legs painstakingly arranged to line up in the same way: two forward, four backward.

"Mrs. Zimmerman is agreeable," Arnold said on his return, making it clear by his tone that if it were up to him, he wouldn't have agreed.

David called for Giannini and Stewart to come and assist him in the search. It might take hours.

Arnold led the way along a wide passageway that continued the pink flocked wallpaper and handsomely framed horse prints. Taking a key from a chain he carried in his pocket, he unlocked the polished wood door and let David into the garage. Some hazy blue light from the window across the main doors cast long shadows across the cement floor in front of the five cars that stood side by side, almost but not entirely filling the vast area of the garage.

After a moment's wait in the darkness, David turned to the silent valet. "Do you think we could have some light here?"

"Certainly," Arnold conceded, as though the idea would never have occurred to him without a reminder. He switched on a central light bulb and two smaller side lights.

The five cars were the Rolls, the Morgan convertible with the canvas sheet draped over its tidy body and tied down with leather thongs, the Cherokee Chief, the little Ferrari, and a large Oldsmobile he hadn't noticed before.

"Where does the Jaguar sit when it's at home?"

"No particular place," Arnold said, determined to be helpful. "Wherever there is room."

David walked slowly around the periphery. There was a groove all the way round, slanting into four drainage outlets, one in each corner. That would make cleaning the cars much easier. The floor and walls were spotless. The garage was a little cooler than the house, but not much, since it was kept warm by a series of space heaters.

Arnold still hadn't suggested that David remove his overcoat. "When was the last time you saw the XJ-S?" Arnold had not budged from the connecting door, so David had to shout to be heard.

"Sunday the 1st," Arnold too raised his voice.

"Where was it?"

"It was here," Arnold indicated the far lane to his right. "The Laidlaw Cartage people came to ship it to Bermuda. I was supervising their removal of the vehicle."

Naturally.

"How did the car look to you then, Mr. Nagy?" David had returned to his starting point, taking small steps all the way and paying attention to the fine-scrubbed floor in case he caught a glimpse of glitter off a piece of glass or heard a crunch under his shoes.

"I beg your pardon?"

"I mean, how close were you to the car, and did the car look any different to you?"

"I was approximately where I am now," said Arnold, not unexpectedly. "And the car was as it had been since it arrived here last fall. At least the parts I could see."

"You couldn't see all of it?"

"Of course not. It had been covered with its padded canvas blanket, battened down for the flight. Occasionally a car can be damaged in transit by even the best company in the field. The XJ-S is a very sensitive automobile."

"Who would have attended to covering it?"

"Michael Ward. He was in charge of the upkeep of the cars."

"Did you actually see him do it?"

"No," Arnold said peevishly. "The boy needed no supervision. He was one of the best staff we have had here and we would still have him, had it not been for your harassment."

No sense in engaging Arnold in an argument over young Ward, though it might be pleasing to arrest Ward on Murder One. "Who telephoned for Laidlaw?"

"I did. At Mrs. Zimmerman's request."

"When did she ask you?"

"Let me see... Friday, I think. They wanted the car in Bermuda for the following weekend."

"Wasn't that an unusual request?"

"Unusual?" Arnold allowed his tone to rise. "Why would it be unusual? The XJ-S was Mr. Zimmerman's favorite car. He wished to drive it on his holiday. Last summer they took it to France twice. By air. So why not Bermuda?"

"The fact remains, Mr. Nagy, that a man was murdered in Mr.

Zimmerman's most beloved car and I'm trying to establish who did it." David sighed. "Where was Arthur Zimmerman that night?"

"I'm afraid you will have to ask him that yourself, "Arnold said firmly. "I do not keep track of Mr. Arthur's movements, as I do not manage his household. All I can tell you is that Mr. Arthur did not arrive here until Sunday morning. He remained in his room most of that day, and resurfaced for the party in the evening." Though Arnold's face betrayed no emotion, it was easy to see he was no great fan of Arthur, a fact that was liable to endear Arthur to David Parr almost immediately.

"And Mrs. Zimmerman? Where was she Thursday night?"

"During the same hours? She was with Mr. Zimmerman at the party."

"The guard, did he report anything unusual that night?"

"No. On the other hand, Thursday night was his night off, as well as mine and the upstairs maid's. He was off after 6 P.M."

A loud noise like a whistle issued from an instrument shaped like a small plastic barbell, attached to the wall. Arnold picked it up and said an ascending "Yes" into one end. Then he said "Yes" once more. "Your colleagues have arrived," he told David.

He pressed a button to open the triple doors of the garage and floated to the entrance, where Giannini and Stewart appeared in a couple of minutes. They both had their collars up to cover their ears and had stuffed their hands into their pockets. It was a blistering cold afternoon, but David guessed they were also responding to the general splendor of Zimmerman's house. They felt out of place.

"Constables Stewart and Giannini," he said to Arnold. "We'll start to examine the garage now, Mr. Nagy. Perhaps you could move all the cars out to give us a hand."

Arnold winced.

"Now, there's a good man," David said patronizingly. He got some minor satisfaction from that wince.

TWENTY-EIGHT

While Giannini and Stewart prepared the garage for Forensics' once-over, David returned to the house for a reluctant guided tour by Arnold. Except for the gun, he had no notion what he was looking for. If Zimmerman had killed Singer and had made such a botch-up of the murder scene, he was probably amateur enough to have kept the gun. David also hoped he'd find some unusual papers along the way, but that was all to do with the why. In this case, more of an intellectual interest, because even if Zimmerman was proven the murderer, he could hardly be charged.

The first place Arnold showed him was the library, a much more pleasant spot than the entrance, but, like Judith, he found it uncomfortable. Not a room you'd choose if you wanted to curl up with a good book.

Arnold maintained his position by the door again, neither helping nor hindering David's progress.

After about half an hour, he was forced to conclude that Zimmerman too must have found his library unfriendly. He kept no personal documents there, not one letter. Not even a bill or a bank statement. Certainly not a gun.

The rolltop Queen Anne writing desk by the window contained not one scrap of paper and no writing utensils. The whole room was like a stage set, unlived in.

Before proceeding to the study, he tried out the antique gold-encrusted telephone on the Queen Anne to call Chuck Griffiths. He was expected to return from a lunch meeting at 3 P.M. Parr thanked the secretary, making sure the import of Homicide Bureau sank in.

The study was not much smaller than the library, but more cluttered. It was not inconceivable that a person could have spent time in it. The baroque Italian marble-top table in the center had

194

apparently been used as a desk: there was a large square piece of leather with green underfelt on one side, a stack of monogrammed papers, envelopes with "Paul Zimmerman" in the left-hand corner, pens, an antique inkwell, a box of colored pencils, and an electric pencil sharpener.

On the bookshelves there were dictionaries, a multivolume history of the Western world, atlases, books of quotations, a set of encyclopedias. The complete *Oxford*. An Andrew Wyeth limited edition. A big brass globe on a revolving wooden stand stood next to the table. David couldn't resist the temptation to turn on its switch to see if it would light up. It did, in blue for the oceans and yellow for the continents. The main cities glowed red, the mountains dark brown.

Arnold cleared his throat noisily.

"Not a bad little toy," David said before switching it off again.

There was an array of black-framed photographs on the wall, mostly pictures of a little girl with ash blond hair, a high, open forehead, a generous mouth, and near-white eyelashes. She obviously enjoyed posing for the camera. Even in the earliest photos, where she couldn't have been more than a year old, she dimpled up for the photographer. A few of the pictures showed her with her mother. There was a strong resemblance of one to the other. Must be Meredith and Brenda Zimmerman. Daddy's girl.

His thoughts were interrupted by a loud clanging noise that breathed instant life into the motionless Arnold, who turned on his heels and dashed out the door, without a word of explanation.

David headed for the two mahogany filing cabinets at the far end of the room and opened, at random, the middle drawer of the nearest one. No telling what else of interest Zimmerman might have filed, after all the bits and pieces Deidre had discovered. The whole drawer was full of files headed "Pacific Airlines," with a plethora of subdivisions with such uninteresting labels as "P & L 1985," "P & L 1986," "Executive Planning Ledger," "Diversification." He flicked through a couple and was disappointed to discover they were indeed what they claimed to be. The top drawer was just as dreary, with long sheets of numbers regarding Monarch Enterprises.

He was about to start on the bottom drawer when Arnold returned with what David now recognized as a smile on his face. He was preceded by a small balding man wearing gold-rimmed glasses and a mink coat and carrying a black leather briefcase embossed with gold letters. His face, round and jovial, turned quite red when he saw Parr bending over the filing cabinet.

"By what right, sir," he demanded, bearing down on Parr, his briefcase swinging, "are you foraging about in Mr. Zimmerman's private papers?" His voice was a high crackly squawk that expressed both indignation and astonishment.

"Foraging," David thought appreciatively, excellent. It implied both that he was aimlessly searching about and that he was an animal. He waited till the little man had planted himself between him and the cabinets, then he slowly removed the search warrant from his breast pocket.

"I am Philip Masters," the little man said with dignity. "Paul and Brenda Zimmerman's counsel." He tried to read the warrant without touching it, then took it from David's hand. "Perhaps you'd be kind enough to explain, Officer," he demanded, his voice a notch lower.

David did. He told him exactly what he had told Arnold, adding that he already had evidence linking Paul Zimmerman to Harvey Singer.

"In that case," Masters said, "there is no need to go through papers relating to business deals involving Mr. Zimmerman's private companies that have no possible bearing on whoever Mr. Slinger...Singer...whatever, was. Right?"

"As it happens, Mr. Masters," David said patiently, "I have every right to examine all of Mr. Zimmerman's papers and fully intend to do so. And I would recommend that you get out of my way so that we can stop wasting each other's time. Unless you prefer I charge you with obstructing justice, a nasty little charge carrying a minimum sentence of — "

"All right." Masters shifted to one side of the cabinets. "But I will remain here protecting my clients' interests." He murmured something else about "wanton destruction," but David assumed that was a last-minute face-saver and let it go. He resumed his random progress through the bottom drawer, then all the other drawers, without finding a single sheet of paper bearing Singer's name. He persevered at the task with rather more attention to detail than he had intended, but Masters's nervousness implied that there were indeed secrets in these files if only he had the key. In the end, he decided to take them downtown later and have someone with expertise in industrial crime go through them. Masters, of course, could challenge the validity of the seize order, if he knew enough. Unlikely he'd had much experience in criminal law. David would wait and see.

"Do you happen to remember where you were the night of February 26th, Mr. Masters?" he asked.

"The 26th? No. I don't think I know what kind of day that was at all. Almost two weeks ago. Before Paul died..." He was sweating profusely inside the smooth mink coat. The smell of perfume, or expensive cologne, mixed with tangy body odor and maybe fear. But why fear?

"A Thursday night," David told him. "You were here, according to Mr. Nagy, working late with Mr. Zimmerman. You stayed till close to 6:30."

Masters looked at Arnold, seeking confirmation. The butler glided toward Masters, eager to explain. "That was the evening, Mr. Masters, you and Mr. Zimmerman were signing papers. There was that young lady here interviewing Mr. Zimmerman."

Judith would have enjoyed the "young lady" bit. He must remember to tell her. She was due back in a couple of hours.

"Yes. Yes," Mr. Masters said. He had unbuttoned his coat, but his face was still red. "That night. That night. Hmm. Hard, on the spur of the moment, to remember the actual things one does. Know what I mean?"

David did, but he wasn't about to say so. Maybe if Masters sweated enough, he'd let slip what was bothering him. He took one more look around the study, then headed for the next room. Arnold and Masters followed closely.

David poked his head into the gallery — Zimmerman was marginally redeeming himself for the reception area and the stagy library — and went on to the split-level living room. The gallery had no obvious hiding places for either gun or papers.

The living room was dominated by the large painting of Brenda Zimmerman wearing black velvet cut low to display her magnificent breasts, a blue hand-held Japanese fan somewhat obstructing the view of her cleavage. Her hair, worn in a knot on top of her head, was spun gold, her eyes an amazing violet, her skin perfectly molded around the curved high forehead and raised cheekbones. Indeed, Zimmerman must have been a man of good taste.

"I have it," Masters said triumphantly. "I drove to the Inn on the Park and had a drink in the bar after I left here. Then I went home. Jane was chairing a ladies' evening for the New Theatre Company that evening. Fund-raising. I was in no hurry to get home. Must have been 8 or 9 before I did. Had some frozen dinner and went to bed early." He followed David to the piano which he was opening to look inside. "Officer, really, I cannot imagine that you seriously believe you're going to find anything in that Steinway."

David opened all the drawers of all the antique tables in the room and found nothing but coasters and ashtrays.

"Was anybody with you?" David asked.

"Not until Jane came home at around midnight, no," Masters said. "Please do be careful with that," he added when David pried open the door of a standing clock. "It's three hundred years old and part of Meredith Zimmerman's inheritance."

The dining room yielded nothing but a recognition of where Paul Zimmerman had died. "His back was to the kitchen door," Judith had said. At the longer of the two dining room tables. There was a swing door to the kitchen, which, in turn, connected to the staff's quarters.

Arnold led the procession up the winding staircase.

"Were you aware that Michael Ward had a criminal record?" David asked Masters.

"Ward? Who is Ward?"

"The young man who took care of the cars," Arnold said.

"Oh yes. Well, no. How would I have known?"

"*We* knew," Arnold said forcefully. "Mrs. Zimmerman works with the John Howard Society for the rehabilitation of former inmates. This particular young man was working out extraordinarily well until..."

"He left without a forwarding address shortly after the murder," David said. Then he thought, wouldn't that have been amazingly convenient for Paul Zimmerman, had he killed Singer and stayed alive to be accused of the crime? He could have encouraged the young man to disappear. Could have paid him a handsome severance.

"You think he killed this man Singer?" Masters asked.

"Possibly," David said.

Upstairs there were two vast bedrooms connected by a sitting room. Each bedroom had a king-sized bed, Brenda's blue with a pink canopy, Paul's blue and brown-striped. The carpets were two inches thick in both rooms, pink and brown respectively.

"It's preposterous," Masters murmured as David began to sift through drawers full of underwear and socks. Zimmerman had over a hundred suits in his walk-in room-sized closet, and they were only his winter wear. Arnold said his summer clothes were in storage. He must have had two hundred silk shirts and ties. Why would a man bother? There were rows and rows of shoes, each pair glossy with fresh polish.

"All this," Philip Masters said proudly, "will go to the poor."

David was turning each shoe upside down to see if something fell out. Shoes made super, though hardly original, hiding places. He thought of Brother Twelve and the Indian and what a bonanza it would be for them to find this lot on some city garbage dump. The detectives still had no idea what Singer had been carrying in his shoe.

Going through the coat pockets David found a photograph of a young woman with red hair and blue-green eyes. On the back, in childish script, it said: "To Paul with love. Forever and ever. Your Martha."

"Who is Martha?" David asked, holding the photograph so both Arnold and Masters could see it.

When neither of them replied, he slipped the picture into his pocket.

"It's Mrs. Charles Griffiths," Masters said, at last. Obviously he had decided David would find out soon enough. "She has no possible involvement in your investigation, therefore you have no right to take the photograph. You do not have the right, sir, to casually pocket other people's property. There are procedures to observe..." He was beginning to gesticulate with his arms, his face glowing with indignation.

"I have the right to take whatever I believe is of material interest to the case, Mr. Masters," David said calmly. "The rules leave the decision as to what is and what is not relevant entirely in the senior officer's hands."

While David began a cursory search through Brenda Zimmerman's endless wardrobe, Masters left to use the phone in the florid sitting room between the two bedrooms.

David wondered how the Zimmermans decided which bed to choose for their conjugal rights. His was much too macho, what with lifelike hunting scenes on the walls, the rows of miniature toy soldiers in the glass window boxes (did Zimmerman play war games?), the display table with antique rifles. Hers was just as determinedly fluffy: all pinks and whites, a dressing room with more jars and bottles than you'd find in your average corner drugstore, the robin's-egg blue and beige harvest tapestry that stretched the length of her bed, the extra-large pink TV set, lamps shaped like lilies, and a profusion of clothes to make Imelda Marcos envious. Perhaps they met in the middle and made out on the resplendent chaise longue?

He merely glanced at Meredith's quarters, concluded they were too sumptuous for a child of ten — or any age — and decided to leave them to last. It was an unlikely place to hide documents, and not one that would be safe for a gun. David would not eliminate the possibility, but there were more likely places to search first.

"What's in the basement?" he asked Arnold.

"Gym. Swimming pool. Tennis court. Sauna."

This time David led the way. He didn't wait for Masters.

The basement was warmer than the rest of the house and just as spectacular. The pool was a bean-shaped green expanse, with orange marble tiles all around; the gym had more equipment than David's club at the Y. The sauna was double the size of the Y's. Between the sauna and the pool there was a long dressing room with separate doors for boys and girls and a series of metal lockers to stash your clothes.

It was behind one of the metal doors in the men's dressing room that David found a gun. It was wrapped into a pair of men's white running shorts, covered by a lot of other white shorts and socks.

He didn't touch the gun. He didn't have to. He knew what it was through the layer of cloth. He lifted it by its muzzle and dropped it, shorts and all, into one of the plastic bags he had brought in his pocket.

To his credit, Arnold made no remark when they were joined by Masters at the top of the stairs. "It's taking unconscionable liberties," Masters was saying. "You would think we live in a police state where you can barge around in someone else's home, grabbing at random whatever you choose." He shook his head rather theatrically and followed David out toward the garage. He had left his coat behind somewhere. His jacket flapped open as he hurried to keep up. "I have the right, Detective Inspector, to ask for a full accounting of everything you are trying to take from this house and will later seek legal recourse for malicious prosecution if I find you have so much as disturbed my clients' — "

"Later," David waved him to one side as he called Stewart over. He handed over the plastic bag with the gun and asked the constable to take it over to the lab. Now. Then he took another look at Martha Griffiths's photograph before returning it to Arnold. "That," he said, "is all I will need for the moment. We will leave a guard at the door to make sure nothing is removed till we have completed the search." He turned to Philip Masters. "I don't suppose, Mr. Masters, you could tell me something about Harvey Singer yourself?"

"Never heard of the man till today," Masters said indignantly. "I told you that."

"Would you know if Mr. Zimmerman had been blackmailed by someone in the past couple of months, or so?"

"Blackmailed?" Masters squeaked. "What do you mean, black-mailed?"

"Were you aware of anyone who might have been blackmailing Mr. Zimmerman and to whom he would have given two install-ments of $50,000 each, on January 7th and February 3rd?"

Masters stared at David. "Why those particular dates?"

"You haven't answered my question, Mr. Masters," said David, watching him intently.

There were beads of perspiration all over Masters's bald pate and gathering along the hairline. He held his hands together in front of his gentle paunch, the fingers almost white as he squeezed them together. This was more than just anger and frustration. What did Masters know that he wasn't telling?

"I don't believe I have to answer your question at this time, Officer," Masters said finally. "I assure you that if I were to answer, it would have nothing to do with this man Singer and his unfortunate death. If I were you, I'd redouble my efforts to find that young jailbird. I have never been in favor of Brenda's interest in causes. Women nowadays feel they must do something useful to justify their existence. Total rot. Why they can't just enjoy what they've got — " He stopped as suddenly as he'd begun, probably regretting his outburst. "Arnold, would you get me a Scotch, please."

That's when David told Masters he had found the gun. That

was the way he said it: "the gun," because that little bit of phony certainty might nudge him into telling what was on his mind.

When Masters said nothing, only stared into space, David returned to the hall to call Griffiths. While he dialed, Masters came in and slumped down on a pink bow-legged stool by the Greek statue to watch him.

Griffiths answered his own phone. He had clearly been warned Parr would call again. "The 26th of February?" he repeated after David told him about the murder and Zimmerman's car. "Yes, they were both at our house for dinner." David could hear him flicking though his diary to confirm the time. "Paul and Brenda arrived rather late. We were on the point of sitting down and Martha was beginning to fuss about where they were. The Goodmans were also here, and the Parkers..."

"Do you remember when the Zimmermans left?"

There was a long silence, then Griffiths asked, "Why?"

"Was it 9 or 10? Perhaps closer to midnight?" David persisted.

"Closer to 10, I think," Chuck Griffiths said. "Yes, I believe they left early. You could check with the others, if you like. It's hard to be sure..."

"That seems unusually early, doesn't it?" David asked. "Especially as you didn't start eating till some time after 7:30. Was there some particular reason why they left?" He had no cause to hassle the wronged husband, but it was worth the effort if it jogged his memory.

"Ah yes," Griffiths said. "Brenda had a headache. That's what it was. She suddenly developed a raging headache and wanted to go home."

"And Paul Zimmerman? Didn't he go with her?"

"No. He finished his coffee and dessert and left about half an hour later. Maybe closer to 10:30."

Still within the time frame to kill Singer and be home before Brenda became worried. Could be a nice bit of planning, that, sending Brenda home ahead. But how would he have managed it? Something in her wine? Maybe he chose that night to tell her about Martha? Bit risky that, to tell your wife you're having an affair with your hostess just before you dig into the main course.

"You're not actually suspecting Paul Zimmerman of killing this man Singer, are you?" Griffiths's voice registered complete astonishment.

"It's only an investigation, Mr. Griffiths. Thank you for your help. I may have to call on you again, but you've already been of great assistance." David hung up. "I'd like to talk to the chauffeur," he told Masters, "and Mrs. Zimmerman as well."

"They are both in Bermuda," Masters said sullenly. The large Scotch Arnold had supplied hadn't lifted his spirits one ounce.

"I know," David said.

"I'm quite sure Mrs. Zimmerman has never heard of Singer, nor has Geoff Aronson," Masters persisted.

"Mrs. Zimmerman has already made a statement to police officers in St. George, Mr. Masters. I merely wish to confirm a couple of details. I could call her while you listen in as her counsel." David was trying to be as accommodating as he could.

"She's still in a state of shock. I wouldn't advise it..."

"In that case, I'll have to go to Bermuda myself, won't I?"

Masters liked that idea even less. "Doubt if they'd send you all that way," he pondered, "just to ask a few questions. Especially as your prime suspect is already dead. What's the point?"

That was smart for a little corporate lawyer in a state of shock. David smiled. "You could be right there, Mr. Masters, but the department does like to tie up its loose ends. You have a choice. Either we call now, or I go tomorrow."

Masters gave up. He finished his drink and dialed the Bermuda number. David let him struggle though the introductory pieces. He'd done it himself three times already, and Staff Sergeant Graham's warning about Brenda's vile temper had done little to help.

There were a lot of pauses at Masters's end of the dialogue. With a bit of luck, David thought, Brenda would be letting off excess steam at the lawyer and be calm enough to answer his questions when it came his turn. When Masters got round to his own suspicions that Michael Ward might have taken the car and done the deed himself, Brenda Zimmerman went on for at least two minutes. That was her reaction to his telling her about the gun, as well.

"She says she can't believe you found a gun here," Masters said, cupping the phone with his hand. "She never knew Paul had one."

"We'll check it out," David said, reaching for the receiver. "Mrs. Zimmerman?" he asked, when Masters gave it to him at last.

"What the hell...," Brenda said softly. She sounded bewildered, rather than angry. "Philip says you have some more questions. Well..." Her silky, girlish voice immediately made David think of the painting in the living room.

"Detective Inspector David Parr," David said. "I did promise Mr.

Masters this wouldn't take long. A couple of questions about the night of February 26th, if you wouldn't mind. Can you please tell me where you were and what you were doing that evening after 9?"

"Dinner at the Griffithses' that night. Don't remember what time...Hmm...Oh yes. Yes. I had a most terrible headache. I don't get headaches, you know. Never. Only that night, like needles in my head." She spoke so softly and slowly he had trouble catching the separate words. "Had to go home early. That's right. I think."

"Do you remember what time that would have been?"

"Hmm...No. Can't say I do. They were just finishing the meat. Some sort of gluey goulash. Sticksville. Martha was trying to please Paul by making goulash..." There was a tiny choking sound at the end of the line, then silence.

"Mrs. Zimmerman?"

"Paul hated goulash," she said quite firmly. "Loathed it."

"How did you get home?"

"Geoff." Another gap, then: "Yes. Geoff drove me home."

"And went back for Mr. Zimmerman?" David prompted.

"No. I think I gave him the rest of the evening off. Thursday, you said? Usually he was off Thursday nights."

"Do you know what time Mr. Zimmerman returned?"

"I'm afraid...no, not that I recall. I took some pills so I could sleep. I had that horrible headache. Couldn't have been too late, though..." She trailed off again.

"Would I be able to speak with Geoff now?"

"No. He's gone for the day, I think. Maybe if you call again..." She faded into silence.

"It's been very stressful for her," Masters said when David hung up the phone. "Paul's not even gone two weeks yet. And now this." He slapped the base of the statue with one hand and looked at David accusingly. "She's on tranquilizers."

David was tempted to say something mildly apologetic, but he didn't. He left abruptly for headquarters.

TWENTY-NINE

The cat was curled into a soft ginger ball, its whiskers shivering expectantly as it stared up at Judith. Its expression, if cats can have expressions, was one of casual inquiry. It was settled on top of the TV set, in what must be a warm or particularly inviting spot for cats. Judith didn't know a thing about cats, never having owned one or even lived under the same roof as one.

Marsha had a cat, aptly named Jezebel, who required constant attention and companionship, and who hated cat food. Judith was puzzled about Marsha's devotion to the cat but tended to explain it to herself by imagining Jezebel was a substitute for children. Everyone needed to be needed by someone.

Judith, on the other hand, had all the reassurance she could handle. She had kids. That's why the TV set was turned to something called *Family Ties* with an actor called Michael J. Fox, who looked about the same age as his mother, only shorter. In Hollywood age is measured by height.

She dropped her suitcase in the middle of the living room, decided to ignore the expectant cat, and raced upstairs to the sound of Madonna emanating from Jimmy's room. She was so excited about seeing them again after five days that she forgot to knock on Jimmy's door, flung it open, and barged in with a "Hello there, thank God you're home." Jimmy was doing some sort of a dance in the center of his room — head bent, arms out, fingers clicking. She wrapped him in her arms and hugged him tight.

"Jeez, Mom, where did you think I was?" he grumbled, but he did look pleased to see her, which was all the encouragement she required. "Did you go to Paris? For real?"

"New York and Paris," Judith said, still holding on to him, breathing in his familiar smell of chewing gum and Head & Shoulders. "Have you grown again?" He was about an inch shorter than Judith, and catching up fast. He'd probably be as tall as James eventually. But not yet. Judith wanted so badly to cling to what was left of the little boy who had once clung to her. "I missed you," she said, overcome with memories of Jimmy waddling around in his diapers.

"Missed you too," he said, giving her a flat-palmed pat-pat on the back. "Was it fun in Paris?"

"Not much. I kept thinking of the time we were there together." *Gotta learn how to let go.* "Anyway, I was working. Where's Anne?"

"Talking to the guy with the fangs. We left in such a hurry, she didn't say goodbye. They've been making up for it the last hour." Jimmy shifted his weight from one foot to the other, the closest he could come to dancing while talking to his mother.

"Fangs? You mean the 18-year-old from UCC?"

"Oh, he's history. No, I mean the guy with the buck teeth from Northern. Someone should have stuck a retainer in his mouth when he was ten, then he'd only be ugly, not buck-toothed too. Skis like an avalanche, though; sweeps everyone off as he comes by. No turns, can't control his skis."

"How's your skiing?"

"Great. Great. Love it." He punctuated each word with swaying movements that combined dancing to Madonna and swishing downhill. "Dad says we should join the club so we can go up every weekend. Maybe buy a chalet in Collingwood."

"Sure," Judith said. "Did he give you the money?" But she was sorry she'd said that when she saw the hurt expression on Jimmy's face. She'd promised herself on the plane not to go on about James, especially to Jimmy. She'd fallen in love with James once, when she was young, why shouldn't Jimmy? She grinned to pretend she'd been joking. "I'll go find Anne and make us all something to eat. Left a frozen lasagna for tonight. Still like that stuff, don't you?"

"Love it," Jimmy said. "Dad didn't think we should have that Italian gloop. Too much starch is bad for a man's libido — you know..." He was watching her warily as he prattled on about energy and carbohydrates.

Judith let her eyes wander around the room with its many familiar shapes — the mountainous hockey gear, Wayne Gretzky smiling encouragement on the wall, the brown bear called Paddy with his Blue Jays cap, the pile of dirty clothes in the corner, the 1986 team photo with Jimmy in his goalie outfit. The memory of that third-rate cannabis came flooding back and made her want to cry.

"What is it?" Jimmy was asking, his voice cracking as it often did when he was feeling emotional. "What's wrong?" When she didn't reply, he made a big production of a resigned, long-suffering sigh. "You want to go another round on that grass shit, right?"

"I don't think so," Judith said unhappily.

"You still figure I'm lying? That's it, isn't it? Isn't it?" His voice alternated high and low as if he had a bad case of laryngitis, and Judith reached out again, her hands touching his tight bony shoulders; there were tears in her eyes because she loved him and because she was suddenly furious at herself for having suspected him. Jimmy didn't lie about important things, only about minor stuff like breaking a plate or why he was late home from school when he'd hung around at the Towne Mall with his friends.

"No," she said with conviction. And it suddenly struck her that the whole business with the cannabis could have been planned distraction, could have been set up by the person who'd climbed into the house last Tuesday night. At first the policeman had said there were signs of entry via Jimmy's window. Then the baggie had got them all sidetracked. "It could," mused Judith, "be all of a piece."

"It could?" Jimmy asked.

"What if the same person who forced his way in to see an early draft of my Zimmerman story came by again last Friday night to paint our door red?"

"It isn't red, it's got a nice new coat of green," Jimmy said. "How did you have time to do that?"

"I didn't," Judith said. "Someone threw paint at the door, and David repainted it." He had arranged to have the window fixed, too.

"He did?"

She wasn't about to tell him about the swastika. That was frightening. But maybe less so if it wasn't put there by some crazed closet Nazi of her acquaintance, but someone who hated Zimmerman so much he'd tried to veer her off the story. Maybe someone who couldn't stand the thought of a long puff-piece commemorating Zimmerman's multifarious successes, his generosity, his personal forest in Israel, the soon-to-be-restored organ at Forest Hill Catholic.

"Mom," Jimmy was saying. "Mom," when she didn't respond. "Earth calling Mom... What is it?"

And what if the same person hated him enough to kill him?

"Mom?"

"Yes. I was just wondering about that cat downstairs."

"The cat?" Jimmy smiled his most ingratiating smile. "That's Zoë. Dad gave her to me. Sort of a late Christmas present. You know. She's totally trained and everything. She'll be no trouble at all, Dad said you'd be sure to get used to her and Anne and I just love her."

"Hi Mom. Can I go to a party tonight?" Anne called from the bathroom. "It's a sort of start-of-term party. Everybody's going..."

"Anne, the cat," Jimmy shouted.

"Zoë? Isn't she great, Mom? Don't you love the way she's made herself at home?" She had run upstairs three steps at a time, gave Judith a warm little peck on the cheek, and stood by fidgeting with something fluorescent green that had attached itself to her wrist. "You look just great, Mom. Super. Can I?" she asked again, bobbing up and down with excitement. "I haven't seen my friends in over a week and I'm allowed to invite Rog, even..."

"The guy I was telling you about," Jimmy said.

"What am I supposed to do with a cat?" Judith said weakly.

"Zoë takes care of herself, Mom. All cats do. They don't have to be walked and that. Just put out their food once a day..."

"Jimmy's going to do that, and he'll clean out the kitty litter once a day, too, so it won't smell, right?"

Jimmy gave her a dirty look, then returned to his pleading. "All cats need is a bit of comfort and love." *Was that off a record cover? A Christmas carol, so late?* "And she can sleep in here..."

"I'm going to heat the lasagna," Judith said, "then we'll talk about the cat and the party."

On her way through the living room she avoided a confrontation with Zoë.

Then all thoughts of the cat and her anger at James were swept from her mind. David called to say he had listened to Eva's tape and he was going to exhume Paul Zimmerman's body.

THIRTY

There had been two inches of snow overnight. Now in the early morning, it was rain and wet snow, with the temperature hovering above 0. The six men stood around the grave site, their hands deep in their pockets, shoulders drawn up, shuffling their feet to keep warm. David wore his heavy police parka, just like Giannini's, the first time in months he had worn any part of his uniform. Giannini's hood was pulled down over his face, the collar straight up, leaving a narrow slit for his eyes. The young pathologist with Yan had a down-filled winter jacket that was already dripping wet. He'd tried unsuccessfully to find shelter under the slender Manitoba maple by the stone angel that adorned the next grave. All that had marked this spot was a small gray stone with Zimmerman's name on it. The four-cornered granite monument Brenda had ordered was still in preparation, Philip Masters had told David. He had offered no help in finding the grave, nor in helping to calm Brenda when David informed her of the exhumation.

"It's your problem," Masters had said tersely, and hung up on him.

David could still hear the sharp wailing sound that had emanated from Brenda's throat when she had heard.

He had asked Arthur Zimmerman to come to Toronto for the formality of identifying the body. David was glad there was another relative to turn to — he'd always had difficulties dealing with hysterical women.

It had been 6:20 A.M. and still dark when they arrived. Now there were the beginnings of a gray, dismal dawn through the splattering drizzle.

"Lucky it's only been a week," Yan said through gritted teeth. He was smoking one of his nasty Camels. From time to time, as he sucked on it, the glow from the tip of the cigarette lit up his face under the wide-brimmed felt hat he had worn for the rain. "If he had been buried in December, it would take all day to get him out."

The two grave-diggers were halfway into the hole already. "Are you sure you call them grave-diggers?" Giannini had asked in the car. "They have fancy names for everybody nowadays. Hell, even garbage men are sanitary engineers. Grave-diggers, Inspector — how the hell would the guy tell someone at a party what he does for a living? Jeez, imagine trying to get a girl to go home with you..." It was Giannini's first experience of an exhumation. He was only 25. David reflected that they promoted men much faster nowadays then they used to. At 25 he'd still been pounding the beat, no idea he'd make it beyond staff sergeant, which was as far as his father ever got. The wet, cold early morning reminded him of his father's funeral. The grave was somewhere in this cemetery. He never visited it. There had been nothing but distance between them, polite lack of communication. These days, though, he had begun to think more about his father. There had been 50 people at the funeral — all cops, except for his mother and one Crown attorney, who was drunk. He remembered wondering if that was all there had been to the old man's life, gaining the respect of these awkward silent men who didn't even know how to show grief. Otherwise, his life had passed unnoticed.

At least Zimmerman had made a difference.

"Good-looking coffin," Yan said, making a high-pitched whistling noise to show his appreciation.

The lid was polished, glistening black wood with brass braces and a brass plaque in the center. As the men brushed the earth off, Parr could make out the raised lettering: PAUL ZIMMERMAN, 1928-1987.

"Son-of-a-bitch is gonna be heavy," said one of the diggers. He took off his yellow plastic sou'wester and wiped his forehead on the back of his glove. "Mahogany, it looks like."

The lacquered wood caught a glint off the storm lamps' amber light and a touch of yellow from the sou'wester.

"Thing like that would set you back a few bucks, wouldn't it?" said Yan. "Never could understand why people bother spending all that money on something they'll never see, or even get to enjoy. Damn thing rots in a year or two down there, anyway."

"Not mahogany. Lasts for years," one of the grave-diggers said. "It's fifteen to twenty thousand for a good one like this."

The other man had cleared the earth from the side of the coffin and slipped a wedge, then a long canvas belt under it. "Better loosen it some more on your side, Jack."

"Bloody cold," Giannini grumbled to no one in particular.

"It'd go a damn sight faster if you guys lent a hand," Jack told him. "Then we can all go and get warm."

Giannini struggled with that idea for a moment, then shuffled forward an inch or two. "Yeah? What d'ya want me to do?"

Jack's partner showed him where they wanted to push the canvas belt under the casket and out the other side, then attach both ends to the two bright red electric winches. "Have to hold them down so they won't slip. Hard to get them properly anchored with the ground frozen. Can you get the big fella to help?"

David was already there, threading the belt into the red contraption. He figured he knew as much about the system — such as it was — as the cemetery staff. His 22nd exhumation. The two men with Independent Transport moved forward to see if they could help. They had been talking quietly to each other near the van. Parr knew them both from other times they had carried "his" bodies to the morgue. The older one with the mustache liked to tell young cops horror stories about corpses coming to life in their "meat wagon," their long-nailed hands smashing through the glass divider.

The coffin emerged to the shrill whirring of the winches. "I'm going to have myself cremated," Yan said. "My ashes scattered over Lake Ontario. Or up in Georgian Bay where I go fishing in the summer. No coffins, and no chance for some yahoo to carve me up, right, Bernie?" He winked at the pathologist.

They pushed the coffin onto the transport's trolley. Yan put the official seal on the lid.

"It'll be about 10 to 12 hours till they can open him up," Yan said. "He'll have to defrost first so they can drain off the embalming fluid. How long's that going to take?" he asked the pathologist.

"Another four or five hours," Bernie said. "We'll have something for you by late tonight, I hope. At least we should be able to determine if he died of a heart attack."

"Call me as soon as you can," David said. "Giannini's bringing Arthur Zimmerman down to identify him. That's the son. Just get him in and out of there fast, okay?"

He walked Yan to his car and thanked him for getting the exhumation order as quickly as he had.

"You better be right, chum," Yan told him. "Your ass is on the line for this one."

"I know," David said. He was thinking of Masters, more than likely at the legislature right now, waiting for an audience with the attorney-general.

He sat in the car while Giannini scraped the newly forming ice off the windows and the windshield wipers, and he worried about the decision he'd made. Even before the tapes had arrived on his desk, he had come to feel that Zimmerman was murdered. It was instinct, more than anything else, and a conviction that Singer's murder was connected to Zimmerman's. But how? And what was it Singer had known about Zimmerman and that boy in the photograph?

Martelli had called late yesterday evening. He'd checked Singer's old bank account, and no large sums had gone in or out of it in the past few months. The same was true of Singer junior's, and Mrs. Singer hadn't had her own bank account. When she left for Israel, she had cleared out their joint checking account of only $1,200 and left their savings at 12 per cent. That account had remained stable at a $105,000 plus interest for over a year.

On the second visit, Melwyn Singer agreed that his father had been a different man after his trip to the old country. He had become morose and short-tempered. He'd even snapped at one of his grandchildren once, which he'd never done before. The last time Melwyn had seen him was the evening before he left for Toronto. He had been very upset about something, but he wouldn't say what. All he did say was that he had some old accounts to settle. "Accounts" must have been what he'd said to Gloria that Thursday morning, his last. That's why she had the idea he'd gone to see his accountant.

And yes, he had mentioned the name Zimmerman once before. Late last year — December — he had told Melwyn he was going to see a man called Zimmerman in New York. He thought he might have been a relative of an old friend he'd known in Hungary.

As to why on earth Melwyn hadn't told him all this before —

well, that had to do with his mother. She had asked that Melwyn keep these personal matters of his father to himself. She had been most insistent. But now that he knew about his father's murder in the Zimmerman car, Melwyn no longer felt bound by his promise to her. Not only that, he was furious she hadn't told her family and the police what she knew.

If Zimmerman had killed Singer, why had Gloria rushed off to Israel? With Zimmerman dead, what was there for her to fear?

David dropped Giannini at 52 Division.

Arthur was on the 9 A.M. flight from New York. After he'd performed his unpleasant duty at the morgue, David would meet him for coffee at Homicide. Meanwhile, he'd have breakfast with Judith.

THIRTY-ONE

Jimmy had left early for another football-team planning and practice session. Anne was brooding over a breakfast of yogurt and Cocoa Puffs, stirring the brown sugary cereal around and around in a big plastic container of strawberry liquid. Judith was drinking her second cup of coffee, sitting on the living room couch, staring at the ginger cat, which had hopped onto Judith's favorite chair by the fireplace and was kneading the worn brown cushion while it rubbed itself against one arm, then the other.

When David rang the doorbell, she yelled "Come in" at the top of her voice. She'd been expecting him.

The cat stopped what it was doing and glared at her.

"Carpet looks good," David said, throwing his gloves in the corner, zipping off his rubber overshoes, shaking the freezing rain off his parka. "Bugger of a day out there," he added. "Is the coffee on?"

"How did it go?" Judith asked as she went to the kitchen to pour him a cup — black, no sugar.

"Fair, for an exhumation." He went to sit in the chair. The cat bounced gracefully onto the arm and curled up into a ball. "He's at the morgue now. Defrosting. We won't know a thing till late tonight, soonest."

"What about the gun?" Judith gave him his coffee.

"No doubt it has been fired recently, but Ballistics can't tell whether it fired the bullets that killed Singer. We didn't recover enough fragments to be sure. The trouble with bullets is they don't have too many distinguishing features. Besides, a Remington-Peters explodes on impact. They make a nasty mess of the victim."

"Would he have chosen that kind of bullet intentionally? Because he knew it disintegrates?"

"Possibly. More likely, though, because he didn't know better. Only a crass amateur would use a Remington-Peters inside his own car." David warmed his hands on the cup before drinking. It was

214

only then that he turned to look at the cat. "Where did she come from?"

"That's Zoë," Anne replied. She had wandered into the living room. "She's Jimmy's Christmas present from Dad. He promised to get me a big orange parrot for my next birthday — if my marks stay good. You guys talking about another murder?" She was pulling on her lightweight, everybody-has-one, Stollery's woolen coat with only two buttons.

"I sure hope so," said David, thinking of Yan's accurate assessment of his future if he was wrong.

"I put her food out on the counter," Anne told her mother. "It's Whiskers for growing cats. Has all the requisite vitamins and minerals, not like the cheap commercial stuff. Dad left a few tins for her. When we run out, we can get some more from the vet."

"No doubt," Judith said gloomily. "They're likely twice what the other cat food costs, and you hadn't mentioned the bit about the parrot last night."

"Probably won't keep my marks up this term anyway," said Anne. "So why get your hopes up?" She was already at the door, her knapsack flung over her shoulder bulging with books. "See you around 5?"

"Right," Judith shouted. "But there'll be no parrot. Not if you get straight As in every subject. No goddam parrot. I've got this cat to contend with and that's more than enough wildlife in this house, you hear me?" She'd jumped up from the couch and was glowering at her daughter with her best authoritative frown. "The cat's enough."

Anne gave her the brightest of smiles. "So we get to keep Zoë," she said. "Thanks, Mom. See you," she dashed out the door, letting in another gust of wind and snow.

David laughed. "I do believe you've just been had."

"Typical of that bastard to give them a cat," Judith fumed, "knowing I'd have to care for it as long as it's alive. Never thinking how I might prefer to spend my time. Shit. If I go to Eger, I'll have to cajole Mother into taking the kids for a few days, but I sure can't talk her into taking on a blasted cat as well. He knows I have to work for a living. Couldn't keep a cat on what he pays me, let alone the three of us..." She stomped into the kitchen.

Zoë sat on the counter next to her extra-special cat food. She seemed to be looking at it with disgust.

"I could take her, if you like," David suggested. "I like cats. They have an independent streak. And they don't fuss if you're late." When he saw his little joke wasn't working, he joined her in the kitchen and offered to make scrambled eggs for two while she told him about Paris, and everything she could remember about Arthur.

"So you think Ligeti knows what you're likely to discover in Hungary?" David asked when Judith had finished her story.

"I can't imagine them giving me the tickets unless they at least have a damn good guess." She snapped her notebook shut. "And whatever it is, I think it will let Arthur off the hook. No matter what Eva Zimmerman felt about her ex-husband, and I'm still fuzzy on that subject, she's not going to point a finger at her son. Guilt, you know. Whoever she thinks killed Paul, she's not betting on Arthur."

"One piece of her advice I will take, "said David, "is about going to see the rabbi. Rabbis often know more than they want to tell a strange woman who attaches herself to them while they're trying to walk home from a funeral."

He phoned Rabbi Jonas, who was at his Bathurst Street office all morning and happy to interrupt the paperwork for the brief call David promised to make.

"Your scrambled eggs get better all the time," Judith said when she saw him out.

"I know," David admitted modestly. "If I could keep this up, you might change your mind and marry me after all. Are you sure you want to go to Hungary?" he asked.

"Fairly sure. Giles's blessing won't be hard to get. The airfare's thrown in and it might lead to one of those illuminating sidebars he's devoted to, a cute one with a brief description of the tiny town that spawned this giant of industry..."

"Sure talked *me* into it," David said.

THIRTY-TWO

The main door to Beth Elohim was open, but there was no one in sight. The blue marble-tiled foyer stretched in a semicircle. At one end of the half-moon there was a wide marble staircase leading up to a corridor with a series of black doors. The one marked RABBI JONAS was open. David knocked anyway. The outer office was empty except for a desk, three black chairs, a typewriter, and a giant fern that bent over when it reached the ceiling. Rabbi Jonas emerged from the inner office. He was a slight man, around 50, with sparse hair, a hand-tied bow tie, striped shirt with white collar, and granny glasses. Definitely not David's idea of a rabbi.

"You are Detective Inspector Parr?" he asked, squinting at David uncertainly. Obviously, David wasn't his idea of a policeman.

"Rabbi Jonas?" David shook his proffered hand. The rabbi had a mean grip for such a slight man.

"I suppose you're much too important to wear a uniform. The highest-ranking chap I ever met in your line of work was a staff sergeant. He still wore uniform." He showed David into his office, which was much like the outer office, except for the typewriter. "Make yourself comfortable," he suggested. He sat next to David, on one of the two low-slung chairs facing his own desk, and looked at him expectantly. "So, what do you have to tell me about Paul Zimmerman?"

David told him about the XJ-S, what he knew about Singer, and his reasons for exhuming Zimmerman's body. The rabbi kept nodding throughout. "You don't seem very surprised," said David.

"On the contrary, I'm always surprised when bad things happen to good people. It's my job to remain surprised. If you grow to expect the bad things, you become too much of a misanthrope to serve God. Don't you think?"

"I suppose so," David agreed after a moment's thought.

217

"So what can I do for you?"

"I'm not sure," David admitted. "All I know is you were a friend of the family. You were often in the Zimmermans' company. Did he ever confide something in you that set off trouble signals? Did you ever imagine Paul Zimmerman was being threatened? That, particularly in the last two months, some kind of cloud had settled on him?"

"Not exactly," Jonas said. "He never even told me he was dying of heart disease, or that he wished to try another religion — though he did. Yet I saw him and Brenda on the 14th when we kicked off a fund-raising drive for a new university in Israel. There was no indication of change in Paul."

"Did he talk to you about Arthur?"

"Arthur? Sure. But not recently. He used to worry about Arthur's unusual choice of sexual partners, but I think he had become accustomed to that long ago. Not that they were ever going to be close." He stared at David for a moment, as if trying to read his mind. "You're not suspecting Arthur Zimmerman of murder, are you?"

"I don't think we have any particular suspects yet," David lied. He had several.

"There was bad blood between Arthur and his father, I know, but not bad enough to suspect Arthur. I've known him since he was a boy. A gentle soul, quiet, brooding. Eva Zimmerman had once spoken to me about Paul beating the boy. I think that's why she left Paul, in the end."

"And *did* he beat him?"

Jonas nodded sadly. "Yes. I've never understood why some people beat their children. I asked Paul about it, after Eva told me. It was the least I could do for her and the boy. And it wasn't enough."

"What did he say?"

Jonas held up his hands to indicate his helplessness. "He said his own father believed in not sparing the rod. And that Arthur reminded him too much of himself: the same rebellious nature, the covetousness, the envy of others, the inability to face reality... all that, plus the boy was a spitting image of how *he* had looked as a child."

"Is that an explanation?"

"In a way. I believe he was telling me he hated himself as a child, hated the boy he had once been. It wasn't Arthur he was hitting, it was the young Paul, who had envied a friend his good fortune so much he robbed him of his bicycle. He told me a story of how he had longed for a friend's bike once. He had been prepared to kill to get it."

"And did he?" David was thinking of the small black-and-white photograph: the two boys with their arms around each other's shoulders, the image that was to bring back memories for Paul Zimmerman, as it had for Harvey Singer. "*I hope your nights are long.*" Neither man had too many nights left after the arrival of that letter.

"That hadn't occurred to me. They were only kids." Jonas stood up and walked to his window overlooking drab sandstone buildings on Bathurst Street. "There was something he once said. I haven't really thought of it since. But at the time it bothered me. He asked if there were any circumstances when taking a human life was condoned in the Torah. God, he said, did quite a lot of smiting of His own in the old days, as did the Jews, in His name, or to protect His people."

"When did he ask you about this?"

"A long time ago. Let's see... A fund-raising drive for the Appeal. Maybe '55, '56. He cornered me with this stuff, and I was rather impatient with him. After all, we weren't there to engage in Talmudic discussion. I was busy. There were over three hundred people to speak to. At the time, I thought he was talking about Israel, asking me to justify Israel's defense of itself against its neighbors and the Palestinians who have sworn to wipe it out. It's a question I'm often asked, and it makes me angry."

"What did you tell him?"

He shrugged. "I don't recall exactly. I think I told him that everyone is entitled to his life, and to defend it if threatened. One is not, contrary to the American constitution, entitled to the pursuit of liberty or happiness at the expense of others. That's a latter-day concept. But we are, I think, entitled to life."

"Did he ever ask you such questions again?"

"No."

"Did Paul Zimmerman also beat his daughter?" David asked, trying another tack.

"No," Jonas said with absolute certainty. "I've known Meredith since she was born. She doted on her father and, as far as anyone could see, he doted on her. Paul was a busy man. Didn't have a lot of time for his family, but when they were together, you could tell he would never raise a hand to her."

"Isn't that odd?"

"Why?"

"Your average child-beater doesn't usually distinguish between his children. He beats them all." David was remembering all the times he had had to save children from their parents, before they killed them, and deliver them, screaming, to Children's Aid. And how often he was called by the same neighbors, back to the same homes, over and over, till he no longer ached for the children, he had become numb, as the older guys on the force had predicted.

With Homicide, he saw the kids only when it was already too late to help them.

"Paul Zimmerman wasn't very average, and maybe my theory is right. I've not had much experience with child-beating," Jonas said. "Jews, generally, love their children too much to hit them, but I've had some experience in understanding people." He went to sit behind his desk, putting distance between himself and the cop, then leaned back with a sigh. "Especially my people. And Paul Zimmerman was one of them."

It was 11 A.M. Arthur would have been delivered to his office by now. David thanked the rabbi for his time and headed across town to Yonge Street.

The slush had frozen into a solid black mass since this morning, making the road precarious and slow, as people piled up behind the snow removers and salt-spraying machines. This time of year, he thought, it was astonishing that people would live in Toronto by choice.

Arthur was sitting on the same plastic chair Deidre had occupied yesterday. His fur-lined green leather coat was on the seat beside him, as was his matching green traveling case. He smoked a long black cigarette, amusing himself by trying to blow smoke rings. David was struck by Arthur's strong resemblance to Paul Zimmerman and, as well, by the trouble he had taken to appear flagrantly different. He wore an all-white suit with a green cravat, and green zip-up leather boots. His blond hair was sculpted into a high tuft with mousse.

When David introduced himself, Arthur looked up with a bored, tired expression. He did not offer to shake hands.

"You're the pleasant chap who invited me up here for a last peek at the body?"

"I'm sorry about the inconvenience," said David, stiffly. "Identifying the body is a formality one can't avoid in these cases."

"By 'these cases,' I take it you mean where 'foul play' is suspected. Right?" with one transparent eyebrow raised. "That's the cute little phrase you use, isn't it? 'Foul play'? Straight out of *Hamlet* and all."

"Exactly," David said. "I'll try to make it as brief as I can." For both our sakes, he thought. "Only a few questions. There is a restaurant nearby, somewhat brighter than this place, if you prefer."

"How charming. Standard procedure?"

"I suppose." David was determined to be as good-humored as possible. After all, the guy had just seen his father's frozen face and would undoubtedly prefer as a sequel any one of a dozen activities to being questioned by a policeman.

Neither spoke while they struggled across the slippery street through the traffic. David paid for his black coffee and Arthur's cappuccino and blueberry muffin, and they settled into one of the orange booths by the window. David tried a throwaway remark about the weather, but Arthur wouldn't play.

"Why don't we get on with it?" he asked, spooning the cinnamon off his cappuccino.

"Fine. Harvey Singer came to see you in late December last year. Let's start with what Mr. Singer told you that day."

"Why?" Arthur asked, with what appeared to be genuine surprise.

"Because Mr. Singer was murdered on February 26th in your father's red XJ-S, which I understand you were rather fond of driving when you were in Toronto. So let's talk about your *first* meeting with Mr. Singer. That *was* your first meeting?"

"Whoa, now, Inspector — "

"Detective Inspector," said David.

"Now, you're not about to suggest, my dear Detective Inspector, that I bumped off that poor sod Singer, are you?"

"Did you?"

"Shit, you can do better than that. I'm not the only person who drove that little car, and there are others, at least one other person we can both agree on, who had more reason to wish him dead than I did. Or haven't you figured that out yet?" When he picked up his cup, he held his little finger up and apart from the others, displaying a diamond-studded gold pinkie ring.

"He did come to see you," David insisted.

Arthur heaved a deep, theatrical sigh. "Of course he came to see me. I've no intention of denying *that* — since you've already worked it out for yourself."

"Why?"

"He said he had known my father back in Hungary. He got the address from the telephone book, for heaven's sake, and just materialized at the door one evening. If I'd known he was some acquaintance of my father, I wouldn't have agreed to see him. But he didn't call, he just came. The book lists me as P.A. Zimmerman, you see. My initials."

He watched David expectantly. "Don't you want to know what the *P* stands for?" he asked at last.

"Not particularly," David said.

"Stands for Polgár. Some obscure Hungarian village my mother's family came from. Nice name for a boy. So there he was in his hat and coat, with some gift from the old country. I had no choice but to let him in. He told me he and my old man had grown up together. He had some photos to show me. That sort of stuff. Then he left." Arthur started to dig into his muffin with so much relish that David began to think he either was a consummate actor or had an ironclad alibi for the night of February 26th.

"No. I don't think so," said David. "That's not the way it went. He told you something about your father you didn't know before, something you thought might be worth remembering." He was guessing, but if Singer didn't get the money from Paul Zimmerman, it would be a fair guess Arthur had. His own mother had virtually told Judith the guy was adept at blackmailing his father.

"That's where you're wrong, Detective Inspector," Arthur said. "Sure Singer had something to say, but he wasn't about to tell *me*. Whatever it was came to his mind when he saw me. He was saving the telling part for my father."

"Why don't you begin at the beginning, Mr. Zimmerman. Starting with the moment you opened the door to Mr. Singer..."

Arthur ordered another cappuccino and a Danish pastry. He complimented the waitress on the cuisine. Then he smiled wearily at David. "Have it your way," he said. "Singer — Harvey, you said? — arrived on our doorstep exactly as I told you. Don't ask me to remember the exact date, but there he was in a dreadfully old-worldy coat and hat with — would you believe — feathers. My dear, *they* went out with lederhosen after the First World War. At first I thought he was selling something, he carried a box of some sort and a briefcase. So I told him we didn't want any, whatever it was, chances are we already had some. But he just sort of stood there, staring at me as though he'd seen a ghost. Then he said 'Zimmerman Pál,' which is Hungarian for Paul Zimmerman — they get people's names backwards. I knew that, because I'd picked up some of the stupid language as a kid. God knows I tried not to, but it sort of seeped in. I told him no, I wasn't Paul Zimmerman, and he got rather hysterical at that, though why the hell he should was beyond me. *I'm* the one should get hysterical every time someone tells me how much I look like the old buzzard.

"Then he carried on about someone called Feri in Eger, and a whole lot of other Zimmermans, I couldn't quite make it out, so I told him I didn't speak Hungarian and that I was Arthur. I spelled it for him. A-R-T-H-U-R. And I admitted, much against my better judgment, to being the son of the aforementioned. This guy Singer was crying and shaking still, so I asked him in. Actually, I more or less carried him in. What else could I do? He was in such a state, he could barely walk, the poor old sod. I stuck him on the couch and got him a brandy. We're only *human*, you know."

"I know," David said. Why did Arthur feel he had to overact? Was he pushing for some major homophobic explosion from David? Because if so, he was in for a long wait.

"Then he told me he'd known my father. They practically grew up together, though I gathered they weren't exactly friends. And he showed me some stuff he'd brought in the small box he carried. Photographs of boys playing together. And there was a silver-colored yarmulke, and a book with ZIMMERMAN PÁL on it, in block letters, like a kid's writing, and an oval locket, it was old-fashioned silver. Inside was a photograph of a little girl. She had dark hair in ringlets with a big white ribbon. I remember it well, because he told me her name was Meredith. I thought, that's nice, because my half-sister's name is Meredith, too, and I told him that. Then he cried some more." Arthur dabbed at his mouth with the napkin.

"Did you ask him why he was crying?"

"What do you think? Of course I did. But all he'd say was that seeing me brought back memories. And he asked a bunch of questions, mostly about my father."

"What sort of questions?"

"Like where he lived, who my mother was, and about Meredith and Brenda. I was getting pretty impatient with the old bugger by then, because I'd just as soon not spend my time gabbing about my dear old pa — you may have gathered by now he's hardly my personal valentine. So I told him I was busy, but he kept on with the damn questions, like where did we live when I was young, and what did we do for recreation. That kind of shit. So I told him about the blasted butterflies and asked him to get the hell out and chase my father if that's who his fond memories were of, because my memories weren't all that fond. So he left."

"He didn't tell you anything else?"

"No. I figured there was something else he might have told me had I stayed quiet and listened. But I don't know what it was." Arthur spooned the sugar out of the bottom of his cup.

David shook his head. "What then, Mr. Zimmerman, was the $100,000 for?"

"The $100,000?"

"$50,000 on January 7th, and another $50,000 on..."

"How did you know about that?" Arthur was dismayed, but not insulted. "Brenda?" he asked. When David didn't reply, he ordered a small brandy, then told him, drink in hand, that at an obligatory family get-together he'd mentioned Singer's visit to his father. Paul had taken the news so badly, Arthur thought he was going to have a heart attack then and there. He'd turned pale. He shook. His first question was whether Arthur had already told Brenda. He hadn't, because he didn't have anything to say. But Paul didn't know that. So Arthur took advantage of the situation and asked what his keeping silent might be worth to his father.

"Right then and there he suggested he would change his will. You could have knocked me down with a feather," Arthur said. "So when I got back to New York, I figured Singer must really have something hot. I wrote my father a letter and asked him for a bit of extra moolah just to tide me over — you know, till he died." Arthur laughed. "Next thing I know, he sent me fifty thou in cash. By courier. Bingo. Just like that."

"And the second fifty?"

"The first lot had gone so smoothly, I thought there might be more where that came from, so I wrote him again..."

"When was that?"

"Late January, because Jeremy and I were planning a trip to Jamaica for February. Lousy time to be in New York."

"And he sent you another fifty?"

"Like magic."

"And then what happened?"

"He changed his mind about the whole deal, will and all. Or so I'm told. He had Masters go back to the original version, and when I called for a bit of financial assistance to get me through March, he told me there wouldn't be any more."

"When was that?"

"I really don't recall. Mid-February, or thereabouts. I didn't keep notes, and didn't jot it down in my diary. Why would I? I didn't know Singer was going to get himself murdered and I'd have to answer all these dumb questions." Arthur hadn't mellowed much with the brandy.

"All that remains, then, is for you to tell me where you were the night of February 26th," David said.

"Certainly, Detective Inspector. My pleasure. I was at Ocho Rios in Jamaica and you can find at least two dozen lovely people — there's no accounting for tastes, is there? — including some straight hotel staff, who'll swear to that."

Back in Homicide there was a message from Martelli. Melwyn Singer had finally received word from his mother.

"Do you want me to read it to you?" Martelli asked David.

"Please."

"I'll spare you the most touching parts. Real mush, but I'm afraid she means it. Sort of stuff my mother might have written had she been able to write. Real old-fashioned materfamilias. Then she says: 'I'm sorry I had to leave in such a hurry. You know I wouldn't have gone if there wasn't something to force me. I'd never leave you and my grandchildren. You are my life. The Nazis threatened me. There was a letter written in blood on the front seat of my car. It said if I didn't pack myself off to some faraway place within 24 hours, they would exterminate me and my family. It said there were still too many Jews in the world, but they were doing whatever they could about it. There was a lock of hair with the letter. It looked like your Dad's...' She then goes on to urge him and his wife to join her in Israel, where they could at least live with their own people."

"So now we know why she left in such a hurry," David said.

"Sounds like the same lot that putzed up your girlfriend's house," Martelli said.

THIRTY-THREE

"There is no question about Zimmerman's heart. He was a very ill man. The pathologist's report confirms Doctor Meisner's diagnosis: idiopathic hypertrophic subaortic stenosis. Symptoms include heavy breathing on exertion, angina pains, dizziness. The radiologic findings indicate a left ventricular enlargement. The course of the disease would be variable, most likely slowly progressive, but could just as easily cause sudden death." Dr. Yan took a deep breath. "Particularly when inherited," he concluded.

"And how do you translate that for an ordinary citizen?" David asked. He was exhausted. There had been the interview with Arthur. His Chief had had a harrowing phone call from Brenda, declaiming that her husband's exhumation had been an act of blasphemy; David had then spent a nasty half-hour with the Chief justifying the veracity of his sources, without either of them letting on that they both knew the main source was Judith Hayes. There had been a confrontation with Philip Masters who had found some obscure law covering unjustified harassment of the bereaved by investigating officers. There had been a tearful call from Deidre about Masters threatening her with removal from the will if his suspicions proved right about her giving confidential information to a policeman. Finally, PC Stewart had appeared with a balding man of indeterminate age who had been put in weekly contact with his dead wife by Madame Cielo, all for a mere $600 per session, $50 more than his monthly trucker's pension, and more than he could scrounge from friends. He admitted he had discovered Madame was a phony, but felt too embarrassed to complain. Stewart was certain he was the killer, but had no concrete evidence.

"You're hardly the ordinary citizen, Parr," Yan replied. "And that report shouldn't require a translation. Zimmerman had an inherited form of heart disease that can, and often does, cause sudden death.

227

There is a swelling in the dividing wall between the two ventricles, which obstructs the flow of blood and, eventually, chokes up the system. It's unpredictable as to timing, but a relatively quick and easy way to go." Yan lit another Camel, breathed in deeply and leaned his head back against the orange padding of his chair. He had been up close to 20 hours, as had Parr, but the lack of sleep was taking a more obvious toll on him. His skin was dry, stretched, parchmentlike, and there were loose brown pouches under his half-closed eyes. He watched David, waiting for his reaction.

In the silence they could hear the hot water pipes clanging as the building cooled for the night.

"Did they do a complete autopsy?" David wished he'd brought along the mickey of Scotch from the apartment. Looked like he was going to need it.

"Yes, indeedy," Yan said, dragging out the words. "Wasn't easy, with the poor bugger frozen, but there are newfangled ways of quickly defrosting. I'd be glad to tell you about them, if you want to hear..."

"It's okay, thanks all the same." David rested his head on his hands, his elbows on his knees. He noticed his scalp was damp with perspiration, as was his forehead. It would be good to take a long walk to the subway and leave the damn car behind. He'd need to think about what he would say to the Chief tomorrow.

"They did their best cutting him up, minimal disfigurement, and all that. The relatives might want the fluids pumped back in, what do you think?"

"You mean, embalm him again?" David peered through his fingers at Yan. He was beginning to notice, despite his tiredness, that an unusual tone of jocularity had crept into Yan's voice — a cheerfulness that was both unlike him and ill suited to the news that Zimmerman had died of a heart attack.

"Well, that will probably be their choice. I, personally, wouldn't do it to a dog, but then, as you know, I don't believe in these barbaric burial customs," Yan prattled on gaily, still gazing at David through hooded eyes.

"I know." It occurred to David that the coroner was enjoying himself. What could he find to smirk about in this unpleasant ending to one of their longest days?

"We may not want to release the body to them until the day

after tomorrow, though," Yan said cheerfully. "We have a few more tissue samples to get back from Toxicology, hair samples..."

"Why Toxicology, if he died of whatever kind of obstruction in his heart?"

"Oh, that." Yan beamed openly now. "You mean his idiopathic hypertrophic subaortic stenosis? He didn't die of *that*. My goodness, I hope I didn't give you the wrong impression. He *could* have died of that, as easy as this..." He clicked his fingers, not very successfully. "But he didn't. What he died of was something far simpler, easily understood even by an ordinary man: a dash of potassium cyanide, otherwise known as rat poison, and readily available at your ordinary drugstore. He was poisoned."

"Son of a bitch," David yelled at the ceiling, as he leaped to his feet. His first impulse was to hug the coroner, but when he saw the smile on his face, he almost slugged him. He got a couple of plastic cups full of water from the water fountain, and walked around the office, slurping, with a grin to match the coroner's.

"I knew it. I knew it," David lied, pulling his jacket on. He could finally get home. "Can I drive you somewhere?" he asked, feeling suddenly energetic.

"I think I'll finish going through the pathologists' reports, and the tests from Forensics. I'll have it all ready and typed for you tomorrow — but I might take the day off. There's a place up north my cousin wants me to try for ice-fishing. It'll be mild and sunny. Near Parry Sound. Clears the fog out of my head."

THIRTY-FOUR

There had been 16 people at the Zimmermans' lavish March dinner party. That meant at least 15 possible suspects.

The seating, as usual, had been arranged personally by Mrs. Zimmerman. Giannini discovered from Arnold that Brenda liked to design the place cards herself. While he no longer had them — "Why, sir, would we have saved them?" — he was certain she had placed them at the head of each plate before the guests arrived.

The waiters hired by Ferndale Catering Services confirmed they had seen Mrs. Zimmerman put the cards in place.

Two tables had been lined up parallel, Brenda presiding at the foot of one table, Paul at the head of the other. Judith Hayes had sat on Paul's right, Jane Masters on his left.

David was sure he could eliminate Judith from the list of potential killers, but he wasn't sure about Jane.

On the surface, Jane Masters was a pillar of feminine society, member of numerous volunteer boards, government-appointed committees, and fund-raising drives for artsy causes. She was widely regarded as the power behind her husband's charitable purse strings and a steady influence on Paul Zimmerman's own choice of patronage.

She was tall and slender, with a regal bearing that would have taken a lifetime to develop. She received him in the spacious anteroom of her immodest Bridle Path mansion, as if he had come to measure the floors for a new carpet rather than to question her about a murder.

She remembered the evening of March 1st as a pleasant gathering of friends, hopelessly marred by Zimmerman's death. She had not been informed of his heart troubles, but then she wouldn't have expected to be informed. She had gone from the living room directly to the dining room and hadn't left her seat until Zimmerman died. She had noticed he was drinking out of three separate glasses, two for the white and red wines, one that contained an amber liquid she thought could have been ginger ale.

Needless to say, all the glasses had been emptied, washed, and put away long ago. The cook was still in Bermuda with Brenda, but Arnold and the waiters were certain none of the guests had entered the kitchen before or during the first two courses. It would have been most unusual for them to do so.

Jane Masters offered no references to her husband's rift with Zimmerman. She said she hadn't been told of the parting of ways between them, nor did she seem offended that Masters hadn't confided in her. It was his business. Whether he had quit or had been relieved of his duties was of no interest to her.

She had no notion of anyone carrying a grudge against Paul, at any rate no one who would want to murder him.

Staff Sergeant Graham called on the Zimmermans' cook, Mrs. Stoner. She was a cheerful, overweight woman from Jamaica whose nine children had all stayed behind in Kingston. Although she frequently sent them money for "little extras," she was fairly proud that they had made their own way. The youngest was 20 and married, with children of her own. Mrs. Stoner had been with the Zimmermans since '78, came with letters of recommendation from the Kingston Hilton.

"Herself a most unlikely suspect," concluded Graham, "and too busy the night of the party to notice much outside her immediate priorities, preparing a complicated menu."

No one came into the kitchen, except the waiters and the hostess, for a last-minute check. The sole observation of an unusual nature that Mrs. Stoner had to contribute was that Martha Griffiths had tears in her eyes when she came out of the downstairs bathroom across from the kitchen doors.

Rabbi Jonas had sat next to Jane Masters. For now, David had no further questions for him. Mrs. Jonas had been in England, visiting family; she could not return for the party.

Martha Griffiths had sat between the rabbi and Adrian Parker. David went to see her at her club, where, according to Jane Masters, she spent Wednesday mornings. He waited in the lounge while they took a message to her in the swimming pool.

When Martha emerged from the elevator, David immediately understood why Zimmerman would have risked Brenda's wrath. She was much more beautiful than anyone would have guessed from the small photograph in Paul's pocket. (*Forever and ever. Your Martha.*) She was almost willowy with long fragile arms, frail childlike wrists, rich olive skin, her wet red hair curling around her shoulders in thick rivulets. An embarrassed smile lingered on her face as she held her terry-cloth robe together, hiding her lanky bare legs. When she said hello, her lower lip trembled.

David told her why he was there and she began to cry softly. She said she really didn't understand — and David believed her. Murder, sometimes even for the perpetrator, was difficult to understand.

She admitted readily she had fallen in love with Zimmerman. He was the most attentive man she had ever met. He sent her flowers, small gifts from Birks, he'd call every day even when he was out of town. She was sure he had loved her. He might have left Brenda, had he lived. She wasn't going to deny her plans included leaving Chuck Griffiths.

There had been a lot of talk. "You know how it is," she said, gazing soulfully into Parr's eyes, or for a moment he fancied that she had. "We live in a world where not much of consequence ever happens. People like to gossip." She curled up in one of the ocher-colored chairs and tucked her legs under her. The terry-cloth robe opened slightly, revealing a flash of olive thigh.

"Mr. Griffiths must have been quite upset."

"No," Martha said with a sigh. "For quite a while I don't think he took it seriously. He's been rather busy with Loyal for the past four years. When Chuck went there from the law firm, it was a lazy gentlemen's club. Paul wanted him to bring it into the 21st century. Chuck's really good at that. And he still had the properties to manage..."

"When did he start taking it seriously?"

"About a week ago." Martha smiled mysteriously. "I moved out of the house. I doubt if Chuck realized I would, after Paul died. He thought it was a passing romantic impulse. And Paul, as you'll have heard, had quite a reputation for romantic interludes, no-account affairs, you know..."

David nodded wisely. Like Deidre Thomas, for example, but when he asked Martha about Deidre, he felt terribly uncomfortable — and somehow disloyal.

"Exactly," Martha said. "Deidre was another of his casual

affairs. Paul was a man with a lot of libido. I had no problem with that. Once we were married, all that would have changed."

"How did Mrs. Zimmerman take it?"

"Brenda?" Martha brushed the wet hair from her face with a nervous movement. "As you would expect."

"Did Mr. Zimmerman inform her of his intention to marry you?"

She didn't reply, she just sighed. She was gazing at the maroon floor.

"Did he?" David persisted, he thought, boorishly.

"Not in so many words, I don't think. But I think he was going to do it the night he died. He told us all when he invited us to his house that he had an announcement to make."

"So you don't think he told her the night of February 26th?"

"Why February 26th?" Martha seemed surprised.

"That was the evening they went to your place for dinner. Brenda left early."

"Such a dreadful evening." Martha sighed. "Chuck had a few things to go over with Paul about the reorganization of a financial corporation Loyal had just bought. That's all they talked about, the four of them: Paul, Chuck, Adrian Parker, and Jack Goodman. The women were bored out of their minds. I think that's why Brenda left early. She has a low boredom threshold. A bit spoiled, you know. Franny, Alice, and I didn't interfere. We made conversation on the side."

"Do you remember what time Paul Zimmerman left?"

"Not exactly." Tears had formed into droplets on her cheeks. "Seems so long ago now," she whispered. "I can't imagine Paul dead yet. I haven't...I can't...think about it...And now you say he was murdered...I...I...that someone would..." She excused herself and fluttered out of the room, drawing her robe tightly around her hips.

David waited for several minutes, with what seemed even to him to be astounding patience. He reread his notes, reviewed the lengthening list of potential murderers. Then a barefoot woman in black form-fitting exercise pants and multicolored headband informed him that Mrs. Griffiths was too indisposed to continue the interview now. If he had further questions, she could be reached at the Goodmans'.

Susanne Bonnier had sat next to Adrian Parker, facing Martha Griffiths. She and her husband Eddie lived in Mississauga near the lake. It was a sprawling ranch-like house on several levels. The garden swept down to the lake in several formal terraced layers. It must be beautiful in summer, Parr thought.

Mrs. Bonnier was a large, buoyant woman with a cheerful manner and an almost infectious affection for her husband. He was sole owner of Bonnier and Prinz, textile manufacturers, having bought Prinz out. He was about the same shape as his wife; a well-matched pair.

They were both there when Parr came to call.

"I figured sooner or later you'd want to see me anyhow, so why not get us both over with all at once?" Eddie Bonnier told Parr. "We were at the same party. She sat at Paul's table, I sat next to Brenda. Shocking about poor Paul. Bad enough when he died, but then we find out it wasn't of natural causes, as they say. Now who'd have wanted to murder *him*, I ask myself. Right, Susanne?" He wore a sport shirt and corduroy trousers that bagged around the knees.

"Can I get you something to eat, Officer?" Susanne asked Parr. "A little strudel? Perhaps some lemon pie? I made it myself..."

"Thank you, Mrs. Bonnier, perhaps some pie," David asked. He hadn't eaten since yesterday afternoon and his stomach was starting to make rattling noises. Even if the Bonniers had poisoned Zimmerman, which he was sure they hadn't, they were unlikely to take a run at a police officer on duty.

The pie was delicious.

The Bonniers had been friends of the Zimmermans since the early '60s. They met him first at a fund-raising for some cause neither of them could recall now. Susanne had become very fond of Brenda. The two of them enjoyed shopping together, went on golfing trips to Florida, once to the Azores, frequently to the Zimmermans' Bermuda house, to New York. They liked each other's company.

"She is a super girl," Susanne gushed. "Must be simply awful for her with this investigation and all. She was upset enough that Paul was — " she hesitated, then went on genteelly, "no longer with us. She has been frightfully upset about the...whatever it is you've done, Officer? Digging up, you know. I suppose it was necessary, it turns out, because if you hadn't you wouldn't know he was murdered, now, would you? And that's what I told her when she called. But I do think I ought to go spend a few days with her, if Eddie doesn't mind too terribly much." She patted his hand as it rested on the couch between them.

"She'll be right lonely, I think," Eddie said, and asked how they could be of help to the law.

He remembered they had been asked to the party late Friday night, must have been the 27th of February. They had been out at another dinner, came home late, and there was an urgent message from Brenda: Paul wanted them to come for some big occasion he was planning for the following Sunday night.

The Bonniers had made other plans for the evening of March 1st. Susanne didn't mind telling Parr that she wished they hadn't allowed themselves to be bullied into going to the Zimmermans'. She'd never forget the scene of Paul's head in the plate, with the blood oozing about — she'd never eat Beef Wellington again and that was for sure.

"What do you mean, bullied into it?" David asked.

"Ah well, one doesn't wish to speak ill of the dead, but it was a bit like that with Paul, once he made up his mind what he wanted no one could gainsay him. He was used to getting his own way. 'A latter-day Caesar' is what Philip Masters called him — all in good humor, mind you, all in very good humor." From time to time, as she spoke, she glanced at her husband for support or encouragement and got it. "He said that whatever the other thing was it would have to wait, we must cancel it. *His* dinner would not wait. It was the most important occasion in his life in four decades and he wanted us to be there. When Eddie protested, he said it was a matter of life and death."

"And it was...," Eddie said sadly.

"You don't think it was suicide?" Susanne asked. "I'm thinking about the way Paul insisted we all show up for this. Perhaps he wanted some company for his passing. Didn't that sort of stuff use to be fashionable in Roman times? People would invite all their friends and serve a buffet and lots of entertainment, then somewhere in the middle they'd drink some kind of lethal potion or get an asp..."

"Come on, Suse, that's silly," Eddie opined, but Parr could see he was thinking about it.

The only person they remembered leaving the table was Jack Goodman, no doubt on his way to the bathroom.

Jack Goodman had sat between Judith Hayes and Susanne Bonnier. Goodman ran Domcor, one of Zimmerman's longest-held companies, constant star in the *Fortune* Top 500. He'd been in the business pages three weeks ago buying some big communications conglomerate in Chicago. Some wit at *Business Week* had asked him whether he'd now take up raiding. David couldn't remember his answer. *Business Week* also inquired if he was next in line to run Monarch itself. Goodman had said he was very happy with Domcor. Not a bad answer, but it begged the question.

Goodman had moved his corporate headquarters from New York to Chicago in the wake of the Zimmerman takeover in 1986, but he maintained a small pied-à-terre in Toronto, in deference to Zimmerman's habit of holding corporate meetings of the group in the Monarch Building's boardroom. Goodman himself was New York born and bred, a relative upstart from ITT, where he had risen from the obscurity of the sales department to marketing director in seven brief months, then to president in seven more.

All that, David had read in Judith's voluminous notes on the Zimmerman holdings and its stars. Half or more of Judith's notes were quite incomprehensible to him, for which he was profoundly grateful. There was no sense in developing a head for business terminology at such a late stage of one's development.

The Goodmans' pied-à-terre was a vast condominium atop Zimmerman's harborside development — almost adjacent to Domcor's branch offices. They were in Toronto for the weekend anyway, Saturday being the night of the Brazilian Ball.

They were both in their late 50s, tanned, nervously energetic, sporty-looking. Both wore tailored slacks, soft woolen jackets, and topsiders.

They received David in the sunken living room, whose long horizontal lines along the walls in contrasting aquamarine and blue proclaimed a sense of happy, expensive design.

Neither Goodman had ever heard of Harvey Singer. They found it difficult to believe that Masters and Zimmerman would have gotten into a serious fight, since the two of them were so close.

Martha Griffiths was living in their designer apartment — what are friends for? The Goodmans were very emphatic in their belief that Martha and Chuck were going to get back together again.

"They had been in difficulties before, you see," Alice said. "Paul was merely in the right place at the right time. Martha needed a boost to her pride, some warm, loving relationship to restore her self-confidence." She gave her own husband a long flat look, then busied herself with rearranging the glass flowers on the big square table.

Jack Goodman examined his polished nails and said nothing.

"A marriage needs nurturing," Alice continued. "You can't take it for granted, and I'm afraid Chuck's been too preoccupied with the business for the past few years. Isn't that right, darling?" She wasn't about to let Goodman off the hook.

"Mm-hmm," he said at last. "You're not actually suspecting Chuck, are you?" he asked Parr. "I wouldn't have thought he was the murderous kind — at least, not outside of a boardroom." He laughed loudly.

Alice didn't join in the fun. "Brenda's to pick Paul's successor, you know," she told David. "Since he never could choose between the two of them, she'll have to decide if it's Jack or Chuck."

Extensive questioning of the Ferndale Catering Service waiters revealed that they remembered little about the Zimmermans' dinner party — until the host's demise. Both had been at the Zimmerman home on previous occasions. Mrs. Zimmerman had made a point of asking for them by name, because they were familiar with the household already. The waiter assigned to Paul Zimmerman's table did not recall pouring him a glass of ginger ale, but he did say that Mr. Zimmerman had barely touched his wines that night; he had just drunk from his own glass, placed beside the others.

Neither waiter had a criminal record. One was a sociology student in the daytime, the other worked at the Hudson's Bay. They made extra money waitering.

The hors d'oeuvres for the cocktail reception had been supplied by Paul's Fine Foods.

Doctor Meisner hadn't been able to attend the dinner at the Zimmermans' on March 1st. He had been in Israel with his father whose health, at 85, was suddenly beginning to fail. Edna Meisner though, had gone that evening and sat between Philip Masters and Chuck Griffiths. Last week, she had followed her husband when he went back to Israel.

At first Father O'Shea was reluctant to see Judith, as he had been reluctant to see David. He had nothing to add to her story or to

David's investigation. He had barely known Paul Zimmerman. But when Judith expressed an interest in the 19th-century organ, he relented and agreed to spare her a few minutes in the church where she could see and photograph it for her readers.

The organ was on the balcony over the entrance, facing the altar. It was, indeed, something to behold. It had 60 bronze pipes, a massive ivory-inlaid keyboard, and a complicated series of pedals and levers, all contained in a carved oak frame that reached the full width of the balcony.

"It's quite an unusual piece," Father O'Shea told Judith. He was sitting on the organ's carved oak stool, running his hands affectionately over the keyboard. "It was originally built for the Roman Catholic Church in Dresden, around 1840. One of the first organs to provide the complete pedal board of two and a half octaves. The pneumatic lever was added later by Willis, an English builder. It's fortunate we got it before the Allies demolished the city; it would have been a great loss."

"Beautiful," Judith gushed. "Paul Zimmerman must have had a great interest in organs...?"

"Indeed he did. It's what brought us together." Father O'Shea didn't continue.

"How was it you met in the first place?" Judith tried.

"Last year at a meeting of Canadian Aid to Refugees. We were both directors, though Paul Zimmerman rarely had the time to come to meetings. But he was generous with his money. The aid program needs money more than meetings." He stopped patting the keys and faced Judith. He was a handsome man in his mid-50s, thin gray hair, pale complexion, his priest's collar incongruous above a fisherman-knit sweater and beige pants. "Now, what was it you wanted to know, Mrs. Hayes?"

"I was wondering when he decided to...donate the funds for the restoration." She was going to ask when Zimmerman became a Catholic but thought better of it. Too soon to get into that sensitive topic, which the good father had refused to talk about on the telephone.

"I've no idea. We only found out after he died. The church was named in the will. I first mentioned the organ to him after that refugee-aid meeting. Then he came by a few weeks ago to look at it."

"And when would that have been?"

"Let's see...It was soon after Candlemas..."

"January?"

"No. February 2nd, Candlemas. Around the 5th or 6th, I think. I showed him the organ and what kind of work it needed. We already had a master craftsman from London under contract to start the restoration. We were short a few thousand dollars. The Lord works in mysterious ways," he added with a smile.

"Is that when he converted, then?" Judith asked quickly.

"Converted?"

"To Catholicism."

"What makes you think he converted?" the priest asked.

"The funeral was here..."

Father O'Shea stood up. "I'm sorry, Mrs. Hayes, but I did warn you I had a prior engagement. We have run out of time." He offered to shake her hand before he descended the staircase.

"He *did* convert, didn't he, Father?" Judith insisted, following him down the steps.

"You're not a Catholic, are you, Mrs. Hayes?" Father O'Shea asked.

"No."

"In our faith, you see, some of the things said between a priest and another person remain confidential. One of the basic tenets of our religion. I do thank you for coming by." He left through the door to the sacristy.

Forensics reported that there were minuscule glass shards in the dust they had collected at Zimmerman's garage, and that they were of the same source as those the pathologist had dug out of Harvey Singer's chest.

At 7 P.M. on March 11, Michael Ward was picked up in Lethbridge, Alberta. He had $5,000 on him in cash and a social insurance card and driver's license that identified him as Peter Strachan from Vancouver.

They flew him back to Toronto and promised to go easy on him if he revealed where the money came from and what he had to do to get it.

David went one better than that: he told Ward on the way to police headquarters that he would go free, without an additional blemish on his record, if he told him who had paid him to throw the paint can into Judith Hayes's home.

At first Ward refused to cooperate.

Adrian Parker had sat next to Martha Griffiths that night. He had occupied the other end of the host's table, facing him. Parker was a senior partner at Ross, Wilkinson, the giant chartered accounting firm that had tentacles from London to New York, Paris, and Toronto. Parker himself was based in New York but traveled extensively. He was back in Toronto for the final probate of Paul Zimmerman's will, staying in the Royal Suite on the top floor of the Park Plaza, a tastefully furnished extravaganza with a grand piano, a peerless view over the chic parts of the city, all the way to Lake Ontario. He had been Paul Zimmerman's international adviser on new acquisitions — he was proud of having had a hand in all of them, most recently the difficult takeover of Pacific Airlines.

He was a square-shouldered man with a proud paunch, a round face, and a relaxed demeanor that imparted a sense of power. He had found nothing remarkable about either of the dinners, had never heard of Harvey Singer, could think of no reason why anyone would want to murder Paul Zimmerman.

He knew of the rift between Paul and Philip Masters, but didn't consider it detrimental. He thought Masters would settle happily into the Amco chairmanship and a Senate appointment.

He didn't believe that Zimmerman had actually fired Philip Masters. One doesn't just fire a man like Philip Masters, no sir. And as for the veiled allegation that Masters had used illegal means to amass his own considerable fortunes — well, let whoever made that statement come forward and say it to Masters's face.

He hadn't much to say about Martha Griffiths's affair with Paul Zimmerman, other than that Paul was fond of the ladies. Martha hadn't been the first, nor would she have been the last. She was pretty and willing... "You're a man of the world, aren't you, Officer?"

About the night of February 26th: "Chuck Griffiths had had a few difficulties transferring Smelter Financial to the Loyal. Lack of natural integration, management overload, that kind of stuff. Paul and I were giving him advice."

"Was there much tension between the Griffithses?"

"None, far as I could see. Chuck had more important matters to contend with."

"Didn't he care that his wife was sleeping with his boss?"

"Rather crudely put, Officer. But as a matter of fact, I don't believe Chuck gave it much heed. Martha can be a silly woman, she acts like a child. When she settles down, I figure she'll return to the warm hearth. She should have had children, that one. Knock some sense into her."

While Parker had no idea who'd killed Zimmerman, he was sure about one thing: it wasn't Chuck Griffiths. Chuck had too much to lose. There were unsecured mortgages on several properties he had acquired over the years and Paul had happily financed them because of other common interests. Chuck had turned Loyal into one of the best companies in the Zimmerman group; he had drive and imagination. With Paul gone, it was questionable whether anyone else would extend him the same privileges. Loyal, he thought, might be sold by Brenda. And she did not favor Chuck for the Monarch succession.

Paul hadn't briefed him on what announcement he was about to make the evening of March 1st. He had asked him to fly to Toronto for the occasion, and to bring Frances if he could. They had known Paul for over 20 years and that sort of request was a bit of a command performance. It had never occurred to them not to come. When he had pressed Paul about the nature of the announcement, he'd been told it was personal. He thought it might have something to do with Paul's past — an odd assumption, but he knew something had been bothering Paul the past few weeks. In fact, since New Year. "We spent New Year's together, the six of us..."

"You and who else?"

"The Masterses. It had become a bit of a tradition — we all went to Barbados. The Masterses have a place, near the Colony Club. I remember that two nights in a row Paul had these dreadful nightmares. I heard him shout in his sleep and cry out. We had the next set of rooms, and in an old building like that the walls are thin enough."

"What was he saying?"

Parker shrugged. "It was Hungarian. Brenda woke him up and walked him out to the living room on the upper floor. She poured him brandy — as if they had done that sort of thing before."

"Had they?"

"Apparently, yes," Parker said. "I asked her. She said he'd been having nightmares for years, some fear of being captured and killed. I think it was one of those wartime memories he carried. Jewish, from Hungary, you know."

"But why did you think he was going to speak about his past the night of March 1st?"

"He said something odd on the phone... How did he put it?"

Parker cupped his voluminous chin in his hand as he thought. "About shadows still haunting him from the past. So I asked him about those nightmares. He said they had been getting worse of late. He'd heard from someone he thought was dead long ago."

"Was he glad this man was still alive?"

"Glad? Glad? Hmm... No. Now that I reflect on it, I think he sounded frightened. That's odd for Paul. Never a man to scare easily. But there it was." Parker lumbered to his feet and around the room, thinking. "And in the same context, he said he was going to tell us a story on the Sunday. A long story. And he hoped I'd not have too much of the wine till he got to it. Joking. He was always pulling my leg. So when I asked him what kind of a story, he said, 'The kind that dispels nightmares.' Strange, that, don't you think?"

THIRTY-FIVE

Stevie solved Judith's cat problem by moving in for a few days. She had always wanted to try living another person's life, and opportunities like this rarely presented themselves. She promised not to educate Jimmy in the fine art of grading quality marijuana.

David decided to accompany Judith to Hungary on the spur of the moment, having finally convinced the Chief there was something to the Eger connection. Chuck Griffiths wouldn't be back from Hong Kong till the end of the week; Masters had left, again, for Bermuda; Arthur had flown back to New York, despite David's instructions to remain in Toronto for a second round of questions.

Brenda Zimmerman was angry and uncooperative. She didn't seem to believe that her husband had been poisoned. David knew he would have to fly to Bermuda to see her and Masters, but even if the Chief agreed, David wouldn't be ready for her till after he had been to Hungary. The last piece of the jigsaw puzzle was in Eger.

They rented a midsize Skoda at the Budapest airport, bought a stack of trilingual maps, and set off through the main thoroughfare of Budapest to find Highway 3, which would, in under two hours, the rental agent promised, take them to Eger. That wasn't quite the way it happened. They were lost almost as soon as they turned off the road from the airport, and found themselves crisscrossing the Danube via a variety of ancient and modern bridges before they located the first person who spoke enough English to direct them toward Eger. He was a waiter in a Castle Hill restaurant and a self-declared expert on local history. The price David and Judith paid for the backseat directions was listening for half an hour to the story of the city's heroic past, particularly that of the defenders of Castle Hill.

It was a cold gray day with occasional flashes of sunshine. At 10 o'clock, the traffic was light — "takes four to five years to save up for a car," the waiter said — but swathed in blue exhaust. The smell of diesel fuel made Judith gag. The Danube was deep winter green; there were large slabs of jagged ice crashing into the shoreline.

They dropped the waiter off at his restaurant in the medieval heart of Buda, near the Fisherman's Bastion, where the general drabness of the city's thoroughfares gave way to arched doorways, Gothic churches, and cobblestones. He was delighted they were going to Eger. Too few visitors bothered to drive into the Bükk Mountains, not only a beautiful part of the country but another monument to heroic battles fought, though, alas, mostly lost.

They traversed the Danube one more time — "promise me it's the last," David begged — and set off on Highway 3, direction: Miskolc. Though it's only 130 kilometers from Budapest to Eger, they were not yet halfway two hours later. They were stuck behind a convoy of slow-moving trucks, and Judith was afraid to pass them on the narrow winding road that only a Hungarian would call a highway.

It was dark by the time they arrived and checked into the Park Hotel, on a narrow lane off Lenin Street, with no visible exit and mountains of snow blocking the sidewalks. The manager showed them to their old-fashioned rooms personally, when he discovered they were from Canada and didn't speak a word of Hungarian. He was a man of about 40, with brown curly hair and a waxed mustache he had trimmed carefully to curve around his upper lip. He had learned English at university but found little use for it up here. He was delighted to have an opportunity for practice. He made sure they knew of the connecting door between their two rooms and presented each of them with a bottle of the local red wine, a tasty cousin of the Bull's Blood one could buy in Toronto.

Judith's polite questions about the differences between wine for export and for home consumption encouraged the manager to launch into an exhaustive dissertation on the relative merits of the wines in the area, followed by an even longer discourse on the seemingly endless history of Eger going back to the first settlements of Magyar tribes — the original Hungarians — when they arrived from God knows where in the 9th century. It appeared the town had been destroyed by a succession of marauding armies, Tartars and Turks, which made it fairly understandable that its proudest moment was a battle the townspeople actually succeeded in winning sometime in the 16th century. The manager took his name, István, from the victorious commander of the 16th-century townsfolk. He would have conducted them to the barely visible ramparts of the ancient fort this evening had Judith not complained of hunger and lack of sleep.

István then insisted on opening the hotel's huge baroque restaurant to serve them a six-course meal larded with Hungarian hospitality and accompanied by mournful violin music he piped through the aged loudspeaker system. The room itself was designed to hold over a hundred people, and it took both bottles of red wine to warm it up for two. The tourist season didn't start till May. In the winter, István explained, Eger got mainly old people who came for the baths that claim to treat rheumatism and gout.

After he had explored the possibilities of their having relatives in the area, ancestors they were trying to trace, an insatiable curiosity about central European history, an appetite for wine tasting, or a nasty case of arthritis, István asked directly why they had come to Eger. Before David could say anything about the murder investigation, Judith said she was a writer, looking for background information on the Zimmerman family who had lived here before the war.

"Zimmerman," István brooded. "No. They don't sound Hungarian. Not one of the names I've heard around here..."

"Before your time, I think," said David. "They were Jewish. They wouldn't have survived the German occupation. We were hoping to meet someone who knew them."

"Those were confusing times, the war years. In '42, '43 there was the famine that decimated the population. That's the right word, isn't it?" He slapped his knees in obvious enjoyment at having found the right word. "One in ten, right? A lot of the Jews left while they could, the ones that stayed behind were taken off in trucks by the Germans. They never returned," István said. "Maybe some went to Israel." He looked a touch embarrassed by this suggestion, but not enough to admit he knew most of them had ended up in Auschwitz.

"Before my time, as you say," he allowed. "All I know, there aren't so many Jews here now as there were in my parents' time. But there are still a lot of anti-Semites. Funny, isn't that?" When neither guest laughed along with him, he asked if they'd like to meet Józsi bácsi — he would remember more about those years. He had started at the hotel as the hall porter just before the war and never had another job, not even a promotion since. "Some men are happy with their lot from the start. No ambition, no desire to set goals. Not so good for the country," he told David earnestly. "We need wider horizons, more growth — you know what I mean? We're the capitalists of the East. We prove you can create wealth without exploitation, all it takes is a bit of know-how."

Józsi bácsi — "'bácsi' means uncle; that's what we call older people we know" — was on duty till 11 every night, which could have been viewed as some kind of exploitation by a woman better versed in political theory than Judith claimed she was. In any event, he was delighted to join the boss and the two foreigners for a glass of wine (or two). His English was limited to "Hello" and "Tank you verymuch," both of which he used liberally, but he spoke a passable French, not unusual, István said, for people of his vintage in these parts. Judith judged him close to 80 but rolled back a decade when he offered to arm-wrestle David after the second glass of Bikavér.

His black tunic, decorated in gold braid and tassels, displayed an array of silver medals that, on close examination, turned out to be football firsts. In the '30s, he had enjoyed a flash of national fame as a regional soccer star. Now he coached the high school team in the mornings. He had short-cropped white hair and a thick neck with prominent tendons that tensed when he became excited. This happened chiefly when he talked about soccer to István in Hungarian. István gave up on translating midway into an argument about two goalies vying for selection to play on the national team.

In her best high school French, Judith asked whether he remembered a family by the name of Zimmerman in Eger before the war.

He did remember, although he certainly didn't know them himself. They were summer and weekend residents only. Lived in a big house on Golya Street, near the Turkish baths.

The baths, István interjected, the most elaborate Turkish baths in Europe, were built in the 17th century by Sultan Valide. He thought David and Judith might like to see the excavations in the morning.

"I'm sorry, we don't have time," David said.

"We'd love to," Judith corrected him. It wouldn't do to dampen István's enthusiasm. "We're tired from the trip now, but tomorrow we'll be rested. Won't we, David?"

"I suppose...," David said uncertainly.

István served a transparent syrupy liquid, called Pálinka, in brandy snifters and encouraged Józsi bácsi to go on about the Zimmermans.

Père Zimmerman had been in some kind of business in Budapest, running a factory, or a string of factories, more likely. They were mighty rich for hereabouts. They entertained a lot, but mostly people from the capital. Józsi bácsi remembered the big limousines, American cars. They were scarce between the wars. The locals still used carriages — those who could afford them. As for himself, Józsi bácsi used to travel by oxcart or on horseback. Those were the days — none of the rush of today, wanting to get places faster. Never had understood why everyone was in such a rush, we all get there in the end, whether by horseback, oxcart, or big Yankee cars.

After the war broke out and the Arrow Cross party became powerful in Budapest, the Zimmermans moved to Eger. There had been two children, a boy and a girl. Józsi was already a football hero. Once the boy had asked for Józsi's autograph for his collection. He had spent a great deal of time in Vienna when he was little and had a book of autographs that included some foreign names, musicians, he thought, as well as Hungarians.

His name was Pali, Józsi bácsi thought. A small boy with glasses, not much good at sports.

"You should talk to Sári Markhot, she would know more about them," Józsi suggested. "She made clothes for Mrs. Zimmerman. She's still here, I think. Worked in a shop down Jókai Street. Now her daughter runs it. They live above the store."

István wanted to know what sort of story Judith was writing and why. When she told him that Zimmerman had become a millionaire several times over in America, he offered to accompany them to the Markhots'. Right now. Why wait till the morning? They would need a translator, and he was busy then. "Very clever, those Jews," he confided to Judith as she struggled into her winter coat. "Always fall on their feet. The Nazis trucked them away in 1944."

Eger hadn't been a particularly friendly place for them, he said. Always a town of Christians. Founded as a home for bishops by a king of the Hungarians made into a saint, Eger's proudest building was a cathedral that vied for grandeur with Cologne's. Each time the Turks demolished it, the Christians started it up again with new towers, new adjacent palaces for their priests. Even today, there are eight churches in the town for 60,000 people, "and religion hasn't had a high profile recently." István himself wasn't particularly religious, but he still made the sign of the cross as they passed the ancient Franciscan basilica looming out of the darkness on their left. "One can't be too sure," he whispered. "These stones have been here for a long time. Perhaps those old monks were on to something."

On the way they discovered that the streets of Eger were still much as they had been in the Middle Ages; few had room for cars, and only officials and other "important people" had telephones. What was the point when you could just as easily walk over to see someone at home? If you had to call long distance, you could do so from the post office or the hotels.

The Markhots' dressmaking shop was across the street from the double-towered church of the Minorites (another bit of furtive obeisance by István — "a habit, that's all"), lit up by the faint yellow of the wrought-iron street lamps. The store window was protected by wrought-iron braces on the outside. The entrance was dark, but there was light upstairs behind the gauze curtains.

"Even the old people go to bed late in Eger," István said as he knocked on the glass door. "Not much happens here during the winter. We sit in the coffeehouses or we visit one another. Some people go skiing in the Mátras."

Judging by the look of surprise on the old woman's face when she appeared, he was inventing his stories as he went. She hadn't been expecting any visitors and wasn't overjoyed to see them. Still, István was convincing enough to gain them entry after a lengthy exchange in Hungarian. "I told her it was a matter of life and death," he joked to David, as they were led up the narrow winding staircase to the small room at the top, which gave off a pungent smell of cooked cabbage and musky perfume. Inside there were two beds, a table with an old porcelain lamp, two armchairs with embroidered backs, a row of painted plates along one wall facing an impressive array of portraits of the Virgin Mary and, in the corner, a tall black cross.

Sári Markhot looked to be around 70. Her skin was heavily lined, sallow, the eyebrows jutting out over her watery eyes. Her back was bent, the shoulders drawn up around her head. She glared belligerently at the two foreigners who had intruded on her evening.

István kept talking and smiling.

"He'd make one helluva salesman," Judith said when the old woman's expression softened.

"She doesn't understand a word of English," István said. "Her daughter does, but she's in Czechoslovakia buying linen for the spring season."

Sári Markhot gestured for them to sit on the beds while she boiled water for tea. She produced blue china cups with gold rims and the dark residue of many years of tea stuck to their bottoms. She put lemon wedges in the saucers.

"She says there isn't much to tell about the Zimmermans," István told them. He had taken one of the armchairs while David and Judith sat side by side on the bed, fondling their warm teacups. Sári Markhot spoke in a flat monotone, occasionally gesticulating with one hand, drawing her black lace shawl close around her head and shoulders. The little room was cold despite the iron burner she had lit when they came up. "They used to live on the far side of the castle, a big white house with a garden that needed two people to keep it trimmed. There were a lot of roses. Madame liked flowers. She wore summer dresses with flower designs. Often she brought the patterns right from Vienna where her husband had a flat. She was a talented woman. She drew. Played music. They had a grand piano in the living room and she often played and sang for the guests. The children had tutors in French, English, and German, and they both studied music like their mother. She was thought a great beauty, Sári says. She had the figure of a young girl. She loved silk."

"Ask her about the children," David suggested.

"The little girl was called Meredith." Both István and Sári pronounced it the way Eva Zimmerman had, flat vowels and a hard *t*. "She was like her mother, all song and happiness. Everybody loved her. She had dark brown hair she wore in ringlets. Her clothes were all stitched by hand. Big, wide — how do you say — ballerina skirts, with tight waists and ribbons. She loved those ribbons, in her hair, at her throat, tied around her waist. Even on her shoes..." Sári Markhot's hands flew from her hair to her neck and, with a girlish movement, to her own broad waist, and she smiled at the memory.

"Does she remember Paul Zimmerman?" David asked. "Pali?"

"She says he was a quiet boy, shortsighted, small for his age. The family hoped he would be a soldier one day, like his father had been during the First World War, but he took no interest in fighting. He read a lot. He had a special violin he'd received for his birthday some years back, he liked to play it. Sometimes his mother accompanied him on the piano. He played Viennese waltzes, Dvořák, even Liszt. She didn't use to make his clothes — his father bought them from his tailors in Budapest or Vienna. All the local boys used to tease him about the way he dressed. Stiff high collars. Tight jackets."

David showed her the photograph of the two boys he had been given by Deidre. "Is this Paul Zimmerman?"

She held the picture up to the lamp, studied it for a moment, then nodded a lot. "Yes," István said. "That's him. She says the picture looks like it was taken around 1940. All the children in the back garden. They built a pool in 1939. The children in the neighborhood would go around there and play. The other boy, he was around a lot. They were friends."

David stood over the old woman's shoulder and looked at the picture with her. She was still talking and gesticulating about the magnificence of the Zimmermans' garden.

"Ask her, would you, to point at Paul Zimmerman for me, Pál, Pali, you know," he beamed encouragement at Sári, who appeared to understand, because she pointed at one of the boys in the photograph. She smiled and looked up at David.

"Is she sure?"

"Sure, sure," István said, and Sári nodded vigorously, her bent arthritic right finger pointing at the smaller of the two boys, the one who wore the baggy singlet to hide his childish belly. His right arm reached over the taller boy's shoulder. He was squinting into the camera, grimacing against the bright sunshine.

"Who is the other boy?" asked Judith. She was now also standing, crowded around the small photograph with the others. "Does she know who it is?" She pointed at the tall blond boy who so amazingly resembled Arthur Zimmerman.

Sári Markhot handed back the photograph. She shook her head and said something to István in rapid-fire Hungarian that translated as, "She doesn't think she can remember his name."

"Perhaps a local boy?" David prompted.

István shook his head. "She can't remember at all," he insisted. Though Sári added a whole lot more in her angry Hungarian, he seemed to have lost interest in translating.

THIRTY-SIX

At first they had both been too exhausted to sleep. They sat in David's bed trying to make sense of who Paul Zimmerman really was. What was it Sári Markhot had said to Istaván that had turned the formerly voluble travel guide into such a tight-lipped interpreter? He had remained quiet on the way home, and when Judith pressed him to explain why Sári had suddenly become angry when she saw the photograph of the two boys, he claimed he hadn't noticed.

"Hungarians are passionate people. Very patriotic. She was recalling the invasion of Eger. By the Germans, of course. We call the Russians 'liberators.' There is a difference," he declared.

Lenin Street was pitch dark by then; even the Park's neon sign had been extinguished. Judith's leather-soled boots skidded along the ice-covered paving stones.

"We don't use salt on the old streets," István said. "It would damage the ancient paving. They have been here for five centuries and will, we hope, remain for five more. That sort of thinking puts everything in perspective, don't you think?"

"Most things," Judith agreed. She doubted if a feeling for local history would have helped Eger's Jews as they were trucked off to the death camps.

Around 2 A.M. she filled the huge lion's-footed bathtub with sulfurous hot water and immersed herself, trying to relax into sleep. She drank the last of the Pálinka and counted Hungarian sheep over snow-covered fences.

When she returned to the bedroom, David was already snoring — a gentle, rhythmic sound she would normally have found irritating, but tonight it seemed comfortingly familiar in a strange town too far away from home. For the sake of propriety (you never quite shake off the ill effects of a Protestant childhood), she crumpled the sheets and turned down the blankets in her own room, then curled up next to David under his soft down duvet.

They woke at 7 to a bright sunny morning and crisp mountain air that testified that the Park didn't subscribe to the decadent capitalist indulgence of individual room heating. A smiling maid, wearing two sweaters under her woolen apron, provided a sturdy breakfast of brown buns, strawberry jam, thick Turkish coffee, and warm milk.

At 8 A.M. they had a visit from Comrade Szabo of the Eger constabulary. He had brought Józsi bácsi with him to translate in French that he was delighted to welcome such a distinguished member of a brother police force — *mes frères* — to his humble town.

"So that's why they had to have our passports overnight," David said. "They check your credentials. Do you suppose they know why we're here now?" He extricated his fingers from his brother officer's fierce grasp.

"I doubt if the system works that well," Judith said. "It would take them days to make all the right connections between Eger and Toronto. All he knows is that you're a policeman and I'm a journalist, and that's bad enough. I doubt if we'll be able to shake him for as long as we're here."

Józsi bácsi looked as though he had continued the evening well past the time David and Judith had left for Jókai Street. He also resented being dragged out of bed long before his usual time. He put heavy emphasis on words like *distingué* and summarized chunks of flattering information about the Toronto police force into, "He wants you to know he has studied Toronto's gendarmerie. Probably spent the whole night on it, *le pauvre*."

Szabo asked if there was some way in which he could be of assistance, and Józsi bácsi suggested they accept his offer, otherwise he'd simply follow them around, incognito, an exercise that often made the police a touch testy. Particularly Comrade Szabo, who was much too fat to inch along the walls unnoticed. His job included keeping an eye on important visitors.

Sympathetic to the myriad ways in which police must bend to bureaucrats, David agreed, provided Szabo stayed out of their way after leading them to Ferenc Lantos and his sweetshop on the site of the old Singer home.

The shop turned out to be a large blue-tiled coffeehouse with an extensive display of homemade Viennese cakes and confections, American ice cream, and Turkish delight. During the summer, Józsi bácsi said, its blue and white awning extended over the sidewalk, but now the customers were all contained inside the crowded room. There were tiny round tables closely packed together, men and women in stylish knits huddled over stained tablecloths. The echoing din of loud conversation. The pungent smell of close-packed bodies and fresh-brewed coffee. The whole was dominated by a massive, silver-plated espresso machine with four black handles and a steaming spout for milk. Above it, a discreetly small photograph of Lenin. All around on the walls, large reproductions of paintings of men in battle dress striking heroic poses. Before saying goodbye, Józsi bácsi pointed out that the Petöfi Kavéház was a favorite hangout for artsy students and writers. The manager was kind enough to let them sit around all day discussing fine points of poetry and philosophy over a single cup of coffee and a piece of cake. Appropriately, the place was named after a famous Hungarian poet — a romantic and a revolutionary. Such excesses were now fashionable only among the very young and the very old.

Ferenc Lantos appeared to be both manager and waiter; his wife, Edith, as he later introduced her, made the cakes herself. He spoke good English, a prerequisite for higher pay in the coffeehouse business. "The government," he told Judith, "wishes to encourage us to learn languages so we can attract more foreign tourists. The difficulty is, not many foreigners come here in the winter no matter how much English we learn." He served them chocolate cake with hard caramel topping and espresso with heavy cream. He didn't think there had ever been anyone in his shop from Canada, and he wanted to hear all about the Rocky Mountains. He was planning a trip there when he retired.

He was a small man with a paunch and a rosy complexion, around 55. He walked with a slight limp. When he sat down to join the overseas guests, he took off his long white napkin of an apron, revealing a pair of daring blue checked pants he said he had bought three years ago in London. They were sure to be in vogue soon here, he said. Eger was somewhat behind "the fashion mainstream." "A little place. Out of the way." But it had charm and tradition. He prattled on about relatives in various parts of the world who missed the kind of cooking they had been used to at home, and, even more, the hospitality, the ambience, and how glad he was to have stayed behind in '56 when the majority of the *bourgeois* left. All that until David told him they had come looking for information about Paul Zimmerman. Then he stopped talking.

He gestured to his wife to take his place while he filled the espresso machine with more hot water, strolled around chatting to other happily occupied customers, then came back to stand behind his wife's chair and stare quizzically at the newcomers from Canada. His face, moments before openly cheerful, now held an expression of guarded suspicion.

"You did know Paul Zimmerman," David asked again, "didn't you?"

"Not very well," Lantos said, after a moment's hesitation.

"Gloria Singer showed me the photographs. I thought perhaps you could tell us something about him."

Lantos seemed surprised. "She showed you pictures? Why?"

"I guess she thought they might be useful for the investigation."

"What you mean, investigation? I don't understand." Lantos looked back at the blue-uniformed Szabo who was sitting at the next table, eating chocolate cake and reading the paper while he waited for the distinguished Canadian visitors to finish talking. He didn't seem to be paying any attention to the conversation.

"What he means is, we are looking into Paul Zimmerman's life. I am writing a story for an American magazine," Judith interrupted. "Obviously Mrs. Singer thought you could help us. You knew Paul when you were all boys, you and Harvey were friends with Paul, weren't you?"

"Not specially close friends," Lantos said impatiently, "Harvey must have told you. The two of *us* were close friends. Zimmermans spent only summers here. We swam in their pool. That is all. I don't understand why so many want to know about Paul now. After all these years. He was a nice kid, but not special. You people in America have such a — how you say, gravelike, ghoulish? — curiosity. Terrible thing, of course, his dying like that, but those were terrible times for all of us here. Hell, in 1944 we ran out of most rations. Not even bread, or flour to make bread. No meat by spring. The Germans came looking in March, the peasants had nothing left to give them but their cows. So after that we had no milk. People were dying. Like flies, you would say. Christians and Jews both."

"His dying *like that*?" David asked. "How *did* he die?"

"It wasn't only him, it was all of them. The whole family. It was the times you blame, not any one person, and Feri was only a boy himself. I know he wouldn't have thought they would be killed. I knew Feri. He wasn't that kind of a person." He wiped his brow with the back of his sleeve. "Only 16. He and Paul were the same age. We were all at the same school. All went swimming at Zimmermans' pool in the summer and when they moved here from Budapest in '39 or '40. Sometimes they allowed us in the house. Mrs. Zimmerman didn't think we should play inside much. Their house had pretty antiques. She wanted Paul to get fresh air. She thought the sun would make him grow strong..." He broke off for a moment and returned to the counter to adjust the espresso machine.

"Feri?" Judith asked. "Who the hell...?"

David put a restraining hand on her arm. "Don't ask him now. He thinks we know more than we do. If you let on we don't, he might clam up like István did."

When Lantos returned, he brought a drawing with him. It was in browns and blues, light lines and shading with a pale blue wash background. The picture showed a young boy with a serious face and carefully combed brown hair. He wore a white shirt, open at the neck, and held a football on his knee.

"That's Mrs. Zimmerman's drawing of Harvey. He was invited in more often than the rest of us, because his parents made friends with the Zimmermans in Budapest. Harvey's father was in the boats, but they weren't so rich like the Zimmermans. Harvey used to tell me how big the Zimmermans' rooms were, and how he was afraid to touch things in case it got dirty. He would sit quietly and listen to Paul play violin, and watch Meredith play with the cats. Paul's father was industrialist. He built houses and factories. After Paul decided he didn't want to be in the army, he was going to go into his father's business. He was terribly good at school. After the war broke out, he had private tutors to teach him the extras we didn't have at our high school — like music. He spoke French, German, English, and some Latin. He was studying ancient Greek. I remember Feri used to argue with him about Latin being the most useless thing anyone could learn..."

He put the picture on the table in front of him and glanced at it from time to time as he talked. "Harvey was my best friend. We were younger than Paul and Feri. Only 14. I didn't care he was

Jewish, and I don't think my parents cared. They never said anything at home about the Jews. But the climate was...You know...
We thought the Germans were just planning to take the Jews to
some camp till the war was over. For a long time, I think everyone
believed that. We wanted to believe it. When the Singers asked if
Harvey could stay with us while they went to the camp, my mother
wouldn't take him. She said the air would do him good." He
laughed, a harsh, mirthless sound. "You know, she was afraid of
what might happen if the Nazis found out we were hiding a Jew. So
they sent him to Budapest where Mr. Singer had a friend who took
him in for a while. Saved his life, you know. He spent only a few
months in Auschwitz." He wiped his eyes. "God, I was so glad to
see him alive."

"I guess Paul wasn't so lucky," said Judith.

Lantos gazed at the patch of linoleum floor between his feet.
"No, he wasn't."

"They were taken off in trucks?"

Lantos shook his head. "No. They went into hiding at one of
the peasant houses up in the north part of the town near the Donat
cemetery. Nobody knew they were there, and after all the Jews had
gone — 1,600 people — no one thought of looking for them. Hell,
they almost made it through the war. It was late summer of 1944,
July, I think, when they found them. The Germans retreated in
September. Another two months and they would have been safe.
Life is so full of those missed chances, don't you think?"

Judith nodded sympathetically. She knew he was referring to
his own missed opportunity, not standing up to his mother about
Harvey Singer's fate.

"What happened when they found them?" David asked.

"They were all shot," Lantos said with a sigh. "All of them. The
Nazis lined them up in front of the house and just kept shooting till
they were dead. Meredith was only twelve then. She was such a
beautiful young girl. We were all in love with her. Every boy who
ever spent summers around the Zimmermans' pool. Feri asked her
if she would marry him when she grew up."

He held his forehead in both hands, fingertips tapping the skin
lightly, then pressing into it. He bent forward, put his elbows on
the table, and remained in that position for some moments.

"Nobody escaped?" Judith asked.

"Nobody. Afterward they locked the peasants inside their

house and set fire to it. They burned them alive... My mother said how clever she was she didn't let Harvey stay, because look what happened to them and they were only peasants. For sure. But I thought better to burn to death than think about what they done to Harvey..." He wiped the table with his apron, though it hadn't needed cleaning. "More coffee?" he asked.

Judith shook her head.

"We have to get on with life, you know." Lantos added that homily for something to fill the silence.

David brought the photograph out of his pocket and put it on the newly cleaned spot. "Is this Feri?" he asked, pointing to the chunky boy with the blond hair, his chest pushed out to make himself seem bigger and stronger.

Lantos leaned over and studied the photograph for a moment. "Yes," he said. "That's him. I gave the picture to Harvey — he wanted it so very much. The other one's Paul. They were always together. I remember Feri started talking about the Zimmermans' coming, as early as April every year. He made plans for the things he and Paul would do. One spring he bagged a hundred butterflies for Paul's collection. He didn't have much to look forward to, Feri. The Baloghs lived in the west toward Bogács. He had to come a long way to school — when he came. Five kilometers, I think. Maybe farther. His father was a laborer in the vineyards. He died when Feri was still very young, ten or twelve. They struggled to stay alive. I thought that's why Mrs. Zimmerman let him around their house so much. She felt sorry for him. She used to give him things to take home. You know, clothes, food. My mother sent a loaf of bread now and then. Afterward we wondered if that was why he did it. Envy, maybe. He had a lot of pride, Feri did, for a peasant boy. He didn't like the handouts, but he took them because they needed to eat."

"He told the Nazis where to find the Zimmermans?" Judith asked.

Lantos nodded. "He led them to the house. Some say he was there when they were shot. He watched. Afterward, the Arrow Cross guards decorated him as hero of the Vaterland. They pinned his picture up on the school's noticeboard as example of true hero. They had a party for him in the old Park restaurant. They drank the last of the wine from the hotel's cellars. They shot bullets through the plaster angels in the ceiling. Next day, I saw Feri riding around on Paul Zimmerman's new silver bicycle. That was the last time I saw Feri."

"What happened to him? Do you know?"

"He was killed when the Russians came in. Our liberators, you know." He glanced nervously at Szabo again. The policeman registered the same lack of hearing as last time. He had finished reading the paper and was sitting back in his chair, his hands folded on his belly, staring into space. His orders, David concluded, must have been to keep in sight; they didn't include trying to make sense of what they were talking about.

Lantos leaned forward, his face mere inches away from David's. "They weren't much better than the Germans, you know. They were angry because the Germans had blown up the bridges and the railway lines. They had taken all the live animals they could find, and every last bit of grain they could threaten from the peasants. So when the Second Ukrainian Army marched in, victorious and hungry, there wasn't anything left for them to eat, and they couldn't bring foodstuffs in too easily because the bridges and the railroads were gone. They wreaked their own version of chaos, they shot their share of the population, and moved on toward Budapest. Feri was killed by them. So was his mother. She had been hiding a bit of wine in a cellar and the Russkies found it. They used to get awfully angry if you didn't give them everything you had."

"When Harvey was here, did you talk about all that?" Judith asked.

"Oh yes. He wanted to know everything about everyone. I'd saved some old pictures of him and his family from before the troubles started. And a few things from the Zimmerman house. An old book of Paul's. A silver locket. That was Harvey's first time back home since the war. Never wrote me or anything in all those years. Hell, I don't really blame the man, after what happened to his family, but I sure would have liked to know he was alive. He did so well for himself in America." He shrugged. "The way it goes. Kept this drawing of him, too. In the kitchen here. About the same place where his old living room used to be. You know their house was here?"

"Why did he take all the Zimmermans' things?" Judith asked.

"He said he'd read about some Zimmermans in the papers. He now thought they might be relatives, and they would like to have them. He showed them to you?"

"Yes," David lied. He had been about to tell him about Harvey's death, but Lantos was depressed enough already; he decided to save it for a while. Instead, he asked Lantos what he meant when he said so many people wanted to know about Paul Zimmerman all of a sudden.

"There was Harvey and Gloria in December, the woman in January, and now you — all in a few weeks, it seems. For 40 years no one so much as mentioned him around here, and then all this interest. We don't like to talk about that time. Doesn't look good for the town. Feri Balogh was one of us."

"Who was the woman in January?" David asked.

"I don't know her name." Lantos shrugged. "She was just passing through, she said. Didn't stop in Eger."

Judith dug around in her handbag where she kept her research pieces and took out a folded page from a magazine. She smoothed it out on the table and pushed it over toward Lantos. "This woman?" she asked.

"Yes, that's her," he said with a smile. "A beauty she was."

THIRTY-SEVEN

There are no direct flights between Budapest and Bermuda, and no easy connections. That's why it was eighteen hours before David Parr and Judith Hayes finally made it to Xanadu.

Staff Sergeant Graham bestowed on them both his official blessing and his unofficial cruiser escort, but he stayed outside among the hibiscus while they entered behind the uniformed maid. She gave Judith a shy smile of recognition and bobbed her head in David's direction. This time, though, she didn't welcome them to Bermuda. All she said was that they were expected in the conservatory.

Brenda Zimmerman was wearing a long-sleeved navy blue dress with a severe high collar that hid her slender neck. Her blond hair fell in straight lines to her shoulders. Her skin was even paler and more translucent than the last time Judith had seen her. The lines around her mouth had deepened, the darkness about her eyes made her face seem skeletal. She sat upright in one of the green and pink chairs near the pool. She was reading a fat leather-bound book that she reluctantly lowered to her lap when David and Judith entered.

Philip Masters stood close to the windows, looking out at the lush greens and purples in the garden. He turned slowly when David wished them a good afternoon, stuck both hands into his pants pockets so his pinstriped jacket flared out behind him and his black waistcoated belly stuck out in front like a raven's feathered crop. "It's taken you long enough," he said belligerently.

Judith mumbled something about it being difficult to make plans from such a remote place as Eger.

"That isn't what he meant," David said. "He's talking about coming to the end of the investigation, aren't you, Mr. Masters?"

Philip nodded almost imperceptibly.

The white cane canary cages had all been covered with dark green woven cloths. The room, lit by the soft amber light of the late-afternoon sun, was still.

"When did you find out that your husband wasn't Paul Zimmerman?" David asked.

Brenda looked up at him slowly, as if the movement of her head was painful in the extreme. Her violet eyes were clouded, unfocused; they reminded Judith of Eva's unseeing eyes.

"Early January, I think," Brenda said quietly. "I can't remember the exact date. Late afternoon. I was on my way somewhere — funny how I can't remember where I was going and why, don't you think, Philip? It's so strange how everything has faded into these vague sepia colors. It's as if my life had always been bright pinks and definite greens and blues, and suddenly the color drains out of it all. Nothing is as it seemed before..." She slammed the book shut and put it beside her on the chair. "I remember he stepped out in front of the car when I was halfway along the Bridle Path on the way to... It doesn't matter, does it?"

"No," David said. "He stopped the car. He told you his name was Harvey Singer. Told you about Feri Balogh and Paul Zimmerman." David spoke as if to a child, gently, cajoling.

"Let her tell it her way," Philip said. He had come to stand behind Brenda's chair, his hand resting on the top of its pink cane back.

"I don't know why I stopped the car, really," Brenda continued. "He seemed such a harmless little man. Well dressed. Had a hat with a feather in the band, a briefcase, big fur-collared overcoat. Respectable. I thought he lived along the street. Maybe he needed help starting his car. January, the batteries die. He seemed distraught. Shaking. So I let him into...my life." She was rubbing and intertwining her fingers, turning her rings. "That sounds rather dramatic, don't you think? Yes. Very dramatic. Death is very dramatic, though. Have you read very much Shakespeare, Inspector?"

"Not for a long time," David said.

"A pity," Brenda pronounced sadly. "I didn't believe him at first. No one would have. It was such a fantastic story. I was married to a man called Balogh, who had once been Paul Zimmerman's best friend, but had betrayed him for a bicycle. Watched while he died. Would you believe that? About someone you know and love? That he was a Nazi, a killer?" She looked imploringly at Judith. "How would anyone believe that? Paul had been so generous to all those Jewish causes.

"I had rolled down the window and Singer was standing there in the snow. He had a bunch of faded old photographs and a yarmulke; he said they were the real Paul's. Harvey Singer begged me to ask Paul myself. I told him he was nuts and I drove off. But I did. Later that night, after he'd had one of his terrible nightmares, shouting in Hungarian, as he so often did. He used to wake shaking and sweating, crying sometimes. He was so frightened. And I had begun to think maybe the crazy guy had been telling the truth. You know how it is, sometimes, in the night, even your worst fears seem plausible. I felt guilty for even allowing myself to think it. I blurted out the question to Paul, all at once. God, I wanted him to deny it so much. But he didn't. He got up and he left. Didn't say where he was going. Didn't come back for days."

"And you told Philip then?" David asked gently.

"I had to tell someone. Philip loved him as much as I did. Or so I thought. Good old faithful Philip. He tried to convince me I was an idiot to give any credence to Singer's ravings. He told me he would make inquiries about Singer. The man must be an escaped lunatic. And about Paul's reaction, he said how would I feel if Paul accused *me* of being a murderer? Wouldn't I leave the house? Wouldn't I feel hurt and astounded? But Paul didn't seem either hurt or astounded, he seemed angry. He left me without a word. It was early morning, still dark. We were in his bedroom. He was covered in sweat from that horrible nightmare. I had held his hand as I had so often done before. When he got out of bed, I tried to hold on but he pulled away. He dressed in the dark. I kept asking him again and again. He didn't reply. When I turned on the light he was pulling on his overcoat. Never even glanced at me when he left. No matter how hard Philip tried to convince me, I couldn't put it out of my mind.

"That's why I went to Hungary. Saw the man in Eger who had given Singer all those pictures and things of Paul's. Lantos. He runs the sweetshop. But you know that already, don't you?" She looked from Judith to David and back again, her eyes pleading for understanding. "I visited the graves afterward. The Zimmerman graves that the priest from the little chapel had dug himself. He dug for days before he had enough of them. He dragged the bodies there, one by one, alone, in the summer's heat. No one would help him,

you see. They were all afraid to be seen touching Jewish corpses."
Her voice caught. She swallowed hard.

"I had some relatives who died that way. Shot. In Germany where
my family came from before the war. No one buried them. I met
the priest. A small man, hard to imagine how he did it. They weigh
so much, dead bodies." Her voice caught again. She brushed her
face with her fingers.

"He's still at the same chapel. Now and then he puts flowers on
the graves, when he collects more than he needs for food from his
congregation. Lantos saw to it the graves were kept clean. Weeded.
A little grass on each. Four graves, side by side, each with a single
headstone the priest brought over from the walls of the old castle.
They never had any visitors. Though the whole town knew. They
were ashamed, the priest thought. Then they forgot. Paul — no...
that other man I married — he knew where I had been and why.
When I came back, he was waiting for me at the airport. Geoff
Aronson stood outside the car and waved me in. He told me then.
He told me everything. Only part he left out was why he had done
it. He never understood that himself. He had been very young. Just
16, in 1944. He was a child. I hardly remember being 16, do you,
Officer Parr? He had wanted that silver bike so badly; he never
wanted anything so badly in his life. He had grown up without
love — a hard working man's son, the only support for a silent
widow. Do you remember all the mistakes of your childhood? All
the envy, the little acts of personal revenge? There was a girl called
Millie I went to school with. She was such a beauty, so popular,
so cute, athletic, you know...I used to fantasize that she died.
Violently. In Hungary in 1944 such fantasies could become real.
'Between the idea and the reality, between the motion and the
act...'" She stopped talking, lowered her head, her shoulders
slumped forward.

They all waited in silence.

When she lifted her head, she looked straight at Judith, as if she
had just remembered Judith was there. "You know about love,
don't you?" she asked.

Judith nodded.

"He was in love with Meredith Zimmerman. His first love. At 16
love can seem so desperate. Do you know, Romeo and Juliet were
only 15? Meredith was 12, but she knew her mind. She told him
she could never love a Gentile, it was against her religion. She

rejected him. Years later, he wondered if that was why he had to prove over and over that he could be attractive to women. He was angry at her. At all of them. They had seemed to be his friends, and now they were telling him...she was telling him...he wasn't good enough for them. Maybe that's what it was. I don't know. Oh God...how I've tried to understand why...as if that bit of understanding would lessen the horror."

She buried her face in her hands for a second. When she resumed she was steady, her voice a monotone. "He told the Nazis — the Arrow Cross — about the Zimmermans' hiding place, before he'd had a chance to think. It all happened too fast. They were heading for the farmhouse, with him running behind them. Too late to change his mind. It was over in seconds. Afterward, he was a hero. And proud, somehow — the only time in his life, till then, that he'd felt important. People looked up to him. No longer the poor laborer's son, the kid who didn't have the right clothes, who couldn't bring his lunch to school, the object of charity. Briefly, he was somebody. When the Germans left, he headed for the hills. He changed his name and his identity. Joined the flood of refugees from Eastern Europe."

"Why did he take Paul Zimmerman's name?" Judith asked.

"On the spur of the moment. He ended up in an American camp. They grilled everyone and you had to have the right answers or you could be sent back. He could never go home again. The whole town knew what he had done. And he couldn't be Feri Balogh — there were trials for war crimes, and recriminations. He needed a new identity. He knew everything about Paul Zimmerman, it was easy to take his place. That's what he told me."

"Did you know then he was going to kill Harvey Singer?" David asked.

Brenda shook her head. "He didn't mean to do that. It was an accident. You have to believe me. What more can I lose now? Why would I lie?" She twisted around so she could look up at Philip, who clutched her shoulder and squeezed it hard enough she winced.

David sat down on the chaise longue facing her. "How did it happen?" he asked, his voice gentle as before.

"I let Geoff go after the Griffithses' dinner and picked Paul up half an hour later at the corner near their house. I was driving the Jaguar. Singer had asked for a meeting with Paul, and I wanted to go along. To help him, if I could. I didn't hate him, you know,

Inspector. I couldn't ever hate him, though I knew what he had done. He was good to me and to my little girl. Do you remember in *Julius Caesar*, when Mark Antony is talking about the dead Caesar who had been a killer but was also an honorable man, and he says, 'The evil that men do lives after them,/The good is oft interred with their bones.'? It's very easy to forget the good he had done, as Paul Zimmerman, and remember only what Balogh did."

"What happened?" David asked.

"We picked Singer up at his hotel. Paul thought he was going to ask for money, as Arthur had, but that wasn't what he wanted. He'd been to see Wiesenthal, the Nazi-hunter in Vienna, and told him everything. Wiesenthal couldn't help him because he didn't think they could ever get Paul to trial. It would take years even to obtain a hearing from the Canadian government...so he had decided he had no option but to kill Paul himself. That's why he came to Canada."

"He said all this when he got into the car?" Judith asked.

"Yes. He pulled the gun out when Paul started to drive. There was a struggle as we drove along the waterfront, where the warehouses are. I think Paul was trying to protect me, more than he wanted to protect himself. He knew he was dying anyway. The gun went off, but Singer kept struggling like a madman, then Paul shot him again." She brushed her hair nervously out of her face. Her once perfect silver nails were short and broken. She wore no nail polish.

"You helped him tear the labels out of Singer's clothes, threw his shoes in the garbage bin. You took the photograph out of his shoes. You have it still?"

Brenda shook her head.

"Another picture of the boys?" David asked.

"It was one Lantos had found after the war. A picture of Paul on that damn bicycle. He wore the Arrow Cross uniform and the red swastika armband. I burned it."

"And next day you cleaned up the car and arranged to ship it to Bermuda," David prompted.

"At most that would make her an accessory after the fact, Officer," Masters said. "Extremely hard to prove in a court of law that Zimmerman didn't make the arrangements himself."

"Yes," David agreed. "And that would also be true of the first break-in at Ms. Hayes's house on the 3rd, though we can admit to each other, Mr. Masters, that you went there to find out how much Zimmerman/Balogh had told her. You were concerned about the story. Of course, we can't prove that you planted that bag of marijuana in her son's room."

Masters neither agreed nor disagreed. He kept staring at David, still as a photograph.

"But young Ward will, under pressure, testify that you later paid him to try and frighten Ms. Hayes into abandoning the story altogether."

"But he didn't," Brenda said. "I paid him."

"Brenda," Masters commanded, but she brushed him aside.

"It doesn't matter," she said. "I'm so very tired. Why don't we get it all over with?"

"When did he decide to tell everyone who he was?" Judith asked.

"When? I'm not exactly sure. It was because Meisner told him he was going to die," Brenda said. "He wanted to come clean with the whole thing. He wanted to be himself for the last few days, months, whatever was left of his life. He was, he said, sick of living someone else's life. He'd done it for long enough. He'd become all that Mrs. Zimmerman would have wanted of her son. Now he wanted to go back to where he had begun. That's why he went to Forest Hill Catholic. He was born Catholic, he wanted to be buried that way. He called all our friends and you, the lady journalist of his choice to record it all, to have dinner with us and to celebrate Feri Balogh's 17th birthday. He was going to tell you everything." She covered her face with her hands and sat, motionless, her soft hair falling forward.

"You didn't want him to do that, did you?" Judith asked quietly.

"No," Brenda said, her head bent, rocking back and forth in her chair.

"That's why you killed him, not because of his affair with Martha Griffiths," David stated, leaning toward her, his voice kind and steady.

"Martha?" Brenda reared up in surprise. "Poor pathetic Martha — I couldn't care less about her. About any of his affairs. They were minor annoyances, nothing serious. Ever. He was a man of big appetites. It didn't matter."

"You were afraid the truth would hurt you, then, that if the papers reported it you'd be threatened? Is that right?"

The room was so quiet you could hear a trapped bee buzzing against the window.

Brenda shook her head, the hair flying from side to side.

"It wasn't for me," she said. "Don't you know anything? It was for Meredith." She choked on the sound of her daughter's name. "It was all for her. I didn't want her to be a murderer's daughter. Says right here in the Torah, I have a duty to protect my own. That's in your Bible too, Officer, the same words. It's what mothers are supposed to do..." She broke off and started to search through the book she had put down beside her on the chair, feverishly turning the pages till she arrived at where she wanted to be and read. Then she began her search again, her fingers snapping through the book.

Philip Masters came around to reach for her hand and restrain it. "There's no need, Brenda," he said in a calming voice. She fought him for a few seconds but then subsided into a low, groaning sob as the big leather-bound book fell to the pink and blue paving stones, and lay there, face down, its pages splayed open. She tried to pick it up again, but her arm was weak and unsteady. Masters lifted her by the elbow and sat her back in the chair. He picked the book up, dusted it off, and put it down beside her.

Instinctively, Judith went over to her and put her arm around her shoulders. They were frail and burning hot under the thin cloth of her navy dress. The bones seemed to shiver with each breath she took.

Philip Masters abandoned his post by Brenda and sat down on the chaise longue next to David. He sighed and unbuttoned his waistcoat. There were stains of perspiration on his white shirt.

"When did you find out about Zimmerman?" David asked.

"In January...not sure of the exact date. Around the 14th, I believe. When Brenda told me."

"I don't think so," David said. "I think you've known for a long time and you found the information useful. I think you were shocked, for your own reasons, that Zimmerman/Balogh was going to have the whole world know; it would no longer be a card in your private deck. That's why you decided to leave him, isn't it? Because he didn't have to — "

"No," Philip interrupted him. "That's a lie. I didn't — "

"Didn't you?" Brenda's voice came from deep down in her throat;

she lifted her head to glare at him, her tear-stained face contorted with anger and pain. "You've known for years and years. God, how many? And didn't tell me. All this could have been stopped if only you'd said something...the long-faithful damned retainer. And you're a Jew," she shouted at him, then her agitation subsided again. "Poor, poor Philip," she whispered.

"That's what you fought over the evening of the 26th of February," Judith said, "and Meredith overheard. She didn't hear much, but enough to know it was something terrible about her father and enough that she was afraid her mother might find out and be upset by it. That's why she was so agitated when she heard you telling me about the fight with her father, isn't that right?"

Philip said nothing, just stared straight out the still glittering windows at the deep red light in the winter garden.

Judith marveled at his duplicity. And his cleverness. She was overwhelmed by sympathy for Brenda, and she was afraid for her.

"I could ask Meredith Zimmerman, if you prefer," David said.

"No," Brenda yelled.

"There's no need for that," Masters said. "I tried to persuade Paul to stop. There was no need to tell the world about what he did when he was a kid. He had more than made up for it as a man. Why expose himself and all of us to contempt? Why invite the press into some murky secret of his past? But he insisted. He said he wanted everyone to know who he really was. The man had a colossal ego..."

"Then you must have fought because he didn't want you to leave him now," Judith said.

"I had to. I was thinking of my family...," Masters said feebly.

"And that damn seat in the Senate, weren't you, Philip? It was all right while no one else knew about it. *You* could forgive him. Never gave me the chance," Brenda shrieked at him. "And Meredith heard you call her father a cold-blooded killer."

"None of this need involve her," Masters said.

"She is ten years old," Brenda pleaded.

"But when the story comes out," Judith said, "she'll know everything she hasn't already overheard."

"She will never return to Canada. We'll change her name. Live in the south of France. She may never have to know," Brenda said.

"There doesn't have to be a trial," Philip said. "Harvey Singer's killer is dead. There is no accused. You can close the book on it.

There were no witnesses. Brenda slipped the poison into his ginger ale before the guests arrived. And Paul Zimmerman was going to die anyway. She may have saved him from a painful, lingering death. Call it euthanasia. And let's say he finally followed Eva's advice and took his own life. She used to tell him if he was so afraid of his nightmares, he ought to kill himself. He took the poison in the company of his family and friends, perhaps the best way to go. Less painful than a massive coronary — and that's what his future held."

David stood up and spoke to Brenda. "I think you should come with us now, Mrs. Zimmerman. It would save everyone a lot of trouble. Mr. Masters could accompany you. We will take a statement in Toronto."

"No," Philip Masters said firmly. "We will stay here. You think about it, Parr. Justice was done — isn't that what you're here to enforce? Justice?"

"It's the law, Mr. Masters," David said politely. "That's what my job is. They're not always the same."

THIRTY-EIGHT

James occupied the couch with the easy familiarity of a frequent visitor. His head rested on one of the arms, his stockinged feet on the other. He was listening, his eyes at half-mast, to Willie Nelson belting out his song about being on the road again — a fate Judith wished on James even more urgently now than she had all those years ago when he did, finally, get on the road to Chicago.

"Welcome," he said, grandly, when he became aware of her standing in the doorway with her suitcase in her hand. "Come in, come in. I have made a small but nourishing repast for your return. It's essential to eat good food when you've been exposed to too many positive ions. Gets your energy level back to normal. Martinis in the freezer..."

"Where in hell is Stevie?" Judith demanded.

James lifted one warning finger in the air. "Now, now," he said. "You mustn't get so testy, Judith — that's a sign of blocked emotions, okay, excusable for a short time when confronted with the unexpected, but not good for you if you keep blocking them. It's like constipation. Must have a regular outlet or it poisons your system..." He must have seen the beginnings of a snarl, preliminary to imminent attack, on her face, because he added quickly, "I sent Stevie home."

"You *what*?" Judith spluttered.

"I sent her home," James replied calmly. "There was no need for both of us to be taking care of our children — I mean yours and mine, Jude. If you're too busy with your other commitments to stay around and provide the care they need, well, what are fathers for? *I* can be here." He smiled. "And I was."

"I was working, for Chrissakes — " Judith yelled, but she was sorry as soon as the words were out. He had her on the defensive. There was no reason to feel on the defensive. She was the one who had

270

supplied the food and money while James was finding himself . . .

"Now, now," he said again, a quiet little smile on his lips, "you mustn't allow yourself to get so easily upset. There was no criticism intended. I happen to think you're a wonderful woman. You've done a superb job with Jimmy and Anne. No one, I don't think, could have done better. Under the circumstances."

Judith dropped her suitcase onto the carpet where it rolled over like a beached whale and smashed into the stereo set, making Willie Nelson jump from the road to a slow whine about Good Time Charlie and the blues. "All right, James," she said in the most controlled tones she could manage, "what the hell are you doing in my house?"

"It's a long story," he said, sitting up, his elbows on his knees, head bent forward, gazing at his gray toes. "I've been back to Chicago. I mean after the holiday with the kids — "

"Where are the kids?"

"They're . . . around . . ." He fluttered his fingers to indicate it wasn't a big deal wherever they were.

"Where?"

"All right. They're upstairs in their rooms. I checked what time your flight was coming in, asked them to leave us alone for an hour or so. I . . . we have a lot to talk about."

"*We,*" Judith repeated with his emphasis, "have nothing whatsoever to talk about. Furthermore, I'm exhausted. I want to say hi to my kids, I want to change into my pajamas, and I want to go to bed. Can we have our little chat some other time?"

While she was still halfway through that monologue, he had bounded into the kitchen and was now on his way back with a tall martini glass topped up with a bunch of olives. He placed it in her hand. "A peace offering. I dug out all the pimientos myself," he said. "You never used to like them. Or has that changed?"

Judith shook her head. Nothing like a red pimiento center to ruin a perfectly good olive. She shook off her damp high-heeled shoes; they were still sweaty from the Bermuda spring. The martini was just as she liked it. She didn't bother to take her coat off. She wandered over to the armchair facing the couch and sat across from the waiting James. "All right," she said, as conciliatory as she could manage, "what do you want?"

James, who had settled back into his former position on the couch, nodded sadly, as if to indicate that she had spoken exactly

as he had, alas, expected her to speak. "Want...want...want...,"
he murmured. "There is too much want in this world and not
nearly enough give. I'm not here for what I *want*, Judith, it's what I
have to offer that's brought me here. It's what I have to give. All
you need do is accept with grace — not one of your most
characteristic qualities, that — grace..."

Judith gritted her teeth in silence and bit on the olives.

"It is time you and I began to *deal with* our relationship, Jude.
Not that we hadn't tried to before, but we were much younger then
and didn't possess the tools..."

"What relationship?" Judith inquired, swallowing martini, olives,
and venom.

"Oh Jude, Jude," he said softly, "you mustn't blame yourself.
That's the problem with these things, too much apportionment of
blame. Fact is..." he balanced his fingertips on top of one another
as a mirror image, then opened and closed them. A spider doing
push-ups "...there is too much unresolved tension between us. No.
Don't answer me now...," he warded off the nasty little question
she was about to pop, "hear me out, at least. We owe each other a
hearing, don't we?"

Judith finished her martini and stuck her feet on the coffee
table.

"It happened on top of the biggest hill at Collingwood. Big John.
I was looking down at the other skiers from the top, getting ready
for my run, and suddenly I felt apart. I don't mean superior, just
apart. Perhaps lonely. I don't know why, I thought of you then, and
why we had decided to separate. I ran the whole thing before my
eyes, like watching a movie, in slow motion, and none of it made
sense. None. Jude, we never resolved our relationship. We never
tried to find out what went wrong. Never tried to fix the damage.
You know, it's like finding that the walls of your house have cracks
in them and instead of caulking the cracks and painting them over,
deciding to abandon the house and look for a new dwelling. That's
dumb, don't you think?"

"You can't be serious," Judith suggested.

"Mm-hmm," said James, grabbing for her glass and going for
a refill.

This time he returned with drinks for both of them.

"Point I'm trying to make is that I haven't been very happy without you. I know, you'll think it's taken me too long to come to that

realization and that seeing you and Jimmy — and Anne, of course, she is such a super girl, never tire of telling her how beautiful she is becoming. Very important that, for girls her age. It's when anorexia starts and that other thing — bulimia? yes — not having enough confidence in themselves. Growing up is so very hard on young girls. You do remember, don't you?"

Barely. Being over a hundred years old. "What are you trying to tell me?" Judith asked. "Not being a house, I'm not sure what you are planning to substitute for caulk."

"I'm serious," James warned. "I went back to Chicago, after the holiday. It didn't feel right, so I saw my analyst for advice. He's used to my fits and starts. Despondent, then out of it, but this time, he realized I meant it. I miss you all. I want to come back home." He smiled. "That's it."

Judith stared intently into her glass. When no inspiration emerged from that careful study, she looked back at James's cheerfully expectant face. "Oh dear," she said at last.

"Well?" James asked. "What do you think?"

Judith finished her second drink, picked up her shoes and suitcase, and began to climb the stairs toward her children's bedrooms. When she was halfway, she called over her shoulder, "Fuck you, James."

THIRTY-NINE

David took them to brunch at China House. He had asked for an extra-large table with a round server so they could have a whole lot of dishes to choose from. Jimmy ate up all the sweet and sour pork, and Anne had most of the barbecued ribs. They fought over the spring rolls.

They had both seemed relieved when James at last returned to Chicago. The offer, he had told Judith, would stand for a month. Meanwhile, at least she could be sure his monthly checks didn't bounce. That, in itself, was a small gain.

"You remember Madame Cielo?" David asked.

"Mmm." Between mouthfuls.

"It was the retired trucker. Giannini found her account book in his house. Poor bugger hadn't been afraid to kill her, but he was afraid to incinerate the blasted book. Felt it might have contained some kind of spell. You know, you cast them over an object and they can attack its attacker. Very handy, I'd say, in case of burglary. Pity we can't patent it..."

"You still haven't decided about Brenda Zimmerman, have you?" Judith asked.

David bit into a piece of crackly duck, then wiped the grease off his face. "What's to decide? Even if the Chief didn't think it was a mindless waste of departmental energy, extradition from France could take a long time..."